=

THE SUITCASE MAN

by

MICHAEL K FOSTER

MICHAEL K FOSTER

Also by Michael K Foster

DCI Jack Mason Crime Thriller series

THE WHARF BUTCHER

SATAN'S BECKONING

THE SUITCASE MAN

CHAMELEON

POACHER'S POCKET

DEATH PLUNGE

THE DEADLY MOORING

Novellas

DCI Jack Mason in the early years

HACKNEY CENTRAL

Remobooks

First edition published in Great Britain 2018 by UK Publishing.
Second Edition published in 2023 by Remobooks.

All characters and events in this book, other than those clearly in the public domain, are fictitious and any resemblance to real persons, living or dead, is purely coincidental.

A CIP catalogue record for this book is available from the British Library

ISBN: 13: **978-1-9161210-7-2**

Typeset in Bookman Old Style *(Body)* and Sears Tower *(Titles)*
Editing, design, typesetting, and publishing
by Remobooks

For Marilyn

MICHAEL K FOSTER

"A child that is not embraced by the village will burn the village to feel its warmth."

African Proverb

MICHAEL K FOSTER

Chapter One

Gateshead 2014

Shortly after nine o'clock, Detective Chief Inspector Jack Mason slid from the unmarked police vehicle and stood for a moment. Eyes transfixed on the building opposite, he observed the large group of onlookers now gathered at the police tape. Gripped by curiosity, they were waiting for answers that would never come. Hopelessness seemed the order of the day, along with a feeling of disquiet. Whoever had chosen this area to carry out their dastardly deeds had chosen well.

The flies were the giveaway. Thousands of them, along with the overpowering stench of rotten flesh. No matter how many precautions he undertook, murder scenes always had the same effect on him. Now kitted out in protective coveralls and a face mask, Jack Mason entered the house with a feeling of trepidation. To the casual observer, this wasn't the swankiest street in town, and the people who lived here weren't rich either. Whatever had taken place here was now a full-on murder investigation.

Having secured the outlying area, the next forty-eight hours would be crucial. Piecing together the last moments of any incident was the crux to solving most crimes, but securing the evidence and material that otherwise would be lost in the early stages of an investigation was vital.

Mason took a deep breath and poked his head in through the open doorway. Sunlight dancing through a chink in the curtains, he gazed at the corpse in revulsion. It wasn't a large room, drab, with plain painted walls and cheap second-hand furniture. The living room carpets were shabby in places, and badly stained.

'Not a pretty sight,' the crime scene manager said by introduction.

Mason turned sharply towards the familiar voice. Early fifties, with an unruly shock of jet-black hair, Stan Johnson was eccentric. Not one for mincing his words, he was more than capable.

'Do we know who she is, Stan?'

'Her name is Jennifer Oakwell.'

'What do we know about her?'

'She was living alone, apparently. We've done a few checks, and neighbours confirm her ex-husband is serving time in Durham prison.'

'That complicates matters.'

The SOCO shook his head resignedly. 'It gets worse.'

'Worse?'

'There's been a second incident.'

'Incident?' Mason was never a man to waste words.

Doctor Colin Brown, a lean, long-backed, balding man with a stern, flushed face, and thick bushy sideburns, peered back at him from the corner of the room. 'Upstairs,' the doctor said, pointing a latex finger at the ceiling. 'There's blood everywhere, but we've yet to find a body.'

Johnson was right. It wasn't a pretty sight. The dead woman's body was bloated and showing early signs of blistering. He could see the wrists had been bound to the chair armrests using heavy duty duct tape, and her ankles strapped to the base. Blood everywhere, her head had fallen back slightly, and the tongue forced out of the mouth. He'd seen evil before, but nothing compared to this.

Mason pointed to the centrally positioned straight-back chair. 'Another grudge attack, do you think?'

'Who knows? Tragically, she suffered from stab wounds to her head, neck, back, and chest wall, which led to the puncturing of her lungs and heart chamber.' The doctor ran his spatula over the dead woman's upper body and shifted in his stance. 'He used a long-bladed weapon by the look, but don't quote me on that.'

The doctor's voice sounded weak, as if someone had rattled his cage.

Johnson added, 'I suspect someone may have disturbed her killer at some point.'

'Any sign of a struggle?'

'Based on the amount of force used, I'd estimate the entire incident lasted only a few seconds.'

Mason bristled, pen poised. 'Over the top, don't you think?'

'Whoever they were, they seemed determined to leave their mark behind.'

Mason turned inquisitively to face the police doctor. 'What mark is this?'

'They've drawn smiley faces on the upstairs walls, using the victim's blood.'

'Christ! That's all we need.'

Johnson shook his head disparagingly. 'Those were my sentiments, Jack.'

'What about neighbours? What do we know about them?'

'University students mainly. It's half-term, and many have gone back to their parents' homes.'

Mason stood for a moment as Johnson explained. Five feet-nine with powerful shoulders and a large moon-like face, the chief inspector was old school. A no-nonsense copper who wouldn't take no for an answer, he was well-known to the criminals he'd helped put away.

'Who found her, Stan?'

'A close friend of the family. She was on her way to work but when Oakwell's phone kept ringing out she called by.'

Still grappling with his emotions, Mason's voice betrayed an eagerness to reject the awful truth.

'What time was this?'

'Around half seven this morning.'

'Has she made a statement to that effect?'

'Not yet, she hasn't, but I wouldn't go there if I were you. The woman's in a state of shock.'

Mason brushed an annoying blow fly from his face and tilted his head back in thought.

'She obviously has a key to the property.'

'She has.'

From what Mason could see, the dead woman looked mid-fifties. Not tall, plump, with a rounded face and square jawline. The front of her dress was torn, and dried blood covered her breasts and lower limbs. It was far too early to establish a motive, but once he knew more about this woman's background, it would be a simple matter of legwork.

He watched as the doctor's attention shifted to the woman's hands.

'How long has she been dead?' Mason asked.

'I can't swear to it, but no longer than a week.'

'That's a heck of a long time, Colin.'

The doctor glanced back at him, then down at the dead woman's feet. 'Let's see what the post-mortem throws up. No doubt the pathologist will fill in the details. If it's Doctor King, she's usually pretty quick, so we may have a few answers later in the day.'

Mason peered over the top of his notebook. 'Her ex-husband could have an important bearing on the investigation, so we may need to keep an open mind on proceedings.'

'Indeed,' Johnson replied laconically. 'We've already run a cursory data check on him, and he's serving a twenty-year stretch for armed robbery. His name's Frank Wiseman, and he's a nasty piece of work. Six months ago, he was involved in a minor dispute over prison privileges. A few days later a scuffle broke out in the prison canteen, and Wiseman beat the living daylights out of one of the prison officers.'

'CV's come little better than that,' Mason groaned.

'No, I guess not.'

The real horror lay in the upstairs front bedroom. Blood everywhere, graffiti-filled walls; it was like stepping into a slaughterhouse at the end of a long day's shift. The room smelt of fear, reminiscent of another case he'd recently worked on. Whoever had died here had undoubtedly met a horrific ending. Of that, he was certain.

Looking round, Mason felt the knot in his stomach tighten. There were no physical signs of forced entry, and someone had shut all the windows. If the victims knew each other, he would need to establish a link. Thinking this through, his report would come later, after he'd cleared his head of unpleasant thoughts. The problem was, Mad Frankie Wiseman didn't exude charm. The man was a moron, but not to be taken lightly.

As he made his way downstairs, he let his mind drift. Despite not ransacking the house, the killer had a definite point to prove. Where was the second body? He wondered. Without that, there was no way of telling what had happened here.

Before leaving, he checked in with the crime scene manager and made a few observations. More importantly, to Jack Mason, was the little cafe on Bensham Road. It was Friday and, with his weekend fast slipping away, he would need some thinking time. He closed his notebook and turned to deal with more pressing matters.

Chapter Two

It was chucking it down, and the air felt oppressive as though a thunderstorm were brewing. Three floors up at Gateshead Police Station, overlooking Matalan car park and the Magistrates' Court, DCI Mason glanced at a new set of crime-scene photographs he'd pinned to the investigation evidence board. It wasn't looking good. Two murders, one body, and a shitload of unanswered questions. Some crimes left a nasty taste in his mouth, and this was one of them.

Now turned forty-six, Jack Mason had risen through the ranks at an early age. Not all had been plain sailing, though. When he was six, his father had walked out on his mother. After the marriage ended, he was raised on a rough council estate in the East End of London. A rebellious child, had it not been for a caring uncle, God knows where he would have ended up. Having messed up badly at school, his sole ambition was to be a police officer. The competition to join was tough, and Mason didn't have a single qualification to his name. In what had been a hard-fought slog, he'd somehow muddled his way through the police entry exams.

Now onto his second mug of coffee, he glanced at the small, assembled team of trusted police officers now sitting in front of him. They were a mixed bunch. Many were old school with several years' experience under their belts. He liked to think he had created a bond between them, but was now having doubts. Not all were perfect, and several came with baggage. At least they were reliable, and that's all that mattered.

He opened his hands expansively as he addressed the team. 'This isn't the most difficult crime to solve, and there's a mountain of evidence to be getting on with.'

Savage raised his hand to speak.

'Yes, Rob?'

'What do we know about the dead woman?' the sergeant asked.

'Her name's Jennifer Oakwell, and she worked as a receptionist in the Bensham area. After failing to turn up for work last week, around eight-fifteen on Saturday morning, a friend discovered her at her home on Rectory Road. While bound to a straight-back chair with heavy duty duct tape, she had been viciously stabbed to death.'

'Are we saying she'd lain there for a week?'

'That's correct.'

'And nobody heard or saw anything?'

'No, nothing,' Mason confirmed. 'Uniforms are conducting door-to-door enquiries, but they've nothing to report so far.'

Savage exhaled noisily. 'What about post-mortem results? Anything back yet?'

'According to Dr Gillian King, the senior Home Office pathologist, Oakwell suffered multiple stab wounds to the neck, back, and chest. The main cluster of wounds was to the left chest region, penetrating the right ventricle and aorta. There were four stab wounds to the left side of her neck, two severing the carotid artery. This was a violent attack, and no one should be in any doubt.' Mason let the silence linger for several seconds before continuing. 'Looking at the report, there were multiple knife wounds to the back, two of them penetrating the lungs, and one piercing the abdominal viscera. These were classic downward arc stab wounds, and of some considerable force. We know her attacker is right-handed, and approximately five-ten in stature.'

'What about the murder weapon?' asked DS Holt, in a broad Geordie accent.

Tom Hedley, the senior forensic scientist present, looked up briefly. 'The wounds to the back and chest are elliptic and consistent with the use of a double-edged knife. Small contusions found above and below each of the stab wounds suggest the weapon had some sort of finger guard attached to it.'

'Sounds like he'd lost control,' said detective Manley, making his presence felt.

Mason nodded. 'It would appear so, Harry. Unable to defend herself, any of a dozen wounds would have been fatal.'

The silence that followed was short-lived.

'Could someone have used a combat knife?' quizzed Manley.

'Yes, that would fit perfectly.'

'Any further developments on the second victim?' asked Holt.

'No, not yet. We still haven't recovered the body.'

Hedley pointed to the evidence board. 'Looking at the SOC photographs, you'll notice there's a lot of arterial blood spread over a wide area. Stabbed numerous times, the second victim now fought their way to the landing, where another brutal attack took place. Judging by the blood trail, someone dragged the victim's body to a position at the top of the landing stairs before removing it from the premises.'

'Blimey,' Manley gasped. 'This bastard doesn't hang about.'

'Apparently not,' Mason replied.

Tom Hedley deflected the comment with a thin smile. 'These weren't random killings. These murders were planned. I'm convinced of that.'

'So why leave Oakwell's body behind?' asked Savage reproachfully.

'At some point, something may have disturbed him.'

'True,' Mason agreed with a nod of the head, 'but he still had plenty of time to return and finish the job.'

Hedley shuffled awkwardly. 'It could be a case of witness elimination, of course.'

Harry Manley shook his head dejectedly. A muscular man, early forties, with a thick bushy mop of black hair, the detective constable was the joker in the pack. 'It's possible, but the suspect is more likely to be sending out a warning, don't you think?'

Mason gave a thin, wintry smile. 'You're right, Harry. That would account for the smiley faces he's drawn on the bedroom walls.'

'What more do we know about her ex-husband?' asked Holt.

Mason explained in a little more detail. 'For those not aware, Jenifer Oakwell's ex-husband is a notorious gangster called Frank Wiseman.'

The noise levels heightened.

'What. Mad Frankie?'

'Yes, Rob.' Mason took a sip of his coffee, then said. 'Shortly after Wiseman was sent down for committing a string of armed robberies across Tyneside, Jennifer divorced him. Codenamed Operation Black Rock, the officers involved in the case described the gang as well organised and violent. After targeting a string of local betting shops, supermarkets, and outlying sub-post offices, the gang's overall takings were over ten million quid.'

There was silence in the room, broken only by Rob Savage's heavy breathing.

'What's your take on it, boss?' the detective sergeant asked. 'Do you think there could be a connection to Mad Frankie here?'

The smell of death still clinging to him, Mason took a deep breath. At times, the mechanics of a murder investigation could be quite overwhelming, but the visual memories of a crime-scene even more difficult to eradicate.

'The thing to remember is that none of the gang had shown the slightest remorse. The violence was extreme, with victims being hit with iron bars or guns held to their heads. As a result, they were each given a sentence ranging from ten to twelve years. As I recall, it was a long drawn out trial, lasting well over ten weeks.'

'I can't speculate on that,' said Holt, 'but what I can say is, because of Wiseman's previous convictions and the fact he'd masterminded the entire operation, the judge sentenced him to a minimum of twenty years.'

Mason nodded. 'Thank you, George.'

Manley blew through his teeth. 'The word on the street is that nobody has ever recovered the money the gang made off with. Well over ten million quid. Some believe it was squirrelled away into Swiss banks, others say that dodgy bookkeepers made a killing from it, laundering it into offshore accounts. The thing is, anyone caught with their fingers in the till usually faces the consequences with these people.'

'You're clutching at straws, Harry,' said Savage, shaking his head. 'We're talking ten years ago.'

'That's my point,' Manley replied cheerily. 'Apart from Mad Frankie, the rest of the gang are now out on parole.'

Mason dutifully stroked his chin in thought. Manley had a point, and a good one at that. Even though Frank Wiseman was still behind bars, it didn't mean he wasn't active. He made a mental note of it and pushed it to the back of his mind.

'Looking at the SOC photographs, apart from heavy bruising to the victim's ankles and wrists, there doesn't appear to be any other surface injuries.' Mason dug his hands in his pockets, the ripples of a grin racing across his face. 'With no signs of a struggle, could Jennifer have known who her assailant was?'

'If she did, why did he kill her?' asked Holt.

'Therein lies the motive, George.'

'It could have been a mistake.' Manley shrugged.

The room fell silent again.

'This second victim,' said Holt, pointing to the evidence board. 'What about personal effects? A wallet, driving licence, a mobile phone perhaps, or something with an address on it?'

'We found nothing,' Mason answered.

Manley's face lit up. 'Who's saying he wasn't giving her one?'

'If he was, then Dr King uncovered no semen traces in Jennifer Oakwell's body.'

'Bugger,' Manley huffed.

'All is not what it appears,' Mason confirmed with a wry smile. 'Find the missing body and we're halfway to solving the crime.'

'What I want to know is, what was the second victim doing there?'

Mason stood for a moment. Manley had unwittingly raised another valid point. Why kill Wiseman's ex-wife? Could she have been acting as a go-between? This case wasn't as simple as he first thought, and he wasn't ruling out revenge.

'What are we doing about these gang members who are currently out on parole?' asked Manley.

'We need to speak to them, Harry. Establish what each of them were doing on February the twenty-first.' Mason paused for effect. 'We also need to check out all CCTV camera's in the vicinity. Who else was in the area around the time of the murder?'

'Leave that one with me,' Holt acknowledged.

As the team left the room, Mason put his head in his hands and muttered under his breath, *God! What a mess.*

CHAPTER THREE

David Carlisle checked his scorecard and did a quick mental calculation. Hole eighteen, how to approach it? Two hundred and twenty yards. A long par three, with out of bounds left, right, and long. In anyone's game, this was the hole that could ruin an excellent scorecard. There were trees down either side of the fairway, and large bunkers protecting the green. Minutes earlier, detective Manley had sliced his tee shot into the long rough. It was a lousy position, full of potholes, an impossible spot to recover from.

Sucking in the air, Carlisle took out his trusty 3-iron and stepped up to the tee box. Aligning himself with the flag, he pushed his tee into the soft ground and stepped back a pace. His colleague had struck a perfect tee shot from this very position, and straight down the middle of the fairway. After landing heavily, it had carried a further thirty yards before pulling up just short of the eighteenth green. This was a pressure shot, and the tension was mounting.

Addressing the ball, Carlisle took a practice swing. Having watched the trajectory of his opponent's ball, he would aim left. If the wind carried his ball towards the right-hand side of the fairway, he was in with a chance. It would require a stroke of genius - but could he make it happen? As the head of his club connected with the ball, it soared into the air like a rocket. Seconds later, after hitting the fairway, it bobbled twice and pulled up short of the bunker.

Perfect, he thought.

'Cracking shot,' Harry Manley called out.

'Thanks mate.'

As the next player stepped up to the tee box, you could have heard a pin drop. Wearing a bright orange sweater, matching trousers, and black brogue golfing shoes, Holt was out to impress.

'Easy, George,' Mason chuckled, 'there's sixty quid resting on this shot.'

'No pressure then,' Holt replied cheerily.

After taking a massive divot out of the tee box on his practice swing, the sergeant addressed his drive with a little more caution. As the club struck the ball with a resounding thwack, it shot into the air and disappeared into the treeline. Seconds later, it came to rest in a bunker.

'Bollocks,' Holt cursed.

'Looks like another bucket and spade job,' Mason chuckled.

'Sod off,' the sergeant replied. 'It's not over yet.'

As Holt dropped his 5-iron back into his caddy bag, he swung to face them. 'To tell you the truth. I don't fancy your next shot either, boss.'

Muted laughter broke out.

Carlisle hadn't got off to a good start that morning. Had it not been for a fluke bounce on the fourteenth green, he would have been well out of the running. When he was younger, he could hit a 250-yard drive to within three feet of the hole. Not anymore. Fast approaching forty-four, his reactions were slowing, as was his concentration. He'd never intended to be a private investigator; it had happened by chance. After taking voluntary redundancy from the Northumbria Police, he'd set up his own investigation business. Nothing ambitious, just enough to earn a few quid and see him through to retirement. The problem was, he struggled to find any consistency and many of the cases he took on were late night surveillance operations. Not exactly challenging work, he found boredom his biggest enemy.

Having given up hope of ever finding Harry Manley's ball, Jack Mason declared a penalty stroke. Then, just when they were least expecting it, the detective suddenly pointed to a small patch in the long grass.

'Here, lads.'

Holt looked on in bewilderment. 'Are you sure that's your ball, Harry?'

'Well, this is where it landed.'

'I thought your ball was white. This one's pink?'

'What the hell?' Mason tormented. 'He'll win bugger all from there.'

Fast losing patience, Manley slammed his golf club into the ground and swung to face them. 'Really? Watch this—'

Three shots later, Mason was proven right.

Now down to three contenders, the chief inspector was in a rich vein of form. Taking out his trusty 9-iron, he addressed his ball with an air of confidence. It was another crap shot, and Carlisle had fared little better. The moment his ball hit the back of the green, it disappeared into the treeline.

All eyes now turned to George Holt.

With little room to manoeuvre, the sergeant shuffled his feet in the bunker sand and addressed his ball with a lofty wedge. As an enormous cloud of sand flew into the air, his ball dropped to within an inch of the eighteenth hole. It was a magnificent recovery, leaving the sergeant with a simple tap in.

Mason checked the scorecard.

'Bugger me. That shot will add sixty quid to your wallet.'

'The winner was never in any doubt,' Holt smirked.

They all fell about laughing.

'Well done, gentlemen,' Mason acknowledged. 'This calls for a small celebration.'

Manley was quick to react. 'Does that mean you're buying the drinks in, boss?'

'Sod off, Harry. Tradition has it the winner gets the first round.'

Things were livening up, and after changing into more suitable clothes, they made for the bar. Still unsure why Jack Mason had invited him here that day, Carlisle trod with caution. Behind the unbending charm was a ruthless streak. Mason was thick skinned, and extremely difficult to weigh up. Everything had to be done his way, which left little room for manoeuvre.

'What do you know about Mad Frankie Wiseman?' asked Mason outright.

'Not a lot. Why?'

The chief inspector cocked his head to one side. 'I'm told you recently did some work for his son.'

'I did. His lawyers asked me to resolve a minor problem they were experiencing.'

'What kind of problem?'

Carlisle felt the cutting edge of Mason's tongue. 'Why? Is there an issue?'

'There could be.'

'If you must know, Wiseman's son was getting a lot of grief from a nearby council estate in Wallsend. A group of young thugs were threatening to burn his pub down if he didn't pay the protection money they were demanding.'

'And what was your part in this?'

'Surveillance work mainly. Low key stuff, talking to local residents.'

'So it was the family lawyers who hired you, and not the son?'

'That's right. Frank's lawyers were keen to get rid of the problem.'

'You certainly pick your clients,' Mason grunted. 'What's wrong with going to the police nowadays?'

'Knowing Frank Wiseman, the police would be the last people he'd want to deal with.'

Mason thought for a moment. 'True.'

'Besides, his son was trying to make a clean sweep and didn't want to involve his old man.'

Mason grinned. 'So, they hired you to sort things out?'

'You could say that, yes.'

'Some things never cease to amaze, my friend.' Mason wiped the beer froth from his lips and turned to face him. 'What about the son's mother? Did you ever bump into her at all?'

'No, we've never met. Why?'

Mason cradled his glass. 'Knowing Mad Frankie, it was lucky you didn't.'

'Oh, and what makes you say that?'

Mason took another swig from his glass. 'It's not general knowledge, but a few days ago, a vicious knife attack resulted in the brutal murder of Frank's ex-wife.'

'Is that what all the fuss is about?'

'Uh-huh. Jennifer Oakwell was her maiden name.'

Carlisle reflected on this. 'How the hell did you keep that away from the media? They're usually good at sniffing out rotten apples.'

'It goes with the territory.' Mason tapped his nose. 'If you want my advice, I'd steer well clear of Wiseman's lawyers in the future.'

'I will.'

'Good, at least that clears one issue up.'

Now deep in thought, something had piqued his colleague's interest. However much Mason could annoy you, he still had his positive sides. He tried to remember how many years they'd worked together on the force. They were much younger back then, and active members of London's Metropolitan Murder Investigation Team (MIT). The work was dangerous, but in 2001, when the unit disbanded, they both went their separate ways.

Carlisle rested his weight on the arm of his chair. 'If I can help, you know where to find me, Jack.'

'I'll bear that in mind.'

'What else can you tell me about Jenifer Oakwell?'

Mason looked at him sternly. 'It's strictly a police matter at this stage, but that could all change in due course.'

He did not elaborate.

CHAPTER FOUR

Jack Mason stood in the shade of the arcades cloister and checked his phone for messages. There was none. Now, at 08:50, glorious sunshine bathed West Road crematorium in Newcastle. Not the best start to his day. He could hear the distant hum of the rush hour traffic but could not see it. Soon to ease off, things would return to normal again. Whatever normal meant.

The chief inspector had barely paid attention to the garden of remembrance that morning; his mind was on other things. Security was tight. It had to be. Mad Frankie Wiseman was a high security risk, a category A prisoner who wouldn't think twice about beating your brains out for the fun of it. But what might go wrong? Very little with this amount of security, he argued.

Among the hundreds of mourners paying their respects that morning were several of Newcastle's most notorious felons. It was a large turnout, a solid show of force for a gangster's ex-wife who had been brutally murdered in her own home. If this was an inside job, whoever killed her would be nervously looking over their shoulder right now.

Dressed in a smart black mohair suit, white button-down shirt and black silk tie, Mad Frankie Wiseman descended the Group 4 prison van steps, flanked by four burly prison guards. Eyes hidden behind Ray-Ban sunglasses; the gangster's face bore the look of indifference. Words were being uttered, but he couldn't catch them out. Now under a heavy security screen, Mason watched as the guards whisked the prisoner through a west wing side door and into the chapel beyond. No one spoke. It was a tense stand-off. They were dealing with professional criminals here, people at the top of their game.

As the two police motorbike outriders sped off towards the rear of the cemetery, the Group 4 prison van pulled out behind them. Positioned strategically along the perimeter wall, a formidable presence of armed police officers was visible. Wearing their familiar black combat overalls and black Kevlar body armour vests, the dog teams were keeping a low profile. If there was trouble to be had, it would start after the service and not before it. Not one to drop his guard, the chief inspector had prepared for every eventuality.

Then, glancing up, he caught his first glimpse of the beautiful horse-drawn hearse. Pulled by a pair of handsome, black Belgian horses, they carried black drapes on their backs and wore tall black ostrich feather plumes on their heads. From the high open top seat, he noticed the driver and groom were impeccably dressed in traditional Victorian livery. No expense spared, Mason thought. Mad Frankie's ex-wife was getting the best that money could buy.

He knew from experience that events such as these always carried a prominent element of risk. It was the budding, reckless young wannabes who scared the living daylights out of him. These were the mindless thugs who turned up in outlandish twenties pin-striped suits and posed like henchmen in an Al Capone movie. And another thing, he reasoned, why were funerals always such morbid affairs? Having spent the past twenty minutes listening to piped religious music invading his privacy, it was doing his head in. He'd often wondered what kind of music they'd play at *his* final send-off. Something livelier, he hoped. Maybe Iron Maiden or Guns N' Roses.

The moment Mason moved towards the chapel door, he felt his coat sleeve being tugged. He turned sharply to find Tony Fox glaring at him. Not the nicest individual to lock horns with on such a solemn occasion, Fox controlled the north side of the city.

'Nice of you to turn up, Jack. Friend of the family, was she?'

'No, just keeping a watchful eye on proceedings.'

'It's always nice to know the police are looking after my interests,' Fox chuckled.

'That's what we're paid to do.'

The two men stepped to one side.

'It's a sad affair,' said Fox, feigning empathy.

'Someone out there had it in for her, and whoever he is, I want the bastard taken down,' Mason growled.

Fox looked down at him and smiled. Six feet six, and built like a brick, he stood head and shoulders above everyone present that morning. It wasn't common knowledge, or maybe it was. Tony Fox had gay tendencies towards young boys who frequented his nightclubs. Not that anyone complained. They didn't. And those who had had been eternally silenced.

'Now here's the thing,' said Fox, menacingly chewing on an ivory toothpick between gleaming whitened teeth. 'Why would someone go to all the trouble to murder such a sweet, innocent young lady like Jennifer Oakwell?'

'I've no idea, Tony. You tell me.'

The gangster's eyelids flickered enough to display his contempt. 'It's not the same city anymore. Not since these Eastern Europeans moved in.'

'Pissing in your pot, are they?'

Fox shrugged. 'You know me, Jack.'

'I'd like to think so, Tony.'

Fox glanced into the distance and sighed. 'This killing will spark off an entire load of unnecessary trouble, and I don't like what I'm hearing.'

'And what's that?'

'You know how it goes, Jack. The sooner we take this bastard off the streets, the better we'll sleep at night.'

Mason stroked his chin, pondering the gangster's statement. If a useful snippet of street gossip was about to come his way, he'd be eternally grateful. Not that he was expecting any; he wasn't.

'These foreigners you talk of. Could they be behind this?'

Eyes like daggers, Fox glared down at him. 'Don't put words into my mouth. It doesn't suit you, Jack.'

'You know me, Tony. It goes with the territory.'

Inside, Mason was bristling, but he stayed calm. His mind all over the place, he turned to face his adversary. 'How's the second-hand car business doing these days?'

'Why do you ask?'

'There's an awful lot of high-end rollers going missing lately, and we're having to keep a watchful eye on the ferry terminals. Someone out there is stealing them to order. Mind, I can't say as I blame them, not with some of the amazing prices they're fetching. There's an enormous demand in the Middle East, and a waiting list as long as your arm. How times have changed.' Mason kicked the gravel under his feet as if to make his point. 'Someone's making a killing. Maybe it's these foreigners you talk about. Who knows?'

'Well, it ain't me. I can assure you of that,' said Fox, exuding disdain.

'Your name never crossed my mind, Tony.'

Fox made a little stabbing gesture with his finger. 'Who told you I was dealing in second-hand cars again?'

'Nobody did. I just thought I'd mention it, that's all.'

The gangster tapped the side of his forehead with a finger. 'I'll bear that in mind.'

Mason stared at him in silence for some moments.

'If you hear anything, you know where to find me.'

'Quid pro quo.'

'You could say that, yes.'

'I'll look out for...' the gangster's voice tailed off at the last syllable.

Joined by a pug-faced associate with short, cropped hair, and a mouth full of gold teeth, there followed a long, awkward silence between them.

'It's been nice talking to you, Tony.'

'Sure. Enjoy the rest of the service,' Fox replied menacingly.

The lump in his throat, now the size of a tennis ball,

Mason turned on his heel. Fox proved himself to be a clever sod, not to be underestimated or misjudged. There was nothing more to be gained here. Once everyone was inside the chapel, he would slip away unnoticed.

Minutes later, and sitting inside the undercover pool car, Mason suddenly realised who he'd been mixing with. There were some hard lessons to be learnt here. Mistakes would be made, new deals struck, but no one was untouchable. Not even Tony Fox.

CHAPTER FIVE

Tommy Harris wasn't a talkative man. If the truth was known, he preferred his own company. Close to retirement, Tommy had salted enough money away to eke out the rest of his days in relative comfort. Never one for taking holidays abroad, he thought them too expensive. The last time he'd done that was a bus trip to Paris with his wife, Peggy. Blimey, that was almost ten years ago, Tommy chuckled. Local B&B's were as far as they ever got nowadays. Preferably by the coast. Somewhere, they served generous portions of fish and chips, and the beer was cheap.

He'd arrived early for work that morning, and Monday had started cheerfully enough. Now onto his second pot of tea, Tommy finished his drink and realised he'd better check the weekly maintenance log. It wasn't a taxing job, and the hours were perfect for him. Halfway along Forth Street and within easy walking distance of Newcastle Central Station, the storage company was ideally located close to the city centre. What many people didn't know – or perhaps they did and weren't letting on – was that Tommy was born in India and educated at Seahouses Middle School. Aged eighteen, he'd followed in his father's footsteps and joined the British Army. Apart from a short stint in Northern Ireland, he'd never fired a gun in anger. He'd won a silver medal to prove it and kept it hidden in a bottom drawer. The problem was, ever since leaving the army, nothing exciting had ever happened to Tommy. Until now, that is.

He lifted his arm and checked his watch. Nine fifteen, and the start of another week. Things weren't going as planned, and there were widespread rumours of an impending change in ownership. How much was true was difficult to tell. It was a great company to work for, and judging by the five-star reviews, there wasn't a bad word to be said about the place. The thing was, Tommy was an expert at choosing the right locker size and giving the customer a good deal. Described in the brochure as the size of a hatchback car boot, the small storage lockers were the most popular. Not so with the larger storage rooms. At two-hundred and fifty square feet, they were similar in size to a thirty-foot lorry trailer. And, according to Tommy's calculations, these were the most profitable units to fill. However, they were rarely available for rent, and the customers who took them out had mostly moved overseas to live. And that was another thing he liked about his job. If a client failed to continue their quarterly payments, he would end the contract. As for the locker contents, Tommy always found it to be a nice little earner when he auctioned them off.

The early morning sunlight flooding through the office window, he logged on to his computer. Scrolling down through the list of complaints, he made a mental note of them. The ladies' toilets still had a broken hand dryer, and there was a problem with the main entrance CCTV cameras. It was then he spotted the kitchen boiler was out of action again. Not good, he thought. It had failed for the third time in just as many weeks. He'd been onto the suppliers at least a dozen times and was sick to death of their excuses. Why couldn't they repair it, or send him a replacement? Since he had repaired the corridor lights, he could mark those off his to-do list.

Then, scrolling down, he saw what the electrician had been whingeing on about. A nauseating smell coming from Locker Room 2. Never a dull moment, he mused. You fix one problem, then another crops up in its place. It was probably the street drains again. The last time this had happened, someone caught one of the local kebab shops on Grainger Street tipping hot boiling fat into their drains. Damn foreigners, he cursed. Why couldn't they conform like the rest of us? Still, Monday wasn't the busiest day of the week to get things done. That was on Friday. It was all linked to the trains – people storing their hand luggage whilst touring the streets of Newcastle. At least it made sense if nothing else did around here.

The electrician was right. There was a nasty odour coming from Locker Room 2. A pungent smell that made him retch the moment he stepped into the room. Just out of curiosity, he checked the toilets. Nothing. Then he poked his nose down into the kitchen drains. Nothing there either. Returning to his desk, he ran his cursor over the long overdue. There were five in total. All pointing to Locker Room 2. The thing was, some people never returned to collect their belongings, as the overdue rental costs far outweighed the value of their possessions. It was a regular occurrence, and time the company put a stop to it.

The first locker Tommy opened in Locker Room 2 was

number 21. Crammed full of rucksacks and personal effects, there wasn't much in the way of value either. Pushing his head in through the open locker door, he caught a strong whiff of sweaty feet. Clearly, these people weren't coming back.

The moment he opened locker 56, his stomach lurched. In all the years that he'd worked for the company, Tommy had experienced nothing like this before. An obnoxious stench that instantly took his breath away. Pinching his nose between finger and thumb, he slid the large blue suitcase towards the front of the locker. It felt heavy. Using his finger, he poked it and observed its peculiar movement. Taking a closer inspection, he noticed it was pad-locked and secured with two thick luggage straps. He tried to lift it and immediately wished he hadn't.

Gulping the air in snatches, Tommy steadied himself as he moved towards the open door. No matter how hard he tried to rid himself of bad thoughts, the sweet, sickly smell of death still clung to him. Torn between doubt and hesitation, he finally arrived at the corridor's end. Unsteady on his feet, he clawed his way towards the main entrance, but not before throwing up.

Who brought it here? He questioned.

Shaking violently, he tried to stay focused, but the thought of what lay hidden inside the suitcase refused to go away. His world falling apart, his whole body felt as though a thousand insects were crawling over him. His mind running amok, he recalled the struggle the customer had in lifting it into the locker that night. A stocky man, he wore a black hoodie pulled down low over his head and black lens sunglasses. The rest became lost in a sea of confusion, and fear prevented him from even going there.

What to do next?

Alone with his thoughts, Tommy felt as if he had lost hours somewhere. Terrified, the more he thought about it, the more confused he became. Despite the mysterious contents of the blue suitcase, he was powerless.

It was still there, waiting for him in Locker Room 2.

CHAPTER SIX

Within hours of the storage company owners contacting Northumbria Police, Warwick Street was awash with newspaper reporters. News travelled fast, and the number of outside broadcast vans had grown considerably. The discovery of a headless torso wasn't an everyday occurrence, either. The city was in shock.

Sitting in his car, David Carlisle had watched the press conference unfold from his iPhone. All the major networks were present. It was a big turnout. With popular news presenters vying for top positions, the events were being transmitted live to the entire nation. In front of a packed media gathering, DCI Mason gave a brief statement appealing for witnesses to come forward. Dubbed "The Suitcase Man," the public's insatiable demand for answers was unnerving and the press were loving every minute. It's what sold newspapers, what pushed editors to write riveting headline stories.

Dressed in full police uniform, the acting superintendent appealed for calm. Even a heavy police presence had brought little comfort to the student community. Rumours ran rife, and anyone seen dragging a suitcase around the streets of Newcastle was immediately stopped and questioned.

It was ten o'clock when David Carlisle finally entered the Gateshead Police Station. Harassed by zealous reporters, the desk sergeant wasn't his usual happy-go-lucky self. According to Central Control, the station was being bombarded with hundreds of hoax claims concerning the killer's identity. If there were any positives to be had, blood samples recovered from Jennifer Oakwell's property matched that of the headless torso. All that remained now was to find the victim's missing body parts, and the rest would fall into place.

Taking the stairs two at a time, Carlisle reached the third floor amidst a hive of activity. These latest developments had certainly fired up the station's imagination, and everyone was demanding answers. The problem was no one had any to give. The moment he entered Jack Mason's office, the profiler felt the urgency of the situation.

'No doubt you'll have heard about these latest developments,' said Mason anxiously.

'I have. I watched the media conference on my phone.'

'What did you think?'

'To tell you the truth, I thought you came across as a right shifty bastard.'

Mason grinned as he shuffled a few papers around an untidy desk. Not the best start, Carlisle thought. Divergence was the chief inspector's favourite distraction.

There was a brief pause.

'This latest discovery has sparked off all kinds of unimaginable panic, and Forth Street will never be the same.'

'No, I guess not.'

Mason took a sip of water from a glass, then rounded on him. 'Remind me of your involvement with Frank

Wiseman's son. What exactly did you do for these people?'

'I thought we'd already discussed that issue.'

Pen poised, the DCI glanced up at him. 'We have. This is for the official record.'

'If you must know, I worked for his son's solicitors. Low key stuff mainly. Undercover surveillance – reconnaissance work.'

'What else did you do for them?'

'What do you mean by that?'

Mason looked down at his notes. 'What was the nature of your investigations?'

'Wiseman's son was having a spot of bother with a group of local thugs. They were threatening him with violence if he didn't pay up.'

'Drugs related, was it?'

'No, these people were trying to extort money from him. If he didn't pay up, they threatened to punish his family and burn his pub down.'

'Did they not know who his father was?'

'They did, apparently.'

'And they still threatened to go ahead with it.'

'I believe so.'

Mason shook his head in disbelief. 'So, how did you finally resolve the problem?'

'Let's say a few people owed me favours.'

Mason's eyebrows rose a fraction, the serious side surfacing. 'This wouldn't involve one of Frank Wiseman's associates, would it? The reason I ask is there could be a connection here.'

'Do you genuinely believe these murders are linked to

his son's threats?'

'No, I didn't say that.'

'Linked to whom then?' the profiler quizzed.

'I'm not at liberty to say. It's strictly a police matter.'

Mason was bluffing, and Carlisle had picked up on it. Two could play at this game, and it was time to get to the bottom of it.

'Without seeing the case files, how do you expect me to comment?'

Mason put his pen down and poured some more water from a jug. He admired his colleague's tenacity but thought it a waste of time. Knowing how the system worked, Carlisle was well aware of the way the chief inspector ran things. First, he'd prime you full of bullshit, then attempt to pick your brain. And yes, these recent murders had all the hallmarks of a gangland killing, but it was far from the truth. Whoever the suitcase man was, he'd certainly stirred up a hornet's nest.

'This latest victim has yet to be identified,' Mason confirmed. 'Find the answer to that, and we're halfway to solving our problem.'

'You think it's that simple?'

'Probably not.' Mason raised a finger, then tapped his computer screen. 'We know Jennifer Oakwell was the killer's intended target, as he dealt with her first. In attempting to dispose of the second victim's body, we now believe he was side-tracked at some point.'

Carlisle swallowed hard. 'You're not suggesting the killer intended to return to the storage locker and recover the suitcase, are you?'

'That's how we see it.'

'He left it a bit late, don't you think?'

'What do you mean, late?'

'According to media reports, the body stank to high heavens.'

Mason took a few moments before answering. As things veered off course, the chief inspector grappled with the unexpected turn of events.

'This was a gangland execution, and that's why they removed the victim's head and hands. It's a classic method these people use. Eliminate the witness... get rid of the evidence.'

'It would have been far easier to bury or burn the body, don't you think?'

Mason hesitated. 'Who knows how they intended to dispose of it?'

'So, what is it you want from me?'

Mason's brow corrugated. 'I'm fascinated by this work you did for Frank Wiseman's solicitors. The guy you dealt with wouldn't be Tony Fox, would it?'

'I can't say...'

Mason explained. 'Fox runs a second-hand car dealership on Bridge Street. It's high end stuff, big turnover, and all of it stolen to order. We've been watching his premises for months now, and a lot of money is changing hands.'

'No. That name's not familiar. What's the connection?'

'Just curious, that's all.'

'Wait a minute—'

Mason interrupted him by raising his hand. 'We also have reliable information that a power struggle is taking place. Someone's trying to muscle in on Frank

Wiseman's patch. If the rumours are true, then there may be a connection between these recent killings.'

'In which case, how can I possibly be of help?'

'You can't,' Mason told him.

'So why did you invite me here?'

The chief inspector stared at him hard. 'It's your involvement with Wiseman's solicitors that intrigues me. You obviously got close to these people, and I was rather hoping you'd shed some light on the subject.'

Carlisle was curious about where Mason's interests lay. Was he exploiting him for information? A go-between? His logical thinking led him to the conclusion that he was. The thought of losing his client's trust was completely unacceptable, and under no circumstances would he allow it to happen.

Chapter Seven

A pall of fear hung over the city that morning, with parts of Forth Street still cordoned off. It was headline breaking news, and tales of a headless torso being dragged around the streets of Newcastle weren't helping either. Sometimes Mason wondered why he bothered to attend media conferences. No matter how hard you tried to cool things down, reporters hyped them up. News travelled fast, and the crowd of curious onlookers now gathered outside the storage building was growing by the minute. What were they expecting to find, for heaven's sake?

Despite all his efforts, Mason's investigations had yielded very little in the way of fresh leads. Throughout that morning, search teams had covered every inch of Forth Street. It was painstaking work, and with hundreds of hours of CCTV footage to sift through, he wasn't confident of making an arrest. Anyone captured on camera, seen dragging a heavy suitcase within a mile of the storage company, was now under suspicion. Not everyone would come forward, of course, and those who declined faced intense scrutiny.

Mason's appeal for sightings of any suspicious activity around the time of the murder had gained significant traction, prompting a dedicated team of undercover officers to be assigned to the case. Uniforms had worked tirelessly too, distributing thousands of leaflets to jog people's memories. Someone out there knew something. It was a matter of weeding them out.

As the nightmare continued, Mason's gaze drifted along the long line of storage lockers. Who could have done such a thing? The trouble was, CCTV covering the company's main entrance wasn't working, nor were the lights in Locker Room 2. The only thing in their favour was the manager had not tried to open the suitcase. It wasn't much, but at least forensics had a clear run of the place.

Savage poked his head into the locker room. 'I've just come from the manager's office, and the guy who brought the suitcase here didn't have a strong local accent.'

'He's not from Newcastle then?'

'Not according to the manager, he isn't.'

'What else did he tell you?'

'He said the guy had one hell of a struggle to lift the suitcase into the locker.'

Mason's eyes narrowed. 'I thought the lights weren't working?'

'They weren't. The manager carried a torch.'

'What time was this?'

'Around seven o'clock.'

'Did he say what he looked like?'

'He's still in a state of shock and can't remember much about the incident.'

Mason checked his watch. Even with a good smothering of Vicks VapoRub under his nose, Locker Room 2 still stank to the high heavens. There was no smell like the smell of decomposing flesh; even the most hardened investigators retched at the first sniff of it when entering a crime scene. As a body decomposed, it released gases, and the two primary chemicals involved were cadaverine and putrescine. Real crime scenes were nothing like the glamorous dramas played out on TV. Working at street level was a whole different ball game. The problem was, it usually took days before the nauseating smell that clung to your clothes disappeared. Even then, it hung in the memory.

The chief inspector slipped out of his white coveralls and brushed the flecks of forensic powder from his trouser legs. Not the best start to his day, he muttered. They'd made progress, but not much. He thought about giving Tom Hedley a call and decided to ring later.

Out in the open, the young constable stood guard at the entrance, tipped his cap in acknowledgment. Normally, Mason would have stopped to chat; not today, though. What little daylight remained, he would need to use sparingly. Despite all his efforts, there was still no simple explanation of how the suspect had arrived at the storage company that evening. Sifting through hundreds of hours of CCTV footage took time, and Mason was having to rely heavily on eyewitness accounts. He knew from experience that someone had planned the whole grizzly affair. *But whom? And why?*

As he let his mind drift, it was something that DS Savage had said that stopped him dead in his tracks. The light closing in, the city would soon take on a different guise. Full of indecision, Mason retraced his footsteps back towards Forth Banks police station. No, he thought. The killer would have arrived here by car. It made sense, if little else did. Then again, he argued. What if an unsuspecting taxi driver had dropped him off? The only thing wrong with that line of thinking was the suitcase would have been extremely heavy to lift out of the boot of the taxi. Not the best option, he reasoned. It would have raised too much suspicion.

***

On entering Forth Banks police station, a familiar face stared up at him from behind the desk screen. Sergeant Bronson was a distinguished-looking man, mid-forties, thin on top, with a sharp, public-school accent. Mason despised the man and considered him a knob head.

'Name?' the sergeant announced.

'Mickey Mouse.'

Fingers poised over the keyboard, the sergeant lifted his head a fraction. 'I need a name, sir. It's procedure.'

'Is DS Wallace on duty?'

'First things first,' the sergeant replied stoically.

Fast losing his patience, Mason held his warrant card up in front of the sergeant's face. 'DCI Jack Mason, Northumbria Police. Is DS Wallace about?'

'Thank you, sir. I'll check to see if he's in.'

The sergeant smiled meekly as he picked up the telephone receiver and punched a three-digit code into the keypad. Seconds later, he spun to face him. 'DS Wallace is on the second floor. It's the first door on your right.'

The operations room was open plan and narrow. Five

desks overlooking the east coast main railway line, and all decked out with flat screen computer monitors. It wasn't a large room, but as police stations went, it had a cosy atmosphere.

He found Wallace staring up at a large wall map pinned to the back wall. From what he could see, his old workmate had piled on the weight since they'd last worked together. Unlike some police officers he'd dealt with over the years, Wallace was a grafter and easy to get on with.

'Hello, Jack. What brings you to this neck of the woods?'

'Business, George.'

Wallace managed a wry smile as they shook hands. 'This wouldn't involve the Suitcase Man, would it?'

'How did you guess?'

Wallace gestured towards an empty seat opposite. 'How can we help?'

A phone rang, and the officer sat at the next desk, picked up the receiver and began taking down notes. Mason cleared his throat. 'This one's a bit of a puzzler. We know the victim had links to Jennifer Oakwell, as we now have a positive DNA match. What we don't know, not even forensics, is who the hell he is.'

Wallace shook his head. 'I take it you still haven't found the rest of the body parts?'

'Not yet, we haven't. And I'm not pinning my hopes on finding them.'

'Whoever killed him is intent on making identification difficult. That much is certain.'

Mason shuffled awkwardly.

'He's a cunning bastard. I'll give him that.'

'Is it possible that he's warning someone?'

'That had crossed my mind,' Mason sighed. 'As have a lot of other things lately.'

'Hindsight's a funny thing, but your killer sounds a bit of a loose cannon in the grand scheme of things.'

The two men looked at one another and smiled.

'It doesn't add up. It's as if—' Mason stopped himself short, his mind switching to other things. 'This has all the hallmarks of another gangland execution. The only problem with that is who in their rightful mind would want to murder Mad Frankie Wiseman's ex-wife?'

'What if someone arranged it?'

'He's not that daft, George. Besides, it would have been far too obvious.'

Wallace thought for a moment.

'Why did Jennifer Oakwell split from her husband? As I remember, she sat in the courtroom during the entire eight-week trial and supported him throughout. Something doesn't sit right. Who in the criminal underworld would dare kill Wiseman's ex-wife?'

'The day Mad Frankie went down, she found herself left facing a twenty-year separation. It's not something to look forward to in any marriage.'

'No, I suppose not.' Wallace frowned. 'And she never re-married?'

'Not to my knowledge.'

'Pity. So, Oakwell was her maiden name.'

'Yes, it was.'

There was a long, drawn out silence.

'What about casual lovers?' asked Wallace. 'Did she

ever team up with anyone?'

'What, you think Wiseman may have a jealous streak?'

'Twenty years is a long time to be cooped up inside a prison cell. Who knows what thoughts and desires lurk in the depths of some people's minds?'

Mason thought for a moment, but said nothing.

'It's not just her sex life,' Wallace went on. 'It's Wiseman's reputation that could be at stake here.'

'That's a good point, George.'

'What about the rest of the gang members? I hear some of them are now out on parole.'

'We've already considered that aspect. The day Wiseman's ex-wife was murdered, they all provided watertight alibis. I'm more concerned about this takeover bid everyone is talking about. Who's trying to muscle in on Mad Frankie's territory?'

Wallace stroked his long-pointed chin, his eyes searching for answers. 'It's been exceptionally quiet around these parts lately, as if the criminal fraternity has gone into hibernation. I could put my feelers out... ask around. I know a few desperate lowlifes who could do with a few extra quid in their pockets.'

'Good man. That could be useful.'

'Tell me,' said Wallace, the look of concern still showing. 'Have you given any thoughts to contacting David Carlisle?'

'Yes and no,' Mason muttered under his breath. 'The Acting Superintendent is the stumbling block there. Sutherland's not at all keen on the idea of bringing specialists in on the case, especially at this early stage of our investigations.'

'Police budgets, no doubt.'

'There is an element of that.'

Wallace nodded. 'She's probably right, of course.'

'I'm not convinced it's the right decision.'

'So where do you go from here?'

'You know me, George. I'm not one to shy away from a problem.'

Wallace stuck a yellow post-it onto the side of his computer screen and swivelled in his seat. 'The last I heard, Wiseman was serving out his time in Durham prison.'

'He still is.'

'In which case, it might be worth paying him a visit.'

Mason let out a sigh. 'Criminals aren't usually that obliging, George.'

'No, I guess not. At least you'll know which side of the fence he's sitting on, and whether he knows anything about his ex-wife's murder.'

Three people, including Wallace, had now made a suggestion for a prison visit in as many days, and he was far from impressed. He would need to sleep on it, consider things before making any snap decisions.

Mason held the sergeant's glance. 'Had it been you, George, how would you have transported a body to the storage company that evening?'

Wallace tapped his pen on the desktop in thought. 'I'd have driven there by car. Think about it. Who in their rightful mind would want to drag a heavy suitcase round the streets of Newcastle with a headless torso stuck inside?'

'Unless you're the executioner!'

'True.' Wallace shrugged.

'Do you think others could be involved?'

'It's possible, especially if this was an organised crime.'

'Who are the most likely candidates, do you think?'

The detective took a deep breath before answering. 'If there's a power struggle taking place, it could only involve a few people. My money would be on Tony Fox, or one of Wiseman's counterparts from the east end of Newcastle.'

'Anyone else spring to mind?'

'There's a guy who operates out of Westgate Road called Carlo Stefano. It may be worth calling him. The trouble is, he has his fingers in an awful lot of organised crime and is difficult to pin down.'

'He sounds Mafia to me.'

'He probably is.'

Mason shook his head.

'So why bother with the storage company? It makes little sense.'

'Why not? I couldn't think of a better place.'

Mason stared at him, confused. It had been a long day.

CHAPTER EIGHT

Whilst the rest of Newcastle slept uneasily in their beds that night, dozens of armed police officers had moved into Forth Street under the cover of darkness. There was no room for error, and police officers had sealed off the entire area as the first rays of sunlight appeared. It was a huge operation. If the killer had arrived at the storage company on foot that evening, then someone must have seen him. It was this aspect that Mason was working on, and couldn't but help feel a surge of optimism wash over him. Not all had been plain sailing, though. Plagued by uncertainty, yesterday's press conference had come and gone. Mason hated media gatherings, claiming they were minefields full of unscrupulous reporters. The problem was, the chief inspector had a nasty habit of saying all the wrong things, and it wasn't good press. Not that it worried him. It didn't.

Pleased with his findings, he checked the street map again. All along Forth Street and buried deep beneath the bowels of the east coast main railway line lay a network of tunnels. It was the perfect hiding place. Built of solid sandstone, someone had turned several archways into going concerns. People ran businesses from here, working beneath the mainline railway as if living the existence of moles.

He watched as a group of armed police officers began

their search of an adjoining property. Dressed in full combat gear, their leader, a sergeant, was giving out instructions. Within seconds, they were inside and searching the property.

'I never knew these premises existed,' Mason said, turning to face DS Savage.

'They've been here for as long as I can remember. It's an additional source of income for the railway company, but I thought they'd closed them down years ago.'

'It's perfect, Rob.'

As the sergeant shone his torch into one of the ventilation shafts, Mason felt his body tense. The air was damp and uninviting. The deeper into the network of tunnels they ventured, the creepier it became. It reminded him of the London underground, high arched ceilings, red brick walls, and a maze of endless passageways.

'What's it like back there?' Mason asked.

'There are several offshoot passages further back, although they don't compare to the ones that run under the city.'

'There's more?'

'I know of a few that still exist.'

'You've obviously been here before, Rob.'

The sergeant regarded him cautiously. A former boxing champion, he wasn't a specialist at anything, more a jack of all trades.

'When I was a young lad, my old man used to bring me down here. It was one of the many weird interests he had. As I remember, there's one tunnel that runs from Spital Tongues colliery down to the River Tyne, which is over two miles long.'

'That's some length.'

'Yeah. Once upon a time, it was used to transport coal to the collier boats, but they mothballed it many years ago. They used them as air shelters during the Second World War, but most authorities have since bricked them up.'

'You live and learn,' Mason said, shaking his head. 'Walk the streets of Newcastle, and you never know what lies beneath your feet.'

'It's another world down here,' the sergeant stressed.

'We ought to inspect. What if someone is hiding in one of the side tunnels you talk about?'

'I'll get one of the dog teams involved,' Savage replied.

Eventually, after what seemed a long time, he could hear the hollow echoes of footsteps. The tunnel curved left slightly, a single chain of emergency lights vanishing into the middle-distance. Then, through one of the offshoot passageways, a small team of police officers emerged.

'We found these two scoundrels holed up in one of the side shafts,' Manley announced.

Mason stepped forward to take control.

'What are they doing down here?'

'Part of the city's homeless community, by the looks.'

Mason gave them a once over but quickly eliminated them from his enquiries. Too many people had fallen through the cracks of society for his like. Securing a safe place to live was always difficult when you were down on your luck. He felt sorry for them, as many were vulnerable. Living rough on the streets of Newcastle meant you were prone to being a victim of violence. It was a statistic he wasn't proud of, but one he had little influence on. Having grown up knowing hardship himself, he knew how easy it was to fall into the poverty trap. Life was a vicious circle, and there was no simple solution.

Having caught a whiff of the suspect's stale breath, Mason took a step back. Cheap supermarket wine – another debilitating disease associated with the homeless community.

'What are you people doing down here?' asked Mason, inclining his head.

'This is our home mate. Is there a problem?'

'How long have you been down here?'

As if to confirm his statement, the shorter man grinned through blackened teeth. 'Six months ... could be more.'

'Anyone else call this place home?'

'Not to my knowledge.'

'How can you be sure?'

'We'd have known if they were.'

Not the sort of place to call home. Sleeping rough in the middle of Newcastle could be harsh. Like two startled sewer rats, the strangers stared at him as though he'd arrived from another planet. The smaller of the two looked ex-military. He had that anxious look, emotionally detached, as if suffering from some form of post-traumatic stress disorder. Probably a fallen hero involved in some sort of military combat in the past. Avoidance of places, people, were the most common symptoms as Mason had so often found. It was a sorry state of affairs, and few people gave a damn about the homeless nowadays.

'Who else hangs around this area at night?' he asked.

Neither spoke, which was understandable under the circumstances.

Mason turned to Manley. 'What did your sweep of the other tunnels throw up?'

'Apart from these two, nothing.'

'Let's bring them in for questioning. While you're at it, see if the duty sergeant can't rustle up some bacon and eggs. They look as if they could do with a hot meal.'

Mason slumped back against the wall, thinking. The main tunnel was an endless black hole of deep rumbling noises. Not the nicest place to hang around in, he thought. It reminded him of the nightmare from hell.

As he moved back into Forth Street, one of the locals confronted him. A stout man with an overhanging belly and black shiny leather shoes.

'Are you the tenant?' Mason enquired.

'I am. What are you people looking for?'

In what was now a well-oiled operation, a team of police officers poured out of one of the adjoining archways. If the killer was using this place as a bolthole, they might even catch him red-handed. Mason smiled inwardly, knowing his imagination was taking flight.

'Are these units always kept locked at night?'

'Yes. Why do you ask?'

The lead investigator was having to think quickly.

'What about CCTV?'

'There is none.'

'Any reason?'

The tenant shrugged but said nothing.

'What about these two miscreants? How do you explain their presence on your property?'

'With all due respects, Inspector—'

Annoyed with the man's attitude, Mason took out his warrant card. 'Take another look. It's Detective Chief Inspector. Any more derogatory remarks, and you'll feel a size ten boot up your arse.'

Not for the first time, Mason had lost the plot, and the man standing before him was probably squeaky clean. Not good, he reasoned. Why did he always fly off the handle at the slightest provocation? Was this down to his marriage breakup, or sheer frustration? He would need to calm down, think things through logically instead of recklessly jumping to conclusions. And that was another thing that concerned him. He was back to his old drinking habits again. The giveaway was his trembling hands, which prompted him to seek control.

'Have you been watching the news lately?' Mason asked.

'I might have been. Why?'

'In which case you'll have heard about the body we found at the storage company.'

The tenant shrugged. 'Is that what this is about?'

Mason glared at him. 'No doubt you've made a statement to that effect?'

'No, I haven't.'

'Why not?'

'I didn't think it was necessary. Besides, it's been weeks since I was last down here.'

Mason took a long, wistful look at the opening to the

tunnel and tried to curb his emotions. 'Okay, you'll need to accompany me back to Gateshead Police Station.'

The tenant was about to speak, but quickly thought the better.

'It's the law,' Mason said brashly. 'It's what we're paid to do.'

'Really? And you thought the best way to solve it was by being as rude as possible, did you?'

Mason curbed a powerful urge to take the man to the ground and have him cuffed. 'If you would kindly accompany us, SIR, then you can help us with our enquiries and be on your way.'

Chapter Nine

Sutherland's eyebrows raised ever so slightly as she studied the coroner's report. Not an unattractive woman, mid-forties, with a slim waistline and fresh complexion, her piercing blue eyes seemed to draw you in. Tom Hedley, the senior forensic scientist, explained that her hair would change colour every other week. At least she was approachable, which was more than Jack Mason could say about most senior officers in the division. A former pupil of Queen Elizabeth High School in Hexham, her father was an ex-Coldstream Guards officer. A strict disciplinarian, with contacts in high places, gossip had it that at some stage in his career he'd served as equerry to the Queen. If true, there was little wonder his daughter had made such impressive progress as she did.

Mason sat quietly, waiting for the punchline.

'This male torso we found in Forth Street,' she began. 'Can we put a name to him?'

'Not yet, we can't, ma'am.'

Sutherland was punctilious about the use of professional titles, and Mason hated it. It wasn't his style of policing, and the word Ma'am always sounded empty and insincere. He watched as she annoyingly tapped the end of her pen on a case file before turning to face him. 'Are you sure this is a case of witness elimination?'

Mason grinned inanely. 'If not, then someone's in a mighty hurry to step into Frank Wiseman's shoes.'

'Speaking of criminals, Jack. Where are we with Wiseman's associates? I hear they have released several of the gang members on parole.'

'Yes, that's correct, ma'am.'

Sutherland fell silent briefly before continuing. 'I'm informed that nobody has ever recovered the money the gang stole during the post office raids.'

'I believe that's the case.'

'Could Wiseman's ex-wife have anything to do with this?'

'It's feasible, but highly unlikely.'

'We need to keep a watchful eye on these people. The money is still out there somewhere.'

'We are ma'am.'

'And?'

'They all have watertight alibis and had nothing to do with these murders.'

'Keep trying. These people cannot be trusted.'

'Yes, ma'am.'

Mason brought her up to speed with the latest developments. When he'd finished, she remained silent again, then said. 'Perhaps a visit to Durham prison is in order. Let's see what Mr Wiseman has to say for himself. He's bound to know something about his ex-wife's murder, surely.'

'I doubt he'll talk.'

'I agree, but at least we'll know if he's still active.'

This was the fourth person in as many days to mention a prison visit, and he was far from impressed.

Experience had taught him that interviewing inmates was never a clever idea, let alone category A prisoners. No, he thought. He would refuse to go down that avenue again.

'I'm not convinced it will work, ma'am.'

'It must be worth pursuing, don't you think?'

Notebook open, pen poised, Mason's look was unyielding. 'And how do you propose we go about that? It's not as straightforward as you think.'

Sutherland's face visibly stiffened. 'Talk to the prison governor. See what he offers.'

Mason cringed, but said nothing.

'Tell me,' she said, the look of despair still showing. 'What was the outcome of yesterday's Forth Street operation?'

'There's been a positive response, but nothing of any significance has shown up.'

'What about ANPR?'

'No, nothing.'

'And the storage company's CCTV footage?'

'The main entrance cameras haven't worked in weeks, and the manager hasn't a clue what our suspect even looks like, let alone give a description of him.'

'He must have filled in a witness statement, surely?'

'He did, but the name and address the perpetrator gave him doesn't add up.'

'Well, there's a thing,' she mused, her eyebrows raising in curiosity again. 'What else did he say?'

'The man was vague, and none of what he told us is of any use.'

'And yet he still remembers a *blue* suitcase being

deposited at this storage company that evening. It can't all be worthless information.'

Mason grimaced, a smile without humour. 'The fact is, we still haven't established how the suitcase initially arrived at the company that night.'

'Being so close to the railway station, I would have thought someone dragged it there.'

'I'm not so sure about that. According to the manager, the suspect had difficulty in manhandling it into the locker.'

The acting superintendent glanced up at a series of SOC images pinned to her corkboard. 'It's rather a large suitcase and definitely looks awkward to lift.'

'And the suspect isn't a tall man.'

She hesitated as she wrinkled her nose. 'Then again, it has sturdy wheels, which suggests someone could have easily dragged it there.'

'It may well have been,' Mason replied.

'We need to revisit the storage company. Let's see if we haven't missed something.'

Mason made a note of it, annoyed at having to go back over the old ground again. He lifted his head as if resigned to the fact. 'I'll get someone over there right away, ma'am.'

Sutherland pushed back in her seat, walked over to the filing cabinet, and pulled out the top-drawer. Unimpressed with her approach, Mason was finding it difficult to relax. It was then he noticed she was wearing flat shoes. More for comfort than fashion, he guessed. He smiled inwardly as she lifted several case files out from its folder and returned to her seat.

'Shortly after Frank Wiseman was sent down, his wife started the divorce proceedings. Their relationship was far from good, and during the court hearing, he showed little interest towards her. Not that Wiseman had any choice in the matter,' Sutherland said, as she flicked through the pages of the report. 'They had a son. Robert. He was twelve. What with a father in prison and a mother keen to celebrate her newly found freedom, it wasn't the best environment to be brought up in.'

'I would agree, ma'am.'

Sutherland's shoulders sagged. 'She didn't hang about either, according to the report. Shortly after the divorce, she reverted to her maiden name.'

'Most women usually do,' Mason said.

Having just gone through a stressful divorce himself, he'd become quite an expert on the matter.

'Yes, but having gained resident parent over Robert, according to Social Services, it wasn't a very pleasant mother and son relationship either.'

'No. I guess not.'

Sutherland's eyes narrowed a fraction. 'It also mentions that Robert spent most of his childhood living with an aunt in Whitley Bay.'

'We've already covered that aspect, ma'am. Robert went to High School there but didn't do well in his final exams. After leaving school, he was in and out of jobs before finally ending up running a pub in Walker.'

'Ah, yes,' she nodded. 'As I remember, he got into a spot of bother over it.'

'He did. Local impressionable thugs trying to squeeze protection money out of him.'

'Do we know who they are?'

'We do.'

Sutherland flicked through the pages of the report and then turned to face him. 'Are things back to normal again?'

'Yes. For the moment they are.'

'We need to dig deeper, Chief Inspector. Find out what Oakwell got up to after the divorce settlement. Why someone would want to kill her still isn't clear. To me, this implies that every little detail could hold the truth.'

'We've already looked into her past, ma'am, but nothing has come of it.'

'It's my understanding she had alcohol issues.'

'She did.'

'And you're still adamant this is a case of witness elimination?'

'Unless we've missed something obvious, ma'am.'

Sutherland shook her head despondently. 'This isn't as easy as I first thought. There's still a lot of unanswered questions surrounding the case. Family issues. Jealousy. Mistrust.'

Mason trod cautiously. 'The question remains, why did the killer choose the storage company in the first place?'

'Convenience, I would have thought. Proximity to the city centre... easy access to the railway and Metro systems.'

'If I may say so, I suspect it's risky dragging a suitcase around the streets of Newcastle with a body stuck inside. Why would someone do that? It makes little sense.'

'What if they stored the body there for someone else

to pick up?'

'It's possible, ma'am.'

Sutherland closed her case files and pushed them to one side. 'If anything, you need to concentrate your efforts on establishing who the second victim is. Once we uncover that, we'll have a better understanding of what the connection is.'

Mason experienced that sinking feeling again. Pity, he thought. He could have done with a few imaginative thinkers on the team. People like David Carlisle, someone who could move with fast changing situations. As usual, Sutherland's head was still stuck inside the rule book and seemed reluctant to venture away from it. At least the case was on his own turf, which offered some consolation.

'I forgot to mention it earlier,' Mason said, keeping his voice low. 'But it was the profiler, David Carlisle, who initially got involved with Wiseman's lawyers over his son's protection racket.'

'I thought it was his father's pub?'

'No, ma'am. Robert owns it outright. Besides, he's the innocent party in all of this.'

'You mentioned none of that in your report.'

'With all due respects, I didn't think it had anything to do with the case.'

Sutherland kept silent for some moments. 'If there is a power struggle to take place, then Frank Wiseman is bound to feature heavily in it. These people have a knack of keeping control over their empires, even when serving time in prison.'

'I couldn't agree more. It's a case of protecting your

assets until your release date.'

'What if someone killed his ex-wife because of it?'

Mason shrugged, but said nothing.

Sutherland gave him another stern look. 'Let's see what your visit to Durham prison throws up. Who knows, it may open up a whole new line of enquiries.'

Little chance of that happening, Mason groaned. Answers were few, and they were running out of ideas. Lateral thinking was the way forward it had to be. If not, then it was back to the drawing board.

As the meeting ended, the chief inspector felt utterly deflated. With morale at rock bottom, any hopes of an early breakthrough seemed a million light years away.

CHAPTER TEN

Over the centuries, HM Durham Prison had housed a dark legacy of infamous criminals, sending chills down the spines of all who entered. Household names like the Kray twins, whose names struck fear and fascination in equal measure. What many people didn't know was that the prison had a haunting history, with over one-hundred men and women meeting their fate on the gallows there. Ninety-one had taken place at the prison or nearby courthouse, and eighteen in public. Not that execution concerned Jack Mason as he strolled into Old Elvet that morning. He was more interested in what Mad Frankie Wisemen had to say.

As he walked into the prison's main entrance hall, the air was heavy with the unmistakable scent of mistrust. Far removed from the everyday hustle and bustle of normality, this was another world. At the reception desk, he showed his warrant card, and the staff asked him a series of questions as part of the standard security procedure. Next, an inquisitive dog approached him and gave him a thorough inspection, as if suspecting him of being involved in the drug trade.

Not finished yet, they placed his personal effects, including his wallet, car keys, and mobile phone, in a long plastic tray and stored them in a security locker for safekeeping. After a walk-through body scan and pat-down search by an overzealous female security officer, Mason felt awkward and conspicuous.

'Follow me,' the waiting prison officer announced.

Led through a series of high security doors, they entered a windowless room normally set aside for interviews. 'Make yourself comfortable,' the prison officer announced. 'They shouldn't be long.'

Mason nodded and took up a seat.

The room was imposing with an overpowering sense of suspicion. Staring up at a 42-inch plasma screen used as a video link to connect to outlying courts, he felt he was being watched. Prisoners who came here were in trouble with the law, that much was obvious. Although much of the building had maintained its original character, several new features had been added. Security was tight. It had to be. Durham Prison harboured many notorious criminals serving life sentences, including child killers and sex perverts.

Several minutes passed, then Mason heard keys jangling. Flanked by two prison officers, Mad Frankie Wiseman entered the interview room handcuffed. Dressed in a standard blue prison shirt, black trousers, and wearing a pair of comfy deck shoes, the inmate's left hand bore a heavy bandage, protecting what appeared to be a broken finger. Staring down at him, the inmate muttered something inaudible and slumped in a chair opposite.

'Mr Wiseman,' the lead detective began. 'I'm DCI Jack Mason, Northumbria Police. I'm here to ask you a few questions, if I may.'

The voice sounded worn out and gruff, like a smoker's.

'Are you for real, or what?'

'I'm sorry?'

Wiseman gave him a stern look. 'It's me who asks the questions around here.'

Mason's instincts told him not to rush into it. Stay calm, he reasoned. It was difficult to get his head round the fact he was dealing with one of Newcastle's most notorious gangsters.

The chief inspector lifted his head as he spoke. 'What is it you're wanting to ask me?'

'Don't fuck with me,' Wiseman growled. 'You know what I want.'

Mason remained silent for a moment. It was a tense standoff, a pure battle of wits. Mad Frankie had obviously kept himself in decent shape over the years, as most long-term prisoners usually did. It's what kept them apart from the rest of the inmates, what segregated the wheat from the chaff. Flexing your muscles was a big part of the prison mind-set, as it not only showed your ability to smash someone's brains in, it established your prison credibility. No, Mason thought, he would need to keep a cool head, even though it rubbed against the grain.

'I'm sorry to hear about the recent loss of your ex-wife.'

'Are you?'

'If someone had murdered my ex, I'd be furious.' Mason let it sink in. 'Just so as you know, we are doing everything in our power to catch the sick bastard who did this.'

'I'm listening, but I'm not liking what I'm hearing.'

'If there's anything—'

Wiseman interrupted him by raising a hand. 'Let's cut the crap. What is it you're after?'

'I'd appreciate some honest answers, Frank.'

Wiseman cocked his head to one side. 'It doesn't work like that. Not around here, it doesn't.'

'Really?'

'Yeah. This is a fucking prison, not a university challenge quiz show.'

As his grip on the tubular chair tightened, Mason's gaze drifted towards Wiseman's heavily bandaged finger again. If trouble broke out, he'd reach over, grab it, and watch the bastard scream.

'When did you last contact, Jennifer?'

'Not since the divorce.' Wiseman almost laughed. 'I was glad to see the back of her.'

'What about relatives?'

'No. They don't bother me anymore.'

'Did any of Jennifer's family ever stay connected? A prison visit perhaps, or the odd Christmas card?'

'Why would they?'

'Just curious.'

'Let's get one thing straight here,' Wiseman said as he leaned across the table and exhaled heavily. 'I've never talked to my ex, not since the divorce settlement. What she got up to, and who she went out with, was none of my concern.'

'What about the sub-post office cash that's gone missing? Was Jennifer involved in that?'

Wiseman stared at him hard.

'What money is this?'

'The cash you people stole in the post office raids.'

'How the fuck would I know? I've been cooped up inside this wretched shithole ever since you heartless bastards sent me down.'

God loves a trier, but this was ridiculous. He would need to cool things down. Try a different approach.

'I was talking to Tony Fox the other day about the European crime gangs who are moving into the north side of the city. The word on the street is they're trying to muscle in on your old stamping grounds.'

'So what?' Wiseman shrugged.

'I just thought I'd mention it. That's all.'

Wiseman flexed his huge biceps in another show of contempt.

'What else did Tony tell you?'

'Not a lot. Although he mentioned there's a lot of money been changing hands recently.'

'What's that supposed to mean?'

'I don't know. You tell me.'

Wiseman said nothing, but his face said it all.

'What information do you have about the young guy who was also murdered in Jennifer's house? Do you know who he is?'

'Without a name, how the fuck would I know?'

'He must have been there for a reason, Frank.'

'Was he?'

'He was. I just thought you may have heard something.'

Wiseman's eyes narrowed a fraction. 'Isn't that what you people get paid to do... find these things out?'

The prisoner smiled, knowing full well he didn't have a name to give. Wiseman was sizing him up, acting dumb and trying to establish how much the police actually knew about his ex-wife's murder.

'Let's hope he was a friend of the family, and not one of your local thugs.'

'So why bother to ask?'

Mason gave a little shrug. 'I'm just making general conversation, that's all.'

'You don't come across as a very intelligent copper. What the fuck do you think he was doing there?'

'I've no idea. You tell me.'

'Whoever killed this young lad obviously knew where to find him.'

Plausible, Mason thought, but highly unlikely as everyone on the force knew Jennifer Oakwell was the killer's intended target. He still hadn't the heart to tell him as much. Not yet. That would come later when he was treading safer ground.

'Someone's got it in for you, Frank. Whoever killed your ex was extremely angry over something. Blood everywhere, carpets and walls, it wasn't a pretty sight. What puzzles me is that whoever killed her took nothing from the property. I wonder why that is. Why were they there?'

Wiseman looked at him like a man who had swallowed a wasp. 'You're the fucking copper. You're supposed to know how these things work.'

'True.' Mason nodded.

'Tell me,' said Wiseman, their faces almost touching, 'why do you think he killed the fat slag in the first place?'

'An old score to settle, perhaps. Or maybe—' Mason broke off mid-sentence.

Murder in his eyes, Wiseman shot to his feet.

'Know this. Whoever killed Jennifer, we will feed to the pigs.'

'And who will do that, Frank?'

'You'd be astonished.'

'Nothing surprises me anymore,' Mason said calmly.

Being face to face with a notorious gangster wasn't the most exciting experience in Mason's life, but it came mighty close. This was another world, a world where every minor victory was hard fought. It was all about posturing, flexing your muscles and trying to gauge what the other person was thinking.

'Tell me, Jack. Have you ever experienced being badly beaten up just for doing your job?'

'Several times. Why do you ask?'

'Do you know what it feels like to be beaten up by a real professional?'

'I know what happens to them,' Mason grinned.

Wiseman glared at him. Eyes glazed over, pupils dilated, his voice ice cold. 'I'm not talking about a bar brawl here. I'm talking about the real deal.'

'So am I.'

'What then?'

'The last guy who gave me a hiding, we got thrown together down a dark alley one night.' Mason scowled at him. 'Just the two of us. No witnesses. That's how I like to deal with your so-called professionals. He's in a wheelchair now. They tell me he drinks through a straw and needs to be spoon fed three times a day.'

Wiseman said nothing, but Mason guessed what he was thinking.

'Is there anything else you wish to talk to me about?'

The prisoner nodded weakly. 'No. I've heard enough bullshit for one day.'

'Any messages for the outside world?'

Wiseman flashed him an angry look. 'Why don't you piss off back to your cosy little office and leave me to get on with it?'

As the door closed firmly behind him, Mason could hear the other inmates kicking off. It was show time, and Mad Frankie Wiseman was putting on a five-star performance. It was all about timing and striking the right balance. Not the greatest interview he'd ever conducted, but getting the prisoner to talk was often enough. No, Mason thought. With any luck, the feelers would be out, and the streets of Newcastle would soon cough up some answers.

If not, another dead body.

CHAPTER ELEVEN

Mason dragged his sore head from the pillow and gazed at his watch through one eye. Monday morning, and the start of a brand-new week. His tongue felt like coarse sandpaper, and the back of his throat dry. No more overindulgence, he groaned. Honest to God. It was 10:00, and he'd missed the morning team briefing, a meeting of his own instigation. Cursing his own incompetence, he'd considered calling the office, but quickly thought better of it. The world's worst liar, he was useless at making excuses and his stories never sounded convincing.

Unsteady on his feet, he staggered into the kitchen and made towards the fridge. Grabbing the remains of yesterday's milk, he gulped it down in the belief that it would pull him around. He was mistaken. Seconds later, he was straddling the toilet full of remorse and self-pity as the recycling process contacted the porcelain pan. Suffering the mother of all hangovers, the previous night's events were awash in a drunken stupor. All he could remember was boarding a taxi outside some sleazy back-street Chinese restaurant in Wallsend. The rest was a series of vague recollections, obscure incidents lost in a sea of alcohol confusion.

His phone rang.

'Is that you, boss?'

'Uh-huh.'

'It's DS Savage. Are you okay?'

Mason's tone sounded pitifully woeful. 'What time did we finish last night, Rob?'

'Two-thirty in the morning, boss.'

Mason swayed and grabbed the bathroom towel rail to steady himself. 'What's happening?'

'Where are you now?' Savage asked inquisitively.

'Why, what's up?'

'Don't tell me you've just crawled out of bed?'

'What gave you that impression?' Mason lied.

'You sound just like I feel... shit.'

Mason quickly improvised and pretended to have a more convenient strategy. 'I'm checking on the witness statements; what are you up to today?'

'I'm over at the waste and recycling plant.'

'Really. What's going on?'

There was another long pause at the other end of the phone.

'We've found another dissected body. A young man, late teens. His hands and feet have been bound with duct tape, and he's a bit of a mess. And, before you ask, we've been trying to contact you ever since the call came in.'

'What time was this?' Mason croaked.

'Eight o'clock.'

'Blaydon, you say?'

'Yes. I'm here with forensics.'

Mason felt as though his head was about to lift from his shoulders. He could barely think straight, let alone make conscious decisions. Having slept curled up on the sofa bed most of the night, his movements were sluggish, and he was struggling to stay upright.

What to do next?

'Who's with you, Rob?'

'Detectives Manley and Carrington, and the SOC photographer Peter Davenport.'

'Who's the Scene of Crime manager?'

'Stan Johnson. Why do you ask?'

'He's a good man. And the duty police doctor?'

There was another long pause, a moment of hesitation. 'It's Doctor Hindson, I'm afraid.'

'Holy shit. That's all we need,' Mason cursed.

'I couldn't agree more. He's not the best person to work with.'

'Tell me about it. The old sod exudes arrogance from every pore in his body. He's not liked either.' Mason collected his thoughts. 'Hold the fort, Rob. I'll be with you in thirty minutes.'

The moment he hung up, Mason grabbed a bottle of aspirins from the kitchen cabinet and dashed his face with icy water. Still in denial, this couldn't have happened at a more inconvenient time. Throwing his jacket onto the backseat of the undercover Ford Focus, he reluctantly slid into the driver's seat. Despite the drink driving laws, he gazed through the mud-spattered windscreen and sighed. Where to begin? Another body on his hands, a shitload of explaining to do, and the mother of all hangovers.

Well, he thought, might as well get on with it.

***

Several constables stood guard around the immediate crime scene, which was enclosed by a perimeter fence on all sides. By the look of things, forensics had arrived in a Mercedes-Benz Sprinter Van — their attentions already drawn towards a large yellow skip full of household rubbish. Having spilled onto the road, it was now being gone over with a fine-tooth comb.

His head full of self-pity, Mason signed the crime sheet log and made his way towards the knot of police officers now gathered in front of a large blue skip.

'What have we got?' he asked.

The constable dutifully tipped his peak cap in salute, then rolled his eyes. 'Young man in his early twenties, sir.'

'Do we have an ID?'

'Not yet. Forensics are working on it.'

'Who found him?'

'One of the site lorry drivers... around seven-thirty this morning. He was about to hook his vehicle up when he noticed body parts sticking out of the skip. At first, he thought it was a tailor's dummy, but on closer inspection, that's when he raised the alarm.'

Pen poised, Mason lifted his eyes from his notebook and levelled them at the constable. In no mood for conversation, he was trying his utmost to stay upright.

'Anyone with him at the time?'

There was hesitation in the constable's voice. 'Nobody that I'm aware of, sir. These guys work pretty much on their own. It's a large unit, and according to the site manager, the recycling compound was closed over the weekend for routine maintenance checks.'

Mason pointed to a large gathering of seagulls hovering over the back of a stationary skip. 'Who's working the outlying area?'

'Uniforms are,' Savage said, fast homing in on him.

A surge of nausea ripped through him, but he contained it. The lead investigator had not felt this lousy in a long time. Moving towards the front of a dumper truck, he gulped at the air in snatches. They couldn't move or touch anything, not until Home Office pathologists had completed their findings. There was still plenty to be getting on with.

Mason steadied himself. 'How long's the young lad been dead?'

'Hard to say. Not more than a couple of days.'

'What sort of state is the body in?' he asked.

'Best look for yourself, boss.'

To stave off the inevitable, Mason pointed to an enormous mountain of garden rubbish. 'How does this stuff arrive here?'

'Vans, tow trailers, the boots of people's cars, you name it...'

The moment he stared at the body, his mouth filled with bile. Not the prettiest of sights. The stench was unbearable and carried an odour of sour dreams. He could see that someone had stuffed the head into a bright orange carrier bag and thrown it into a skip full of rubbish. On closer inspection, the face had a waxlike appearance. The skin was drawn tight around the cheekbones, with the eyes wide open and the mouth frozen in a cry of revulsion. He'd seen mutilation before, but nothing compared to this. Then, when he looked up, he encountered an even more disturbing sight — someone had opened a black suitcase, revealing its contents.

Moving in closer, he could see that a frenzied knife attack had riddled the upper torso with puncture marks. Someone had sliced the arms from the shoulders and had bound them together with duct tape. Not as he was expecting to find, he pocketed his notebook and moved towards a small group of police officers huddled around a large open skip. His mind running amok, a site of this size, would surely keep records.

'Okay,' Mason announced. 'I want a list of everyone employed at the site, particularly those who worked here over the weekend. And, when you've done all of that, I need statements from anyone who dropped rubbish off here on Friday. Do I make myself clear?'

Nods of approval gathered the pace.

'Who's in charge of site security?' he asked.

'The site manager's the best person to talk to about that,' DC Manley replied.

'Have a word with him, Harry. Check out what arrangements are in place. CCTV cameras, log sheets, etcetera, etcetera.'

'Will do, boss.'

'While you're at it, take DC Carrington with you. Let's check out the lorry drivers who work here and don't take no for an answer.'

Mason mulled over the facts. Perhaps this wasn't a gangland killing after all. Maybe the profiler was right. One thing was for sure, he would need to understand it, and fast. Christ, he cursed. Just when he thought they were getting to grips with the case, the killer had struck again.

Savage grinned. 'You look like I feel, boss.'

'No thanks to you,' Mason groaned.

'You shouldn't drink so much,' Savage replied, his voice dripping with disdain. 'It can have detrimental effects on your physical well-being.'

Mason brushed the sergeant's sarcastic quips to one side. 'If this murder is linked, we must engage in some deep contemplation.'

'I hate to mention it,' said DC Carrington. 'But Dr Hindson believes the head and hands belong to another victim.'

'What?'

'Something's not right. Hindson's convinced that someone has kept some of the body parts in a freezer. No doubt the post-mortem will tell us more, but surely he can't be right?'

Mason swung to face Savage.

'What's going on, Rob?'

'God knows. Now we have a head and hands in our possession. Hopefully, we can identify who he is.'

'That's a valid point.'

'The trouble is, what if the body parts don't match?'

Mason looked at him for a moment. 'Try explaining that to the powers to be.'

'I'm sure you'll cope,' Savage grinned.

Mason realised his biggest nightmare and gazed at the torso, feeling unimpressed. The sick bastard who'd done this wasn't right in the head. Perhaps it was time to bring some lateral thinking to the case, involve the profiler David Carlisle. But would his boss agree to such an idea? Probably not.

His phone pinged, and he ignored it.

'This screws up a lot of our theories, Rob.'

'At least the skip driver had the sense to check his load before hitching up his lorry. Had he not, then this would have been history.'

'That's true,' Mason agreed with an element of irritation in his voice.

Savage blew hard. 'If you ask me, there's a definite pattern taking place.'

'I couldn't agree more. The trouble is, we're stuck with a killer who enjoys delivering his victims to us in a suitcase.'

'Do you think these foreigners are involved?'

'Nothing is off the table, Rob. Whoever killed these people was determined to get rid of the evidence.'

'But why mix the body parts up?'

Mason furrowed his brow in an expression of concern. 'If we link this latest finding to Jennifer Oakwell's murder, we could have a major problem on our hands.'

'What are the chances of that, do you think?'

'A copper always follows his nose. Instinct is eighty per cent truth, the rest is bullshit and falls into insignificance.'

The approaching blue flashing spinner-lights told them more officers were arriving.

'Sounds like the experts are on their way,' Savage groaned.

Mason stared into the distance. 'Yeah. Soon the entire area will crawl with keen wannabe police officers eager in the belief they're about to solve their first big murder case. In a few hours from now, after sifting through millions of tons of unwanted shit, they'll probably think differently.'

'I cannot wait.' Savage chuckled.

The mentality of some officers never ceased to amaze, especially in moments such as these. A copper's luck was hard earned, and you could spend days working your backside off without a sniff of a lead. Having pulled round a tad, the lead investigator was feeling his real self again. With any luck, by mid-afternoon forensics would have a clear picture of what actually took place here. Only then could he set the plan.

About to climb into the unmarked pool car, Mason's phone buzzed in his pocket. He checked the display to find Sutherland's name had popped up on the screen. Right now, he knew the square root of bugger-all, but sensed what the call was about.

Never a dull moment, he groaned.

'Morning, ma'am. How can I help?'

Chapter Twelve

It felt good to be back, thought David Carlisle as he entered the Gateshead Police Station that morning. Despite not knowing what the meeting was about or why he had been summoned, the profiler still sensed its importance. Checking in at the front desk, he found the sergeant was his usual jovial self. With only one prisoner in the holding cells, there was an air of calm about the place. Caught red-handed trying to steal a tray of pork sausages from a local supermarket, the culprit was still pleading his innocence when they slammed the cell door behind him. Some things never change, Carlisle mused.

After taking the stairs two at a time, the acting superintendent was on the phone when he entered her office. Taking the last seat, he settled down next to Jack Mason and took out his notebook. Dressed in full police uniform, her hand over the receiver, Sutherland asked if he would like anything to drink.

'I'd love a coffee, black no sugar, please, ma'am.'

Pleasantries over, she hung up and made a little grimace. 'I'll be frank,' she began, in a low, sombre voice that grabbed the profiler's immediate attention. 'I'm unsure how much you know about Operation Walrus, but there's been another major incident.'

'Is this in connection with the one in Forth Street, ma'am?'

She spread her hands on the desk in front of her, and then said softly, 'Yes, and we're now left with another mutilated body on our hands.'

'Where exactly this time, ma'am?'

'Blaydon, over at the waste and recycling centre.' She turned to DCI Mason before continuing. 'It's not general knowledge at this stage, as we're trying to keep it from the press.'

'That's understandable,' Carlisle nodded.

'I don't wish to cause alarm, but I fear we are dealing with the same killer.'

Carlisle remained silent for some moments.

'So you believe there's a link?'

'We do. After conducting a thorough search of the recycling centre, we recovered several more body parts belonging to another victim. It naturally came as a shock, and we're still trying to piece everything together.'

'Do we know who the victims are?'

'One of them we do,' she answered directly. 'Blood sample previously taken from Jennifer Oakwell's property is a match for body parts recovered from the killer's second victim – the one we found at the Forth Street storage company. His name is Colin Henderson, and he was a nineteen-year-old undergraduate who was studying computer graphics at Newcastle University.'

'How were the body parts found?'

Sutherland's bottom lip quivered slightly. A keenly intelligent woman, she was usually bursting with enthusiasm; today she wasn't. Having spent much of the morning studying crime scene photographs and listening to police officers' first-hand grizzly accounts of dismembered body parts, she seemed overwhelmed by it all.

'From the evidence so far, it seems the perpetrator has removed the head and hands of the latest victim, but they severed the legs mid-thigh and placed them inside a large black suitcase alongside the victim's torso. Looking at the photographs, the killer seems to adopt the same method of disposal.'

'I presume the head and hands are missing from the latest victim?'

'Yes, they are,' she replied, her surprise clear as she locked eyes with him.

The profiler wanted to tell her they were dealing with a psychopath, but refrained from doing so. That would come later, when he had more facts at his disposal.

'For some unknown reason, the killer deliberately mixes up the body parts, which suggests that he meticulously plans his murders.'

'Is he not trying to dispose of the evidence?'

'He could be, but there's something more profound going on.'

A deep sigh eluded her lips, heavy with unspoken emotions. 'I was having reservations about what his intentions were.'

'What about forensics, any indications as to his method?'

Sutherland raised her eyebrows a fraction before continuing. 'After we carried out a thorough fingertip search at the recycling plant, we found nothing. It's a difficult one. Identification is proving more challenging, as you can well imagine.'

'He's highly organised, ma'am. It's part of his ritual, and he's deliberately keeping you guessing.'

Sutherland peered at her notes, as if searching for divine intervention. 'According to Tom Hedley's forensic report, after this monster had dismembered Colin Henderson, he'd kept some of the body parts in a freezer.'

'That is an interesting new twist,' Carlisle said, shaking his head.

'Yes, but what does it tell us about him?'

'He sounds like he's on a murder rampage. Whatever his reasons to kill, he's obviously gained a passion for the taste of blood. That's how some killers react. To them it's a game. By mixing the body parts up, he's not only keeping you guessing, he's spreading untold fear whilst deliberately maintaining control.'

'That's all very well, but why the hell does he do it?'

The profiler sat shocked at Sutherland's sudden outburst. This latest incident had obviously rattled her, but that was understandable given the circumstances. This was fast turning into another horror story, and unless he could give the problem his full attention, he was wasting his time.

'What makes him tick?' Carlisle replied thoughtfully.

'Yes, that would be very useful.'

'May I ask how someone removed the limbs from the victim's body?'

Sutherland glanced at Mason, who nodded for her to continue. 'According to the post-mortem report, the killer used a powered saw. The type used by surgeons.'

'The same one he used on Colin Henderson?'

'Yes, we believe so.'

'That is an interesting development.' Suddenly, he remembered something. 'And what initially drew your attention towards Colin Henderson being a university student?'

'It was quite by chance, actually,' Mason interrupted with a smile. 'When Newcastle University broke for half-term recess, everyone thought he'd returned to his parents' home in Nottingham. He hadn't, of course.'

'When did they realise he'd gone missing? Who raised the alarm?'

'When Henderson didn't show at his parents' house, they naturally became anxious. They'd tried calling him, but his phone kept ringing out. After talking with other family members who hadn't heard from him in weeks, they contacted the police. The rest was a matter of legwork and gathering the evidence together.'

'Do we know what Henderson was doing on Jennifer Oakwell's property at the time of her murder?'

The acting superintendent took a sip of water from a glass and wiped the corner of her mouth. 'She's a friend of the family apparently, which may account for his visit there before returning to Nottingham.' Sutherland checked her notes. 'The course of our investigations has since led us to a student bedsit in Bensham, but after a thorough search of the property we found nothing to cause alarm. In the meantime, Henderson's university mentor released a statement to the press, which confirmed he was a hard-working young man. He was well-liked by all accounts, and his sudden disappearance was strictly against the grain.'

Carlisle cocked his head to one side. 'Right place, wrong time, by the sound?'

'It would appear so.' Sutherland leaned forward, both elbows on the desk. 'It seems we have another vicious predator on our hands, Mr Carlisle.'

'Indeed, you do, ma'am. But how can I possibly help?'

'What makes you say that?'

'Well,' Carlisle began, trying his utmost not to sound overly enthusiastic. 'You seem to have everything under control here.'

Sutherland blushed. 'It may appear that way on the surface, but we're looking for expert advice.'

Carlisle considered this. One thing was for sure, these weren't gangland killings, as the police firmly believed. Organised crime executions were usually no-nonsense affairs. Swift. A bullet to the head or a knife to the throat. These murders felt sinister, more controlled. Whoever was responsible was suffering from delusional paranoia. They had to be. If not, who in their rightful mind would pick up a powered saw and dissect their victims' bodies as if they'd worked in an abattoir? No. This wasn't an everyday occurrence, and the person responsible was a sensation seeker. A cold, calculated killer. Someone who enjoyed his trade.

'What about Jennifer Oakwell's close-knit family and friends?' he asked.

Mason rounded on him. 'Why would you want to know that at such an early stage in our enquiries?'

'Well,' the profiler said, pointing to the scene of the crime photographs loosely pinned to Sutherland's corkboard. 'Whoever killed these people certainly knew where to find them.'

Sutherland managed a thin smile. 'That's why we believe Jennifer Oakwell was his initial target.'

'I'm not so sure about that either, ma'am.'

'How can you possibly say that without even seeing the case files?'

Carlisle unfolded his arms. 'Call it intuition, ma'am.'

'Is that a criminal profiler thing?'

'Undoubtedly.'

Sutherland looked down at her notes, as if taken aback.

'Is this the sort of case that would appeal to you?'

'It certainly has potential, ma'am.'

'You don't sound overly enthusiastic. Any reason?'

Carlisle sensed a contract was about to be tabled and tried to contain his emotions. It was time to cut to the chase. 'This latest suspect you talk of. What do we know about him?'

'Not a lot,' Mason interrupted, 'but we have a person in mind.'

'Does this person have a name?'

Mason looked at him like a dog with a bone. 'He's a local miscreant called Thomas Wilkinson. He's not a prolific offender as such, more a public nuisance than anything.'

'Any involvement in drugs?'

Mason sat back in his seat. 'Let's not go there at this stage.'

'Any reason?'

The chief inspector shook his head but said nothing.

'We received a tip-off only yesterday afternoon,'

Sutherland confirmed. 'Wilkinson was last seen drinking in the Eagle public house late on Thursday night. It's a gay bar on Scotswood Road. We know Henderson went there and believe the man he met with was on speaking terms.'

Mason cut across them. 'It's probably worth mentioning that Wilkinson is legally homeless. As far as we know, he's sleeping rough and is sofa surfing for short periods with family and friends.'

Carlisle removed his spectacles and puffed on the lenses before giving them a quick wipe. The likelihood the killer still had unfinished business to fulfil worried him. Serial killers started slowly and built up confidence until reaching a point where the killings became more frequent. Three unsolved murders. One concerning a bright university student, another the ex-wife of a notorious gangster, and a third involving a suspected homeless male who was yet to be identified. Crude as it was, why the killer had gone to great lengths to dismember only male victims puzzled him. Were these people known to the killer, or did he have a personal grudge against young males? Whatever his motives, Carlisle felt a conflicting surge of emotions as if something were terribly wrong.

He stared at the photographs again. On the face, these crimes bore all the characteristics of a serial killer at work. Loath to admit, he'd already decided about taking on another case. Business was business, and if they offered him a contract, he could certainly do with some extra cash. What Mason didn't know, or perhaps he did, was that his private investigation company was in free-fall. Things were extremely quiet at the moment, and the competition for new business was challenging, to say the least.

'Well,' said Sutherland, shaking her head dutifully. 'Is this case something you may wish to consider?'

'It certainly presents an interesting challenge, ma'am.'

'Can I interpret that as a yes?'

Carlisle trod cautiously. 'Before committing to something I may later regret, would it be possible to take a quick peep at the case files?'

Mason rounded on him. 'I'll talk to you in the morning about that.'

Sometimes it was better to take it on the chin, act dumb and say nothing. If he had an answer, right now he couldn't think of one. The only positive was the press still hadn't picked up on the story. Some serial killers were notorious for keeping newspaper clippings and viewed them as a record of their achievements. Others took trophies and souvenirs from their victims, and he hoped that this wasn't the case.

Carlisle stood to leave. 'What time is your meeting in the morning?'

'Nine o'clock. Meeting Room One.'

'See you all there then.'

Mason couldn't stop smiling, which pleased the profiler immensely. At least someone was happy of his help.

Chapter Thirteen

Jane Collins simply adored cats, and the moment a stray kitten walked in through the open office door, it was only natural she would pick it up. Grave mistake. David Carlisle hadn't lifted a finger since eleven that morning and could sorely have done without this. Not a cat lover, there was always the problem of what to do next.

Switching to profiler mode, he guessed the young kitten's survival rate was based on a combination of mathematics and probabilities. If his calculations proved correct, the kitten would find its mother again. Perhaps she was lying low somewhere; out hunting for food. And yes, there were plenty of stray dogs in Laygate to scare the living hell out of her.

'I take it you've found nothing?' asked Jane.

'No. Not yet.'

'Did you check the waste ground at the bottom of the street?'

'It was the first place I looked,' Carlisle replied.

'You poor unfortunate thing,' said Jane, now talking to the kitten. 'What are we going to do with you?'

Carlisle shuffled awkwardly. 'Well, he can't stay here if that's what you're thinking.'

'What do you propose we do?'

'Simple. We stick him outside with a bowl of milk and

wait for his mother to appear.'

'That's utter nonsense, and you know it,' Jane retorted. 'The poor little thing wouldn't last two minutes on his own.'

'It's not my problem,' the profiler shrugged.

Jane leaned back against the metal filing cabinets and stared at him quizzically through narrow eyes. There was no simple answer to this, but he wasn't giving in lightly.

'I'd take you home with me if I could,' his business partner said, addressing the kitten again, 'but I doubt my two Siamese cats will take kindly to you moving in with them.'

Bored with it all, Carlisle returned to his computer. Having cleared his head of feline thoughts, he reverted to the business in hand. These latest murders had all the hallmarks of a gangland killing, but there were too many flaws in that theory. Jennifer Oakwell had died in the hands of a narcissistic killer, he was certain of that. Besides, gangsters preferred executions when eliminating their adversaries. A bullet to the head, or a shallow grave in the country to conceal the body.

He was still searching for answers when the stray kitten appeared on his desk. At first, he thought he was imagining things. Without giving it a second thought, he picked it up and dropped it back down on the floor. The next thing he saw, after turning his head, was his iPhone crashing to the floor.

'You little bugger,' he shouted.

***

It was late afternoon when the profiler finally walked through the press office forecourt in Sunderland. Now running late, he was met at the reception desk by an obnoxious middle-aged blonde with heavy mascara and thick ruby red lips. Offered drinks from a quirky dispensing machine, he settled down in the reception lounge and took in his surroundings.

He didn't wait long.

Mark Patterson was a tall, elegant man, with wispy chestnut-brown hair swept back at the sides. A retired police officer now turned senior newspaper editor, Patterson had an extraordinary talent for sifting out scandal. Could it be possible he knew something about these murders, some small connection or thread? Determined to find out, it was this aspect that had brought him here today.

'What can I do for you?' asked Patterson, taking up a corner seat overlooking the busy main road.

'I'm looking for information, Mark.'

'Is this in connection with Frank Wiseman's ex-wife?'

'How did you guess?'

'The last I'd heard, the Northumbria Police had approached you.' Patterson tapped the side of his head. 'The mere mention of that sad bastard's name was enough to send shivers down my spine.'

Carlisle's phone kept ringing, and he switched it to silent.

'Heard anything about this power struggle that's taking place over in the West End of Newcastle?'

'You know me, Davy,' his colleague said mischievously. 'I like to keep my readers informed.'

Carlisle managed a smile. 'Any names?'

'I'm told a lot of Eastern Europeans are moving into the area, and it's causing a great deal of friction. People are jockeying for position, and nobody knows how to put a stop to it.'

Coffee and biscuits arrived, and Patterson filled him in with the details.

'What are these foreigners up to exactly?'

The senior editor moved his hand dismissively. 'There are agents and runners all over the place, and a lot of fake passports are changing hands. It's big business, unlawful, and local authorities are extremely concerned. The trouble is, the Home Office is loath to get involved, and local community leaders have all but washed their hands of it.'

'Human trafficking, do you think?'

'Cheap labour and prostitution more like.'

'What about Border Force?'

'It's not their problem, seemingly. Besides, they're stretched to the limit with illegal immigrants at the moment.'

'That doesn't surprise me. What the hell is going on?'

Patterson habitually whistled through his teeth. 'Nobody seems interested these days. Freedom of movement isn't all it's made out to be, and we're no longer in control of our borders. It's not the genuine asylum seekers who are causing the problem, it's the undesirables who follow in their wake.'

Not wishing to get drawn into a political debate, Carlisle chose his next words carefully. 'Is Frank Wiseman's old territory still under threat?'

'It is, especially from people like Tony Fox.'

'That doesn't surprise me.'

The senior editor brushed the biscuit crumbs from his trousers and leaned forward. 'Fox is ambitious, and not to be trusted. If he can't buy his way out of trouble, he reverts to using force. That's how he works; he makes things happen.'

'Capable of murder, do you think?'

Patterson roared with laughter. 'He's more than capable of that.'

'What about this recent Forth Street incident? Could Fox be involved?'

'I presume you're referring to this Suitcase Man?'

Carlisle nodded.

'I doubt it.'

'Any reason?'

'It's not his style. Fox is a sly bastard, and he knows how to play the system.'

'Are we talking bent lawyers here?'

Patterson lowered his voice. 'Nothing surprises me about Tony Fox anymore. The man has his fingers in too many pies. Ten years ago, when Frank Wiseman's gang did a hit on several sub-post offices, they'd made off with over two million quid in used banknotes. Given the ease in which Fox salted away the money, the gang thought they'd got away with it. They hadn't, of course, and that was their biggest mistake.'

Carlisle shrugged. 'What went wrong, do you think?'

'The police had a snitch in their midst. A guy called Sam Monday. It wasn't common knowledge, but it was Monday who gave the police the breakthrough they'd been looking for. He told them everything.' Patterson laughed. 'And I mean everything. Who was involved in the raids, who the contacts were, and who masterminded the entire operation? A few days later, after they'd rounded up most of the gang members, it was the end of Wiseman's empire.'

'No doubt Frank wasn't pleased.'

'He wasn't. When word got out that someone had deceived him, Wiseman was furious. It was payback time, and that's when Fox got involved.'

'Yes, but this was ten years ago.'

'It was, and Fox has hung around on the side-lines ever since. He's not daft. That bastard never misses a trick. Like I say, he knows how to play the system.' Patterson stared at him hard. 'The only way to eat an elephant is a piece at a time.'

'So, you think someone brought Fox in specifically to do a job for Mad Frankie?'

'Who else could take care of it? Fox was one of Wiseman's most trusted lieutenants, and always featured heavily in the gangster's plans. It was the opportunity he'd been waiting for. A chance to make a name for himself.'

'So that's how Fox rose through the ranks as he did.'

'To cut a long story short, within a week of the post-office trial ending, the nameless whistle-blower disappeared without a trace. It was the talk of the Tyne, and no one has seen him since.'

Carlisle felt a ripple of excitement running through his veins.

'What happened to him, do you think?'

Patterson nodded. 'Rumour had it that someone shot Sam Monday through the head and buried him in the outside lane of the A1(M). They were conducting motorway improvements, so I guess that story fits.'

'What about the police? Surely they would have known he'd gone missing?'

'They did, but it was pure speculation. Besides, who'd dig up a brand new hundred-million-pound motorway hoping to prove a point?'

'No, I suppose not.'

'Whichever way you look at it, Fox had it all worked out.'

Carlisle thought about this.

'As I recall, Monday was under some sort of police protection scheme. They gave him a new passport and identity and promised to whisk him off to another country. Could that not account for his sudden disappearance from the scene?'

'It may well have been, but there were so many rumours doing the rounds that nobody knew who to believe.' Patterson checked his watch. 'The media were full of it, and you can't imagine the number of newspapers the story sold.'

'No, I guess not.'

His colleague wrinkled his nose. 'You asked me if Fox was capable of murder. Well, here's my view. It was Tony's crew who buried Monday in the outside lane of the motorway. Fox had contacts in the construction industry – people who owed him favours.'

'On what evidence?'

Patterson tapped the side of his nose. 'Think about it.

They don't call it Monday's Highway for nothing.'

'Can't say that I've ever heard it called that before.'

'It's not widely known.' His colleague gave him a strange look before continuing. 'One thing for sure, I wouldn't like to get on the wrong side of these people.'

'Could Fox be running the show whilst Wiseman's inside?'

'The thing to remember is most of the gang are now out on parole.'

'So I've heard.'

Patterson furrowed his brow as he pondered the issue. 'There lies another problem, as there were dozens of people involved in the raids. The thing is, no one knows where the money is. Some claim someone salted it away in Swiss bank accounts, while others insist they buried it. Whoever's story you believe, there's no simple answer.'

Carlisle considered this. 'What about Tony Fox?'

'Hard to say. If you're wanting to find out more, I'd stay well clear. Walls have ears, and you never know who's listening.'

'Do you know what? You're the second person who's told me that?'

Patterson pushed his empty cup to one side. He'd received sound advice. There was more to this than first met the eye. Gang wars were one thing, but cheating on fellow criminals was a lethal cocktail that no gang member would tolerate.

Carlisle was silent for some moments.

'What puzzles me is how Tony Fox paid for his nightclubs. They don't come cheap.'

'I wouldn't go there either if I were you.'

'Oh. And why not?'

'You're only asking for trouble.'

'How do you think he paid for them, then?'

Patterson stared at him and smiled. 'From what I can gather, Fox makes most of his money from dealing in second-hand cars. Most of them stolen to order, and all shipped overseas. No doubt he has other lucrative ventures; who knows what he gets up to?'

'Quite a lot, according to the police.'

Patterson drew back in his seat. 'If anyone in the criminal underworld knows who committed these murders, it's Tony Fox. But don't quote me on that.'

'Thanks, Mark. I'll bear that in mind.'

Patterson stood to leave.

'Time's precious,' he said, staring at his watch. 'I hope I've been of help. If there's anything else, you know where to find me.'

'There is one other thing,' Carlisle confessed.

'Oh! And what might that be?'

'What do you know about stray kittens?'

The senior editor looked at him gobsmacked. 'I'm a newspaper editor, not a vet.'

'Just asking.'

'Why? Do you have a problem?'

'I do, but let's not go there.'

Chapter Fourteen

Having spent the best part of the night reading through Jennifer Oakwell's case files, Carlisle felt worn out. It was seven-thirty, and as TV presenters continued to deliberate over the state of the nation's economy, he sat back in astonishment. If it wasn't one thing, it was another. Sometimes he wondered if people weren't rigging the stock markets - making vast fortunes out of shifting money around. Not that he could influence anything; he couldn't. But it annoyed him immensely.

The moment the toaster popped on the kitchen unit, Benjamin was on to it in a flash. Paws outstretched, the young kitten had caught the flying slice of toast in mid-air. His newfound companion was certainly in mischievous spirits that morning, and the distractions were driving him mad. Having watched his new feline companion climbing up the living room curtains in a show of utter contempt, he'd considered fitting blinds. If that didn't work, he would need to take a positive stance. Not that Benjamin cared, he thought everything was a game.

The profiler arrived at Jennifer Oakwell's terraced property in Bensham just as the rain fell. Not the best place to visit at nine in the morning; he could sorely have done without this. Now holding open the driver's door, Mason burst out laughing.

'How the hell did you get those scratch marks on your face?'

'Don't even go there.'

'Have you been in a fight, my friend?'

'Yes, with a twelve-week-old kitten.'

Mason burst out laughing, but the profiler couldn't see the funny side.

Still off-limits, the blue and white cordon tape attached to the victim's door was fluttering in the breeze. Despite all the locks being changed, Mason had a key. It wasn't the best arrangement; he realised that, and the profiler would have preferred to view the property alone.

Darkness embraced them the moment they stepped into the narrow hallway. Never-ending and sameness, the air felt oppressive, tinged with a musty smell that clung to his throat like a thousand nightmares. This was the moment the profiler cherished above all else in his job: stepping into a serial killer's domain.

The living room was small, high-ceilinged, austere, with plain emulsion walls and a north facing bay window overlooking the main street. At the far end of the room, next to a small bookcase, stood a flat plasma TV screen. At odds with the rest of the furnishings, and now taking centre stage, was a large, strait back chair.

Mason pointed to it. 'This is where Jennifer Oakwell finally met her maker. Ankles strapped to the chair legs, wrists bound to the armrests, the cause of death was recorded as sharp force wounds to the back, neck, and chest.'

'Nasty!' Carlisle cringed.

Mason outlined the heavily blood-stained carpets and sighed. 'To say this was a frenzied attack would be an understatement. According to the coroner's report, the killer inflicted no less than thirty stab wounds to the victim's upper body. We've done some background checks and strongly suspect the killer's right handed and approximately five-ten.'

'What do we know about the murder weapon?'

'We suspect someone used a double-edged combat knife. Made from high carbon steel, it had a spear point four-inch fixed blade and some sort of protection guard to it.'

'Any fingerprints?'

Mason turned sharply to confront him. 'Not according to forensics. The killer wore surgical gloves. They're a common brand that most pharmacy stores sell. There's plenty of footprints scattered around the place – size eight to ten Nike trainers. A popular brand, these have no distinguishing wear to the soles, which suggests they're reasonably new.' Mason's eyes toured the room. 'As you can see, it's pretty cramped in here, so there's not much room for manoeuvre.'

'Any sign of sexual motive?'

'No, nothing of that nature.'

'What about masturbation?'

'Funny you should mention that,' said Mason, sounding decidedly pleased with the question. 'This one is more intent on dismembering his victims, which I find rather disturbing.'

Carlisle mentally put himself in the killer's shoes. Unable to protect herself, Jennifer Oakwell's ending must have been horrific. But why bother to restrain her, and how did she get into that position in the first place? The only thing that struck him as odd was the use of a kitchen chair. There were no signs of a struggle, no forced entry, and the perpetrator stole nothing valuable from the property. Having killed her, and now in a heightened state of frenzy, had events overtaken the killers thought patterns? At least it made sense if nothing else seemed to at this stage. The more he thought about it, the more convinced he was the answer lay in the upstairs bedroom.

'Initial impressions?' asked Mason.

'What about neighbours?'

'We've received no reports of anyone hearing or seeing anything suspicious.'

'I find that odd. I would have thought someone would have seen something.'

'The fact she'd lain here for the best part of a week sort of backs that theory up.' Mason gazed at him through narrow eyes. 'It wasn't a pretty sight, I can assure you. Flies everywhere, the early signs of bloating, and a smell that beggared belief.'

'What about curtains and house lights?'

'The curtains were closed. As for the lights, the house was in total darkness when Oakwell was discovered.' Mason pointed to the hallway. 'We found her friend's fingerprints all over the light switches.'

Still early days, Carlisle was still waiting for his brain's synapses to kick in and provide him with inspiration. Then he remembered. 'According to the post-mortem report, they didn't find any alcohol or drugs in her body, and there weren't any superficial bruising to suggest a struggle had taken place. Don't you find that odd?'

'Not when duct tape bound her to the chair, as it

severely restricted her movements.'

'So how did she get into that position in the first place?'

Mason folded his arms, a defensive stance.

'Maybe he threatened her, and she froze.'

'Possible, but highly unlikely, don't you think?'

'Of course, someone could have knocked her unconscious.'

Carlisle moved to the corner of the room and glanced around. 'If she was conscious, then surely she must have put up some sort of resistance?'

Mason said nothing.

On reaching the upstairs landing, the chief inspector hummed with nervous energy. 'There's a lot of arterial spray and cast off everywhere. Walls, ceilings, and floors.' Mason pointed to it. 'Henderson had obviously fought his way this far before collapsing to the floor. Now in a state of shock, the killer remorselessly set about his business. This was unquestionably a prolonged knife attack, and every single thrust was driven deep into the young lad's body.'

'And the angle of the wounds?'

'Good question.' Mason took up a new position at the top of the landing, as if to demonstrate the killer's actions. 'We believe he straddled his victim, which obviously makes him right-handed.'

'Yes, of course.'

Turning his attention towards the graffiti adorned walls, Carlisle bent forward to take a closer look. This wasn't a vendetta killing. This crime had all the hallmarks of a psychopath at work. Child-like smiley images drawn using the victim's blood weren't normal. He closed his eyes and searched for a moment of inspiration. Who was this man who could show such utter contempt towards humanity? No, he thought. The act was too final. Too well organised, as if planned.

All the warning signs were there, the little idiosyncrasies that psychopaths fostered. Normally, these people developed with each passing murder, growing in confidence as they tried out more bizarre techniques. Curious, Carlisle checked the blood spatter again. Then realised this wasn't his first; these killings were far too advanced.

The profiler fell silent for a moment. Motive was a further problem: why such a frenzied attack? And another thing, he noted, moving around, there was an awful lot of victim blood transfer. Had the killer moved freely between the two murder scenes? Full of misguided thoughts, was this the point at which the executioner had turned his attentions back to Jennifer Oakwell? No, he argued, even though the evidence pointed to Oakwell being his intended target, there were too many unanswered questions.

Mason stared at him subdued.

'As you'll have noticed, there's an awful lot of arterial blood spatter radiating out from where Henderson's body lay.' Mason bent down as if to re-enact the scene. 'Plunging a four-inch steel blade repeatedly through flesh and muscle thirty odd times would have been extremely tiring work.'

'So, he wasn't dismembered here?'

'No. Not here, he wasn't.'

Alarm bells ringing in Carlisle's inquisitive mind, he stooped to inspect the floor. If the killer had used the same roll of heavy duty duct tape to restrain his victims, he'd obviously come prepared. Then again, he argued, according to forensics, there was no duct tape residue found on the dead woman's face or hair. If nothing else, no one had gagged her.

Then it hit him. What if she knew her killer?

'He's organised, Jack,' Carlisle said, thinking out aloud.

'What do you mean, organised?'

'These murders have all the hallmarks of a serial killer at work.'

'How can you possibly say that?' said Mason in his usual assertive manner. 'This is an open and shut case of witness elimination. I'm convinced of it.'

'In which case, why not remove Jennifer Oakwell's body from the premises?'

Mason stared at him, clearly confused. 'Simple. The killer was obviously disturbed.'

'No, Jack. Jennifer Oakwell wasn't his intended target.'

'What! You think Henderson was?'

'I'm certain.'

'That's ridiculous; even the forensic evidence doesn't point to that.'

'Something's not right,' said Carlisle, turning to face Mason. 'Too many pieces of the puzzle don't fit.'

'Like what?'

'Pitch dark, no one around. Her killer had all the time in the world. He planned this. Whoever he is, he has an extremely big ego. To him it's a sport, his way of keeping us guessing and that's why he's mixing the body parts up.'

'Let's not get carried away here.'

It wasn't easy to dismiss Carlisle.

'Just because the evidence points to the woman being silenced doesn't mean she was the intended target.'

Mason rolled his eyes, and Carlisle knew he'd overstepped the mark.

'This isn't a straightforward case, I realise that, and that's why we brought you in to assist.' Mason gave him a friendly pat on the back. 'Don't overcomplicate things. Let's stick with the programme, and less of this professional mumbo-jumbo.'

'Fine by me, but why did the killer keep moving between the two crime scenes?'

'It's pretty obvious I would have thought. After he dragged the young lad's body to a position at the top of the landing stairs, that's when he removed him from the premises. We know that from the blood trail he left behind.'

'So why not remove Jennifer Oakwell's body whilst he was at it?'

'As I mentioned, something probably disturbed him.'

'Okay, so what's his motive for killing Henderson?'

Mason shrugged. 'Wrong place, wrong time, I would suspect. He simply got in the way.'

At least Mason was forthright in his answers and didn't pull any punches. No, he thought. It was time to settle their professional differences once and for all.

'No, Jack. He killed Colin Henderson for the same reason he killed his latest victim.'

'And that is?'

'I've yet to decide.'

'So, you don't have a motive, then?'

'Not yet. But something has him incredibly worked up and agitated.'

'Christ! Even I could have told you that.'

'Think about it. He's targeting young males... cutting their bodies up because he's angry about something. It was Jennifer Oakwell who got in his way, not Colin Henderson, and that's why he left her as he did.'

Mason stared across at him, gobsmacked.

Chapter Fifteen

After setting up an incident room to deal with university students returning for the start of the summer term, the police were busy. It was painstaking work, and not all students were willing to cooperate. Information was police lifeblood, no matter what form it came in. Despite all their efforts, it was a fellow student who had given Jack Mason his first real breakthrough. Colin Henderson had experimented in narcotics. Not in a big way, but he'd dabbled in them.

After checking thousands of DNA records, a team of genealogy specialists finally produced a match. Their last victim, the one they'd found at the Blaydon waste and recycling centre, had finally been identified as Thomas Wilkinson. A local miscreant well-known to them, Wilkinson was no angel. Things were moving at speed, prompting dozens of new lines of enquiry.

Mason ran the word serial killer ritualistically around the tip of his tongue. He toyed with it, twisting its meaning until mentally conjuring up a picture of what it entailed. Physically exhausted after viciously stabbing his victim to death, the killer then tried to dispose of his body. To say Henderson was blissfully unaware of the terrible fate that awaited him would have been a foolhardy judgement. He had stared death in the face.

That much was certain.

After driving north, DS Savage parked opposite a large red brick building and switched off the car's engine. Set back from the rest of the urban sprawl, Fat Sam's nightclub was the in-place to be seen. Soon every police officer would familiarise themselves with the area, and Westgate Road would never be the same.

Struggling to contain himself, the chief inspector reflected on what he'd been told so far. If nothing else, the area reminded him of the West End of London. People here held a deep mistrust towards strangers. There was a subtle difference, of course. This was North Tyneside, and Tony Fox territory.

Mason gave Savage a withering look.

'Are you sure this is the right place?'

'I'm positive, boss.'

'Christ, what a dump. To think I spent the best part of my youth visiting places like this, it's a wonder I'm still alive.'

Mason banged on the heavy steel door, and a familiar face appeared round the corner. Not the sharpest tool in the box, Rolex Roy was a former member of the Newcastle Gremlins – a notorious hooligan gang that followed the city's football team. Having switched his allegiance to become a nightclub bouncer, Roy had rapidly gained a reputation for peddling counterfeit watches.

'Inspector Jack Mason,' the nightclub bouncer grinned. 'What brings you to this neck of the woods?'

Mason looked straight past him and pointed towards the main entrance door. 'Is your gaffer at home?'

'Yeah,' Roy nodded. 'He guessed you might call.'

Seconds later, they were inside and descending a steep, narrow staircase. From what Mason could see, Fat Sam's was a warren of sleazy alcoves. It had low ceilings, strobe lighting, and a multi-million-pound sound system nicked from a well-known Manchester strip club. He'd visited some dives in his career, but nothing compared to this.

Nerves jangling on edge, they entered the inner sanctum. Clearly off limits, this place was a mindboggling fortress. Reinforced windows, alarmed doors, and security cameras covering every inch of the building, there was little chance of escape. Warned by his area commander to go in heavy-handed, Mason had urged against it. Things didn't add up, and he was now having second thoughts.

It was Tony Fox who spoke first. 'What's your problem, Jack? Pissed the bed, have we?'

'I'm seeking information, Tony.'

'What kind?'

Mason pulled a crumpled photograph from an inside pocket and placed it on the desk in front of him. 'I'm looking for the person who killed these two young men.'

'What about them?' Fox answered guardedly.

'Recognise their faces?'

'Never seen them before. Who are they?'

'It might pay you to inspect,' Mason insisted. 'The guy on the right is called Colin Henderson. He was a friend of Jennifer Oakwell. Frank Wiseman's ex-wife. Nice lad, university student who was doing really well for himself.'

'You know me, Jack. I run a tight ship.' Fox stared

down at the photograph and shuffled awkwardly. 'I swear on my mother's life I've never seen this person before.'

'What about this young man?' Mason said, pointing a finger at the second image.

'Nope, never seen him before either. Who is he?'

'His name's Thomas Wilkinson. Rumour has it he dabbled in cannabis and injected himself full of crap. In and out of prison, he was a regular in here.'

'Can't say as I've ever seen him before.'

'Think carefully, Tony. Your licence could depend on this.'

'What the fuck? I'm clean. What do you think goes on around here?'

'That's why I'm here, Tony. To find out.' Mason hunched his shoulders in a show of contempt. 'With so many cameras around the place, your security must be pretty tight.'

Fox swallowed hard. 'What does that shit mean?'

'It means we may have to search your premises.'

'You'll find nothing here.'

'What makes you think that?'

'Anyone caught handling illegal substances on my premises is automatically banned for life – even the police.'

'And which life is this?' Mason smiled.

'Ask around,' Fox insisted. 'Check for yourself.'

'We already have, Tony.'

Fox smiled in defeat and quickly changed the subject. 'I hear you've been in talks with Mad Frankie Wiseman.'

'I have, but that's none of your business.'

The gangster swallowed hard. 'My oh my, we are

tetchy today.'

Mason's eyes toured the room. Apart from a strong whiff of cheap aftershave, the place reeked of cigar smoke. It hung in the air like a forgotten memory. Men's clubs, after dinner speeches, and the odd Rotary Club dinners he'd attended.

Unimpressed with Fox's credentials and attitude, DS Savage pushed forward. 'The man responsible for killing these two young men needs to be taken off the streets.'

'That's your fucking job, not mine?' Fox said, spinning to face the sergeant.

'Never mind the crap. Wilkinson felt at home in this shithole.'

'What are you implying?'

'We're close to making an arrest, and if you know who's responsible, now's the time to make a name for yourself.'

Fox laughed. 'There's a million people out there who fit the description of this so-called Suitcase Man. If I could help, I would, but I can't. It's as simple as that.'

'Is that so?' said Mason, annoyingly shaking his head.

Fox looked at each of them.

'Why don't you throw a name at me?'

'You know we can't do that.'

'Then how do you expect me to help?'

Silence.

'It's not that simple, and you know it,' Mason replied.

Fox stared at them. Like most gangsters that Mason had come across, they thrived on attention. His friend at the press office was right. If anyone in the West End was involved in these murders, Tony Fox was high on the list.

Savage leaned in closer. 'We have it on good authority your club's been shifting bucket loads of shit lately, and I'm talking top-quality.'

'Who told you that crap?'

'You'd be surprised,' Savage said with a smile. 'The thing is, we're thinking of closing you down.'

'What the hell are you rabbiting on about now?'

Mason watched as the muscles around Fox's neck tightened. Head and shoulders above the detective sergeant, he wasn't a guy to be messed with. The problem was, whatever Fox put his hand to invariably involved narcotics. Perhaps he didn't know who the killer was, but that was the nature of the beast.

Fox muttered something inaudible, having thought through the implications of them closing his club down.

'What is it you people want?'

'Names, Tony.'

'Which names?'

'Tell me about these East Europeans who have moved into the area. What have you heard?'

'Nothing,' Fox insisted.

'Have you talked to any of them lately?'

'About what?'

Full of contradictions, the gangster was refusing to cooperate. It wasn't looking good, but Mason wasn't giving in that easily.

***

Twenty minutes later, and the chief inspector was thumbing through the pages of his little black notebook.

It was 11:30, and the day ahead looked another long one. Sitting alongside him in the undercover vehicle, Rob Savage was weighing up the facts. Fox could not be trusted. Everyone knew that. But was he telling them the truth?

The sergeant blew through his cheeks. 'If these aren't gangland killings, then where do we go from here?'

'Whatever his motives, the killer's a loner who wears the mask of sanity.'

'He could be anyone.'

Mason stretched his back. 'Yeah, which makes our investigations even more challenging.'

'I'm thinking as you do, boss. There are far too many people tied up in this.'

'You're right. Which way to turn is the problem?'

These past few weeks hadn't gone at all well. Instead of looking at the bigger picture, the team had got bogged down in the criminal underworld. People were complex, and they needed some quality thinking time. Despite all their setbacks, Fox remained their prime suspect. Trying to preserve an image could cost the gangster dearly, and there was always someone out there willing to step into his shoes.

Mason turned to Savage.

'This case reminds me of the Dennis Nilsen murders.'

'How come?'

'Nearly all of Nilsen's victims were students or homeless dropouts picked up in bars. After he killed them and cut them up using butchery skills he'd learned in the army, he had very little recollection of what he'd done. Until 1981, Nilsen had access to a large garden, so he could burn their bodies. Then, after moving to an upstairs flat in London, he had problems of where to get rid of them.'

Savage held his gaze. 'I seem to remember the case. Didn't they catch up with him after he'd blocked the sewerage drains with body parts?'

Mason shrugged, emphasising his point. 'These individuals are such egotistical sods they couldn't care less how many people's lives they destroy.'

'How did they eventually catch up with him?'

Mason explained in a little more detail. 'When the police raided Nilsen's London flat, they discovered a suitcase full of human remains. After tearing the rest of the building apart, they found body parts hidden beneath the floorboards.'

'Blimey.'

'I know, and I suspect that's what we're up against.'

'Do you think we could have a copy-cat killer on our hands?'

It was typical Rob Savage, thought Mason. Jump in feet first without the slightest hesitation. 'I doubt it, but we know our killer stores his victim's body parts in a deep freezer.'

'It may be worth posing the question.'

'I'm not sure about that, but what if he runs out of freezer space?'

'Christ!' Savage gasped. 'So that's why he's trying to get rid of the body parts?'

'It's just a hunch.'

Savage's whole demeanour changed suddenly.

'Where the hell do you dream your ideas up from, boss?'

'That's why I'm a DCI with loads of money.'

The sergeant smiled, then fell silent for a moment.

'What if he's cutting them up at home? A garden shed. A garage perhaps?'

'He probably is.'

'Shit,' Savage replied, 'and we're still missing body parts.'

'I wouldn't get too hung up on it if I were you. He's probably disposed of them by now.'

'This is pretty gruesome stuff, and I've never given it much thought. You're right about one thing, though. What if he lives in a house without a garden?'

'It's another way of looking at it.'

Savage drummed his fingers on the steering wheel and laughed. 'Don't spoil it, not when I'm warming to the idea.'

'Something's not right, Rob.'

'I know, and I'm getting bad vibes about this one's evil intent.'

Mason understood the sergeant's train of thought, that a sexual assault had never taken place, heartened him. 'He's an opportunist who kills on impulse. I'm certain of that.'

'Yeah, but what triggers him?'

'His pleasure comes from inflicting sexual torment on his victims, driven by sadistic urges. His type has a point to prove and nothing gets in their way.'

The sergeant's eyes were full of unnerving coldness. 'You know what? That's a bloody good point. The fact he drew smiley faces on Jennifer Oakwell's walls shows he's angry about something. God forbid we're dealing with another Wharf Butcher here.'

'Don't even go there,' Mason replied.

They both sat silent, thinking.

Chapter Sixteen

The years had worked on Peter Carter's features like a caricaturist's pen. Not an assertive man, Carter had always shied away from the limelight, believing he was just ordinary. Now eighty-one, he accepted the fact that most of his life was now behind him. His colleague had worked for the Port of Tyne Authority as a ship's pilot for thirty-seven years, but a colourful career was tragically cut short owing to major heart surgery. Forced into early retirement, Carter had rented a stone-built cottage with magnificent views overlooking Cullercoats Harbour. Living out a frugal existence, his sole passion in life was painting seascapes of his beloved North-East Coast.

Cleaning the last of his paintbrushes, he dropped them into a large earthenware jar and turned back to their previous conversation. He reminded Carlisle of an old recluse he'd once met. A hermit who'd lived out his days on Holy Island collecting seashells and selling them back to holidaymakers as lucky charm bracelets. He'd made a small fortune from it, but always claimed he was penniless. He wasn't, of course. After he passed away, his entire estate had been willed to a local children's hospital in Newcastle. Two million pounds, and not a penny less. It was an enormous sum of money, and the charity was eternally grateful for his act of kindness.

'So,' Carter began, 'you'd like to take your father out

on a sea fishing adventure?'

'That's if you're still up for it.'

Carter's frown lines corrugated. 'Why the sudden change of mind?'

'Dad's always fancied his hand at sea fishing and has gone on about it for years. He's not getting any younger and is unsteady on his feet these days.'

'That answers a lot,' said Carter thoughtfully. 'Sea fishing totally differs from river angling, of course, and is a lot more challenging.'

'I realise that, but I thought the North Sea air might do him the world of good.'

'If it doesn't finish him,' Carter chuckled.

'Try stopping him.'

Peter Carter had been a family friend for as long as Carlisle could remember, and his pride and joy was a forty-foot motor yacht called *Thunder*. When Carlisle was an impressionable schoolboy, he'd sailed out to sea on her. Moored up in South Shields, she had twin Mercury Marine engines that could cut through water like a knife through butter. Those were the days. Packed lunches wrapped in greaseproof paper, bottles of fizzy pop, and a box full of rag worm for bait. It was a life-changing experience, the stuff of childhood dreams.

'Tell me,' said Carter. 'Did your father ever catch that sea trout he was after?'

'You mean, Herman?'

'Ah, yes. I remember that name now,' his colleague said, stroking his chin. 'The last time we met, your father never stopped talking about it. I've often wondered whether it was true or just a figment of his imagination.

It's funny how some stories stick in your mind.'

Carlisle smiled resignedly to himself. 'As far as I'm aware, Herman is still swimming around in the River Coquet. Mind, my old man has snapped many a fishing line attempting to catch him over the years and has never given up trying.'

Carter stared at him in disbelief.

'It must be one hell of a fish.'

'According to my old man, it is.'

'How old did you say your father was?'

'He's coming up to seventy-nine.'

'Where have all those years gone? It seems only yesterday we were playing cricket for the local parish team, and there's just a handful of us left now. Most have passed on to greener fields sadly.'

His voice trailed off as if reliving a memory.

'It must be over twenty years ago now.'

'You don't have to remind me.'

Carlisle gave a curt nod as Carter stroked his chin in thought. 'You had just joined the Metropolitan Police, as I remember. A young whippersnapper, keen as mustard at having passed your entry exams. Your father was so proud of you; he could never stop talking about it.'

'You're right,' Carlisle remarked, 'none of us are getting any younger. It was around that period we went on a fishing holiday to Scotland. Loch Tummel, a beautiful stretch of water surrounded by big tree country and rolling hills. We were looking for pike, which was a pretty exciting predator to target for a beginner. Dad was an experienced angler and knew the ropes.'

Carlisle's phone pinged, and he checked the display.

'Hello?' he asked. 'Who am I talking to?'

'Angelica.'

The voice on the other end of the line fell to a whisper on the last syllable of her name. At least she'd told him that much.

'How can I help you, Angelica?'

'It's about the body the police recently found.'

She had a foreign accent. Eastern European, he guessed. Now on the edge of his seat, he took a deep breath and focused his mind. 'Which body might this be? There's been quite a few lately.'

There followed an awkward silence between them, a gathering of wits. She was hyperventilating, as if having a panic attack. Also, there was shouting in the background, and he made a mental note of it.

'The one they found in Forth Street,' she finally replied.

Carlisle felt an adrenaline rush. 'Is that close to the railway station in Newcastle?'

'That's the one.'

He could hardly believe his ears. Feeling on edge, he questioned what other dark secrets this young woman might have in store. Just out of habit, he opened his notebook and flipped through the pages until reaching a space. Why hadn't she gone to the police before now? Strange, he thought. Foremost in his mind was how to build up a rapport of trust between them. Force the issue and he could easily lose contact.

His phone crackled.

'Are you still there?'

'Uh-huh.'

Carlisle sensed the hesitation.

'I need to share some information with you,' she said brashly.

'And what might that be?'

The line went silent suddenly. This type of call was a regular occurrence these days. The city was full of rumours. False sightings of potential serial killers walking the streets were commonplace. But this caller appeared genuine, as if desperate to share her information with someone. Pencil in hand, Carlisle scribbled down the details and tried to build up her confidence. She was young; he imagined. How young he had yet to decide. His head full of dangerous thoughts, he felt he was playing a game of Russian roulette.

'Have you spoken to anyone else about this before now?'

'No,' she replied.

'Not even to the police?'

'No police, you're the only person I will speak to.'

Carlisle remained silent for a second, thinking.

'Okay,' he said. 'No police. That's a promise.'

'Do I have your word on that?'

'Yes, of course you do.'

'Good,' she replied.

Carlisle lowered the tone in his voice, using a more sympathetic approach. 'One question if I may, Angelica. How did you come by my name?'

She hesitated, then said, 'I saw your advert in one of the local newspapers and ran a check on you. You're a private investigator, are you not?'

'Yes, I am.'

The background noises had kicked off again, as if an

argument had turned ugly.

'Perhaps we could meet somewhere?' he suggested.

'Not today.'

'When then?'

There was another long pause. 'I'll call you back later.'

The man in the background screamed out at her in a foreign tongue. More Eastern bloc than Germanic, he thought. Carlisle pondered his next move.

'Tell me—'

The connection went dead.

He checked the display. Number withheld. Whoever Angelica was, she seemed pretty desperate to talk to someone. Why hadn't she reported this to the authorities before now? Why had she chosen him, of all people? Then again, he reasoned. No matter how small or seemly insignificant her information was, it could be of major interest to them.

'Trouble at mill?' said Carter, his face showing concern.

'I'm sorry, Peter.'

'Damn phones.'

Carlisle looked at him, feeling uncomfortable.

'There's never a dull moment, I'm afraid.'

'I guess not.'

He watched as the old man gathered a few empty plates and returned to the kitchen. Still thinking about his conversation with Angelica, he gave Jack Mason a call. The ring tone had nearly played out when the DCI answered.

'I'm in a meeting – can I call you back?'

Carlisle could barely breathe, let alone talk. 'There's been a fresh development, Jack.'

'Give me a few minutes,' the chief inspector replied.

The line went dead.

Chapter Seventeen

David Carlisle had taken the Metro train that afternoon, which seemed a pleasant change from driving in heavy traffic. Besides, parking in Newcastle was expensive, but finding a space was an even bigger headache. Thinking about his forthcoming meeting with Angelica, he made his way down Grey Street before turning right into High Bridge. Now a listed building, people reputed the Old George Inn to be one of the city's oldest surviving pubs. Not the best meeting place. He would have preferred a more tranquil setting.

Despite her secretive stance, Carlisle did not know what Angelica looked like. Was she an attractive young woman, or just plain and ordinary-looking? He knew he'd recognise her voice, especially over the telephone. Sometimes it was best to keep an open mind about these things, not get carried away. Foremost on his mind were Angelica's latest revelations regarding the Suitcase Man. What else would she disclose? What other dark secrets was she holding back from him?

On entering the cobbled courtyard, the Old George Inn was busy. All the bench seats were taken, and people were standing around chatting. Close to the main entrance, a busker was playing an old accordion rather badly. He had collected a little money, and no one was paying a blind bit of notice to him. His dog, a flea ridden mongrel, lay stretched out on a blanket looking bored out of its mind.

Intrigued, Carlisle glanced across the crowded room. He ordered a pint of Theakston's Old Peculier and found a corner seat. Now back in the swing of things, he hadn't felt this way in a long time. Not since his days in the Metropolitan Murder Team (MIT). Those were the happiest years of his life: a trained criminal profiler tracking down psychopaths, and the occasional hostage-taker who threatened national security. Above all else, there was nothing like getting inside a serial killer's head and trying to unravel the mystery that made them tick. It was like a drug to him, and he couldn't get enough.

Well, he thought, he only had himself to blame. Half-past three and still no sign of Angelica showing. Of course, the team had warned him against meeting her, but he felt he was on to something.

Then the barman's voice cut through the rest.

'David Carlisle?'

'That's me.'

'It's for you,' he said, handing him the pub phone.

The profiler instantly recognised the broken English on the other end of the line. 'Is that you, Angelica?'

'We agreed no police.'

'I came alone. What's your problem?'

'Someone followed you.'

There was an uncomfortable silence between them.

'That's ridiculous,' he protested.

'There's a man at the end of the bar wearing a blue baseball cap and dark horn-rimmed glasses. Can you see him?'

'Yes, I can.'

'He's an undercover police officer.'

'That's impossible. How could you possibly know that?'

'If not, then why has he been following you these last fifteen minutes?'

Carlisle stared at a thickset man entrenched at the end of the bar and saw a flicker of recognition in his eyes. He wasn't a gambling man, but guessed it was one of Jack Mason's old cronies sent to check on him.

'Where are you now?'

'Never mind that,' she replied. 'Do you still wish to meet me?'

'Yes, of course I do.'

'Then listen carefully.' Her voice was brusque. Agitated. 'There's a little Costa coffee shop inside the Central railway station. Meet me there in twenty minutes.'

With that, she hung up.

The barman rolled his eyes. 'Frustrated girlfriend?'

Carlisle feigned a smile and handed back the pub phone. It was time to leave.

The Cloth Market wasn't overly busy at this time of day. Mainly office workers and business owners moving between appointments. Sliding his hands into his pockets, he made towards the Haymarket before doubling back on himself. One thing he'd learned in his chosen profession was how to remain invisible. If undercover officers were following him, this was the perfect place to lose them. On reaching the bottom of Westgate Road, he stepped up his pace and slipped into one of the many narrow back-lanes.

Why did fate choose me? He questioned. This was ridiculous. Which side of the fence were the police sitting on? Knowing his movements were now under scrutiny, his head was so mixed up with half-cocked rumours he was doubting his own judgement.

Then he realised. Mason was using him as bait.

***

Two miles north, DCI Mason looked at his watch and smiled. What Henry Bannister didn't know about the criminal fraternity wasn't worth knowing. A born loser, Bannister's major source of income was off-loading cheap cigarettes to the local community. Brought over from Amsterdam in vast quantities, thousands of pounds were exchanging hands, and none of it was traceable. Black market trading was a lucrative business, and everyone wanted in on it.

Parked in the visitor's bay, it wouldn't take long before word got around. The mere presence of a police undercover vehicle was enough. That aside, the tower block wasn't the friendliest environment to hang around in, either. Not at any time. Mason was letting too many people see his face and wasn't sure how to handle it.

Since the lift doors were broken, he opted to use the emergency stairs instead. Walls full of graffiti, doors in disrepair, the levels of anti-social behaviour in this neighbourhood were exceptionally high. Despite warnings not to defecate in corridors or walkways, the place stank of urine and something a little stronger.

Readjusting his priorities, on reaching the tenth floor, Mason moved along a dimly lit corridor until finding door 1025. He rang the doorbell. Seconds later, a man answered wearing a black polo neck sweater. He looked dishevelled, as if badly in need of a night's sleep.

'How are you, Henry?' Mason asked.

'All the better for seeing you, Jack.'

'Someone giving you grief, are they?'

'You could say that, yes.'

Ignoring him, the chief inspector was under no illusions his informant was a dangerous felon. Moles had a knack of trading information, occasionally to the press, but mainly to the police. Cultivating informants was tricky, and it took years to build up a degree of reciprocal trust. It was all about belief, and giving your informant the benefit of the doubt when the occasion arose.

Mason stuck his foot over the threshold to stop the door from closing. They had not crossed paths in a long time, but all that was about to change. Bannister had overstepped the mark, double crossed the police and was about to be taken off the streets. Soon, the lead detective would have a massive void on his hands and would be desperate to find a replacement.

'This person who's giving you grief,' Mason remarked. 'Do I know who he is?'

'Ah-huh. He's one of your local bizzies, Jack. He's a right pain in the arse.'

'How can I possibly help?'

'It depends.'

Seconds later, he was inside and staring out through the living room window. Double glazed with toughened glass, the views from up here were stunning. Mason had a keen eye for spotting opportunities, and the signs pointing towards them were always unmistakable. Piled high on the living room floor were dozens of spurious cardboard boxes. Of various shapes and sizes, they had no official labels attached to them, nor formal identity. Curious, he took a step back, made a show of inspecting them, but refrained from pressing the matter.

'Tell me who this PCSO is, and I'll have a word.'

'I'd appreciate that, Jack.'

'Before I do, there's something I need in exchange.'

'Like what?'

Mason turned sharply to face him. 'Information, Henry.'

'What kind of information?'

'That's a new one,' Mason growled. 'You rarely question me.'

'Everything has a price, Jack. Even you should know that.'

Bannister looked fit enough, despite being in his early sixties. He had a heft, but the years had given him a stoop. Although the man seemed at peace with himself, Mason knew otherwise.

'If that's how you wish to play it, that's fine by me.'

'What do you mean by that exactly?'

'Asking a PCSO to turn a blind eye on your little cigarette scam could cost me all of twenty grand.'

'That's bollocks!'

'But is it?' Mason sighed as his eyes toured the room. 'Doing you a favour means I'm putting my police pension on the line.'

'Life's tough, Jack.'

'I couldn't agree more.'

Bannister stared at him with deep-rooted suspicion. 'What is it you're after this time?'

'The trouble is, offloading dodgy cigarettes carries a hefty penalty nowadays. It's as bad as piracy – worse than lying to a judge. Handling contraband is crown prosecution stuff, and I doubt Her Majesty would take too kindly to you swindling her out of thousands of pounds of taxpayers' money.' Mason suppressed a grin. 'People have hanged others for less.'

'Who said this stuff was contraband?'

'Why don't we open a box and see?'

'Why would I do that?'

Mason was enjoying himself.

'If this isn't kosher, it'll get burnt in an incinerator. You know that. It's the law of the land. I'm not a gambling man, but I'd say you're taking an enormous risk here. So why don't we open one, Henry?'

Bannister's eyes narrowed a fraction. 'What is it you're wanting to know?'

'What do you know about this so-called Suitcase Man?'

His informant remained silent for a moment. Paying moles was a cost-effective method of securing valuable information, but the risks were enormous. People like Bannister were driven by greed to engage in intelligence gathering, as they could earn a lot of money from it.

'You mean this geek who's chopping people up?'

'That's the one.' Mason nodded.

'Not a lot. Why do you ask?'

'I need a name, Henry.'

'Easier said than done.'

'Oh. And why is that?'

'Cos this one doesn't hang about.'

Mason had had a toothache the previous night. It had been in remission so far today, but now it was troubling him again. He paused, watching Bannister's eyes closely and guessed what his informant was thinking. 'I know. But this bastard needs to be taken off the streets before he commits further atrocities.'

'I thought that was your job, Jack.'

Mason looked at him hard. 'Don't push me, Henry.'

'I'm not. But what you're asking isn't easy.'

'Just give me a name, and I'll see to it my mates don't close your illicit operation down.'

'What operation's this?' Bannister replied nervously.

'Don't mess with me. This sneaky little business you're running must be a nice little earner. We're not daft, Henry. You've been under our radar for months. We know what you're up to in Amsterdam, and everything's now on camera.'

Bannister swallowed hard. Suddenly, the general conversation was over, and Mason could feel the change of intensity in his informant's voice. 'It's rumours, Jack.'

'Maybe, but I'm not liking what I'm hearing.'

'It's pure bullshit.'

Mason gave him a neighbourly tap on the shoulder. 'I'm trying to look after your interests here. All I need is a name.'

Judging by Bannister's response, he wasn't a happy customer. Caught red-handed with a room full of contraband, there wasn't a lot he could do.

'I'll ask around, see what the word on the street is.'

'Don't take too long over it. The clock's ticking, and I need a name.'

'You know me, Jack. If I can help you, I will.'

Mason moved towards the door.

'It's been a pleasure talking to you, Henry. I'll see myself out.'

'Gan canny, Inspector.'

'I will.'

Mason had barely crossed the threshold when he heard the dead bolts snap shut behind him. It was that kind of neighbourhood.

CHAPTER EIGHTEEN

Inside the little Costa coffee shop on Newcastle Central Station, Carlisle had found a corner seat. There were dozens of young women passing the time of day and drinking coffee, but which one was Angelica?

His phone pinged.

'Raise your hand above your head, Mr Carlisle,' the young woman's voice instructed.

'And—'

'Now I see you.'

'Where are you?' asked Carlisle inquisitively.

'When you step out of the Costa cafe, turn left towards the main entrance and wait for me under the train arrivals board.'

His phone went dead.

Carlisle suddenly felt like the actor in the film Phone Booth, where telephone calls were controlling the main protagonist. Whoever Angelica was, she certainly knew how to send his adrenaline racing. But there lay his problem. This was the best lead in town, and just because Jack Mason's team were shadowing his every movement, he wasn't giving in that easily.

His mobile pinged again.

'Mr Carlisle.'

He spun sharply. 'Where are you?'

'I'm twenty metres away,' she replied.

'How will I recognise you?'

'Walk back towards the station's main entrance.'

Still holding the phone close to his ear, Carlisle did as instructed. Then, through a gap in the crowd, he spotted her. A petite young woman with blonde hair and ice-blue eyes, she carried a large black bag slung loosely over her shoulder. Dressed in a plain red coat, black jeans, and wearing red baseball boots with long white laces, she conveyed a mystical presence. Being a private investigator was all about trust – putting your client at ease. This meeting felt different, full of dark secrets and suspicion. Then he understood why. There were no CCTV cameras in this section of the station – just electronic notice boards.

He walked towards her. Warily.

'You must be Angelica?'

She remained silent for a moment. 'I won't keep you long, Mr Carlisle. As you'll have gathered by now, I'm not from this country. Where I live, you learn not to make contact over the telephone. It's far too dangerous. You are a private investigator and will know all about the electronic surveillance devices. You never can be too careful.'

As far as he could tell, Angelica was alone. But that didn't mean they weren't being watched. He steadied himself, but the way she looked at him was unnerving.

'So,' Carlisle began, 'what is it you wish to talk to me about?'

'You're moving too fast. How do I know I can trust you?'

Carlisle considered the question but wasn't about to

answer. Whoever she was, she had certainly done her homework. One false move and Angelica would disappear into the throng.

'I'm here at your request,' he replied calmly.

'What do you know about Eastern European gangs?'

'Not a lot. Why?'

She told him more. About Britain's proximity to the Netherlands, which was now regarded as the epicentre of the EU's narcotics industry. Gang leaders, it seemed, were using smuggling routes to traffic their illegal human cargoes to England. Despite her age, Angelica – if that was her real name – displayed remarkable knowledge. Too well, he thought. This was a dangerous game she was playing, but she spoke with confidence, as though she understood the situation perfectly.

As more of her story began to unfold, Carlisle had to pinch himself. Venom laced her voice, but she delivered her words with a guardedness and an underlying sense of enigma.

'Tell me what you saw on Forth Street,' he asked outright.

She looked at him with frank surprise. 'Can I trust you?'

'Yes, of course you can.'

Her posture had changed, and he sensed uncertainty. 'It had just turned seven o'clock when the car drew up into one of the side lanes in Forth Street. It's headlights switched off, I could still hear the engine running.' She checked over her shoulder again. 'Most men are usually friendly when you approach them, but some like to feel in control. It's a defensive stance, as most customers have secrets to hide. This time felt different, though, as if something nasty was about to happen to me. It was then I questioned him.'

'Question whom?'

Her shoulders slumped, and she glanced coyly away. 'Men often pull up in cars to talk to us girls. It's a safe area, Mr Carlisle. That's how we operate.'

He thought about it, but not for long. Forth Street wasn't a known red-light district, yet she claimed she was posing as a prostitute. Then again, he reasoned, tucked back from the hustle and bustle of city life, it was the perfect environment for a woman of the night to operate.

He refrained from pressing the matter further.

'What happened next?'

'The moment I approached the driver's door, his electric window wound down. I knew he wasn't interested in sex. You can always tell by the tone of their voice.'

'What did he say to you?'

'He was foul-mouthed and nasty about it. He told me to clear off, or he'd fetch the police to me.'

'And did he?'

'I was scared. Some men can be extremely violent towards you, and I try to steer well clear of those types of customers.'

Although she spoke English fluently, the profiler was convinced that she was East European. Her face was angelic, as her name suggested, but that's where the similarities ceased.

'What did he look like, this man?'

There was panic in her voice, and fear in her eyes. 'Not

like the rest.'

'What do you mean by that?'

'I didn't get a good look at him,' she replied warily. 'I was terrified. It was dark, and I was working alone in the area that night.'

'Sorry,' Carlisle replied almost apologetically. 'So, what did you decide to do next?'

'I moved to a safer spot... but still kept a watchful eye on him.' She turned her head towards him but spoke as if he wasn't there. 'I knew something wasn't right. I could tell from the tone of his voice. At first, I thought he was waiting for one of the other girls. That's what some men do. They like to stick with the same girl every time. It's much safer that way, and they know what they're letting themselves in for.' She steadied herself. 'When none of the other girls showed up, and he didn't drive off, that's when I panicked.'

Carlisle thought about this.

'Was he a regular client, this man you talk of?'

'No. I'd never seen him before.' Her eyes widened as she turned towards him. 'If any of the girls feel uncomfortable about a client they're meeting, we text the car registration details to each other. Things can go wrong, and a quick text puts our minds at rest.'

Clever move, he thought.

'And did *you* text anyone that night?'

'Why would I do that? I certainly wasn't getting into his car.'

'No, I suppose not.' He thought of something. 'What makes you think he had anything to do with this recent murder?'

The look she gave him told him he'd overstepped the mark. He apologised.

'There was something sinister about him. Something that did not fit. Then, when I walked away, that's when he got out of his car and moved to the rear.' She glowered, as if reliving the moment. 'He was gangly looking, tall, and wearing a black hoodie pulled low over his face. After he opened the car boot, he stood for a moment before struggling to lift a large blue suitcase out from it.'

Carlisle felt a sudden adrenaline rush.

'A *blue* suitcase. How did you know it was blue when it was dark?'

'The boot lid was lit up.' She frowned. 'It looked extremely heavy, from what I could tell. It had two thick luggage straps to stop it from bursting open, but it still bulged at the sides.' There was a sudden eagerness in her voice. 'Moments later, he dragged it into the storage company.'

'Why haven't you gone to the police with this information before now?'

'No police,' she panicked.

Annoyed at himself, Carlisle studied her face. Her eyes were heavy, and her lips drawn tight, conveying worry. He needed more thinking time, but things were moving too quickly.

'Are you in some sort of trouble with the police, Angelica?'

She did not answer.

'If you are, I can help you.'

She arched her back, a stretching motion. 'I would

need to consider that.'

'Please do. Take your time.'

She smiled. 'I know I can trust you, but I don't have a lot of confidence.'

'That's understandable.'

'Thank you. It means so much to me.'

He stared at her hard. 'Are you here illegally?'

'What makes you think I am?'

'Just asking, that's all.'

He felt for his phone. Either she didn't realise it, or just didn't care, but if she didn't replace her SIM card at some stage, he could trace her call.

'No more questions,' she insisted.

Carlisle felt sorry for Angelica, as if she were stuck in a negative downward spiral. Much as he hated to admit, there were some elements of her story he disbelieved. Not all, but some. He was usually good at weighing people up, but this time felt different. There was a darker side – far removed and difficult to comprehend.

'This man you saw. How would you best describe him?'

She turned sharply to confront him. 'Now you're making me nervous.'

'But I'm trying to sort this out.'

She waved her hand dismissively. 'Please don't follow me, Mr Carlisle. That would be a very foolish thing to do.'

She pivoted and walked away.

'Angelica, wait.'

Her pace quickened.

'Angelica,' he called out.

He tried running after her, but within seconds, she'd

melted into the crowd.

It was a funny old world, thought Carlisle. You could spend weeks trying to force an opening, then everything fell into place. If nothing else, he now had a reasonable explanation of how the victim's body had turned up at the storage company that night.

Before he left the train station, he gave Jack Mason a call. Seconds later, the automatic voice recorder kicked in.

'You have reached the phone of DCI Mason. I'm sorry, but—'

Chapter Nineteen

Jack Mason spread his hands out on the table in front of him, palms face down. It had taken the chief inspector all of twelve minutes to reach the Costa cafe on Newcastle Central Station. Now into his second cup of coffee, Carlisle eased back in his seat. Knowing his colleague as he did, this was far from a simple conversation. Even though he had the upper hand, that meant nothing. Mason was hot-headed, temperamental, and could fly off the handle at the slightest provocation. The problem was hot leads had a nasty habit of going cold and you had to react quickly to them.

'First things first,' Mason said, his voice filled with trepidation. 'Care telling me why you haven't contacted me before now?'

'What do you mean?'

'You were meeting a key witness who is probably withholding vital information.'

Sitting awkwardly, his colleague's frustration was understandable, having given his surveillance team the run around that morning.

He glanced at his watch – a diversionary tactic.

'Well?' Mason insisted.

The profiler braced himself and tried to remain calm. Still no mention of their agreement to work together on this one, he was feeling isolated. Sometimes he got the impression he was talking to a brick wall, and the DCI wasn't listening. His colleague was thick-skinned, inflexible, and seemed unwilling to yield ground.

'It wasn't my call, Jack. What else was I to do?'

Mason paused just as the coffee cup reached his lips. 'I'm still listening.'

'Look,' Carlisle replied, sucking the air. 'Whatever problem this young woman is facing, she's determined to call all the shots.'

'So, it seems,' Mason mocked.

Carlisle lowered his voice, realising that people were looking at them. 'She categorically refuses to talk to you people and will only speak to me. What am I to do?'

Mason scooted his seat, his expression showing contempt. 'Here's my problem. I've got a shitload of angry senior officers on my back, and every one of them demands answers. What do you suggest I do? Tell them I've got an eighteen-year-old prostitute who thinks she knows who the killer is?'

Carlisle remained silent.

'You should have rung me earlier,' Mason insisted. 'At least run it past me.'

'If you think I'm going to call you every time this young woman springs a surprise meeting on me, it will not happen.'

There, it was said.

Mason's eyebrows lifted a fraction. 'You're forgetting who's in charge here, my friend. Three people lay dead, and I'm determined to get answers to every one of them.'

'I realise that, but I've told you everything I know.'

Mason stroked a two-day stubble as if pondering over

his next line of attack. 'Prostitutes aren't the world's most reliable witnesses. Most are natural born liars; it goes with the profession. And another thing, who's saying she's not here illegally?'

'Wait a minute!'

'How do you know we can trust her?'

'We don't.'

'That's my point,' Mason said, stabbing a finger in his direction. 'This young woman is rational about a lot of things, but is she telling you the truth?'

'She is, I believe.'

'That's utter bollocks.'

Carlisle remained silent.

'Besides, prostitutes normally tout for business by poking their heads in through a driver's open window. It's a little trick they use. Once a client gets a whiff of their perfume, it's normally a done deal.'

'Speaking from experience, are we?'

'Don't push me,' Mason groaned.

Late afternoon and Newcastle seemed darker than ever, reflecting the DCI's mood. It was pointless arguing; there was nothing to be gained from it. Mason was goading him, and all he could do was sit there and take it.

'There has to be a glimmer of truth in what she's saying, surely?'

'Okay. How come she knew he wasn't one of her regular clients and yet can't give you a facial description of him? Then there's the question of timing. You told me it was seven o'clock when he approached her, which she could have read about in any of the newspapers.'

'What are you implying?'

'She's a liar,' Mason insisted. 'Can't you get that into your thick skull?'

'You're making a grave mistake, Jack.'

'Do you think so?'

'I know so,' Carlisle retorted. 'Her account is too detailed, even down to the colour of the suitcase and the two luggage straps that were wrapped around it.'

Mason swung to face him. 'You mentioned nothing about two luggage straps before.'

'I would have done had you given me a chance.'

'This city is full of rumourmongers. If this was the killer's car she claims to have recently seen, then why wasn't it picked up during our CCTV sweep of the area?'

'He could have driven there on false number plates.'

'True, but highly unlikely, don't you think?'

'Well, that's what I would have done.'

Mason eyed him with suspicion. 'She's a liar... goddammit. I wouldn't trust her as far as I could throw her.'

Carlisle pursed his lips, knowing full well he was getting nowhere. Mason was a creature of habit, notorious for makeshift plans. Confused at first, then angry with himself, he tried to focus his mind. And yes, serial killers were egotistical predators who would stop at nothing to accomplish their goals. Whoever had killed these young men could be driven by sexual lust. And yet, he argued, sex wasn't his primary motive. The killer was systematic and carried out most of his crimes away from his area of residence. No, he thought, his behaviour patterns were far too consistent – he was winning over his victims' confidence before killing them.

Mason gave him a look that said it all. 'You should know the procedure by now. You'll need to come in and make out a written statement. In the meantime, I'll get Forth Banks Police Station to run a few checks on the area. If Angelica is a working prostitute as she claims, she'll not be too difficult to pick out.'

Carlisle stood to leave.

Trying to read into Jack Mason's mind was like staring into a black hole. He would need to work on it, find a better way of relaying future information. As it was, he now had a lot of explaining to do, besides a written report to fill out.

God, what a mess. He could sorely have done without this.

CHAPTER TWENTY

Naked, stretched out on the cold bathroom floor, Wasp inhaled the sickly sweet smell of death. Physically exhausted and emotionally drained from his recent overindulgence, an overwhelming sense of calm washed over him. Beautiful strains of music filled the air – *The Tempest* – coming from another part of the building. He loved the sound that a full symphony orchestra made as it played out its dark brooding passages, and this part of the performance was truly magnificent. He particularly adored the string articulation, tranquil, unlike the overpowering climax that followed. That would come next. Nature breathing its fury as the sea moved from calm breezy moods to the thundering gust of a tempest was Sibelius at his best.

Alone in his thoughts, Wasp stared at the young man's lifeless body, now sprawled out on the bathroom floor. Two weeks of watching him – following his every movement – fantasising.

'Death is a door through which everyone must pass,' he whispered. *'Death is inevitable.'*

Not stocky, wiry with short, cropped hair, he fingered the knife. Building a rapport and trust between you and your client was a big part of the excitement. It was all about timing, choosing the right moment to execute your plans. Sometimes he felt an uplifting affiliation towards his victims, as if not deserving to die. Regrets seemed futile, as events had inevitably overtaken him. Exhausted, he would sleep later. After he finished his work here.

Wasp stared at the bathroom tiles and smiled. Blood everywhere, ceilings and walls, all of it his own doing. The sight excited him. A feeling of power and control, for which he always felt grateful. Separating the vulnerable from the rest of the pack was the simple part. The next bit was much trickier – forcing them into the kill zone. Then Wasp remembered his Facebook account. Blimey! He'd almost forgotten about that. It was time to open a new account – seek another potential candidate. The timing felt right, and he couldn't have chosen a better moment than this. Planning was essential, as it had been quiet around the estate these days. Most people had lost the art of conversation, which was always a good thing.

Not long now!

His heart racing, he reached over and wrapped his long slender fingers around the cold plastic handle of the saw. It felt good. Exhilarating. Just as it had done on every other occasion. He tilted his head back slightly, rolled his eyes till only the whites were showing. The moment he pressed the start button, his mind flew into hyperdrive. This was far better than drugs, more invigorating than anything he'd ever experienced.

He toyed with the start button and sensed the tiny vibrations running through his fingertips. There was nothing like the sound of a surgical saw slicing through a human body at sixteen inches per minute. It felt good.

Stimulating. Flesh was easy to cut through, but other parts of the body were more difficult. He always wore a visor for that, as pieces of flying bone could easily blind a person.

Wasp wasn't daft.

Heels trailing the tiles, head lolloping to one side, he dragged the limp corpse the short distance towards the edge of the bath. Overcome with emotion, he felt an unexplainable surge of adrenaline rushing through his veins. Not for the first time, he needed to take a rest.

Slowly at first – hands gripped firmly under the young man's arms – he hauled his victim onto the lip of the bath. Once the legs had cleared the floor tiles, only then would he release his grip. Eyes wide open in utter astonishment, he watched as the body slid effortlessly towards the drain plug. It was perfect. He couldn't have positioned it any better.

'Nearly done,' he whispered.

Silent for a moment, Wasp mentally walked through the various scenarios he'd meticulously planned in his head. The next bit would be tricky, and this was the most important part. Steadying himself, experience had taught him always to grip the surgical saw in your right hand, as it was much easier that way. More accurate. Less chance of slipping.

Then, grabbing hold of the victim's arm with his left hand, he made his first incision. Not hurried. Precise. Just as the surgical book had taught him. As the blade sliced smoothly through human membranes, he guided the blade effortlessly along the suture line.

'Looking good,' he smiled.

Chapter Twenty-One

The moment he stepped into the Northumberland Arms in Newcastle city centre, the profiler's taste buds were alerted. It was lunchtime, and the place reeked of chicken curry and other tempting aromas. A regular haunt with off-duty police officers, today it was full of pensioners. Two meals for the price of one, not bad considering. He ordered a beer and spotted an empty table nearby. Running your own private investigation business could be a dreary existence. Endless hours spent snooping around some seedy partner's nocturnal activities could drive a man mad. Not today.

The profiler had been so tied up with work these past few weeks, he'd almost forgotten it was Monday. The weekend had flown by, and he still had a lot of catching up to do. Earlier that morning, he conducted a cognitive interview with Tom Hedley's forensic team and felt pleased with the end results. Not an exact science, they had cobbled together an e-fit image of Angelica, which he thought bore a remarkable likeness. All that remained now was to circulate the image to every police force in the land. Someone would recognise her, surely.

Pint in hand, he squeezed into one of the many side booths overlooking the bar. As he sat pondering his options, nothing could convey the horror, nor the dreadful loss the victim's families must be going through. God's will was one thing, but man's madness was another. As he took another sip of his beer, he tried to put things into perspective. In a way, he felt sorry for Angelica. Yes, she could exaggerate, but that didn't make her a liar.

Not everything was rosy in the garden, and Mason's ability to irritate people had caused him a serious challenge. But that wasn't the only issue. Organised crime gangs were much broader and more complex than they were ten years ago. In the wake of the Soviet Union collapse, Russian mobsters had moved into Europe's major cities and were causing havoc amongst decent folk. Drugs, human trafficking, and financial scams were the scourge of modern-day society. People had grown tired of it, but frontline policing was ill-equipped to tackle the problem.

He could not be sure, but the man stood next to the gaming machine carried a familiar look. Not a conspicuous man, his demeanour was the giveaway. Dressed in a blue open neck shirt, jeans, and black leather bomber jacket, he blended in well. Then it twigged. This was one of Mason's latest recruits, a fresh face brought in to strengthen their ranks.

After finishing his drink, Carlisle exited the pub into bright sunshine. Adjusting his sunglasses, he stood for a moment before heading towards Neville Street. Joined by countless office workers, a sudden break in the weather had certainly created a vibrant atmosphere.

On reaching Grey's Monument, the profiler caught sight of the ominous figure now following in his tracks. A tubby man in his late forties, he looked at odds with the world. Unable to shake him off, on passing the cathedral, he ducked into the multi-storey car park and boarded the elevator. As the doors swished shut, he took stock of his surroundings. The atmosphere was tense, and ascending to level four, the relentless noise of cars zooming by and horns blaring grew louder. His heart pounding with anticipation, his whole body felt tense.

Stepping onto the cold concrete, he heard voices. As the elevator lights flickered, he felt the slight vibration as the lift began its ascent. Alone once again, he heard footsteps approaching and hung in the shadows. It was an anxious moment, and as the man levelled with him, he emerged from the shadows, his voice threating.

'This is as far as it goes,' he shouted.

The stranger stopped in his tracks.

'What's your problem?'

'I should ask you that. Why are you following me?'

Reaching into his pocket, the officer pulled out his warrant card and said, 'Detective Constable Carver. I have every reason to believe...'

'Cut the bullshit,' Carlisle angrily replied. 'Who sent you?'

'What the hell are you on about?'

'I know what's going on. Tell Jack Mason not to bother next time.'

Annoyed with himself, Carlisle took the steps to the ground floor. On reaching the entrance ramp, he searched for the backup officer. They usually worked in pairs; swapping places was common practice as it reduced the chance of being spotted. Not this time.

'Why are you following me?' demanded Carlisle, as he

directly confronted the second officer.

'Who the hell are you?'

The man had an attitude and was cocky with it. Carlisle had become an expert at evading surveillance, losing count of how many times he had slipped away undetected. He remained vigilant, and never once let his guard down.

Unsure if the officers were grossly incompetent, he stepped from the shadows. 'The game's up,' he scoffed. 'It's time to return to base.'

'Carry on like that, and I'll arrest you for obstructing a police officer in the execution of his duty.'

'Try pulling the other leg.'

In one swift movement, Carlisle brushed past him as if he never existed. Confused at first, the officer stared at him, speechless. Descending into the depths of the Metro station, the profiler doubled back and discovered a more secure environment. Reaching the ticket machine, his mobile pinged.

Sure enough, it was Jack Mason.

'Where are you now?'

'I thought you might tell me that.'

'Yeah, well?'

'The next time you put officers on my tail, try using someone with brains.'

'Enough of this "Get Carter" stuff,' Mason interrupted, his voice cutting through the tension. 'There's been another development.'

Inside, Carlisle was bristling, but he stayed calm.

'Like what?'

'I need you to drop everything you're doing and meet

me in twenty minutes.'

'Where exactly?'

'I'm over at the "Sticky Table" cafe in Gateshead.'

'Is this about Angelica?'

'No. This is far more serious. We need to talk.'

The connection went dead.

Now it made sense. The two undercover officers were merely there for his protection. He'd cocked up big style, and mistrust had triumphed. As he retraced his footsteps, his father's words echoed in his mind. The truth hurts, lies poison, but suspicion is torture.

CHAPTER TWENTY-TWO

The cafe wasn't full. A sprinkling of pensioners, a young mother with kids, and an obese lowlife who gave him a look that said: *who the hell are you staring at?* Carlisle was never keen on the place. The service was crap; the food was always cold, and the ambiance non-existent. Besides, he liked his coffee warm, not swilling around in a saucer full of cracks.

He found Jack Mason in a corner seat overlooking the busy shopping precinct. Engrossed in a handyman magazine, he barely lifted his head as he took up a seat opposite. Sometimes he felt the chief inspector enjoyed making him feel inferior. With his crumpled grey suit, his colleague paid little attention to police protocols or the requisites of case law.

'Another body has turned up,' the DCI said coldly.

'Where this time?'

'Close to a council estate in Byker.'

Carlisle paused in thought. 'Another vicious knife attack, was it?'

'How did you guess?'

'When was this?'

Eyes glazed over after another heavy night's drinking session, the chief inspector peered over the top of his magazine. 'Around six this morning... a man out walking his dog.'

'Thank God it wasn't schoolkids who found him.'

'Not the best start to his day, I'd wager.'

'No, definitely not,' Carlisle agreed.

Mason cleared his throat. 'Any thoughts?'

'I had a feeling he would strike again, Jack.'

'Really?'

'It was always on the cards. This one has a bee in his bonnet over something, and will not stop until he fulfils his fantasy.'

His colleague shrugged nonchalantly, as if it was no big deal. 'Tom Hedley's sifting through the crime scene, so I'm hoping for some positive news.'

'Has anyone said anything to you yet?'

'Not to me they haven't.' Mason folded his arms across his chest in a defensive stance, signalling his displeasure as he put his magazine down. 'This sadistic bastard finds delight in presenting us with his victims, neatly packed inside a suitcase.'

'He's aptly named. I'll give him that.'

'I dread to think what the media will make of it. The city's already in fear, and this latest news will go down like a lead balloon.'

'What's the Acting Superintendent's reaction?'

Mason flicked the crumbs from his jacket. 'Hard to say. The last I heard, she was waiting for the Home Office pathologist's report to land on her desk.'

Wise move, the profiler mused. Things were getting out of hand, and the police hadn't a clue where the killer would strike next. Easing back in his seat, he trod cautiously, aware of Mason's pensive mood.

'What state was the body in?'

'Multiple stab wounds to the upper torso and neck. Someone had hacked him to pieces, but this time, none of the body parts were missing.'

'That's new,' Carlisle said, spinning to face him. 'He usually likes to keep us guessing.'

'Who knows what he's thinking?'

'Do we know who the victim is?'

'His name's John Lawrence, according to our DNA database.'

'That could be useful. Do we have anything on him?'

Mason stared at him oddly. 'When will it end? That's what I keep asking myself.'

'He will not stop now.'

'No. I wouldn't have thought so. What's upsetting him? That's what I'd like to know.'

His colleague posed a valid question, which made him pause and reflect. Psychopaths were grandiose, thinking they were smarter than anyone else. They were not only charming and manipulative, they could hide behind the mask of normality and yet commit the most heinous crimes.

'Jack, he's completely altering the rules. With each passing day, his confidence grows, and he elevates his performance.'

Mason let out a loud, exasperated sigh. 'That's the last thing I need right now. I've got dozens of officers out looking for him, and yet he still slips through the net.'

He understood Mason's frustrations, but refused to be intimidated. With a killer on the loose, they had no other choice but to act swiftly before he struck again. As he let his mind drift, he recalled the heinous crimes of

Jeffrey Dahmer, an American serial killer who lured his victims back to his small urban apartment with promises of sex and drugs. In late 1987, he took his second victim back to a hotel room and drank. When he eventually awoke to find him dead, Dahmer had no recollection of the previous night's activities. As Carlisle remembered it, Dahmer transported the body in a large suitcase back to his grandmother's basement, where he dismembered the corpse before disposing of the remains. This case had a similar ring to it, and he was slowly beginning to piece together a mental picture of what the killer was about.

Mason, with a stern expression on his face, carefully adjusted his position. 'We have scheduled an emergency meeting in MR-1 at 08:00 tomorrow morning. The Acting Superintendent wants you to write a summary report on the killer's behavioural patterns. Nothing elaborate, so try keeping it simple.'

'I'll give it my utmost.'

His colleague leaned in closer. 'Before we attend tomorrow's meeting, let's spend a few minutes in my office together, going over the agenda and preparing.'

'Anything particular in mind?'

'Why does he select mainly young males? Why does he dismember their bodies?'

'Is he already known to us?'

'That's a valid point. We're bound to be asked those questions, so we need to be prepared.'

'What time?'

'There's a press briefing at ten o'clock. Let's make it seven.'

'Busy times, eh?'

Mason screwed his face up. 'There's not enough time in the day, my friend.'

'What about the Acting Superintendent? What does she have to say?'

With thoughts elsewhere, Mason stared aimlessly across the room. 'She wants me to conduct a press appeal, but I'm not keen on the idea. Not at this stage in the proceedings. People are looking for answers, not appeals for information.'

'Crimewatch, no doubt?'

'No. Tomorrow's press briefing.' Mason rounded on him. 'She's also looking for information regarding this woman you've recently been in contact with.'

'Good. She's finally coming round to my way of thinking.'

'No, quite the opposite,' Mason said guardedly. 'She's scaling that side of the operation down.'

'What?'

'Well, not in as many words.'

'So why bother to go public?'

'Tactics apparently. She wants to hoodwink the public into believing that we're on to something.'

'I cannot fault her logic, but what if Angelica's telling the truth?'

'That's her problem, not mine.'

Carlisle thought for a moment. Despite everything that Angelica had told him, there wasn't a single prostitute working on Forth Street, according to Jack Mason. Someone had moved all of them on years ago. The pressure was mounting, and everyone was reluctant to trust his judgement these days. Whichever way he looked at it, he was now out on a limb.

'Is there anything I can do in the meantime?'

'Not that I can think of.'

'So, where does that leave me?'

Mason looked at him, then stared out of the cafe window.

'Make sure your report's ready in time for tomorrow's briefing. No waffle.'

'I will.'

There was something unnerving in Mason's calmness that unsettled Carlisle. He looked unruffled by it all. No doubt he'd be defending his corner, as most senior officers did. This time felt different, though, as if the chief inspector had a hidden agenda up his sleeve.

'Angelica's story doesn't stack up,' Mason said. 'She's like a million other wannabes out there... eager to have her two minutes of glory. You need to tread carefully, my friend. Whatever she's up to, don't get sucked into her web of deceit.'

Like hell, Carlisle thought. There had to be some truth in her story. After all, he was the profiler the man brought in to assist the police in their investigations. He'd often wondered what went on behind closed doors, and now he knew. Far too many senior police officers were keen to build a team of fall guys around them. People like Jack Mason, individuals they could readily lay blame on. To get to the top required guile. It was a game of kidology where only the strongest survived.

'So, what's your programme for the rest of the day?' asked Carlisle quizzically.

'I'm still awaiting Tom Hedley's report to filter through. In the meantime, there are a few details I need to catch up on regarding John Lawrence's background.'

'Anything so far?'

'Not a lot. That's why I'm working on it.'

'Good luck,' Carlisle beamed, as he stood to leave.

Mason fixed his gaze on him. 'I'll call you if anything of interest crops up.'

He knew what needed to be done. Achieving it was the difficulty.

CHAPTER TWENTY-THREE

The mountain of paperwork had grown considerably these past few weeks. It was the first thing the profiler noticed when he entered MR-1. The longer this case went on, the more reports the team seemed to generate. It was a vicious circle, and somewhere beneath the pile of case files lay his psychology report concerning the suspect's mental state. He'd tried keeping it simple, but behavioural psychology wasn't the easiest subject to write about, particularly one involving a serial killer who was targeting young men. Despite his simplistic approach, the profiler had grave doubts whether the team would fully comprehend the profound significance behind it.

Except for Dr Colin Brown, all the usual suspects were present that morning. It was a large turnout – *full of hot-air and contradiction.* This was the nineteenth team briefing of Operation Walrus, and they still had a lot of ground to cover. It had taken the best part of a week for DNA results to filter through, and trying to find the right person to talk to was impossible. As far as Carlisle was concerned, the case was stagnating, bogged down by police protocol. If progress were to be made, they would need to look at the bigger picture.

Throughout the comfort break that morning, the acting superintendent had stood in front of the evidence board as if seeking divine intervention. Dressed in uniform, her tense expression hinted at the challenges she now faced. Nothing was going to plan, and the pressure was showing.

'Should we not consider extending our door-to-door enquiries, ma'am?' Colin Magrath, a police control room operator, asked.

Sutherland's eyes softened a little. 'Not at this stage. Not until we have more information at our disposal.'

'In which case, perhaps a recap of the timeline is in order.'

'Yes, I would agree,' she said, turning to Jack Mason. 'Perhaps you can enlighten us, Chief Inspector.'

Mason acknowledged with a nod. There was an air of anticipation as he sauntered towards the evidence board. Turning to face them, he gave a little shrug as he spoke. 'Friday, April 11, Thomas Wilkinson, a well-known local petty criminal, is last seen drinking in the Eagle bar on Scotswood Road. Shortly before closing time, around 23:15, he finishes his drink and leaves via the pub's back door. Where did he go? Who did he meet?' He paused for effect. 'What we know is, three days later, his torso turns up at a waste and recycling centre in Blaydon. Hidden inside a large black suitcase, along with the rest of Colin Henderson's body parts, a thorough search of the site revealed nothing.'

Sutherland raised her eyebrows a fraction. 'Just to add, we know the killer used the same powered surgical saw to cut his victim's body parts up... but where did he purchase it?'

Despite her composed demeanour, Carlisle detected an underlying nervousness in her voice. He wanted to say something, anything, but the words got stuck in his throat.

Mason continued. 'At 22:15 on 20th May, Lawrence was seen leaving the Blue Bell public house in Gateshead. Twenty minutes later, at 22:35, a high street camera picks him up again. Worse for wear after a heavy night drinking session, he appears to be heading towards Gateshead Metro station... but we cannot be certain at this stage.' The chief inspector gestured towards the evidence board. 'So, if he wasn't intending to catch a Metro train that night, what other arrangements had he made?'

The noise levels heightened.

'Boss, what about the CCTV footage from the surrounding area?' asked Holt.

'No, nothing. We've drawn a complete blank.' Mason grimaced, then opened his hands expansively as he spoke. 'Three males, all aged between nineteen and twenty-five, and all killed using the same murder weapon. What links them?'

It was Rob Savage who spoke next.

'Every bar within a two-mile radius of the Tyne is now under scrutiny. If the killer is local, and we believe he is, our aim is to find that connection.'

'Thank you, Rob,' said Sutherland calmly. She stood for a moment, as if to let it sink in. 'Apart from a grainy image, what else do we know about the killer?'

'According to the PM report, John Lawrence suffered multiple stab wounds separated into three distinct clusters. Neck, back, and chest,' said Savage, in a gruff Geordie accent. 'Two of the three stab wounds to the left side of the neck severed the carotid artery. The victim, suffering from heavy blood loss, now attempts to stem the blood flow, and that's when someone stabbed him in the back.'

Tom Hedley pointed at the evidence board. 'Looking at the crime scene photographs, these are classic downward arc stab wounds and of some considerable force. His attacker is right-handed, and approximately five-nine. At this stage in the proceedings, we know the victim fell backwards to the ground, and wounds to the upper chest suggest the attacker straddled his victim before repeatedly driving the knife home with both hands.' The senior forensic scientist paused in reflection. 'Stab wounds to the back and chest are elliptical, which confirm the knife was double edged. What is of interest are small contusions found above and below each of the puncture marks, which point to some sort of finger guard attached to it.'

'Could this be the same double-edged combat knife?' Mason asked.

'Yes, that would fit. What is of significance is, the wounds are consistent with those found on the previous victim's bodies.'

Sutherland's face contorted, betraying a hint of discomfort. 'Has anyone got anything further to add?'

'There is one other point, ma'am,' said DC Carrington. 'Fibre strands found on the latest victim's body are consistent with those discovered at two of the crime scenes.'

'What about fingerprints?'

'No, ma'am. We believe the killer wore surgical gloves.'

Detective Harry Manley, who had been silent all along, suddenly became animated. 'He must be a pretty strong bastard, if you ask me.'

'How do you make that out?' asked Mason.

'What is the average human body weight?'

'I don't have a clue.'

'One-hundred and seventy pounds, boss.'

The room held its breath.

'If you say so, Harry,' Mason nodded. 'What are you driving at?'

'Dragging a heavy suitcase over uneven waste-ground would take an awful lot of effort, don't you think?'

Tom Hedley looked bemused by Manley's statement. 'More awkward than anything, I'd say.'

'True,' Sutherland nodded, a smile of gratification showing.

Manley looked at Hedley, puzzled. 'He could be a fitness freak. Who knows what we're up against?'

'What else do we know about the suitcase, Tom?'

'Common type, purchased from the same charity shop in Low Fell, ma'am.'

Mason spread his hands like a Baptist priest offering an Amen. 'Just for the record, we've interviewed everyone at the charity shop, and they all seem to remember a young woman purchasing it. She paid by cash, so we don't have a bank trace to a card.'

The mere mention of a young woman hit Carlisle hard. Something didn't fit, and that concerned him. He watched as Sutherland jotted something into her notebook and put her pen down.

'Are we on to something here?'

Carlisle puffed his cheeks out, daunted by what lay ahead. 'The weapon used is an important factor, as the use of a combat knife shows a great deal of pent-up anger. There is a significant difference from a psychological standpoint to that of shooting someone, of course.'

Sutherland stared at him. 'Yes, but there was nothing in your report to suggest it was part of his behavioural pattern?'

'It's not an exact science, ma'am. The killer could suffer from an inferiority complex or may have failed miserably in his life. There are far too many variations to consider in order to make an honest prognosis.'

'Is he hedonistic?'

'I doubt it. I get the distinct impression he's not at all popular with the rest of society. He's probably a loner, someone shunned by his counterparts. We know he's egotistic, hence the smiley faces he's drawn on Jennifer Oakwell's walls.'

Tom Hedley raised a hand to speak, and Sutherland gave a nod. 'Yes. Tom?'

'What drives him?'

'That's a strange one,' Carlisle admitted.

'In what way?'

'Motive's the problem. It's as if the killer is being egged on by someone or something.'

'Could a partner be involved?'

Carlisle drew breath; the questions were coming thick and fast.

'It's possible, but I'm still not convinced.'

Eager to move on, Sutherland moved to the evidence board again. 'Three young males, all killed by the same murder weapon, and all dismembered using the same surgical saw. Apart from Jennifer Oakwell, there's a distinct pattern taking place.'

Mason cocked his head to one side. 'Young men, all picked up from bars and nightclubs. What does that tell us?'

'According to the toxicology report,' said Hedley, 'Both Thomas Wilkinson and John Lawrence had unusually high levels of alcohol in their blood.'

Carlisle eased forward in his seat. 'If he is using alcohol as a stimulus, it certainly shows his ability to manipulate vulnerable men in a drink-fuelled environment.'

'That's a valid point,' Hedley conceded. 'Perhaps we should look into it.'

Carlisle shook his head as the coffee slipped down his throat like bitter mud. At least someone was agreeing with him, which was far more than he could have hoped for half an hour ago.

'It's my view he's gaining his victims' trust, only to exploit it mercilessly in the most horrifying way.'

'Ah.' Mason gasped with a grin. 'We're coming back to this Dennis Nilsen theory of yours.'

'*Dennis Nilsen!*' Sutherland pronounced. 'Now that is an interesting case analogy.'

As Mason continued to ponder over the evidence board, a profound silence engulfed the room.

CHAPTER TWENTY-FOUR

Winter was going out with a bang, Jack Mason felt as he stared out through the unmarked police car windscreen. The high winds had finally abated, but his garden fence had taken a terrible battering. Perhaps it was a man's thing, but he couldn't give a damn about climate change. When he was younger, he would spend hours gardening with his mother, and there was always lots to do. His mum, God bless her, always ensured they had plenty to drink during the long, hot summer days, for which he was forever grateful. Ginger beer was his favourite. It always sounded such a manly drink, as if part of growing up. Innocent thoughts, he mused. Nothing unpleasant.

Thinking back to those halcyon days, he always preferred Saturdays as the day of the week, when he spent most of his spare time congregating on the end of station platforms or crawling around grubby railway depots and collecting train numbers with friends. In what had become a national pastime for thousands of young schoolboys, for the price of a platform ticket, he could spend a whole day searching for those illusive engine numbers he was so desperate to capture. Times had moved on, and not for the better, in his opinion. Today's teenagers were saturated by social media and mobile technology, which left little to the creative imagination. Six hours a day spent texting, chatting, or surfing the web wasn't good. Entrenched in unrealistic expectations, cyberbullying had reached a breaking point, and nobody knew how to deal with it. Teenagers today had far less control over their lives compared to his generation, and life in the fast lane didn't live up to its expectations.

'Well,' Mason began. 'What do you think?'

Savage's dark expression said it all. 'It's hard to tell from the outside, boss.'

'These bastards are hiding behind locked doors in the hope we'll bugger off. We need a search warrant – take them by storm and expose them for what they truly are.'

Mason's head turned as another souped up vehicle sped effortlessly past them. A Ford Mondeo this time, with yellow spoilers and flash silver trims. Seconds later, it vanished from view, and the street fell eerily silent again. Nothing was going to plan. Everything that could go wrong had gone wrong. Two days spent poring over Fat Sam's nightclub was sorely testing their patience. It was desperate stuff, and if they didn't get a breakthrough soon, they'd end up with more blood on their hands.

Mason watched as the nightclub doors cracked open a fraction, and a familiar figure emerged. A short man, with huge biceps and a face resembling a bulldog.

He wound the window down for a chat.

'Is your gaffer in?' Mason announced.

'What if he is?' the man replied.

Mason slid from the driver's seat and held up his warrant card. 'This is a police matter, Roy.'

'Really?'

'We're not here to check the fucking gas meters... there's a good lad.'

There was doubt in the man's eyes. Hesitation.

'Follow me,' the man said finally.

Two floors down, and the chief inspector was treading unfamiliar territory. The air reeked of cigar smoke, and something a little stronger. Cannabis, he suspected. As the man pushed on ahead, he heard a click and a rasping sound as the security gate swung open.

'Wait here,' the man said.

There was a short, embarrassed silence as the nightclub owner, Tony Fox, stared at them through an open doorway. 'Why, if it isn't Jack Mason and his sidekick, Detective Savage? What's on your mind? You people are never away from my premises nowadays.'

'It's not membership we're after,' Mason announced.

'What then?'

'I'm here to close you down.'

The gangster signalled towards two of his minders. No one was going anywhere. That much was obvious.

'What do you mean, close me down?'

'Simple. We're suspending your licence.'

'Nobody in their right mind would dare do that.'

'It's not looking good, Tony. The word on the street is a young man who frequented these premises is lying on a coroner's slab.'

'So what? That's your problem, not mine,' said Fox.

'Is it?'

'You know it is.'

Mason gave him a withering smile. 'We've been monitoring your premises for months now, and it's time to shut shop.'

'You're beginning to sound like a fucking broken record,' Fox laughed.

'Cut the crap,' Mason retorted. 'We have it on camera.'

'I don't believe a word you're saying,' Fox replied, his voice dripping with disdain. 'We've been down this avenue before, you and me.'

'I'm in no mood for small talk. It's more serious this time.'

The nightclub owner fidgeted uneasily and stared across at them. 'Touchy today, are we? What's on your mind, Jack?'

Mason pulled out an e-fit image from an inside pocket and slid it towards the gangster. The room felt cold and uninviting, as if someone had turned the air-conditioning to full blast.

'Recognise this young woman?'

'More photographs,' Fox sniggered. 'You should have been a photographer, Jack.'

'Just answer the question.'

The gangster shook his head. 'Nope. Never seen her before. Who is she?'

'Her name's Angelica, and she's East European.'

'What's she been up to then?'

'We're keen to talk to her about a body that turned up on the streets of Newcastle.'

'Sounds about right,' said Fox, all white teeth and insincerity. 'I wouldn't trust these foreigners as far as I could throw them. What is it with these people?'

'Never mind the lecture,' Mason interrupted. 'Where can I find her?'

Fox remained silent for a moment.

'She probably arrived here through the back door like the rest of them.'

'Meaning?'

'Human trafficking runs rife in the city. There's a significant amount of money to be gained, and young women are an added advantage, as they are more vulnerable to exploitation.'

'Sounds just like the second-hand car market,' the chief inspector replied smugly.

'Funny.'

Mason pointed a finger at Fox and there was an icy shrillness in his voice. 'Someone in your organisation knows who she is.'

'Maybe they do, but it ain't me.'

'Who then?'

Savage flinched as he eyed up the two bouncers who had now appeared in the doorway. One was small and chubby, the other tall and fair. Maybe they carried guns... maybe not. Either way, neither looked too friendly, Mason thought.

'You need to look closer, Jack. Smuggling gangs receive good money to transport these illegals across our borders. Once here, that's where the financial transaction ends.' Fox fell silent for a moment, then said, 'If it's trafficking this young woman is involved in, it has fuck all to do with me.'

'Who mentioned anything about trafficking?'

Fox suddenly brimmed with confidence. 'You know me, Jack. We go back a long way. Trafficking means bringing these illegals into an ongoing situation, and a lot of women are being forced into prostitution. It's not my style, even you know that.'

'You're well informed, Tony.'

The gangster shrugged as he tried to cover his tracks.

'Not really. It's just what I've read in the papers.'

'That's a new one. I didn't know you could read.'

'I always had top marks at school, Jack. That's what made me what I am today.'

It was Mason's turn to laugh.

'What, a defunct second-hand car dealer whose nightclub is about to be shut down?'

'There's no smoke without fire,' the gangster replied sharply.

Mason's dark expression said it all.

'So, you think this woman could be here illegally?'

'I didn't say she was.' Fox made a grinding noise with his teeth, as if bored by it all. 'I was merely making a point. Anyway, how do you know her real name's Angelica?'

'We don't. That's what she calls herself.'

Fox glowered. 'These are troublesome people to deal with, and I steer well clear of them. They slip across the borders like the March winds, and nobody can put a stop to them. Not even the politicians.'

'Let's not go there,' Mason shrugged. 'Just throw me a name.'

'You know me, Jack. If I could, I would. But I swear on my mother's life that I've never seen this woman before.'

'Sounds very much like the last favour I asked you to do for me, Tony.'

The gangster's head dropped. 'Yeah. But nobody's heard Jack shit who killed those two young men. Even my crew knows nothing.'

'What about your friends on the east side?'

The gangster shot him a look. 'It's difficult these days, as no one will talk.'

'What about Mad Frankie Wiseman? Could he be involved?'

'How the hell would I know? The last I heard, he was banged up in Durham.'

Their eyes met.

'I know, and Mad Frankie is far from happy about this takeover bid. Some say you have it coming to you, Tony.'

'Who told you that shit?'

Mason tapped the desk with an index finger. 'There's an easy way out of this, Tony.'

'Oh, and what might that be?'

'What if you talk to your counterparts on the north side? Find out what they know about this Angelica woman. You never know, I might even turn a blind eye to closing your nightclub down.'

Fox stood to his feet before he spoke. A towering man, he was head and shoulders above Jack Mason. 'You're talking through your arse again.'

'Don't make me angry, Tony. We know our latest victim visited your nightclub, as we have it on camera,' Mason bluffed.

Fox took in a long intake of air and tried to recover his composure.

'These foreigners won't take too kindly to me asking them questions about this Angelica woman... especially if she's one of their own.'

'Yeah, but my neck's not on the line here.'

'Hold it right there,' said Fox. 'Who said I'd talk to these people?'

'Your face tells me otherwise.'

'It's like that, is it?'

'Afraid so,' Mason smiled.

'It's not that easy, and you know it.'

'You look nervous, Tony. Do these foreigners frighten you?'

Fox laughed. 'Give me a fucking break; it's about time you visited Specsavers.'

'There's nothing wrong with *my* eyesight or my sense of smell,' Mason replied.

'What the hell's smell got to do with this?'

Mason wrinkled his nose. 'Nothing. But on stepping into the building, I swore I could smell cannabis.'

Fox moved to protest, but quickly thought the better.

'Let's talk about this arrangement, Jack?'

'Who mentioned anything about an arrangement?'

'Nobody. I just thought I'd mention it, that's all.' Fox looked anxious as he swore through gritted teeth. 'What the fuck's going on, Jack?'

'Murder, for starters, and one that entails your premises.' Mason's glare hardened. 'I need a contact name. If not, I'll hit the accelerator hard.'

'And in return?'

'I'll see to it you stay open.'

An uneasy silence showed a reluctant agreement.

Fox picked up the e-fit image and studied it again. The confidence had gone, and the gangster was struggling to form his words. 'Like I say, these people are nasty bastards to deal with.'

'I'm sure you'll cope.'

The bodyguard standing in the doorway glared across at them, perturbed. His eyes were sharp, and never still. One wrong word and things could turn ugly.

Mason gave Fox a look of daggers. 'You have three days, Tony.'

'You're joking.'

'After that, I'll be round with a dozen of my best men to close your nightclub down.'

Fox glared at them, annoyed. 'Let's hope Angelica is her real name. If not, we're both up the fucking creek.'

As they made their way across the dance floor, Mason felt a deepening sense of unease. Heavily outnumbered, they still had a long flight of stairs to climb, and it was an awful long way to the top.

Chapter Twenty-Five

Friday 23 May 2014

It had rained incessantly throughout the night, and the sky over Newcastle hung as a solid grey curtain. The rain bouncing off the roof of his Rover P4 100, Carlisle slid from the driver's seat and made a dash towards the grey stone-brick building opposite. Earlier, Tom Hedley had won him over with his encyclopaedic knowledge of the forensic techniques. Latent fingerprints found at two of the crime scenes were a perfect match. It was a huge step forward, enough to send a ripple of excitement amongst senior backroom staff.

The task force had assembled at five-thirty that morning, and everywhere was crawling with police. Close to the waste ground where John Lawrence's body had been found, CCTV footage captured a slightly built man passing a local corner shop in the early hours the previous day. Wearing black tracksuit bottoms, hoody, and white Nike trainers, the suspect was dragging a large suitcase behind him.

Carlisle checked his watch. Now nine-thirty, and there was ample time to persuade local magistrates to sign a few more search warrants. It was Friday, so there could be possible delays. Beyond the yellow barrier tape marked CRIME SCENE DO NOT CROSS, the profiler spotted the slightly built figure of Peter Davenport. Rain bouncing off the brim of his cap, the SOC photographer seemed oblivious to the appalling conditions. Further afield, close to school gates, he noted a small team of forensic officers. Fully suited up, they were crawling on hands and knees in an extended line and methodically searching for clues. It was painstaking work, but a fingertip search could throw up all kinds of results. Not today, though. What little evidence there was to be had got washed away in a sea of mud.

'If it's DCI Mason you're looking for,' the constable announced, 'he's over at the old lorry park.'

'And where might that be?' Carlisle enquired.

'It's at the rear of the building, sir.'

Bracing himself, Carlisle drew in a long intake of air and made towards the main entrance gates. Close to a series of loading bays, several police vehicles had parked. Dominating the skyline, a colossal metal girder structure cast dark, elongated shadows across the entire proceedings. It reminded him of a piece of modern artwork he'd seen in a local art exhibition.

From what he could see, many of the outlying buildings had fallen into disrepair. Little more than a demolition site, this once thriving chemical plant was a mere ghost of its past. Picking up the pace, he soon spotted the mobile incident command truck. Tucked back against the outer perimeter fence, its bright interior lights illuminating the way ahead. On closer inspection, someone had propped a set of mud-spattered steps against one of the side doors, hinting at recent visitors.

He moved towards them.

'Nothing yet,' Mason announced, peering down at him through the open doorway.

'Why here, Jack?'

'This is where the killer parked his vehicle yesterday morning. Looking at the date and time display on the camera footage, it confirms he passed Dean Street on foot at precisely 02:32.'

'Anyone caught dragging a suitcase around at that unearthly hour would have surely attracted attention.'

'Not really.' Mason shrugged.

'Oh. And why not?'

'It's not uncommon to find someone heading for an early morning flight check-in. Not everyone can afford an overnight hotel – especially around here.'

Carlisle considered this. 'How do we know it was the Suitcase Man's vehicle?'

'There is no public transportation operating that time of day, and we've conducted a comprehensive search of all the taxi services in the area.'

'He could be local, of course.'

'It's possible, but why dump a body on your own doorstep?'

'He's not that selective, Jack.'

Mason shook his head. 'You're right. I wouldn't put anything past this evil bastard.'

Something had clearly got under his colleague's skin. He sounded abrupt and was exhaling heavily. In a way, Carlisle felt sorry for him. People were demanding answers, and he didn't have any to give. The media wasn't helping either. This latest killing had drummed up an awful lot of public fear, and most of it pure fantasy.

The profiler leaned in, his eyes scanning the detailed street map, its edges securely pinned to the worn corkboard of the command truck's rear wall. Why this estate? Why here? Was this a random selection, or was this all part of a predator's bigger plans? He tried to think logically. If their suspect were transporting his victims around in a Transit van, it meant the kill zone could be miles from the drop zone. There was no simple explanation, and this case was far more complex than anyone had envisaged.

The door swung open, and DS Holt joined them.

'Just the man,' said Mason, stepping to one side.

'You talking to me, boss?'

'Who else?' Mason groaned. 'I need you to do a quick sweep of the area. Take a few officers with you. Try the local bars and find out who hung around after closing time. While you're at it, make a list of everyone who works night shift in the neighbourhood.'

'Anywhere in particular?'

Mason pointed to a small section of the map where they found Lawrence's body. 'Start somewhere here and work your way back towards this area. Ask around, establish if anyone heard or saw anything suspicious that night. According to eyewitness accounts, we know our prime suspect was last seen in this area around 02:50. If so, where did he go after that?'

Holt touched his forehead in an imaginary salute and turned towards the door.

It had barely closed when DC Manley appeared. Notebook in hand, rain dripping off the detective's long parka, he looked a forlorn figure.

'Any luck?' Mason asked.

Manley stood for a moment before answering.

'I think we're onto something, boss.'

'Like what?'

'Like a set of number plates that were nicked from a local resident's Transit van.'

'When was this?'

'Late Thursday night. Shortly after ten o'clock.'

Mason eyed him with suspicion. 'Both plates?'

'Yeah, front and rear apparently.'

'Nice work,' the chief inspector grinned.

The profiler shuddered inwardly, sensing the vulgarity. If this was the killer's doing, he was obviously covering his tracks. He thought about it, but not for long. If the killer stole the number plates from the north side of the estate, it meant he must have taken a different route back to his vehicle that night.

Inside the tiny, cramped command unit, the air felt oppressive. He didn't know why, but the profiler felt a close affinity with the killer. How quickly things could transform? One minute he was wallowing in the dark, the next his mind was running amok.

Manley allowed himself a brief, smug smile as he wiped the rain droplets from his face. 'Perhaps we should broaden our search, boss. Take in the north side of the estate.'

'No. Let's stick with the original plan.' Mason made a little sweeping gesture with his hand. 'You need to release the stolen number plate details to the media. In the meantime, I'll get Road Traffic to set up a few discreet checks using ANPR. If this is our suspect's doing, and there's no reason to believe otherwise, he can't be far away.'

Manley peered up at the wall map, his wet finger circling a large area. 'How much of the estate do we need to cover?'

Mason reached over and pulled out a couple of well-thumbed images from a pile of case files, and placed them on the table in front of him. Next, he consulted the map.

'CCTV coverage confirms a forty-minute gap from the time the suspect passed the corner shop to the time this person came into view.' He pointed to the image. 'Who is he? What was he doing in the area that time of night?'

'I suspect the streets would have been pretty muted, don't you think?'

'Let's not forget it could be a shift worker we're dealing with.'

Manley smacked his forehead with the flat of his hand. 'Do you know what? I never gave that a thought.'

'Someone out there knows who he is, surely. Talk to local shop keepers – find out which tradespeople made deliveries. While you're at it, we need to talk to all the local taxi drivers in the area. Ask around. Anyone who arrived here by taxi that night needs to be brought in for questioning.'

'You're right. Local gossip might throw up a few interesting leads.'

Carlisle watched as Mason dug his hands deep into his pockets and glanced up at the timeline. Not a good sign, he thought. Still wrestling with the notion that they'd paid too much attention to Fat Sam's nightclub, they were having to play catchup. It was the trivial things that worried the profiler the most. Like the lack of detail that was given to the geographical movements of the killer. They were looking in all the wrong places and needlessly covering old ground.

He stood for a moment. A part of him hoped that Jack Mason would finally come to his senses, but there was little chance of that. Not now. Compromise would be the last thing on the chief inspector's mind. No, he thought. He would need to produce a plan, but right now, he couldn't think of one.

The rain had eased when Carlisle finally stepped out of the command truck. Squinting left, he noticed one of the forensic team was carrying a plastic evidence bag in his hand. Although it appeared insignificant, the discovery of one crucial piece of evidence changed everything. If there was a breakthrough to be had, it would come from the most unlikely of sources. Then he remembered. The latest body parts had arrived here in a suitcase bought by a young woman using cash. Who was she? Why choose a Low Fell charity shop?

It was time to make tracks.

CHAPTER TWENTY-SIX

The superintendent had thought better of seeking the public's help over the stolen Transit van's number plates. Someone had given her sound advice. If this was the killer's doing, the more control the police had over proceedings, the greater chance they had of catching him. There was no simple solution, and with dozens of roadside checks in place, Gateshead Police Station had not been so busy in a long time.

Six miles south, near to the Washington northbound motorway services, little did Constable Clarke realise what he was about to get involved in that morning. It was rush hour, and after pulling over dozens of unsuspecting van drivers, nothing had come of it. Further afield, he watched as fellow officers were re-directing drivers towards his designated holding area. Following the temporary line of cones, in what was a well-managed operation, one lane of the A1(M) motorway was closed to north-bound traffic. With long tailbacks, tempers were fraying.

Clipboard in hand, the constable felt an air of authority as he approached the latest arrival. After a cursory glance at the tyres, he tapped on the driver's window with the end of his pen. The solution to solving some crimes often lay in a person's demeanour. If they reacted positively towards him, it meant they were genuine. If not, it meant they had something to hide. It was all down to a person's attitude, and the constable could tell within the first five seconds of questioning someone what type of person they were dealing with.

He waited for the driver's electric window to wind down before firing off that all important question.

'Is this your vehicle, sir?'

'No, it belongs to a friend,' the van driver said in broken English.

'Mind telling me his name?'

'Alex.'

Pen poised, the constable gave him a withering look.

'Alex who, sir?'

'I don't know his other name. He's a friend of a friend.'

'I see.'

Suspicions roused, the officer moved to the front of the vehicle and took down the registration details. He was in no hurry. The driver appeared genuine enough, but something was niggling Clarke. As the offside cab door swung open, he watched as the occupant jumped onto the hard tarmac in front of him. A wiry man, five-ten, with a round rubbery face, he had sticky out ears and an unruly mop of black hair. His T-shirt clung to his body, two sizes too small, while his trousers were baggy and in need of a wash. Officially, this was a murder enquiry and had nothing to do with vehicle checks. But this van was different, as it had come up on the ANPR as stolen.

'Mind telling me the registration number of your vehicle?' the constable enquired.

'I can't remember.'

'I take it that's a no.'

The van driver remained tight-lipped.

Clarke stepped back a pace and signalled for help. Seconds later, blue spinner-lights flashing, a marked patrol car pulled up in front of them. Wearing a Hi-Vis jacket and a no-nonsense expression on his face, the sergeant in charge squeezed his portly frame out from the front passenger seat and ambled towards them.

'Morning,' the sergeant said, by introduction. 'Mind handing me the keys to your vehicle, sir?'

Taken aback, the van driver reached into his trouser pocket and dutifully obliged. His English wasn't good, but he understood the sergeant's demands perfectly.

'What's going on?' the van driver asked. 'Why are you stopping me?'

'This will only take a few minutes, sir.'

A second marked police vehicle only added to the confusion. On poking his head out of the passenger window, the officer inside gestured towards the stationary white van. 'You guys in need of help?'

'We're fine,' the sergeant replied. 'Everything's under control here.'

Bracing himself, Clarke scratched his head with his pen.

'We best check the VIN, Sarge.'

As the bonnet catch sprung open, the sergeant dutifully thrust his head inside the engine block. Sometimes it was better to say nothing, keep an open mind about these things. But there was something odd about the van driver's demeanour, and Clarke couldn't put his finger on it.

'Guess what?' the sergeant announced. 'The VIN doesn't match.'

Bracing himself, the constable instinctively grabbed hold of the van driver's arm. He'd been down this avenue before, many times. Just when you least expected it, the suspect would do a runner. Not today. Clarke had everything under control.

'Do you carry any form of identification with you, sir?'

'Not with me, no.'

'A logbook, vehicle insurance details... a passport perhaps?'

'No. Nothing.'

Clearly the focus of attention, there was a new buzz of excitement in the air. As he stepped closer, there were two trains of thought here. One, the suspect, spoke a little English. The other, he was driving on false plates. Either way, they were about to slap a fixed penalty fine on him or arrest him on suspicion of murder.

The Mercedes Sprinter van's arrival injected a new sense of urgency into the team. He recognised the driver, along with the officer sitting alongside him. Things were on the up, and glancing at his watch, he blew a sigh of relief.

'Mind telling me what's in the back of your vehicle?' the sergeant asked.

The moment the van's rear doors flew open, a crowd of police officers gathered round.

'What is it with you people... what are you looking for?' the bemused van driver demanded.

'This won't take a minute, sir. I can assure you of that.'

'So why search my van? I have nothing to hide.'

'Let me be the judge of that.'

The words had barely left the sergeant's lips before he'd clambered into the back of the van and began rummaging around. The sight of builders' equipment piled high created a sense of organised chaos, and a thick layer of dust coated everything.

'Well, I'll be damned,' the sergeant muttered as he turned to face them. 'Guess what we have here?'

'What have you found, Sarge?'

'A bag of butcher's knives.'

Clarke reached for his handcuffs as a second officer grabbed hold of the suspect's other arm. What had started as a routine check was now a full-blown murder inquiry.

The sergeant's grin broadened. 'Mind telling me who owns this bag of knives?'

'I didn't know they were there.'

'If they're not yours, then who do they belong to?'

The driver looked at him, confused. 'I know nothing about the contents of the van.'

'Is that so?'

'Yes. I'm delivering it to a friend, and he's expecting to meet up with me.'

'Not anymore. Someone reported this van as stolen two weeks ago,' the constable announced in a well-rehearsed authoritative voice.

Clarke watched as the sergeant jumped from the Transit van and dusted himself down. Now in official mode, he cautioned the driver on suspicion of vehicle theft, then led him towards the waiting Sprinter van. As another police officer appeared, he swiftly took control, cordoning off the area. It was a fast moving operation and, with the scientific support unit due to arrive at any moment, Clarke's involvement was almost at an end.

'Excellent work,' the sergeant announced. 'No doubt you'll have plenty to write in your report.'

'Yes, Sarge. I have.'

The officer nodded. 'In which case, I'll catch up with you back at the station.'

Clipboard in hand, Clarke tipped his peaked cap in salute as he jotted the details down. The next twenty-four hours would be crucial. Some suspects talked, others refused to cooperate knowing they would only incriminate themselves. Once solicitors got involved, everything changed. It was all about timing and getting the defendants to respond.

The constable watched as the van's doors closed and the sergeant banged on the roof. Slowly at first, it edged forward before joining the rest of the motorway traffic. Just when the constable thought he was having another bad day, everything had clicked into place.

CHAPTER TWENTY-SEVEN

After another mad hour spent haring around the living room, Benjamin was fast asleep. Having led Carlisle to a merry dance, the profiler had all but given up on him. Having clawed his way into the back of his favourite sofa bed, Carlisle was at wits' end. Loath to admit, he should never have listened to Jane Collins. Nothing was sacrosanct, and everything was up for discussion. He regretted not following his gut feeling instead of falling for his business partner's smooth-talking. Too late now, he groaned. He should have taken Benjamin to the local cat rescue centre and ended it there and then. He never imagined that kittens could be so destructive, and now he had to collect the shattered pieces, along with the remnants of his sofa bed.

By the time he'd finished breakfast, it was getting light. Unable to conjure up an obvious motive for why the suspect was dismembering only male victims, he was having to second guess. What fuelled the killer's rage, and why had he chosen this area?

Turning to his computer, he slotted the memory stick into the USB port and waited for the autopsy images to appear. At a glance, the torso looked bloated; the flesh mottled brown and green. Zooming in, he studied the puncture marks, mainly around the left sternal. He was searching for patterns, something to bring them ever closer. The next set of images showed an open black suitcase, with a broken lock and covered in dust. They described the woman who had acquired it from a local charity shop as being in her late teens. Who was she, he wondered?

Carlisle cupped his hands to his face and tried to think as the killer did. Once he'd cut their bodies into manageable chunks, he had stored them in a freezer. It would need to be fairly large, as anything smaller simply wouldn't work. Disposal came later when things had quietened down. These weren't random acts; these crimes were too well-managed for that. The man they were searching for possessed an uncanny ability to deceive, manoeuvring through social interactions with his exceptional charm.

Back in the real world, he closed the lid of his laptop and rubbed tired eyes. There was a great satisfaction to be had from solving some crimes, but this case was doing his head in. Initially, he believed the killer had chosen his victims at random. Now he was having doubts. Mixing the body parts up was all part of his ritual, a means of gaining sexual arousal. Often referred to as posing, it was not only a conscious criminal action meant to thwart an investigation team, but its real aim was to shock those who discovered the bodies. The perpetrator took great pleasure in acts of sickening violence. This wasn't for the fainthearted; these killings were pure insanity.

He stood for a moment and tried to take in the detail. Had he overlooked something? A small piece of evidence. Then again, he argued. If his killings were controlled, then why did he find it difficult to dispose of John Lawrence's body? Was he disturbed? He could have been. Then again, could his inner fantasies have snowballed out of control?

Carlisle cast those notions aside and pondered on other factors that could affect his decision-making. Annoyed that Angelica still hadn't got back to him, he was feeling let down. Hopefully, there would be a simple explanation, but he wasn't overly confident. Deep down, he felt sorry for her, especially if someone had forced her into slave prostitution. He wasn't alone in his woes. Others now thought as he did.

Frustrated, the profiler gazed at the street map, not wanting to lose heart. He'd lost count of the number of hoaxes the police had received lately. Each requiring a follow up, and many fool's errands. His wasn't the only disappointment. Mason's agreement with Tony Fox had also fallen on deaf ears. Four days had passed since their last visit to Fat Sam's nightclub, and still no signs of Fox getting back to them.

He stared at the timeline and thought about victim selection. What was the driving force behind his actions? Most serial killers were territorial predators who liked to work within their comfort zones. This case was chillingly different, as the killer was using large chunks of the local landscape to scope out his potential targets. Grooming his victims in bars, before taking them to a place of execution, this was no ordinary crime. Not only were his selection criteria consistent, but he was good at gaining people's trust. He knew from experience that some visionary serial killers suffered from a warped form of psychosis, where their delusions and fantasies became twisted commands to kill. However, this person possessed a cleverness that allowed him to navigate this dark realm.

Having changed his mind on so many things these past twenty-four hours, Carlisle was doubting his own judgement. And yet there was a distinct pattern to the killer's modus operandi, and his choice of victims. The more he thought about it, the more confused he became. Yes, there was an awful lot of pent-up anger inside this monster's head, but what was he trying to achieve?

His phone rang, and Jack Mason's number popped up on the screen.

What now, he wondered?

***

The moment the profiler stepped into Jack Mason's office, the whiff of black coffee greeted him. Seated behind an untidy desk, his colleague was deep in conversation. Seconds later, he crashed the receiver down and turned to face him.

'That was the Acting Superintendent, and she's not a happy bunny.'

'So it would seem.'

Mason stared at him blankly. 'She's after an update on the latest developments, and why we're no further forward in catching this fiend.'

The profiler was constantly on the move, adapting to changing situations. Ever since the divorce settlement,

Mason had developed a short fuse. To make matters worse, according to station rumours, he'd hooked up with a married woman. It was difficult to tell how much of it was true, but the memory of his colleague's previous affair still lingered, reminding him of the trouble it had caused.

'What did you tell her?'

'Not a lot.'

The profiler took stock.

'What about this Rumanian guy you picked up at yesterday's roadside checks? Are we any further forward with that?'

'He's not the killer, if that's what you think. Charged with theft of a vehicle and driving without insurance, that's all we can pin on him.'

'That's disappointing. I could have sworn he had a connection.'

'You're beginning to sound like Sutherland.'

'Hang on a minute, Jack.'

Mason huffed as he stared at the pile of papers now cluttering his desk. Incensed after his clash with the area commander, he folded his arms and slouched back in his seat.

'There must be a way of getting to the killer, surely?'

'It's not that simple, I'm afraid.'

Mason lifted his head. 'This research you've carried out on geographic profiling. How reliable is it?'

'We've used it before,' he insisted.

'I know, but what does it tell us this time?'

'Quite a lot, actually.'

'Like what?'

'I've been going back over old witness statements and mapping out potential sightings of the suspect's known movements.' The profiler blew into his coffee and tried to avoid eye contact. 'After adding in the kill zones, I applied some basic statistical concepts to the formula. Mean, and standard deviation, that type of analysis.'

'Christ,' Mason huffed. 'I was asking for an overview, not a bloody lecture.'

'And I'm giving you one.'

Mason held his hands up as in surrender. 'Okay. I'm sorry. So, what's the bottom line?'

'Crime mapping isn't an exact science, but it's becoming increasingly more sophisticated with things such as digital photography, global positioning, and the likes of videography. What I can say with confidence is, there are two areas he's most likely to strike again. One of them comes out at seventy percent, which is quite encouraging.'

'How confident are you?'

'Very, if I'm honest.'

The room fell silent for a moment.

'Those odds aren't bad. When is the question?'

'Sooner rather than later. Once he feels the urge and picks out his next victim.'

'And the location?'

'Within a five-mile radius of Newcastle's city centre.'

'He's got to be local.'

'I cannot be certain of that.'

Mason's face lit up with excitement. 'Do you believe he's attempting to avoid us by operating in a different location?'

'It's possible, and we know he doesn't have a local accent.'

'I'm surprised we haven't caught up with him during these roadside checks.'

'He's obviously avoiding them, Jack.'

Carlisle's mobile buzzed in his pocket, and he checked the display.

Number withheld.

'Hello, is that you, Angelica?'

Mason stared at him from behind his desk and mouthed the words, *'Speak of the devil.'*

'Okay,' Carlisle whispered. 'I'll catch up with you later.'

The connection went dead.

Mason looked at him with contempt. 'I take it she's planning to meet up with you again?'

'She claims to have seen the killer.'

'More lies, no doubt.'

Carlisle sucked in the air. 'Who knows?'

'You know my views on this woman.'

'I know, but I still need to follow it up.'

'You're wasting your time, my friend. When are you meeting her?'

'She's promised to call back.'

Mason shrugged, but said nothing. He was the man in charge of a murder investigation and no doubt the backroom staff would try to get a trace on her call. The trouble was, Angelica's conversations were always brief, leaving no room for elaboration or small talk. The woman wasn't daft and knew how to handle awkward situations.

He flicked through his notebook. 'What about Tony Fox? Has he got back to you yet?'

'No, and I'm not expecting him to either.' Mason put a pencil against his lips and thought for a moment. 'If you want my opinion, this Angelica is taking up far too much of your valuable time.'

'Really?'

'What's your genuine interest?'

A fresh pot of coffee arrived, brought in on a tray by one of the canteen ladies. A squat woman, dressed in a summery frock and loafers on her feet. She smiled and pushed a small plate of cream biscuits towards his colleague.

'Will that be all?' she asked.

'Yes, Margie. That'll do fine, thank you.'

The moment the door closed, Carlisle picked up on their conversation. 'I've been giving these Eastern European gangs some thought. If Angelica's caught up in a human trafficking ring, she could be in a lot of trouble.'

'She may well be, but it has sod-all to do with criminal profiling.' Mason shot him a warning glance. 'Stay clear of her and let the police deal with those matters.'

'But she claims to have seen the killer dragging a suitcase through the streets of Byker.'

Mason huffed. 'We've been over this ground before.'

'Well, that's what she claims she saw.'

'It's another pack of lies. Just like the last time she sent you on a fool's errand.'

Carlisle took a sip of coffee, thinking about the John Lawrence murder. Releasing a photofit to the local press was an act of desperation. It wasn't a good move, and he felt far from comfortable. He eased back in his seat, feeling the tension in his neck muscles.

'I thought we'd agreed to keep certain details from the media,' he said with a hint of frustration.

Mason shifted his weight. 'We have.'

'Then how could Angelica have known it was a GREEN suitcase the killer used?'

Mason's jaw dropped.

CHAPTER TWENTY-EIGHT

A compromise had been reached, and Jack Mason had cancelled his tactical operation to arrest Angelica. Carlisle's remit, if he could call it that, was to unlock this woman's dark secrets and get the hell out of there. A rundown retirement home in Bensham wasn't the safest environment to hang around in, but if police backup was required, then a small group of specially trained officers were close at hand. East European gangs were notoriously dangerous people to deal with, and Mason was taking no chances. Drug wars, individuals going missing, and online fraud scams were all too commonplace, according to national statistics.

Despite last-minute interventions, the rush hour traffic had been and gone when David Carlisle drove into Bensham that evening. Turning right at the bottom of a steep bank, he pulled up in front of a nineteenth century stone building and switched off the car's engine. Hands gripping the steering wheel, he checked his surroundings. There was very little activity – and no sign of the young woman.

On closer inspection, he found a door at the rear of the building. With his shoulder pressed firmly against it, he exerted a gentle force and nudged it open.

'Is anyone there?' he called out.

Silence.

On reaching the end of a long, narrow corridor, his

wind-up torch went dead. Eyes straining through the darkness, he frantically wound it up again. It was pitch black inside, and someone had boarded up the windows.

Where the hell was she?

Why anyone would want to meet him here beggared belief. Given the choice, he would have preferred backup. Spent needles everywhere, a strong whiff of urine. This wasn't the nicest place to hang around in.

Disorientated, the profiler pushed ahead. The room was spacious, with cathedral ceilings and graffiti filled walls. As the last rays of daylight played through a gap in one of the window panels, he made his way into the next room. Life in the gutter could be tough, but this building was full of nightmares, and the denizens who hung around in it filled with hopelessness. Nothing was sacrosanct. All rooms were destroyed. Floorboards ripped up, copper piping torn away, and doors torn from their hinges and used as makeshift drug mixing tables. He'd often questioned why owners allowed such terrible things to be done to their properties. If this building was anything to go by, then no wonder drugs had a terrible reputation.

He heard footsteps in another part of the building.

'Who's there?' he whispered.

Uncertainty gripped him.

'It's me, Mr Carlisle,' a familiar voice called out.

'Are you alone?'

'I should ask you that question.'

At last, he sighed.

Picked out in his torchlight, Angelica looked the epitome of innocence. But there was a darker side to this young woman. Unexplained, and one he craved to uncover.

'What is it you wish to talk to me about?'

'I bumped into that man again,' she replied.

'Which man was this?'

'The one I saw in Forth Street.'

At first, when the coldness had crept into her voice, he shuddered at the vulnerability. She looked so innocent. Helpless. As if she shouldn't be there. Why did no one believe this young woman? And why, he kept asking himself, did she expose herself to such dangers if she wasn't telling him the truth?

He stared at her for several moments.

'What happened next?' he asked.

'He was in Byker this time and getting out of the back of a white van. He had another suitcase with him.'

'What's unusual about that?' Carlisle said, acting dumbly.

'The last time I saw this man, he was dragging a suitcase out of his car, remember?'

'Yes, and the police found a body inside that one.'

'Well, then...'

'You seem to know an awful lot for someone who professes to know so little.'

She stared at him, eyes full of suspicion. 'What are you inferring?'

'Millions of people drag suitcases round towns and cities every day, so how can you be sure this was the same person?'

'It was him.'

'How do you know that?'

'Same height, same top, and the same Nike trainers on his feet.'

'What colour trainers?'

'They were white,' she frowned.

Carlisle's heart sank, and he sensed uncertainty.

'What makes you think there was a body inside the suitcase?'

'I mentioned nothing about a body.'

'But you implied there was one inside. If not, then why mention it?' She managed a smile, but her eyes betrayed insincerity. 'What makes you think I should trust you, Angelica?'

'If you don't, then why did you come here?'

Clever answer, he thought.

'The last time we met, you told me you were working as a prostitute in Forth Street. You said you saw this man, and he was sitting alone in his car. You approached him, and he told you to go away. If not, he would fetch the police to you. You said you were scared, so you hid in the shadows to see what he was up to. Minutes later, he opened the boot of his car and struggled to lift a large suitcase from it. He wasn't a tall man, you said, and he had difficulty in dragging it into the storage company.'

Not unlike before, she was eager to avoid eye contact.

'Why are you telling me this?'

Carlisle moved closer, the hint of a predatory smile on his face. 'Here's my problem. There are no prostitutes working in Forth Street. Someone moved them on years ago. Also, there is no evidence to support your story of a car ever being parked anywhere near where you said it was that night.'

She wavered. 'I am a prostitute, and I do work in Forth Street.'

Wait a minute, Carlisle thought. Hadn't she told him it was dark that night and never got a clear view of the suspect's face?

'What are you hiding from me, Angelica?'

'Nothing.'

'And yet you claim you saw this man again.'

'Yes. I did.'

'Byker, you say. And he was dragging a large suitcase behind him?'

'Yes. This one was GREEN!'

Carlisle, clearly puzzled, fell silent for a moment. Didn't Tom Hedley confirm he found identical matching fibres at all three crime scenes? He dug deeper.

'Tell me,' he said. 'Is Angelica your real name, or is that made up too?'

'Why would I lie to you?'

'I'm a private investigator, remember?'

'Well, then.'

The profiler detected a slight movement in the corner of her eye and knew she was lying. 'Are you in some sort of trouble with the police?'

'What makes you say that?'

'If not, why are you refusing to talk to them?'

'That's none of your business, Mr Carlisle.'

'And it's not a clever answer, Angelica.'

'In my country, we do things differently.'

'But you're not in your country now. You're in England.'

She'd lied to him about so many things that he'd lost all track of the truth. And yet, her description of the clothes the killer had worn was unnervingly accurate. Same hoodie, same colour shoes, and the same method of transporting his victims' bodies around. Then there was the question of the green suitcase. How could she have possibly known that?

Carlisle watched as she placed her hand on the door stanchion. He could not be sure, but she may have applied enough contact pressure to get a latent palm print from it.

He made a mental note.

'I'm sorry for asking so many awkward questions,' Carlisle said almost apologetically, 'but I'm confused.'

'Confused... confused about what?'

'This man you recently saw in Byker. What did he look like?'

'He wasn't tall, about your height...'

Plunged into sudden darkness, Carlisle frantically cranked the wind-up torch handle. It didn't take long, but in those precious few seconds, she'd vanished without a trace.

He checked the building. Inside and out. It was empty.

Then he realised.

***

Less than one hundred metres away, the watchers were busy. Their orders, crude as they were, were to assist the profiler should trouble break out. Hiding in the back of an undercover police van wasn't a bright idea. It felt cramped and uncomfortable, with far too many people moving about. Lifting his binoculars, the officer took in a long intake of air. Parked up outside the old retirement home was an old Rover P4 100. It belonged to the profiler, and they'd been following it for days. Surveillance was key, and while adjusting the focusing ring, he zoomed in on the action. Three kids kicking a football against the old perimeter fence.

Officer two smiled. 'Jumpy tonight, George?'

'No, bored out of my mind.'

'Relax. It's just a bunch of harmless kids having fun.'

'Yeah, toerags more like.'

This wasn't the safest location to conduct a surveillance operation in, which went without question. Yesterday, a street robbery took place. Today it was house burglaries. Drug crime ran rife here, and if you needed a car, you simply stole one.

The officer checked his watch.

'Time check,' the sergeant announced. 'It's twenty-two hundred hours,'

'Roger that,' officer three confirmed, as he wrote it down in the log.

Close to the building entrance, he watched as a young woman appeared through the haze, pushing a buggy. She was far too young to be a mother; he reasoned. Had it been his daughter out walking the streets this time of night, he would have given her a stiff talking-to. He reached over, picked up the handset, and contacted control. As the operator re-routed his call to a mobile phone in Forest Hall, he waited for a connection.

'Jack Mason,' the voice on the other end uttered.

The officer groaned as he heard laughter in his earpiece, and guessed the chief inspector was in a pub. Lucky bastard. What he wouldn't give for a pint right now. Reporting his findings as ongoing, he summarised events and ended the call.

Seconds later, a side entrance door opened. His head stooped slightly forward, the officer lifted the binoculars up to his eyes and zoomed in. The light fading fast; he recognised the profiler as he emerged from the side of the building. With no sign of the Eastern European woman, the officer swung his binoculars back towards the young female, pushing the buggy.

Then the penny dropped.

'That's her,' he screamed.

The distance between them growing, the surveillance officers watched in disbelief as the young woman slipped silently into the night. She was gone, and confusion reigned.

'Are you sure it was her?' asked officer two.

Officer one shook his head as if not knowing and had every reason to do so.

'Can't be sure, but it's too late to do anything now.'

As darkness fell, a haunting silence settled over the scene.

CHAPTER TWENTY-NINE

The moment Jack Mason breezed into MR-1, the team fell eerily silent. Glancing round, he instructed them to remain seated before taking up a central position in front of a large evidence board. Covered with post-its, maps, photographs, and newspaper cuttings linked by red tape, it was easy to decipher. This was the twenty-fifth meeting of Operation Walrus and, no thanks to a spate of misfortune, everyone was feeling the strain. After reading the overnights incidents report, the chief inspector's mood was subdued. Not an encouraging start, thought Carlisle. The team was looking for answers, and no one had any to give.

'Late yesterday evening, law enforcement conducted a sting operation at a disused retirement home in Byker, where they contacted this woman.' The lead investigator leaned over and pointed to an e-fit image pinned to the evidence board. 'Small in stature and operating under an assumed name, we estimate this individual is around eighteen years old. Having talked to Border Control, we now believe she has connections to a human trafficking ring operating out of the Netherlands.'

'Do we have a name, boss?' asked DS Holt.

'She calls herself Angelica, but that's all we know at this stage.'

'Not a lot to go on then.'

'No. I would agree.' Mason turned to Hedley. 'What's the latest response on fingerprints, Tom?'

The senior forensic scientist ran his hand over unkempt hair and pushed back in his seat. He had an owl shaped face, strong jawline, and thick bushy eyebrows. Known for his reserved nature, Hedley seldom spoke at meetings. When he did, there was always a significant reason behind it.

'Latent fingerprints lifted from yesterday's crime scene have drawn a blank. If this woman is an illegal entry, she'll be difficult to pin down.'

'What about Interpol?' asked Mason.

'The same applies. Unless she's committed a criminal offence in Europe, she's unlikely to be on record.'

Mason turned to face Holt. 'Where are we with phone tracking, George?'

'Nothing back so far,' the sergeant replied dejectedly. 'She's obviously using a Pay–as-you–go phone and throwing the SIM card away at the end of each contact.'

The room fell silent.

'What about this new theory of yours?' asked Mason, addressing Carlisle. 'What are you proposing?'

The profiler studied their faces. Clearly at odds with the rest of the team, there were many present who perceived Angelica to be nothing more than a hoaxer. Convincing them otherwise had been difficult, but they were right, of course. He realised that now, but not entirely for the same reasons. Trying to justify his sudden change of mind would be futile, and there was no simple explanation. A relatively new field with few set boundaries or definitions, criminal profiling could be very insular. Not all agreed with the method or the terminology, and the term "profiling" often rested uneasily with many senior officers. This would be challenging, and to a packed room, he would need to explain the reasons behind his new line of thinking.

Mason's voice betrayed his astonishment. 'You're not suggesting this woman is in cahoots with the killer, surely not?'

All eyes were now on him.

'Yes, that's how I see it.'

'What changed your mind?' asked Holt.

'Having met with her last night, Angelica's graphic descriptions of events are so accurate that only an accomplice or someone close to the killer could have known such facts.'

DC Manley shuffled awkwardly. 'If she couldn't identify the suspect in Forth Street, how come she recognised him in Byker?'

'That's a valid point,' the lead detective agreed.

'I've struggled with that myself,' Carlisle replied dolefully. 'It's my belief that Angelica has inserted herself into the investigation in order to drip feed us with vital information about the killer's activities.' The profiler braced himself for the onslaught. 'Why is the question? Does she have an inflated ego and seek recognition for her part in the killings, or does she gain her kicks from it?'

Mason looked at him questioningly. 'And what do you base your facts on?'

'While I may not have expertise in linguistics, I have an uncanny knack for detecting blatant deception. And that's what initially drew my attention.'

'I always knew she was a hoaxer,' agreed Holt, 'but she has a propensity of being in the drop zone at all the right moments.'

Mason remained silent. He didn't do conventional; it wasn't his style. Where most senior police officers hung certificates of achievements on their walls, Mason did not. He proudly displayed only one, a school swimming certificate for breaststroke. And that, according to his cleaner, was nailed to the toilet door.

Savage raised an arm to speak.

'Yes, Rob.'

'Her knowledge of the facts is uncannily accurate.' The sergeant cleared his throat. 'I presume that's where David is now coming from.'

'I concur,' said Sue Carrington, who had sat quietly throughout. 'There's an awful lot of information the media doesn't know about the case, including our links with this woman. Unless someone is drip-feeding her info, there's no other reasonable explanation.'

Holt expressed his doubt that anyone in the building was providing her with information.

Mason turned to Carlisle. 'What finally convinced you?'

'When I challenged her about the white Transit van, she told me the incident took place at a run-down factory close to the Byker council estate.'

'That sounds remarkably like the old chemical plant,' Manley concurred.

'Summat's not right,' added Savage.

Carlisle took stock. 'You're right, Rob. She may suffer from hybristophilia.'

'Ah! *Folie á deux,'* Tom Hedley said, excitedly rubbing his hands together.

Mason stared at them, bemused. 'Are we talking at cross purposes here, or am I missing something? What the hell is hybristophilia?'

'It's often referred to as Bonnie and Clyde syndrome,' the profiler replied, 'and occurs more often in women than men. It's described as a paraphilia that takes on two forms, either passive or aggressive. The aggressive form is what Bonnie Parker displayed when she assisted Clyde Barrow in their infamous 1930s bank robberies in America. It can also manifest as sexual arousal, fascination, or when someone develops a strong affinity with someone who commits atrocious crimes.'

'We're cutting a fine line here, and I'm not liking what I'm hearing,' Mason glowered.

The tension was building, and it was Tom Hedley who unexpectedly came to Carlisle's aid. 'What disturbs me is how she's able to describe what clothes the suspect was wearing. It fits perfectly with our forensic findings.'

'That's another good point,' Carrington added.

The room fell silent as the chief inspector switched his mobile on and frantically searched the Internet. Lateral thinking was one way of looking at it, but complex psychological theories all too often went over everyone's head. There were some present, only a handful, who were questioning Mason's stubborn stance. Carlisle knew what the chief inspector was thinking. His colleague worked on impulse. It was like flipping a coin in a game of pitch and toss when you never knew which side the coin would land on.

Mason held his hand up and read out aloud from his phone. 'It says here that some people believe hybristophiliacs are submissive subjects, while others believe they are narcissistic enablers who are pulled into power. If there is a hint of truth in what you're saying, then what's this woman's role in these killings?'

A chance to explain, thought Carlisle.

'There are two parts to hybristophilia,' the profiler began. 'There's the taboo danger part, and there's this hyper-masculine aggressive element that appeals to some women. Without knowing Angelica's background, if our killer is significantly older, she might perceive him as a paternal figure. Someone to look up to.'

'What if she's not?' Mason replied.

'Then her role would fit perfectly into the Bonnie and Clyde syndrome.'

Manley's mouth slowly twisted into a thin smile. 'Guessing by the number of stab wounds we found on the victims' bodies, he's more likely to be a younger man, don't you think?'

'True,' Hedley acknowledged. 'And there's plenty of forensic evidence to support such a claim.'

Ever the optimist, Mason paced the floor. Short on ideas, and time, he was struggling to come to terms with it. 'I'm still not convinced, Tom,' he said, shaking his head. 'It's a massive shift in direction and doesn't resolve her connection to the killer.'

'And yet it answers a lot of questions.'

'Let's park that theory to one side for a moment and concentrate on this latest killing.'

'And what do you propose to do about this woman in

the meantime?' asked Hedley.

'If you're so concerned, let's put a warrant out for her arrest.'

'On what charges?'

'Being an illegal immigrant, for starters.' Mason checked his watch. 'If Interpol has drawn a blank, and she hasn't got previous, we could be treading on thin ice. Let's see what your forensic results throw up. Latent fingerprints may give us a few answers.'

'What if she skips the country?' asked Holt.

'We'll cross that bridge when we come to it.' Mason looked Carlisle directly in the eye. 'Let's hope this theory of yours leads us in the right direction, otherwise we'll have a lot of explaining to do.'

Carlisle nodded. 'With any luck, she may even lead us to the killer.'

'I doubt that.'

'And why not?' queried Holt.

'A copper's nose, George. And twenty years' service at the sharp end,' Mason replied stoically.

Tom Hedley leaned over as he came to Carlisle's rescue again. 'I must admit I quite like this new line of approach, and the evidence certainly points us in that direction.'

Mason stared at the evidence board as if looking for inspiration. While case files filled the table in front of him, there wasn't a scrap of evidence among any of them to suggest why the killer had committed such heinous crimes, let alone worked with an accomplice.

'Okay,' Mason announced. 'If she is an accessory, what's her involvement? Let's re-examine the facts... find the connection.'

The chief inspector jotted some notes down.

'She's an attractive young woman,' grinned Holt, 'so perhaps he's using her as bait.'

'Your right, George,' Mason said, tilting his head back in thought. 'We need to get the tech boys to run another trawl over the Internet chatroom sites.'

'What about witness statements?' asked Manley.

'No, Harry. If she's in cahoots with the killer, she needs to be brought in for questioning. Find the woman and we'll catch our killer.'

A new buzz filled the air, and the lead detective became caught up in it. As the meeting ended, everyone broke into smaller groups.

Mason approached Hedley as he moved towards the meeting room door.

'What do you think, Tom?'

'I quite like the idea, if I'm honest. The forensic evidence stacks up.'

'Let's hope you're right or we'll all be thrown into the doghouse.'

'It won't be the first time, Jack.'

'No. I suppose not.' Mason groaned.

CHAPTER THIRTY

Leeds – Ripper territory

In search of answers, Jack Mason had driven to Leeds that morning. The West Yorkshire Police had picked up a stolen white Transit van in the Seacroft area, which was now in the hands of the serious crime division. In what was now a fast-moving operation, a lot of progress was being made, all thanks to a rental company in Leeds. Despite his doubts, the lead detective begrudgingly acknowledged the need to entertain the profiler's latest theory with an open mind.

'Turn left at the next junction,' the voice on the Sat Nav instructed.

Got it. Mason smiled.

On the east side of Leeds, behind the facade of this modern office-block building, Killingbeck Police Station covered a large sector of the city, including the infamous Halton Moor estate – the seat of several hardy criminal gangs. Met at reception by a fastidious desk sergeant who insisted on taking his details down, Mason cursed his luck. Minutes later, someone escorted him into a back room and offered coffee.

He did not wait long.

'Ah! Detective Chief Inspector.'

The moment he heard the familiar high-pitched voice, he almost choked on his coffee. A born-again Christian,

Inspector William Greystone was a tall, balding man in his late fifties, with slicked back black hair and touches of grey at the sides. Not the easiest individual to get on with, Greystone was a knobhead as far as Jack Mason was concerned, a man who loved nothing more than to spout religious verse at the most inappropriate times.

'How was your journey south?' asked Greystone.

'The A1M was a nightmare.'

'It seems these motorway improvements are never ending,' Greystone acknowledged, with a shake of his head. 'It's not ideal to have average speed cameras tracking your progress at speeds of fifty miles per hour.'

'No, I suppose not.'

The inspector took up a seat opposite and flicked open the files he'd brought with him. 'I've just had a lengthy discussion with Tom Hedley, the senior forensic scientist up in Gateshead. It seems latent fingerprints found on this stolen white Transit van match those recovered from a retirement home in Byker.' Greystone cleared his throat. 'If this is the foreign woman you're referring to, she doesn't appear on the police national fingerprint database.'

'So it would seem,' Mason nodded. 'She's obviously here unlawfully.'

'Pity,' sighed Greystone, 'I was rather hoping for a quick breakthrough.'

'What about the van driver?'

'Nothing in the way of fingerprints, as someone wiped the van clean. However, during the investigation, we recovered soil samples from one of the vehicle's wheel arches, showing it had been driven off-road.' Greystone conferred with his notes. 'They've been sent to the lab for further analysis.'

'Do we know who the Transit van belonged to?'

'A local lease hire company on Kirkstall Road.'

'What do we know about them?'

'Three weeks ago, they reported that someone stole the van from the Seacroft area.'

Mason did a quick mental calculation. 'Your report stated it was found abandoned, as I recall.'

'Yes. When we first came upon it, it wouldn't start. Whoever nicked it must have realised that something was seriously wrong with the vehicle's engine.'

'It's a wonder someone didn't set it on fire.'

Greystone laughed. 'Their end is destruction, their god is their belly, and they glory in their shame, with minds set on earthly things. Philippians 3:19.'

Unimpressed, Mason jotted down some notes. 'So where was it stolen, exactly?'

'Here in Seacroft, close to the A64.' Greystone's brow corrugated. 'Two builders had leased it to carry out local house renovations. Parked up outside the property with the keys left sticking out of the ignition, it's not surprising that someone nicked it.'

'He's an opportunist, William.'

'It would appear so.' Greystone recovered his composure. 'We also found a set of stolen registration plates tucked under the passenger seat. Your man was obviously intending to avoid detection at some later stage.'

Mason scratched the side of his head. 'If someone stole it in Leeds and drove it up to Newcastle and back, there's every chance he's local.'

'We've already considered that angle. If your suspect has connections to Leeds, then they probably stole the van to order. That's a much safer approach, especially if they switch number plates.'

Mason ignored his comment.

'What else did you recover from the vehicle?'

'Not a lot,' Greystone admitted. 'We found a couple of petrol receipts and a spent roll of heavy-duty duct-tape wedged down the back of the driver's seat. Your suspect obviously overlooked them during his clean-up operation.'

Mason felt an adrenaline rush. 'Is it possible to have a full analysis done on the duct-tape?'

'Of course. Is it important?'

'It could be a crucial piece of evidence.'

'Excellent. Once I receive the results, I'll send you a full written report.'

'Copied in triplicate, if you please.'

'Obviously,' Greystone smiled smugly.

Unlike Gateshead Police Station, this building had a contemporary look. Plush furnishings, state-of-the-art technology, and plenty of parking space at the rear. He preferred a more lived in environment. This building was too clinical to be a police station, he thought.

'Just out of interest,' Greystone said, lifting his head, 'have you uncovered a motive?'

'No, but we're working on it.' Mason ran his hand over the top of his head. 'We've drafted in a criminal profiler to help in that side of our investigations.'

'A criminal profiler?'

'Yes, but I'd rather not elaborate at this stage.'

'Of course, that's understandable.'

'All I can say is that he's worked with us before, so we know what to expect.'

Greystone's expression showed interest. 'Tell me. How does that tie in with the psychological aspects of the case? What do you expect to gain from it?'

'From the evidence gathered so far, we are hoping to reach into the killer's mind.'

'That is interesting.'

Mason debated whether to reveal more detail, but evaded the matter. 'These petrol receipts you found. Anything of interest show up?'

'None that I'm aware of.'

'I presume they had a date?'

Greystone was taken aback. A rank below him, he dutifully fell into line. 'They were all concentrated around the Leeds area, but there is one from a Gateshead filling station that may be of interest. Low Fell, wherever that is.'

Got him. Mason grinned.

For Greystone, everything was a matter of fact. The inspector was a bumbler as far as the chief inspector was concerned, and there was no getting away from it. As their meeting wore on, he fumbled around in an inside pocket and pulled out an e-fit image.

'Ah. The Eastern European woman. We've recently circulated this image to every officer in the force. If she's local, there's every chance we'll catch up with her.'

Mason made a note of it and pushed back in his seat. 'Excellent.'

'What's her involvement in all of this?'

Mason explained as a fresh pot of coffee arrived, brought in by the fastidious desk sergeant who insisted on pouring it out. Mason caught the look of fulfilment. Close to retirement; if not, he'd suffered one hell of a paper round. Sometimes he envied other police officers' roles. Far less hassle, little responsibility, and a shitload of free time on their hands. Then again, he argued. Sitting behind a desk all day didn't exactly appeal. He preferred old school policing, down-to-earth encounters with the real criminals.

Surprisingly, Greystone had fallen over backwards to assist, which was more than he'd expected. Police work was all about contacts, and the more connections you had, the better chance you had of solving a case.

'What more can you tell me about his victims?' Greystone asked.

'Concerning what?'

'This one appears extremely brutal, according to the reports I've read. Is he a medical man, do you think?'

'More a butcher than anything. His methods are pretty crude.'

'In what respect?'

Mason explained in more detail, but declined to elaborate. As the morning wore on, his mind drifted. What if the killer lived in Leeds? What then? Would the case fall outside their regional authority? He doubted it. Besides, the northeast was the location where all these murders had taken place. Ninety-five miles away, to be exact.

Greystone stood to leave.

'This is a nasty business, and I don't envy your task.'

Mason closed his notebook and reached out a hand. 'Thanks for your help, William. You've been most helpful.'

'No problem,' Greystone replied, lapping up the adulation like a ten-year-old schoolboy receiving his first school certificate. 'Always a pleasure to come to your aid in such dark times.'

Mason looked at him oddly. 'Yes, of course.'

'If there's anything else we can help you with, you know where to find us.'

Greystone's contribution had been priceless, and he now had a better understanding of the killer's movements. Despite all that was going on, Tom Hedley was right: the duct tape now played a major role in capturing the killer.

A sprinkling of black clouds had formed over the horizon as Mason drove north towards Wetherby. Feeling peckish, it was then he remembered the New Inn in Scarcroft. It was an obvious choice, since it was less than a twenty-minute drive away. The beer was exceptional, and the food was always excellent. His mind made up, he phoned the office and relayed some further instructions to DS Holt. If he would not make it home before six, he would need some thinking time. At least he could draft his report to prepare for tomorrow's briefing.

Yes, he thought. The New Inn was perfect.

CHAPTER THIRTY-ONE

Throughout the morning, the district of Byker had been a hotbed of activity. With every available police officer drafted into the area, by mid-afternoon, the mobile incident command truck brought with it a temporary respite from the inclement weather. More importantly, it meant that Jack Mason now had coffee-making facilities.

On first impressions, the DCI seemed pleased with the way his operations were developing. They'd plugged a few gaps, opened fresh leads, and made their presence felt. Having split the area into three zones, the chief inspector was exploring every possibility. As dozens of police officers poured into the outlying districts, the hunt for the killer was relentless. They now had had a three-week window to work on, from the time the white Transit van was stolen in Leeds to the time it was last seen in Newcastle. There was no simple solution, it seemed, and he was keen to fill in the gaps. Garages, pubs, restaurants, and supermarket car parks were all under scrutiny.

Officially, this was a Northumbria Police murder investigation, even though the killer had links to Leeds. If nothing else, Mason's recent dealings with the West Yorkshire Police had certainly clarified matters. Any notion the enquiry would be switched to another division had finally been crushed. He was still the man in charge.

Looking around, nine detectives crammed into a tiny incident unit no bigger than a broom cupboard were always going to be a tight squeeze. If nothing else, it showed Mason's inability to plan things.

'You okay?' Mason asked, glancing up at Carrington.

Now wedged between two strapping police officers, the young detective smiled without humour. 'Is this some sort of joke, boss?'

'I know it's a tight squeeze.'

'Tight squeeze!' she gasped. 'There's not enough room to swing a cat.'

'Try spreading some charm around and see if that helps.'

Laughter broke out.

'There's little chance of that happening, not with this bunch of morons.'

Mason gathered a few loose papers together and looked at her quizzically. 'You ever played rugby?'

'No, but my father did. Why do you ask?'

'Was he good?'

'I don't know, I only ever saw him play the once.'

'There's a part in the game called the scrum.' Mason smirked. 'It's a bit like a big man's cuddle. After a lot of pushing and shoving, everyone breaks free and a space opens up in front of you.'

'Not in here, it doesn't.'

More laughter broke out.

'Okay,' Mason said, the serious side surfacing. 'I know we're going back over old ground, but I'm particularly interested in the white Transit van that was stolen in Leeds. Blood samples found in the back of it match John

Lawrence, which tells me the killer used it to transport his body around. Where was it parked? Who saw it? Did anyone see anything suspicious?'

'What else do we know about the vehicle?' asked DS Holt.

'According to the West Yorkshire Police, it has PROPERTY RENOVATIONS splashed all over it.'

'Does that mean we're looking at recent house renovations?'

'Not at this stage, we're not.' Mason let his words sink in.

'Any more feedback on the Low Fell petrol station receipt?' asked Savage.

'The diesel was paid for in cash, so we don't have a bank card trace.'

'What about CCTV coverage?'

'There was none.'

'Typical,' Savage muttered.

Carrington raised a hand to speak.

'Yes, Sue.'

'What are our instructions, boss?'

The chief inspector handed everyone a brown envelope and flicked back over the pages in his notebook. 'You'll be working in pairs on this one, so try keeping it simple. We know the suspect was last seen in the area during the early hours of Friday the twenty-third, around the same time when someone stole a set of vehicle registration plates from a local van. I'm also interested in this Eastern European woman's movements. Was she involved? Did anyone see or hear anything suspicious?'

Carlisle stared down at the brown envelope and noticed that someone had scribbled Sue Carrington's name across the top of it in bold black letters. At least

Mason had got something right for once.

'What more do we know about her?' asked Manley.

'I'm coming to that,' Mason replied.

Outlining his plans, the chief inspector requested a summary of the team's findings, which unfortunately wasn't much. As was often the case surrounding illegal immigrants, there were more questions than answers. Without a surname, Angelica was becoming a bit of an enigma in Carlisle's mind.

Manley turned to Mason. 'Could this woman have been acting as a lookout?'

'I take it you haven't read my report?'

'It's the bairns, boss. They've been keeping me and the missus up all night...'

Annoyed, Mason shook his head despondently. 'Before moving into the estate, she claims to have seen the suspect dragging a green suitcase out of the back of a white Transit van. Caught on camera passing Dean Street at 02:32, our suspect was last seen heading in a southerly direction. What did this young woman get up to in the meantime?'

'That's easy,' Manley grinned, 'she was nicking number plates.'

'Hmm. It's a thought,' Mason mused. 'We need to jog a few memories. Who else was in the vicinity that night?'

It was the coordinator who took everyone by surprise.

'You okay, Ted?' Mason asked.

With very little air circulation inside the command truck, Ted Black's face had turned ashen. Shoulder to shoulder and squeezed tightly together, the heat generated was unbearable. To everyone's relief, Mason signalled for the back door to be opened, and the briefing ended abruptly.

***

Checking his street map, David Carlisle estimated there were at least a dozen pubs within easy walking distance of the mobile incident truck. It was an enormous catchment area, which meant for a busy afternoon. Having to convince himself that this wasn't a bad idea, the profiler remained optimistic.

Carrington sidled up to him.

'You've not been in contact in a while.'

'I've been busy, Sue.'

She gave him a judgemental glance. 'Are you avoiding me, or is there someone else in your life?'

'Neither. Is there a problem?'

'If there is someone, that's fine by me.'

Carlisle stiffened. 'It's funny you should mention that; there *is* someone in my life.'

She looked at him dejectedly. 'Anyone I know?'

'I doubt it.'

Her face clouded over as her eyes rested upon his. 'I always thought the right person would come along one day. Pity, because I thought I was in with a chance.'

Carlisle smiled inwardly. 'His name's Benjamin, and we're living together.'

'Benjamin!' she huffed.

Carlisle burst out laughing.

'It's not what you think. Benjamin's a stray kitten I've

recently adopted.'

'And you're sleeping together?'

'Yes, but not by choice. I can tell you.'

The young detective blushed, having revealed her feelings towards him. It had been months since they'd last worked together. Now an established member of Jack Mason's team, Carrington wasn't pushy like the rest. Apart from getting on well together, he really liked her. He would need to tread warily, as rushing into any sort of meaningful relationship might not end in the fairy tale Carrington was hoping for. She had an enthusiastic little-girl quality that was infectious. Then again, younger women were far less demanding, which suited him perfectly.

It was mid-afternoon when they entered the Cumberland Arms in Ouseburn. The place was heaving, standing room only. Checking his surroundings, Carlisle spotted a space at the end of the bar and made a beeline towards it.

'Police,' Carrington said, holding up her warrant card in front of the young barman's face. 'We're looking for information regarding a recent murder which took place close to St. Anthony's Park. Are you the regular barman?'

'That's me,' he smiled. 'What can I get you people?'

'Nothing,' Carrington replied bluntly, 'but I'd appreciate some honest answers.'

'I gave you people a statement a few weeks back.'

'Yes, I'm aware of that.'

'Listen,' the barman said, lowering his voice, 'it's not convenient right now. Do you mind popping back later?'

Undeterred, the detective reached into her handbag

and dug out an e-fit image of Angelica. 'Ever seen this young woman in here?'

The barman's eyes narrowed a fraction as he turned from his work. 'Can't say as I have. Mind, thousands of pretty young girls get in here every week.'

Annoyed, Carlisle had heard enough. Blindly, he reached over and grabbed hold of the barman's arm. 'Don't be clever, son. Continue to mess us around, and I'll sharp close this place down.'

The barman stood gobsmacked.

'So, what's it to be?'

'I'm sorry?'

Carlisle picked up the e-fit image and slid it towards the barman. 'This young woman we asked you about, she came in here with a fella.'

'Yeah, but... no,' the barman stammered, 'she sounds like dozens of other customers who regularly drink here.'

'The guy she hangs around with is shifty looking,' Carlisle exaggerated. 'Average height, he always wears a black hoodie. He's much older than her and prefers to keep his distance.'

The barman hesitated. 'I'm not sure I should tell you this, but there is a customer who fits that description.'

'And who might that be?' asked Carrington.

'It could be nothing, but he was in here the other night.'

'Alone?'

'No. He was with this woman,' the barman said, pointing down at the e-fit image.

'What can you tell me about them?'

The barman paused long enough to pull another pint.

'I overheard their conversation that night, and she was telling this young lad that she fancied having sex with him. When they went outside, her partner was waiting for them in the carpark. He sounded a real nasty bastard.'

'What happened exactly?'

'As far as I know, the young lad got away from them.'

'And what's this young lad's name?'

'Reggie.'

'Reggie who?' Carrington demanded.

'How the hell would I know? He's never been back since.'

Carlisle checked the sign above the bar and pointed to it. 'I see you do bed-and-breakfast here.'

'That's right, thirty quid a night.'

Carrington stared at Carlisle.

'I need to see your guest book,' the detective demanded.

Reaching below the counter, the barman reluctantly handed her a large red diary. Curious, she flipped through the pages before tucking it under her arm. 'We need this as evidence. I'll drop it back to you when we're finished.'

The young man rested his knuckles on the edge of the bar, and there was an urgency in his voice. 'I may need to speak with the landlady about that.'

'Why, is there a problem?'

'It's not for me to say.'

'Perhaps I should have a word?' said Carlisle.

'No, that won't be necessary.'

Carrington handed the barman one of her business cards. 'The next time you see Reggie in here, you're to ring that number.'

The barman looked at her, bemused.

'Does this place operate security cameras?' asked Carlisle.

'No. We got rid of them years ago.'

'What other security arrangements do you have?'

'The pub's burglar alarmed. That's about it.'

Carlisle didn't suppose the barman was really interested, but he still felt the necessity to emphasise the point. 'When Reggie comes in here again, you're to contact that number.'

'Leave it with me,' the barman nodded.

The moment they stepped outside, Carlisle felt a cool breeze on his face. Not more than a ten-minute walk from Manors Metro station and fifteen from Newcastle's Quayside, the Cumberland Arms was ideally located. Halfway down a steep bank, with views overlooking the Ouseburn valley, he couldn't think of a better place to lie low. But there lay a problem: his victims were being kept in a deep freezer which ruled this place out. Then again, he thought. Why on earth would he travel all the way from Yorkshire to carry out his murders? He stood for a moment, thinking about this. Serial killers were territorial and liked to stick within their comfort zones. The closer to home, the better. So, unless he was lining the van's interior with heavy duty plastic sheeting, then home was close at hand.

'Penny for your thoughts?' Carrington smiled.

'Angelica,' he replied. 'If she's grooming these young men with promises of sex, where are they slaughtering them?'

'Somewhere quiet, I'd wager.'

'It makes sense, but they found their van in Leeds. Don't forget.'

'What if they live there?'

'If they do, then why does Angelica always use the Metro trains?'

Carrington wrinkled her nose. 'I've no idea. You're the mind expert.'

'No, Sue. The killer works in Leeds, but home is here in Newcastle.'

She looked at him oddly. 'This profiling malarkey does my head in.'

Carlisle didn't press the matter. It was better to say nothing in these situations. Keep your thoughts to yourself.

CHAPTER THIRTY-TWO

Meeting Room One was buzzing with enthusiasm that morning. Still without a motive, their sweep of the Byker area had thrown up dozens of new leads. Confident of a breakthrough, Jack Mason had brought in two recent additions to the team. Both senior road traffic officers, with a wealth of experience, and ready to tackle any new changing situation. The DCI's plan was to secure the two main arterial roads covering the North East of England. Namely, the A1(M) and A19 north of Middlesbrough. If the killer was commuting between Newcastle and Leeds, he would need to come under their radar.

The moment Tom Hedley appeared in the doorway; the noise levels heightened. Looking like a possessed man, the senior forensic scientist was frantically waving a sheet of paper in the air and trying to attract their attention.

'What is it, Tom?' Mason asked.

'I've just received an email from the West Yorkshire Police.'

'Anything of interest?'

'It couldn't be better news,' Hedley replied excitedly. 'The blood sample found in the back of the stolen Transit van is an exact DNA match to John Lawrence, confirming his presence.'

'Can we be sure?'

'There's absolutely no doubt.'

'Is there anything else you would like to add?'

'Yes. The roll of duct tape found wedged down the back of the driver's seat is the same composition and identical to that used in the Jennifer Oakwell murder.'

'Does it mention the place of purchase?'

'It does, and the manufacturer's batch code tells us they distributed it to several major northeast hardware outlets throughout 2013.'

Mason stroked his chin in thought. 'Is there a list of where exactly?'

'No. It doesn't say.'

'So, we still don't know when or where someone purchased the tape?'

'If nothing else, it tells us he was in the area when he purchased it,' Carlisle assured them.

Mason shot the profiler a glance. 'So he's local?'

'I would say so. Besides, his knowledge of the area and his ability to move around in it suggests he's territorial. This one sticks rigidly to set routines, even down to the clothes he wears.'

'What are the chances he works in Leeds?' asked Hedley.

'It's odds on, he's a tradesperson of sorts.'

'Hold on a minute,' Mason said, raising a hand. 'Let's stick with the duct tape for a second. What else does the report tell us?'

Hedley raised his eyebrows a fraction. 'We know he did a clean-up job on the Transit van, but after further examination, we found small traces of brick dust in the foot-well of the vehicle.'

'What does that tell us?' said Mason, disquiet clearly showing.

'The footpath close to where John Lawrence's body was discovered has an identical chemical composition. Also, the investigators discovered thirty-six types of plant and pollen in the vehicle, one of them rare.'

'Got him,' Mason said out loud.

Hedley allowed himself a brief, self-assured smile. 'If that hasn't convinced you, then fibres discovered on the driver's seat match those found at all three murder scenes.'

Chatter broke out. This was a crucial development.

'We know where John Lawrence's body was found, and how it got there, but we're missing one vital piece of information: who killed him?' said Mason.

'Any mention of this Eastern European woman in the report?' asked Holt.

Hedley elaborated. 'Besides fingerprints recovered from the van's dashboard, investigators found a strand of hair in the seat well. The annoying thing is, after many inquiries, there's nothing to say to whom it belongs.'

'Nothing on our database?'

'No. We've drawn a complete blank.'

'If it belongs to his accomplice, she's obviously here unlawfully,' Mason sighed, 'which begs the question: what nationality is our killer?'

Carlisle was quick to react. 'He's definitely territorial, someone who commits his crimes within a ten-mile striking distance of Newcastle. If his partner suffers from hybristophilia, her infatuation towards him may lead us to his whereabouts.'

Mason proffered a smile. 'Find the woman and we find our killer.'

'Precisely,' Carlisle agreed.

Tom Hedley shuffled awkwardly. 'Easier said than done. Where do you suggest we look? Other than a strand of hair and a set of fingerprints, there's nothing to say who she is.'

Inspector Dick Harris peered hard over the top of his horn-rimmed glasses. His fifteen years with road traffic invaluable. 'For what it's worth, these people are avoiding detection by stealing legitimate plates and putting them on stolen vehicles. The problem with that is, people seldom report legit plates to the police, and it is difficult to pick them up on ANPR.'

'We need to find a way round it.'

Harris nodded. 'We could set up more road checks.'

'Let's do it,' Mason insisted.

DS Holt raised a hand to speak. 'What are the chances of her making contact again?'

'Slim, I'd wager,' Mason replied brashly. 'She'll only do that through, David. If she contacts him, then we've fitted a call tracker device to his phone.'

'It's a waiting game?'

'Unless you can come up with a better plan.'

Carlisle glanced at the dozens of location markers. Emotions were running high, and everyone was getting tetchy. He leaned forward and pointed to the chart. 'Have we heard any more from Tony Fox lately?'

'No, nothing,' Mason shrugged. 'Which reminds me, it's time we paid him another visit.'

'I wouldn't hang my hat on it,' said Holt.

Mason proffered a thin smile. 'No, I suppose not.'

'Perhaps we should go public,' added Savage.

'No. Not at this stage, Rob.'

'Why not? It's worked in the past.'

Mason angled his head in thought. 'Yes, but this woman's a control freak. If we go public, it will only force her to go to ground.'

'What other alternatives do we have?'

Carlisle studied the chart and shook his head in frustration. If their suspects were operating locally, they would need to flush them out. It was an enormous catchment area, densely populated, and with no simple option. He considered this.

'If her real name isn't Angelica, then why has she chosen to call herself that?'

'That's a bloody good point,' Mason agreed.

Holt drew back in his seat. 'Nah, it definitely sounds East European to me.'

'Hang on a minute,' said Hedley. 'When I spoke with my counterpart in Leeds, he told me his wife's favourite restaurant is called Angelica's.'

'That's stretching it a bit,' Holt chuckled.

'Not really,' Mason argued. 'I'm already warming to the idea.'

Manley grinned. 'Me too, boss. A trip to Leeds sounds like a radical idea. Who knows, if we apply some pressure, we might even get a free meal.'

Mason was about to speak when the acting superintendent appeared in the doorway. Dressed in uniform and carrying a bundle of documents under her arm, her expression looked strained. 'Ah, Detective Chief

Inspector,' she said, staring directly across at Mason. 'Have there been any more developments in this white Transit van?'

'Yes, ma'am. We've just received a full written report from the West Yorkshire Police.'

Tom Hedley reached over and handed it to her. She stared at the report for several minutes, then said. 'This is fantastic news. I'm currently on my way over to police headquarters. They are bound to ask.'

Mason nodded, but said nothing.

'What about yesterday's operation? Anything more to report?'

'Not yet, ma'am. We're still working through the detail.'

Sutherland stood thinking.

'This joint operation with the West Yorkshire Police. Where are we with that?'

'Operation *Sparrow Hawk* takes effect from midnight tonight, ma'am. All arterial roads in and out of the northeast will come under the command of Durham Constabulary. If the killer is actively moving between Leeds and Newcastle, he's bound to come under their radar.'

'Good. I'll inform the Area Commander that we're making satisfactory progress.'

She turned, hesitated, then took off at haste.

As the door closed behind her, Mason let out a long sigh of relief. Nothing was ever straightforward these days. Mystery shrouded everything.

Chapter Thirty-Three

Foot hard on the accelerator, the speedometer on 112 mph, Mason took the next slip road towards Corbridge. If his gamble paid off, and it was Angelica sitting in the front passenger seat of the stolen BMW, he might just make a name for himself. Now the most wanted woman on the national crime agency's rogue's gallery, every police officer in the country was on the lookout for her.

'Angelica's Curse,' he softly whispered to himself.

As the road ahead narrowed, Mason caught his first glimpse of flashing blue lights. Fast closing in, his car radio suddenly crackled into life. Seconds later, after taking a sharp left-hand bend, an irate road traffic officer met him. Dressed in a Hi-Vis yellow jacket, and carrying a traffic cone under his arm, he flagged him to the side of the road.

'DCI Mason, Northumbria Police,' he announced, holding up his warrant card.

'There's been a vehicle accident some fifty metres up ahead,' the officer confirmed, 'and we're closing this section of the road.'

'Does this involve a silver BMW?'

'Yes, sir. It does.'

'What do we know about the occupants?'

'As far as I'm aware, we still have a young woman

trapped inside the vehicle, but the driver's done a runner.'

'Is she alive?'

'The last I heard, she was unconscious but still breathing,' a second officer announced, as he appeared from behind a marked BMW X5 traffic vehicle.

'Who's in charge?'

'Sergeant Fallon. He's over at the crash scene.'

On a good day, emergency services aimed to respond within a swift nineteen minutes. Now hot on the trail of a serial killer, Mason was yards away from the seat of the accident. Lengthening his stride, he approached the T-junction with trepidation. As he turned to his left, he noticed a stationary paramedic's vehicle. Blue spinners flashing, doors thrown open in haste, the occupants were nowhere to be seen. Then he spotted the skid marks.

From what he could determine, the driver of the stolen BMW had failed to make a sharp right turn at the T-junction with Jack's Lane. Travelling at speed, it had glanced off a tree, flipped onto its roof, and was lying upside down in the bottom of a dry ditch. Glass was everywhere. It reminded him of a scene out of a Clint Eastwood movie he'd recently watched.

'DCI Mason, Northumbria Police,' he proclaimed.

Barely visible through the tree line, the sergeant stared up at him.

'Sergeant Fallon,' the officer called out. 'There's a bit of a footpath just to the left of your position.'

'I see it,' Mason acknowledged.

At the bottom of a steep ditch, he stood in silence for a moment. Apart from a slight whiff of woodland flora, the air reeked of petrol fumes. Curious, the lead investigator dropped on his hunkers and peered in through the driver's shattered door frame. Peering into this topsy-turvy world of uncertainty, he couldn't shake off the unsettling feeling of chaos. His eyes adjusting to the gloom, he heard the metallic clicking sound of cooling metal.

He paused in reflection for a moment and tried to take it all in. Stretched out over a crumpled roof, a middle-aged paramedic was attending to a young female passenger. Her hair matted with blood, she carried that all too familiar haunted look of death. Suddenly, the situation took a turn for the worse and things didn't look promising. Held in place by the seatbelt, her lower body remained trapped by the mangled passenger door.

'Is she alive?' he whispered.

The paramedic acknowledged with a nod.

'How did you get here so quick?' asked Sergeant Fallon.

'I was on my way to Riding Mill when the response call came in over my radio.'

The sergeant took off his peaked cap and scratched his balding scalp. Late forties, squat, with a square jawline, he had inquisitive mouse-like eyes that were constantly on the move.

'Not the best of situations, I'm afraid.'

'What happened exactly?'

'When I checked the ANPR, this vehicle was down as a red BMW.' The sergeant turned and pointed to it. 'This one is silver, and that's when I suspected it was riding on false plates.'

'A copper's nose,' Mason grinned. 'What happened next?'

'After I pulled them over along the Western Bypass, I recognised the female passenger. When I asked the driver to step out of his vehicle, he took off like a bat out of hell.' The sergeant exhaled sharply, as if replaying the moment in his mind. 'Before we'd even reached the A69, he was doing a hundred and twenty.'

Mason stared at the wreckage. 'How did it end up down here?'

'Approaching the T-junction, he clipped the nearside verge, and the vehicle rolled over several times before leaving the road. It wasn't the greatest manoeuvre. Not at that speed.'

'Where's the driver now?'

'There's a team out looking for him.'

Mason stared out across the open countryside. 'In which direction did he go?'

'East,' the sergeant replied, pointing a finger in the general direction of the distant treeline. 'He'll not get far. There's a helicopter on its way.'

'Were you able to get a clear view of him?'

'Not really. He was wearing a baseball cap and dark tinted glasses. What had started as a minor road traffic violation soon escalated out of control. It all happened so quickly, but I'd certainly recognise his voice if I heard it again.'

'Distinct was it?'

'Yeah. He had a funny sort of Yorkshire twang.'

'Middlesbrough, do you say?'

'No, more Leeds.'

Mason heard the helicopter but could not see it. Then, through a gap in the treeline, he recognised the familiar figure of Stan Johnson. Early fifties with an unruly mop of hair, the scene of crime manager was a welcome addition. A stickler for detail, Johnson was standing at the top of a worn footpath and barking out instructions to anyone and everyone in sight.

Mason stared up at him, and then shouted. 'I'm down here, Stan.'

'Jack. How the hell did you get here so fast?'

'I heard the response call over my radio and joined in.'

Reaching the bottom of the ditch, Johnson turned to face him. 'What have we got?'

'One female suspect trapped in the passenger seat of a stolen BMW. She's suffering extensive head, chest, and leg injuries. There's a paramedic in attendance, and an ambulance is on its way. From what I can gather, the driver's male, around five-ten, and was last seen running away in an easterly direction.'

'He'll not get far,' Johnson confirmed. 'There's a dog team out looking for him.'

'I'd be careful, Stan. It could be The Suitcase Man.'

'Thanks, Jack. I know you've got my back,' Johnson smiled. 'So, who's the female passenger?'

'I suspect she's an accomplice.' Mason's eyes toured the crash scene as if to confirm his statement. 'Based on my observation, the outlook is not positive.'

'It's one hell of a mess, if you ask me. Let's hope she pulls through,' Johnson acknowledged.

'Yeah, but I have my doubts.'

Their eyes met. 'The vehicle was stolen from Tesco's car park in Jesmond around 10:15 this morning.'

'You people don't hang about, Stan.'

'No. Operation Sparrow Hawk has got everyone on their toes.'

'Something had to give.'

Johnson's eyes scanned the horizon.

'If he's out there, Jack. We'll find him.'

'What about the accident teams?' Mason asked.

'They should be with us shortly.'

Every few minutes, Mason's mobile kept pinging. This wasn't the right time or place and switched it off.

The moment the ambulance arrived, he heard the paramedic relay his findings back to the hospital crash team. His words sounded hollow, matter of fact.

'Scalp lacerations to the skull, subdural haematoma.'

What other injuries this woman was suffering, he dreaded to think. Survival hung in the balance, with unpredictable results. It was then he observed a group of Fire Rescue members approaching from the top of a steep bank. There were three in total. One carrying cutting gear, the others a hydraulic jack, crowbar, and rope chains. They would soon have her out of there, and with any luck, she would recover. He wasn't hopeful. Not with severe head trauma, he wasn't.

Stan Johnson was right. It was one hell of a mess.

CHAPTER THIRTY-FOUR

David Carlisle had steered well clear of Jack Mason's celebrations that evening; he thought them premature. Now fighting for her life, he had grave doubts whether Angelica would pull through. It had taken emergency crews all of forty-five minutes to free her from the wreckage of the stolen BMW. Apart from massive blood loss and lacerated flesh, paramedics had difficulty in inserting a breathing tube during the twenty-minute ambulance ride to Newcastle Royal Victoria Infirmary. After a CT scan showed brain swelling, she underwent emergency surgery to remove part of her skull and stop multiple brain haemorrhages.

Now in intensive care, security was tight. The chances of Angelica regaining consciousness and making a meaningful recovery seemed slim. The news wasn't good, and neurosurgeons acknowledged that an early prognosis was extremely difficult, as many patients defied all sense of reasoning. More so in this young woman's case. Her life was hanging in the balance.

Angelica's arrest quickly spread, capturing the public's imagination. Strange as it was, neither the media nor the police had the foggiest idea who this young woman was. At this crucial stage in their investigations, Carlisle was more concerned about what was going on inside the killer's head. The motives to kill were complex, but the outcomes more difficult to comprehend. Still out there, the man was a dangerous predator who would stop at nothing to accomplish his goals. Having run from the scene of the crash, search teams believed he'd flagged down an unsuspecting motorist to make good his escape. Anything was possible, but having gone to ground so quickly, the killer's mind-set would lead Carlisle to think that no other explanation was plausible.

It had just turned four o'clock when DC Carrington finally pulled up outside the snooker centre in Gateshead. Barely a five-minute drive from the High West Street police station, this was their last call of the day. Having worked through a list of potential students known to have been close to Colin Henderson at the time of his demise, classmate Terence Walker was now of major interest to them.

Sitting inside the undercover vehicle, Carrington turned to the profiler as if her mind was elsewhere.

'I'm intrigued by this new CCTV footage that Harry Manley has recently picked up.'

'In what respect?'

'The guy caught on camera bears a striking resemblance to the man seen passing the corner shop near to where John Lawrence's body was discovered.'

Carlisle unbuckled his seat belt and stared out of the windscreen.

'What was the quality like?'

'Not good, I'm afraid.'

'Anyone with him?'

'Just the East European woman.'

'What time was this?'

'Shortly after six on Thursday evening.'

'Rush hour. That is interesting. Which means they could be local,' Carlisle acknowledged.

'Those were my sentiments, but what we really need is the facts.'

Stopped at the check-in desk, Carrington showed her warrant card to a doorman in his late sixties and signed the visitors' book. Seconds later, someone ushered them into a small back room and away from the table action. As luck would have it, their suspect was already sitting waiting for them. Terence Walker looked much older than nineteen. Not a tall man, he wasn't sporty looking either. Around sixteen stone, his enormous pot belly hung over baggy jeans, and his T-shirt was covered in food slops.

Over the years, the profiler had learnt that some thoughts were best kept under wraps. His job was to get inside the killer's head and steer well clear of police affairs. But the small team of detectives who had travelled down to Leeds that morning was an utter waste of time. The killer was still in the northeast, but where he had no idea.

After brief introductions, they sat in a corner seat and away from distractions.

'So,' Carrington began, 'you and Colin Henderson were out drinking the night he was murdered. Mind telling us why you haven't gone to the police before now?'

Walker blushed. 'I was...'

'You were what?' said Carrington, pen poised.

Walker cleared his throat. 'I gave you people a

statement a couple of weeks ago. What more do you want from me?'

'Answers,' she groaned.

Walker shook his head and remained tight-lipped.

'The night Colin Henderson went missing, people saw you drinking with him in the Whickham House on Bensham Road. According to your statement, you alleged a young female accompanied Colin that night?'

'Did I?'

'Don't be clever with me, Mr Walker. We've got it on camera.'

The suspect's face drained. 'What is it you want from me this time?'

The detective presented Walker with an e-fit image of Angelica and asked, 'Is this the young woman you and Colin were with that night?'

'I'm not sure.'

'It's important,' she insisted. 'Take a closer look.'

Walker gave the slightest shake of the head and muttered something inaudible.

'When I rang you earlier, you told me Colin's new partner didn't sit right with you. What did you mean by that?'

'I had difficulty connecting with her.'

Carrington raised an eyebrow. 'You obviously spoke to her.'

'Yes, but she wasn't interested in anything I had to say.'

'Are you suggesting she froze you out of her conversation?'

'You could say that, yes.'

The young man seemed reluctant to cooperate, and Carrington had picked up on it. 'I'm confused, Mr Walker,' she said sternly. 'This was your friend's first big date, and yet you still went ahead, and gate-crashed the party.'

'That's not true.'

'So why join them?'

'Colin didn't fancy going it alone and asked me to tag along with him. It was a confidence thing.'

Carlisle listened as Walker huffed and puffed his way into another tight corner. The more he opened his mouth, the deeper the hole he dug. It was that kind of interview.

'What confuses me,' Carrington continued, 'is why you went to the pub in the first place. It seems only natural they'd aspire to be alone on their first date, don't you think?'

Walker hesitated. 'Yeah, I suppose so.'

'I know so,' Carrington insisted.

Walker looked at her, annoyed. 'If I'm honest with you, this wasn't the first time they'd met in the flesh.'

'Really. And what makes you say that?'

'They'd chatted over the Internet frequently before they met.'

Carrington shot Carlisle a puzzled look.

'This wasn't mentioned in any of your statements.'

'I was never asked,' Walker bluntly replied.

The detective drew forward in her seat. 'This wouldn't be a chat room site that Colin was involved in, by any chance?'

'Yeah. Why?'

'Which one?'

'I've no idea. Colin was involved in several, as I remember.'

'I take it this young woman was offering your friend an enjoyable night out?'

Walker reddened. 'Where is this interview heading?'

'Oh, come on,' said Carrington. 'I'm not naïve. That's why he invited you along with him, wasn't it? You thought you were onto a good thing... didn't you?'

Walker remained silent.

Carrington checked her notes. Something didn't sit right, and whatever it was, she was determined to get to the bottom of it.

'What else did you find strange that night, Mr Walker?'

The young man hesitated, his expression puzzled.

'It was weird.'

'Weird?' Carrington scowled. 'What was weird?'

'This white Transit van that was parked up in the pub carpark; it was facing the entrance door.' Walker leaned back in his seat, his fingers gripping the armrest. 'It was weird, I tell you. Every time I went outside for a ciggy, the guy in the van kept staring at me.'

'Perhaps he was waiting for someone.'

'I wouldn't say that,' Walker shrugged.

'Oh, and why not?'

'Cos...'

'So, you went outside for a ciggy. What happened next?'

'I'll come straight with you,' Walker blushed. 'I do like the odd spliff now and then.'

'A spliff?'

'Yes, but I'm no addict. It was just a bit of cannabis.'

Walker smiled philosophically as if glad to have broached the fact, and Carrington had caught his reaction. 'This man in the Transit van? What did he look like?'

'Difficult to say. He was wearing a hoodie and dark sunglasses.'

Carlisle felt a sudden adrenaline rush.

'How old was he?'

'Thirtyish.'

Only the noise of clattering snooker balls could be heard, and the sound of inaudible chatter. When a car horn tooted in an outside street, it caused Walker to flinch. Then Carrington looked up at him as she spoke. 'I'm struggling to find a connection here, Mr Walker. What does a thirtyish van driver have in common with this eighteen-year-old woman your friend was dating? Is there something you're not telling me?'

The suspect stiffened. 'Look,' he replied. 'I don't like the tone of your questioning.'

'So, this man's appearance spooked you. Is that what you're saying?'

'Yeah—'

'What happened next?'

'When it was my turn to get the drinks, they told me they were leaving.'

'Leaving to go where?' asked Carrington.

'They didn't say.'

'Okay, so what did you do then?'

'I ordered another pint.'

'And?'

Walker drew back. 'When I returned, they'd gone.'

'Gone where?'

'How the hell would I know?'

'What time was this?' Carrington asked flatly.

'Around ten o'clock.'

'And that was the last time you saw Colin?'

Walker lowered his head. 'Yes, it was.'

'This van driver you spoke of. Where was he in all of this?'

'That's the thing. When I went outside to look for them, the van was nowhere to be seen.'

Carlisle folded his arms across his chest and continued his silent observation. Carrington was doing fine. Walker was floundering, and the detective was in complete control.

'Could they have booked a taxi?' she quizzed.

'Colin would never do that. He was a tight bastard at the best of times.'

A ghost of a smile swept across the detective's face. 'Maybe this young woman had a car, and they left in it together.'

'If they did, she was well over the legal limit.'

Pen poised, Carrington drew back in her seat. 'Do you know what, Mr Walker? I find it hard to believe that you've not gone to the police before now with your story.'

Walker protested bitterly. 'I gave you people a statement a few weeks ago and have heard nothing since.'

'Yes, but none of this information was in your previous statement.'

Walker's jaw dropped. 'You people never asked.'

It was easy in hindsight. At the time of Walker's interview, nobody knew that Angelica was the killer's accomplice. Had they done so, then things would have turned out differently. Carlisle consulted his notes.

'After your friend left the pub that night, did you try to make contact at all?'

'I rang his mobile on several occasions, but it always went straight to voicemail.'

Carrington cast Walker a look of disproval. 'Which suggests you were the last person to be seen in Colin Henderson's company.'

'What does that mean?'

Carrington closed her notebook, the official side surfacing.

'Mr Walker,' she began. 'I need you to accompany me back to Gateshead Police Station. And before you say anything that may be used against you in court, I would advise you to find yourself a solicitor.'

'What the hell for?' Walker protested.

'The night Colin Henderson was murdered, apart from the young woman he was with, everyone knew you were the last person seen with him.'

'That's ridiculous. How can you possibly know that?'

Carrington's frown lines deepened. 'This is all new to us, and your previous statement mentioned none of it.'

'What's going on here? I've done nothing.'

'That's for us to decide,' the young detective said, pursing her lips. 'Had you been forthright in the first place, I doubt we'd be sitting talking to you now.'

The suspect lowered his head as though a judge had sentenced him to death. His hands were shaking, and he was perspiring profusely. Now caught up in a murder enquiry, it didn't mean that Walker was the killer. Far from it. From what Carlisle could glean, Angelica had been using the internet chatrooms to lure her victims into a web of deceit. It was a dangerous game, and one with deadly consequences.

It was time to dig deeper.

CHAPTER THIRTY-FIVE

Hardly anyone socialised with Jack Mason these days, not since he bust up with the fancy woman. She wasn't attractive either. Mid-forties, peroxide blonde hair, and lacking in feminine attributes. On the few occasions they'd met, David Carlisle could not think of anything nice to say about her. Taciturn and undemonstrative, she was a woman of few words. He'd often wondered whether his colleague was genuinely looking for love in his life or had fallen off the rails after a stressful divorce. The emotional challenges were immense, and Mason still hadn't got over the feeling of betrayal and mistrust. Marriage breakups could be extremely painful, not to mention his colleagues' ex-wife's solicitors who had put him through monetary hell these past few years.

'Take a seat,' the chief inspector muttered.

It was mid-afternoon, and Carlisle imagined, as he often did, that he was sitting in front of the headmaster awaiting a reprimand. Finding his colleague in an irritable mood had the same effect on his stomach as a dodgy landing at Newcastle Airport. No one claimed he was a bad copper, just that he bent the rules to suit himself.

Dressed in a black open-neck shirt, jeans, and brown leather shoes, he waited for Mason to finish his call. Not the best way to start a meeting, he thought.

'What the hell is up with Sutherland?' Mason said irritably. 'The stuck-up bitch wants me to hold another press conference.'

'Really?'

The chief inspector banged the phone on its cradle in a show of contempt.

'She's got some nerve. I'll give her that.'

'What's the problem, Jack?'

'If you're willing to stick your head above the parapet nowadays, someone will take a pop at you. It's what policing has come down to.'

'Sounds like I got out at the right time.'

'Believe me, things have moved on a lot since your days in the force.'

'In what way?'

'Everyone is answerable nowadays. Its political correctness gone mad. Whatever happened to freedom of speech?' Mason locked eyes with him. 'How can a conservative organisation such as the police suddenly become restrained by the thought-crimes that obsess these so-called political radicals? It's the minority ruling the majority.'

Carlisle was used to witnessing the crushing of people's pride, but this was beyond ridiculous. Things were getting out of hand. Even the morning briefing had ended up a bad-tempered affair.

Mason shook his head in resignation. 'All I need now is another murder on my hands and this place will implode.'

'Can't help you there, I'm afraid.'

'No, I guess not,' Mason conceded, puffing out his

cheeks. 'I've got dozens of officers out searching the city, and not a single sighting.'

'It's the way their minds work. Serial killers have a knack of avoiding us. That's what we're up against, unfortunately.'

'Where the hell is he?'

Rant over, there followed a moment of reflection. Only the sound of the window blinds flapping in the breeze. Trying his utmost not to make a dangerous situation worse, Carlisle trod cautiously.

'He's out there somewhere, Jack.'

'I know, but finding him is proving difficult.'

'Something to bear in mind is, a lioness always protects her cubs no matter what the circumstances are.'

Mason craned his neck. 'Is this another one of your infamous riddles?'

'No, but he's bound to come to Angelica's rescue at some point.'

'And do what exactly?'

'It's difficult to say, but you'll need to keep a watchful eye on the hospital.'

Mason looked at him, puzzled, as though his words were stuck in his throat. 'There's no way he can snatch her out of there. Not with the amount of armed police officers patrolling the wards.'

'The moment he feels ready, he'll make his move.'

'Fool if he does,' Mason groaned.

Carlisle shuffled awkwardly. He'd wanted this to sound like a reminder rather than the suggestion it was. Short on clues and ideas, Mason was pinning his hopes on Interpol getting back to him. Without a name or country of origin, any form of identification was proving difficult. Angelica, it seemed, was making his colleague nervous. That much was obvious.

'Just out of interest,' Carlisle asked, 'how was the BMW stolen?'

'There's mention of some stupid clown returning an empty supermarket trolley back to the collection point.' The DCI forced a laugh. 'They left their car keys in the ignition with the engine running. Can you imagine that?'

'They're making it far too easy for him.'

'Tell me about it.'

'What about fingerprints?'

'He wore leather gloves.' Mason shook his head in annoyance. 'And, might I add, after an extensive fingertip search of the crash scene, we found nothing in the way of blood sample.'

'Lucky escape by the sounds.'

'Remarkable, more like.'

'How come he escaped the accident unscathed?'

Mason twisted his face. 'According to the experts, the impact was all on the passenger side of the vehicle. If she had a handbag or phone with her, he obviously grabbed them before he ran off.'

'He's organised, and intelligent with it.'

'So it would seem.'

'Without proof, how can we be certain it was him?'

Mason's stare hardened, as if taken aback. 'Simple. Footprints found at the accident match those lifted from previous crime scenes. Tom Hedley's in no doubt.'

'So, they were working together?'

Mason grinned. 'Let's see what Tom has to say before we go stating the obvious.'

Carlisle declined to comment, just fought his usual interior battle about exactly when to give up a lost cause. Angelica was key, but his colleague's tone betrayed his frustrations. Still in intensive care, there was no likelihood of questioning her. Patience. They would need bags of it, but Mason was coming up short.

'What's the latest hospital bulletin?'

'It's not favourable, I'm afraid.'

'Is she conscious?'

The DCI's fingers hovered over the keypad. 'Her neurologist reckons it could be weeks before she comes out of her coma, and there's no way of knowing whether there's permanent brain damage.'

'Little chance of an interview by the sounds.'

'It would appear not.'

'What about the suspect we picked up from the Gateshead snooker club?'

'You mean, Walker?'

'Yes,' Carlisle nodded.

'He's not the killer, if that's what you're thinking.'

'No, I didn't think he was.' Carlisle veered from the cutting edge. 'He's definitely holding back on something. I got the impression he was looking for a good time.'

Mason checked his watch.

'This chatroom site that Colin Henderson was involved in. They took down his wall and removed his posts.'

'That's odd. Do you suspect these people were grooming him?'

'We believe so. If not, it's mighty suspicious, don't you think?'

'When did you discover this?'

'When Walker was brought in for questioning, the tech boys seized his phone. Looking at his text messages, Angelica is grooming their victims with promises of sex.'

'I had a feeling that's how she was operating.'

Mason shook his head slowly. 'How will the killer react now that his accomplice is being held in police custody?'

'He'll not stop now. Not whilst he has a taste for it.'

Mason's face dropped. 'Do you think he'll attempt to reach out to her?'

'Nothing will impede a serial killer; even you know that. Apart from missing her adulation, he'll need to work harder from now on. He'll adapt, trolling the chatrooms under a new screen name to ensnare his unsuspecting victims. This one has a mission to fulfil, and that's what worries me.'

'I thought as much,' Mason groaned. 'I was hoping you'd say otherwise.'

'It's the way his mind works. He'll not take to it lightly.'

Mason sat back in his seat, both hands behind his head.

'Something is bound to give, surely?'

'True,' Carlisle replied, barely masking his growing misgivings. 'Any more developments from the West Yorkshire Police?'

'No. Nothing. You were right about one thing, though. Inspector Greystone believes the killer lives in the northeast and travels to Leeds to work. He has a team out working on it, but I'm not expecting a great deal to come from it.'

'You never can tell with these things.'

Mason forced a wry smile. 'No. I guess not. We're still covering the A1(M) in both directions and further restricting his movements. Who knows, with any luck, road traffic will catch up with him.'

Carlisle stared at the map attached to the office wall and pointed a finger at it. 'If he's stealing vans to order, he'll need a place to keep them. Not just the vehicles, but somewhere to carry out his dirty work.'

'A lock-up, perhaps?'

'It makes sense, and it ties in nicely with having a large freezer at his disposal.' Carlisle stood and circled the map with the tip of his pen. 'You may wish to broaden your search to this area. Take in a few industrial estates.'

'We don't have the resources.'

'What other options do we have?'

Mason gave him a studious look. 'Not a lot.'

'What about witness statements? Has anything come of the door-to-door enquiries?'

'Nothing of interest. Why do you ask?'

'Pity. I was hoping for some better news.'

The skin around Mason's mouth tightened as he leaned forward to speak. 'This geographical profiling you're working on. Is there any chance of narrowing the field?'

'In what way?'

There followed a sharp rap on the office door, and DC Manley entered.

'Yes, Harry?' Mason said, closing the lid of his laptop.

'Is this a private confab, or can anyone join in?'

There were smiles, but no laughter.

'What can we do for you, Harry?'

'This Reggie geezer. The one at the Cumberland Arms.'

'What about him?' Mason asked.

'I've been reading through the interview transcripts, and Reggie reckons he met this woman through a dating website called Cherubins.'

'Never heard of it.'

Manley puckered his lips. 'You don't know what you're missing, boss.'

'Sod off. Get to the point.'

'I've been trawling the Internet and may have found something of interest.'

Mason cocked his head to one side. 'Like what?'

'According to the website writeups, Cherubins specialises in Russian women offering a good time and promises of sex.'

Mason laughed. 'I wouldn't have expected them to sell anything else.'

'As I remember, Reggie had met this woman in the Cumberland Arms. I'm not a gambling man, but I reckon it was her. The thing is, why there?'

'I thought Rob Savage was dealing with that?'

'He is.'

'So why are you getting involved?'

Manley let out a long sigh. 'I know it's not much, but when I read that Eastern European ladies were involved, I thought I'd drop by and mention it.'

'Good man,' Mason nodded. 'Leave it with me.'

'There is one other thing,' Manley said as he turned

at the door.

'Oh, and what's that?'

'There's no mention of an Angelica on the site.'

Mason stared at Carlisle. 'I doubt that's her real name, anyway.'

'No, probably not.'

Intrigued, chatroom sites were high on the profiler's priority list. If these people were grooming their victims, then where were they slaughtering them? If there was ever an obvious motive to be had, then jealousy sprang to mind. It made sense, and he was only targeting young males.

Carlisle jotted it down in his notebook and circled it with his pen: *Motive jealousy?*

CHAPTER THIRTY-SIX

Wasp had seen enough for one day. Obnoxious TV presenters, so-called media experts dragging up bucket loads of bullshit about nothing. Who did they think they were? Most hospital security officers were computer based, anyway. Not like the Fat Controller who spent most of his time walking the corridors and challenging people. Drunks mainly, and at weekends. Top security was a different matter, of course. It meant armed police officers dressed in bulletproof Kevlar jackets, press button keypad entry, and heaps of cameras to manoeuvre around. Hospital security was tight. It had to be.

Once again, he meticulously examined the site map. Multiple layers of security guarding the front entrance, including closed circuit cameras and facial recognition technology, made life extremely difficult. More importantly, to Wasp, was the control room. Get a life, he groaned. If those geeks had a purpose in life, it was to stare at a computer screen all day. Bored out of mind, he groaned inwardly as another ambulance drew up alongside A&E and unloaded its sick patient. Blue lights flashing, this was the third arrival in as many minutes. Hospitals were naff since the parking ban had come into effect. Security here was ridiculous, and no one could move a muscle. Not without the Fat Controller knowing.

Wasp wasn't daft, and his name carried a sting in the tail. He had developed an attachment to it. It had an uncompromising, tenacious quality. His shrink thought he had a screw loose, but what did that idiot know? Most therapists were nuts anyway and had a long history of destroying people's sanity. He'd read somewhere that consultants had frazzled millions of people's brains after putting them on toxic drugs programmes. It was devastating stuff, and those parasites were making big bucks from it.

Angry, Wasp stared at the incoming text. Dressed in green scrubs, a stethoscope slung loosely around his neck, he endeavoured to blend in. His new disguise was awesome. He'd fooled everyone. And, according to the site map he carried in his pocket, he wasn't far from neurology. Guarded by cameras, from what he could see, it stood at the end of a long, winding corridor. Auxiliary was the way forward, and he had a spare uniform.

Striding towards one of the side wards, there was only one thing on Wasp's mind. To snatch Angelica from purgatory. She was trapped, handcuffed to a hospital bed, and sedated up to the eyeballs. These freaks didn't have a soul. He firmly believed in that. The drugs they used were powerful, but he'd learnt how to reverse them. It was all clever stuff, mind-blowing really, and he'd mastered the art of their dark secrets.

Now following the direction signs, he pushed on through the double doors marked SURGERY SUITE. It was quiet back here, spooky. Plain glossed walls, polished floors, and an overpowering stench of disinfectant. When he was a kid, he'd suffered all kinds of allergic reactions to chemical cleaning fluids. IEI, they had called it. An idiopathic environmental intolerance to low levels of common substances. It led to depression, and even worse, those dreadful anxiety attacks. He would need to wear a face mask next time – stop the fumes from scrambling his brain.

Gripped by uncertainty, Wasp checked the site layout and tried to get his bearings. No more cameras beyond this point. The rules strictly forbade them.

Easing forward, the fire door clanked as he pushed hard on the panic bar. It wasn't alarmed. Isolated from the rest of the building, he poked his head through the tiny opening and checked his surroundings. He could see the car park a short distance away, and beyond that, the student quarters. What he didn't know, or maybe he did, was just how far it was from the main entrance. Yes, there was excellent ground cover to wheel a bed-trolley around, and plenty of room for manoeuvre. But what lay beyond that?

Still speculating about the Fat Controller, Wasp pushed on regardless. Less than twenty metres away, a short corridor opened up into a large annex which wasn't on the hospital plans. Confused at first, he stared at the site map and tried to get a fix on his position. When that didn't work, a feeling of unease washed over him. He hated maps anyway, and the people who drew them always made mistakes.

Then, beyond the double swing doors, he suddenly pulled up. Not what he was expecting to find. This part of the hospital is where they carried out MRI scans.

Nuclear imaging. Injecting you full of shit called tracers, a known radioactive element that could do all kinds of nasty things to your body. Frustrated, he quickly doubled back on himself. The next corridor he came to was long and narrow, scattered with side wards which ran in every direction. Disoriented, he'd almost given up on it when he stumbled across the neurology ward. Overcome with emotion, he stared up at the sign.

'Not long now, my little sweety.'

Twenty minutes later, after another cursory check, Wasp strolled towards the stolen Peugeot. More than pleased with his findings, he slid into the driver's seat and fired up the engine. He still had a few things to fix, but he'd deal with that later. Once he'd changed into his new disguise, everything would be fine.

Chapter Thirty-seven

Working on a tip-off, DCI Mason had summoned a small select group of detectives to his office that morning. Things were moving at a snail's pace, far too slow for the impatient senior ranks. As Carlisle checked in, the calmness of the front desk struck him as odd, particularly given the considerable weight of Angelica's disappearance on everyone's mind. Snap decisions were being made, and according to the desk sergeant, everyone was keeping a watchful eye on the hospital bulletins. Nothing so far, but the team was ready and waiting in the wings.

Hand hovering over the phone, Mason stared at him from behind his desk.

'Coffee?'

'I'd love a cup,' Carlisle replied.

His colleague mumbled indecipherable instructions into the phone and hung up. Ignoring the sarcastic quips, the profiler sat across from them at the back of the room. The team were in jovial spirits, as if they'd had a tickle on the lottery.

Reaching over, he watched as the lead detective held up an official paper, announcing some favourable news from the Home Office. 'The Eastern European woman turns out to be Estonian,' Mason began. 'Her name is Angelica Glebova, and according to Dutch police, she's wanted for questioning about a series of credit card scams in Amsterdam.'

'Why wasn't she picked up on our database?' remarked Holt.

'It seems the Dutch authorities lost track of her six months ago, so that would account for any delay. Furthermore, I'm reliably informed she arrived in the country with fake documents.'

'What do we know about her background?' asked Carlisle.

Mason gave a little shrug. 'Born into a working-class family in the old Republic of Estonia, Glebova attended a basic comprehensive school near to the old city walls. According to city records, her father died from a heart attack when she was seven, and the family had to move to Kopli. It's a rundown district of Tallinn.' He paused in reflection, as if taking in the detail. 'Overrun by drug gangs, prostitution, and rowdy youths intent on causing trouble late into the night. It's not a delightful place.'

'Sounds like she had a rough upbringing,' said Holt, shaking his head.

'It's the classic background,' Carlisle acknowledged. 'Childhood neglect, and low self-esteem. That's how vulnerable young women frequently get caught up with human trafficking gangs. There's little wonder she's fallen into the wrong hands.'

Mason huffed, 'Let's not loose site she's a wicked bitch.'

The chief inspector's outburst had taken everyone by surprise.

'Do the Dutch authorities have an Amsterdam

address?' asked Hedley.

'Yes, but she vacated the premises six months ago.'

'I presume that's when she slipped into the UK?'

Mason took a sip of coffee and stared down at his notes. 'As far as human trafficking is concerned, the Dutch authorities have no evidence to support such a claim.'

'If she's wanted for questioning in connection with credit card fraud, she's bound to be part of a gang.'

'I would have thought so,' Mason agreed.

Holt shuffled awkwardly in his seat. 'Credit card fraud runs rife in Europe. It's the number one crime at the moment.'

Mason rasped a two-day stubble. 'Let's not jump to conclusions here. We have a name to work with, and I've circulated her details to every police force in the land.'

Carlisle felt pleased with Mason's remarks but chose not to express it. Sex trafficking was one thing, but murder was a whole different ball game. Whoever the killer was, he was hiding behind the mask of uncertainty. Was he a foreigner, too? Someone who had jumped ship and illegally slipped into the country.

Then Tom Hedley's voice cut through the rest. 'Is there any more news on this young woman's progress?'

'She's out of the coma, but is not responding to sights and sounds,' Mason replied. 'They are doing more CT scans tomorrow morning, so hopefully we'll have some better news.'

'Do we know if any permanent brain damage has been done?' asked Hedley.

'Not at this stage, we don't. Any improvement, and the

hospital will be in contact.'

'Shit,' Manley swore. 'That could go on for weeks.'

'It's the nature of the beast, I'm afraid.'

'Sounds like this could go either way,' said Carrington, shaking her head.

'I agree, but we need to look on the positive side.'

'True. It could have been much worse.'

Mason allowed himself a smug smile as he turned to Carlisle. 'Any thoughts about what the killer's next move might be?'

At that, the profiler snapped open his briefcase and pulled out a thick bundle of reports. He opened the top file and stopped at the desired place. 'I've been trying to get a fix on locations where the killer might be hiding. Once the surge of his immense power subsides, he will undoubtedly experience a strong need to satisfy his deepest desires and cravings.'

Hedley cocked his head to one side. 'If Angelica lures his victims through social media sites, then how will he operate without her?'

'He'll work around it, Tom,' Carlisle confirmed. 'It's in his nature to do so. Once these people get a thirst for it, it's difficult for them to stop.'

'Does that mean he'll strike again?'

'Yes, unfortunately.'

Mason's face dropped.

As their conversation splintered into smaller groups, Holt removed a sheet of paper from a folder and placed it on the table. It was a copy of the hospital bulletin.

'What if Angelica makes a remarkable recovery?' the sergeant announced.

Carlisle smiled meekly. 'She'll not talk to any of us, if that's what you're thinking.'

'Not even to you?'

'I doubt it.'

'Is this something to do with hybristophilia?'

'She's obviously infatuated by him, and probably worships the very ground he walks on.'

Mason gave Carlisle a withering look. 'Yeah, but a sheep can be meat, and it can also be wool.'

Carlisle grinned but said nothing.

More coffee arrived, and Mason gave out a few hurried instructions as the meeting wound down. It wasn't a solid plan, Carlisle felt. More of a spur-of-the-moment thing. They were slowly building up a mental picture of how Angelica had arrived in the country, and what she'd got up to when here. As the office emptied, they asked Sue Carrington, who had said very little so far, to stay behind. Something was afoot, and whatever it was, Carlisle was curious.

'This theory of yours about the killer having some sort of lock-up,' the chief inspector began. 'I've been giving it some thought. I'm intrigued by this geographical profiling you've been conducting. If you have any places in mind, I'd like to hear about them.'

'Yes, I do.'

'Good. In which case, I need you and Sue here to do some digging around for me.'

'There's no guarantee it will work.'

'I'm aware of that, but I'm willing to take that risk.'

Carlisle considered this. 'It has its merits, and the killer is predictable.'

'He'll not stop now; you've already told us that.'

'Is this on a full-time basis?' quizzed Carrington.

Mason spun from the window to face her. 'Do you have a problem with that?'

'No. I just like to be clear about my instructions.'

It was Carlisle's turn.

'What about access to properties... search warrants, that sort of thing?'

Mason helped himself to a fresh mug of coffee and sat down at his desk. He knew the DCI had rushed things, but this time felt different. There was a change in his colleague's demeanour, as if he'd thought things through.

'That's where detective Carrington will come in handy, as she represents the police.' Mason made a friendly little hand gesture. 'Besides, you two seem to work well together and you're both level-headed.'

Carrington blushed.

'Does that mean we have a free hand in this?'

'Until I say otherwise. Yes.'

Knowing he was free from police protocols, Carlisle felt a weight lift off his shoulders, and had no need for further questions. He already had a plan and a rough idea of where to start. For what more could he wish?

CHAPTER THIRTY-EIGHT

Detective Carrington swung the unmarked Ford Focus estate onto the garage forecourt in Wallsend and switched off the car's engine. Not exactly a tourist attraction, more a run-down shantytown, the profiler thought. Row upon row of terraced houses, bored kids hanging around on street corners usually spelt trouble. This notorious hot spot was strictly off-limits to strangers. Leaving your vehicle unattended was a risky business, as people would strip it for spare parts and torch it.

She stared at Carlisle. 'Where do we go from here?'

'There's another industrial estate to the north, which majorly interests me.'

'Why do we always visit rundown areas, why not go up market for a change?'

'Because that's where the villains hang out.'

'Get a life,' she sighed. 'I thought we were looking at factory units?'

'We are, trust me.'

It was then a group of young thugs caught Carlisle's attention. Fifteen or twenty of them, closing in on their vehicle. As Carrington eased off the forecourt, he kept a watchful eye on the rear-view mirror. Half-expecting a brick to land through the window, he feared the worst. As the detective's foot hit the accelerator, the engine roared, and the car surged forward, pushing his head back against the headrest.

'Idiots,' she screamed, shaking a fist at them.

As rain fell, twenty minutes later, they emerged from the undercover vehicle and took stock of their new surroundings. He'd visited some dumps in his time, but nothing compared to this. Rundown factory units filled with a sense of abandonment and hopelessness, as if they were relics of a forgotten era.

'Typical,' Carrington huffed. 'Who'd want to run a business around here?'

'Someone obviously did.'

'It's a hovel,' she groaned.

'I know, and I have a bad feeling about this.'

The detective gave him a withering look. 'Just like the rest of the estates we've visited today. Whatever happened to that sixth sense of yours?'

No sooner had they stepped onto the tarmac than a Group 4 security van drew up alongside. Not the friendliest of introductions, either.

'What are you people doing here?' the pug-faced security guard announced.

'Police,' Carrington said, flashing her warrant card under his nose. 'Who owns these units?'

'A property company down south, but they've gone into liquidation.'

'Are none of them occupied?'

'Only the end unit.'

Carlisle made a mental note. 'What can you tell me about Auto Parts Distribution?' he asked, pointing to the crudely hand-painted sign above the door. 'Regular guys, are they?'

'How would I know?'

'Who occupies the building?'

The security guard stared at him as though it were a statement and not a question. 'I can't say that I've ever talked to them. What's your problem?'

'Who would know for certain?' asked Carrington.

'You'd need to check with the head office. What these people get up to is none of my business.'

Carlisle glowered. 'Does your company run CCTV monitoring by any chance?'

'We do. That's how I caught you nosing around.'

'So, where's the control room?'

'It's five minutes away. Why?'

'What about keys? Are you in charge of those, too?'

'That's me.'

'You are a busy man,' Carrington replied, with a hint of sarcasm in her voice. 'We need to look inside.'

'It's against company policy. I can only open up in an emergency.'

'Try murder?' the detective said, pointing up at the camera. 'Is that classed as an emergency, or do you have rules for that too?'

The stupid grin on the security guard's face had vanished.

'Murder,' he gasped. 'Around here?'

'Yes. That's why we need you to open up.'

***

The key had barely turned in the lock before an

overwhelming stench of diesel fumes hit them. It wasn't a large unit, half brick, and half double-stud walls. They'd installed skylights, and the floors were solid concrete impregnated with heavy oil. Running along one wall was a series of steel storage racks, and in front of them a smattering of rusty work benches. Cluttered with old vehicle parts, nothing had moved in months by the amount of dust that had gathered on them. But that wasn't all. It was a white Transit van that had unsettled them. And yes, its number plates were missing. Carlisle knew from experience that this estate had a reputation, but it wasn't unrest that he was experiencing. Get a grip. He shuddered. You're a criminal profiler; this isn't supposed to happen.

'What is it?' asked Carrington.

'It's not long been here,' said Carlisle, pointing at the white Transit van. 'The tyres are wet, and there are puddles on the floor.'

Carrington held her hand in front of the radiator grill as she spoke. 'You're right,' she confirmed. 'The engine's still warm.'

'Which means the owner can't be far away.'

At the rear of the building, they found a door. Curious, Carlisle was expecting to find it locked. It wasn't. Fumbling in the dark, the moment he flicked the light switch, it gave off a strange ominous glow.

The room was 'L' shaped, airless, and the floor was ice cold at the touch. Following in Carrington's footsteps, the place exuded an unsettling aura. The walls, red brick, were windowless, with no exits other than the one they'd stepped through. At the back of the room hung a pair of heavy duty plastic curtains. Crudely nailed to the ceiling by a thick batten of wood, they looked at odds with the rest of their surroundings. As he let his mind drift, the hairs on his neck prickled. Whatever dark mystery lay beyond the plastic curtains, his instincts were pulling him towards it.

Carrington turned nervously to face him.

'Over there,' she whispered.

'What is it?'

'I thought I heard something.'

'Rats,' he replied. 'The damn things are everywhere.'

'I'm not liking this,' she murmured. 'Who'd want to work here?'

As his eyes adjusted to the orange glow, he moved deeper into the building and closer towards the plastic curtains. At first it didn't register. Then it did.

A large deep chest freezer!

Carrington had spotted it too, but her detective instincts had already kicked in.

'Touch nothing,' she insisted. 'We may wish to use it as evidence.'

He noticed that the padlock on the freezer lid was loose and open, so he moved in closer. Smothering the lock with his handkerchief, he gently tugged on the hasp. Next, he lifted the lid. It was heavy. Awkward. On reaching mid-point, he felt a sudden rush of chilled air waft over his face. His mind implanted with malevolent thoughts, the moment the interior lights flicked on, he stooped to take a closer look.

He froze.

Eyes glazed over and staring back at him, Carlisle's

whole body locked solid. He swore he saw the eyelids flutter, a grotesque twitch impossible given the head's brutal separation from the body. Slowly at first, he lifted the freezer lid and felt his stomach lurch. Now lying at the opposite end of the unit, he caught sight of the real horror. Someone had painstakingly arranged the legs down either side of the torso, which had been severed mid-thigh. Toes pointing upwards, the feet looked surreal. It was then he spotted the hands. Whoever the perpetrator was, had meticulously arranged and paired them together using heavy duty duct tape. If the profiler needed proof that these were indeed a serial killer's trophies, he need to look no further.

As his grip on the freezer lid slackened, it slipped through his grasp with a thud.

Carrington shrieked.

'Sorry, Sue,' he whispered.

Terrified, the young detective's face had drained of all colours, and she was uncontrollably shaking with fright.

'You scared the living shit out of me. What's inside?'

'You don't want to go there.'

'Why not?'

'Best ring Jack Mason,' he instructed.

His entire world now pressing down on him, Carlisle was finding it difficult to breathe, let alone think straight. No matter how many corpses he'd dealt with over his career, it got no easier. He'd witnessed mutilation before, but nothing compared to this. This was insanity gone mad. There were no other words to describe it.

'I need to look for myself,' Carrington said, grabbing hold of the freezer handle.

Carlisle looked on perplexed. 'I wouldn't if I were you, Sue.'

'But I'm a police officer. It's my job.'

Slowly at first, the young detective struggled to lift the heavy lid. As the interior light flicked on, he strained his ears, waiting for a response.

He did not wait long!

CHAPTER THIRTY-NINE

Sometimes Jack Mason wondered where time went. Huddled around a computer screen, they'd spent the best part of the morning going back over hundreds of hours of CCTV footage. In what felt like a long and drawn-out session, tempers were frayed, and they had made very little progress. The footage wasn't the best quality either. The images were jerky and constantly kept going out of focus.

Holt at the controls, the detective sergeant annoyingly twiddled with the brightness button which seemed to take an eternity to get right. Still no better, they'd all but given up on it when a woman appeared at the bottom of the screen, pursued by a white Transit van. Mason noted the time and date on the video surveillance footage and watched as the driver slid from his cab and unlocked the roller-shutter doors. His face remained permanently hidden from view as he wore dark sunglasses and a cap pulled low.

Holt's voice broke the silence as he spoke first. 'That looks remarkably like Angelica operating the roller-shutter doors.'

All eyes now moved to the top left-hand corner of the screen.

'Can we sharpen up the image?' asked Mason.

'I doubt it, boss. The quality is crap.'

The moment Holt clicked the pause button, the lead detective shuffled awkwardly. 'Hold it right there,' he said, pointing his pen at the screen. 'That has to be her.'

The room fell silent as minds focused.

'I must admit,' Manley agreed, 'she looks uncannily familiar.'

'Grab a screenshot and let's make a few facial comparisons,' Mason ordered.

'I'm on it, boss.'

The chief inspector exhaled loudly as he latched on to something else of interest. 'There...' he announced, pointing, '... the van's rear driver's side hub cap is missing just as the one stolen from Byker.'

The sergeant zoomed in.

His mind all over the place, Mason leaned over to take a closer look. It was impossible to miss the large advertising slogan that was splashed along its side.

'Well, I'll be damned,' a voice from the back of the room declared. 'Isn't that the vehicle the West Yorkshire Police have been whinging on about?'

The sergeant shook his head in dismay.

'This bastard doesn't know when to stop.'

'Never mind the van,' Mason interrupted, 'where are they cutting the bodies up?'

'Not at the factory unit,' the senior forensic scientist replied stoically. 'He's using it as a storage base.'

Mason exchanged glances with Hedley. 'What are the chances he lives within easy walking distance of the industrial unit?'

'It's plausible.'

'Probable more like.'

Hedley pointed at the monitor screen. 'What do we know about the latest victim?'

'Not a lot. I'm eagerly awaiting the pathologist's report.' Mason furrowed his brow and scratched his forehead while deep in thought. 'I'm receiving reports of other people who have gone missing lately. It needs to be checked out.'

'Do you think these bastards could be about to deliver another body?' asked Manley.

'What are your views?' Mason asked, spinning to face the profiler.

Carlisle, who had said very little, pointed to the screen. 'Catching a psychopath presents a multitude of challenges, each one more daunting than the last. To him it's a battle of wits, and the only way we'll stop him is to catch him red-handed.'

The chief inspector twisted his face in a show of frustration. 'And how do you propose we do that?'

'Extend our search.'

'But we don't have the resources to check on every public house, let alone the thousands of young men who frequent nightclubs.'

Carlisle drew back in his seat. 'There has to be a way. Surely.'

Mason shrugged in a show of contempt.

'Here we go,' Holt suddenly announced, breaking everyone's thoughts. 'They're leaving the factory unit.'

Sure enough, no sooner had the roller shutter doors come down than their suspects appeared at the entrance door. Backs to camera, they moved left of the screen, making any form of facial recognition almost impossible.

'It looks like they're heading for Wallsend.'

'And on foot,' Carlisle noted.

Mason wrinkled his nose. 'That should make your geographical profiling much easier.'

'There,' Manley pointed out. 'That's a better mug shot.'

Holt rewound the tape and grabbed a screenshot of the suspect's face. Suspense hung in the air, creating a palpable tension.

'You were right all along, George,' Mason remarked. 'The quality's crap.'

Manley annoyingly popped another humbug into his mouth and sat back, smiling. 'Just out of interest, the property owners went into liquidation six months ago.'

'If true, that makes these people squatters.'

'It would appear so.'

'So much for site security. What more do we know about Auto Parts Distribution?'

'Established in 2006, they had a wide customer base covering the whole of the North-East of England.'

Manley drew back. 'Van hire, auto distributors, and now factory units. There's a pattern here.'

'Duct tape...' Mason remarked.

Everyone froze.

'Of course,' Hedley nodded in agreement.

Mason rasped the bristles on his chin. 'I want a list of names of every employer who ever worked for them. What they did, how long they were employed by the company, and the distribution outlets in which each of them was involved?'

'Anything else, boss?'

'We'll be asking everyone to give a DNA sample –

completely voluntary at this stage.'

'What about site owners?'

'The killer's an opportunist, and may have known the financial difficulties the company was in. Everyone needs to be checked out.'

Hedley referred to his notes. 'Motive jealousy, do you think?'

'It's difficult,' Mason acknowledged. 'What are your thoughts, David?'

Carlisle stared at the grainy surveillance stills. 'It's clear that he's harbouring his anger, and it's likely that jealousy is the driving factor behind it. To him it's a battle of wits, and the only way we will stop him is to catch him red-handed.'

'You're right,' Manley agreed. 'This individual is on a mission.'

Carlisle smiled meekly, then added. 'Missionary killers' murder because they're motivated to seek revenge or eliminate a specific group of people; they seldom move away from their selection criteria. That said, there's plenty of convincing evidence to suggest that Angelica was grooming their victims through the Internet chatrooms. Working together, these individuals are a lethal cocktail.'

'Hang on a minute,' Mason interrupted. 'If jealousy is the motive, this may account for his anger towards young men. Let's wind the clock back a couple of months. If his initial target was young Henderson, it proves Jennifer Oakwell wasn't part of his plans. So why did he kill her?'

'Witness elimination?' Manley shrugged.

Mason looked perplexed. 'I'm not so sure about that,

Harry.'

'What about this Bonnie and Clyde theory?'

'I'm not convinced about that either.'

Plenty of officers got along fine with each other, but not so in Mason's case. The chief inspector could be a grumpy old sod, and few were prepared to challenge him these days. Not even Harry Manley, which surprised everyone, as the detective constable was renowned for making snide quips.

'Okay,' Mason announced. 'There's plenty to think about here, so let's keep it simple.'

Taking a momentary break, Mason caught up with Carlisle. It was Monday, and the growing bottleneck of weekend crime had finally caught up with them. Every police cell in the building was full, and the duty solicitors were having to work flat out to clear the backlog. By the end of the day, things would ease off, but that was a few hours away.

'Here's my problem,' Mason said thoughtfully. 'According to her doctors, Angelica is now conscious but cannot remember a damn thing.'

'What are her solicitors telling us?'

Mason spoke in a hushed tone, his voice barely audible. 'We've yet to charge her with murder, and I'm in no hurry to do so.'

'And why not?'

Mason tapped the side of his forehead and smiled philosophically. 'On the surface, she appears to be suffering from temporary memory loss. What she doesn't know, not even her doctors, is that a team of trained specialists has been monitoring her progress.'

'You've lost me. I thought she was suffering from post-traumatic amnesia.'

Mason gave him a hapless look. 'She's not. That's what she wants everyone to believe. Having gained the trust of a sympathetic ear, she's beginning to open up. The nurse she's confiding with is not who everyone thinks she is. She's a trained psychologist with a shitload of qualifications. She's a plant, our best option for gaining insider information, and I aim to keep it that way.'

'You kept that quiet, Jack.'

Mason glanced back at the empty corridor, as if to check his surroundings. 'Some of what she's telling us is lies, but there is some truth mixed in. Shortly after she arrived in this country, she claimed that someone had coerced her into prostitution.'

'That's exactly what I thought had happened to her.'

'You were mistaken,' Mason said flatly. 'She's a liar, and I wouldn't trust her as far as I could throw her.'

'What else have you uncovered?' quizzed Carlisle.

'She claims to have been in a steady relationship with an older man, but has yet to mention his name. Most of what she's told us so far doesn't stack up.' His colleague looked at him sternly. 'It's my view she's trying to disassociate herself from the killer.'

'It's time we talked to her.'

'Try telling her solicitors that.' Mason gave him a pensive look. 'If anyone can get close to this Estonian woman, it's my psychologist. She's excellent at what she does, but it's now down to a waiting game.'

'Time's a luxury we can ill afford, Jack.'

'I'm aware of that, too.'

'He's angry, which means he's unpredictable.'

'Unless you have an alternative plan, what other options do we have?'

Carlisle didn't have an answer for that.

CHAPTER FORTY

It was Monday, and the soil sample found at the factory unit had drawn Jack Mason's investigations back to Byker, a district north of the River Tyne. The team's intensified hunt for the killer had kept the forensic team busy. Things were coming along nicely, and having formally identified the body found in the deep freezer as Kevin Price, a 26-year-old local engineer who had recently returned to Newcastle after holidaying in France, they were working flat out. Reported missing after failing to turn up for work, Price was last seen hanging around Wallsend bars.

In order to gather information about the victim's potential involvement with a young woman, detectives, who were aware of his solitary lifestyle, conducted a comprehensive house-to-house inquiry. Without a crime scene, the team was severely hampered, so establishing the victim's last known movements was crucial.

Sitting inside the undercover Ford Focus, Mason took another swig from a water bottle and stared at the building opposite. It was mid-afternoon, and his police radio had gone into hibernation. Earlier that day, reports of a stolen white van had scrambled the team into action. He'd heard nothing since. There was always something for which you could not account, and he understood that. Now parked several blocks away from where John Lawrence's broken body was found, Mason was feeling the strain. If this was the killer's drop zone, he could be onto something.

Thinking this through, Kevin Price's violent ending had hung heavily on the chief inspector's mind. His was a harrowing experience. One piece at a time. A sickening puzzle of trying to match dismembered body parts, only to find pieces were missing. A hand here, a leg there. It was stomach-wrenching stuff that he could have done well without. Mason was never keen on visiting morgues or path labs, but sometimes it came with the job.

Now facing the biggest murder inquiry in his entire career, he knew exactly what was going on inside chief constable Gregory's mind when the Yorkshire Ripper was at the height of his killing spree. When they finally caught up with Peter Sutcliffe – a Bradford lorry driver and a former grave digger – he had already committed thirteen horrific murders. God forbid the Suitcase Man was aiming to reach such staggering notoriety; it didn't bear thinking about.

The moment his radio spewed out some inaudible instructions, he caught the gist of it. A mile east, a stolen white van was heading his way and moving in heavy traffic. As a precautionary measure, Mason had banned all marked cars from the area but wasn't pinning any hopes on it. If this were the killer's vehicle, they would need to remain alert.

He heard a sharp rap on the nearside window and flicked the door release button. Moments later, the profiler slid into the passenger seat.

'Heard anything?'

'We're getting reports of a stolen white van heading in this direction.'

Turning abruptly, his colleague swung to face him. 'Sounds encouraging.'

'Don't get carried away; this is the third van today.'

'Really?'

Mason craned his neck as he peered out of the rear window. Nothing yet. There was a tall, red brick building to his left, offices to his right, and double yellow lines on both sides of the street. Directly up ahead, the road narrowed. Beyond that was a mini roundabout leading towards the town centre. Not the best place to stop a vehicle, but nowhere was perfect.

'Anything come of your enquiries?' Mason asked.

'No. Nobody recognises him.'

'Pity. We're close to the location where they found his body.'

'Why here?' the profiler quizzed.

'More importantly, Sutherland wants me to charge Angelica with murder.'

'That's premature, don't you think?'

Mason twisted his face. 'I've expressed my concerns in no uncertain terms. Not that she'll take a blind bit of notice. The stupid woman seems determined to go ahead with it. Media interviews, reconstructions, you name it, the area commander wants it.'

'It's not a clever idea, given the current conditions. It could spark him into committing all kinds of atrocities.'

Mason shook his head. 'Once Sutherland gets her teeth into something, there's no stopping her.'

'The killer won't give up now, Jack.'

'I know, and that worries me.'

'Mind, I can't say I blame you for putting up a fight.'

It was time to settle their differences, find out the profiler's inner thoughts.

'If you could change one thing right now, what would it be?' the chief inspector asked.

'That's a hypothetical question.'

'Maybe, but you're not tied down like the rest of us.'

'What's bothering you, Jack?'

Mason let out a deep sigh. 'What with Sutherland's crazy demands, it's impossible to duck under the radar these days.'

Carlisle burst out laughing. 'Get a life. You're blowing this out of all proportion.'

'I'm trying to be serious for once.'

'So am I.'

Mason exchanged glances. 'Let's park that to one side for a moment. The team's overstretched, and even you know it. Knowing where to concentrate our resources is my biggest concern. The killer's cunning and he'll be watching us like a hawk.'

'The one thing I've learnt about serial killers is, they stick rigidly to set plans. This one's no different, and his method hasn't changed one iota since his partner's arrest.' Carlisle made a little sweeping gesture with his hand. 'If I were in your shoes, I'd concentrate my efforts on the people who previously occupied the factory lock-up.'

'What, you think the killer could be an ex-employee?'

'Think about it. If you didn't know why the factory

unit had remained empty all these months, you wouldn't dare store body parts in it.'

'That's a valid point, but checking hundreds of distribution outlets will be a massive drain on resources.'

'He's local, Jack. He knows his way around this city. Finding him will prove difficult.'

'I can't disagree with that.'

Carlisle grinned. 'I'm not a gambling man, but it wouldn't surprise me to find he's still working in the auto parts trade.'

'Is that what you believe?'

'Yes. We just need to be patient, that's all. Without Angelica's help, he's bound to make a mistake. It's only a matter of time.'

'You and I should talk more often, my friend.'

Carlisle smiled. 'I doubt you'd listen, Jack.'

Mason lifted his eyes to the rear-view mirror, just as a white van came into view. He checked the ANPR, and sure enough, he discovered it was stolen. But that didn't mean a thing, as the killer had a nasty habit of switching number plates.

The chief inspector pressed the clutch and turned the key in one swift movement.

'Hold on to your hat,' his colleague grinned.

The moment the van's red taillights grew brighter, Mason swung in behind it. Eyes glued to the rear-view mirror, DS Holt's undercover pool car was up close and intimate. Too close for Mason's like, and he switched on his hazard warning lights to signal his intentions. Seconds later, Holt's unmarked vehicle pulled out of the pursuit.

Carlisle checked the satnav, then said. 'If he doesn't

join the Coast Road at the next junction, he could head for the Freeman Hospital.'

Mason felt an adrenaline rush.

'How far is that away?'

'Barely half a mile.'

Sticking rigidly to the speed limit, at the next mini roundabout, the van up ahead swung left. At least the driver hadn't spotted them, which was always a good sign.

'He's turning onto Freeman Road.'

'What the hell is he playing at?'

'He's checking the lie of the land, I'd wager.'

Mason slowed down as he reached the hospital turn, then stopped at the car park entrance. Thirty feet ahead, he watched as the driver turned into the first available parking space and came to a halt. He drove up behind it and boxed it in.

'Police,' Mason shouted, holding up his warrant card and hammering on the van driver's door. 'Mind telling me the registration number of your vehicle?'

The driver wound his window down and stared at him, confused. 'Beta, Gamma, Victor, Ninety-Six.'

'It's not what it says on the tin.'

Jumping out of his cab, the van driver moved to the front of his vehicle. Seconds later, he turned to face them. 'Some bastard's switched the number plates.'

'Is this your vehicle, sir?' Mason asked.

'No, it belongs to the company. I'm a delivery driver for FastTrack.'

His mind all over the place, Mason felt his stomach churn. 'Tell me,' he said, 'where do you normally park your vehicle at night?'

'Outside my house. Why?'

As soon as he noticed the switched plates, he grabbed the suspect's arm. 'Mind telling me where that is?'

'Yeah, Barry Street in Walker.'

Mason turned to face the profiler. 'Sounds like our friend is active again.'

'If it is him.'

Mason managed a wry smile. 'If not, I'll show my arse in Fenwick's window.'

The van driver stared at them, confused.

CHAPTER FORTY-ONE

Within weeks of Thomas Wilkinson's dismembered body being discovered at a local waste and recycling centre, a miscreant named Andrew Martin had come to Mason's attention. The evidence was thin, but the team believed Martin had hung around with Wilkinson's associates, and technically didn't have a job. Apart from claiming social benefits, Martin was conducting dodgy door-to-door drug deliveries to fuel his habit. Although their suspect seemed an unlikely source for an intensive surveillance operation, when Jack Mason received information he was dealing in high end car theft for Tony Fox, it all made sense.

As the cell door swung open, Andrew Martin moved awkwardly towards the interview room. There were no smiles, no friendly banter, just dogged determination. Brought in for questioning the previous evening and held on suspicion of murder, Martin looked exhausted. After a thorough search of the suspect's property, a knife found hidden inside a bag of clothes was currently under scrutiny. Anticipating a quick result, Mason remained optimistic.

The moment DS Holt activated the recording tape and announced the time, date, and those present, the atmosphere was strained. Sitting directly opposite, the chief inspector was in no mood for compromise. He thrived on interviews such as these and could always tell when a suspect was out of their comfort zone – they always reminded him of a frightened rabbit trapped in a car's headlights.

Mason stared at his interview notes. After a moment of consideration, he turned to address the suspect. 'Let's talk about your friend, Thomas Wilkinson.'

'What about him?'

'Care to explain where you were on Friday, April eleven around seven thirty pm?'

'I was out drinking. Why?'

'According to your previous statement, you were watching TV at a friend's house that evening.'

'If you say so.'

'I know so. After conducting a thorough search of your bedsit, we found a vital piece of evidence that places you near the crime scene around the time of Thomas's murder.'

'Like what?'

Mason shuffled awkwardly, expecting *no comment* to every question he posed. So far, so good. Things had got off to an excellent start, and he was in no hurry. His next question, when it came, was far more reaching.

'Your account of what happened that evening doesn't add up. You were outside the Globe bar in Railway Street at 07:20, and captured on camera. Also, someone saw you talking to Thomas.'

'No comment.'

'For the tape, I'm showing Mr Martin exhibit AD54.'

The chief inspector slid a monochrome image towards

Martin and assumed an unfriendly posture. 'At 09:30, someone saw you outside the Yard Bar in Newcastle wearing the same black hoodie, jogging bottoms, and white trainers.'

'No comment.'

'This is you, is it not?' Mason said, pointing to the monochrome image.

'No comment.'

'Care to tell me why you murdered Thomas Wilkinson?'

'Fuck you, Inspector,' Martin replied angrily. 'You can't pin that one on me.'

It was desperate stuff. If Martin folded now, they would undoubtedly charge him with murder. But would he admit to it?

'Tell me,' said Mason calmly, 'what did you do with the knife after you killed Thomas? Where did you hide it?'

Martin glared at him. 'That's a crazy statement. There's no way I'd stab my best friend.'

'Who mentioned anything about stabbing anyone?'

'Everyone knows Thomas died of knife wounds. It was in all the papers.'

'You're going to have to stop lying to us,' DS Holt said assertively. 'You're not making a convincing job of it. The fact is, early this morning, we recovered a six-inch bladed weapon from your property identical to the one that killed Thomas Wilkinson.'

Martin was digging a bloody big hole for himself, and his solicitor was allowing it to happen. Strange, Mason thought. Getting the suspect to cooperate was proving more difficult than he thought. What's more, they could only hold him in custody for twenty-four-hours. After that, they would need to apply for an extension, and he wasn't keen on the idea as he still didn't have enough evidence to lay charges.

Furious, he turned to his files and slid another monochrome image towards Martin. 'For the tape, I'm showing Mr Martin exhibit AD43.'

The suspect glared at him but remained silent.

'Just for the record, what were you doing in the Yard Bar at 09:42 that night?'

'No comment.'

'Isn't that on Scotswood Road?'

'You know it is.'

'Did you go there intending to meet with someone?'

'No comment.'

Martin drew back in his seat, his demeanour defensive.

'Just answer the question,' Mason insisted.

'I meet loads of people on Friday night.'

'We're not stupid,' said DS Holt, shaking his head. 'Whilst you've been banged up in custody, we've been busy going over your property. It's what we do best. It's what we're trained to do. The problem is, we've recovered several items of interest, including your computer.'

Martin stared at them through narrow eyes, but remained silent.

'Do you know what?' Holt gloated. 'It's fascinating what computers throw up. Facebook, Twitter, TikTok, people you link up with and never give a second thought to. It's all clever stuff. The thing is, on Friday, April eleven, around five thirty, you were engaged in an interesting chatroom conversation that we have been monitoring. It's all there, Mr Martin.'

'If you say so.'

'We know so. You'd met up with a Joseph Trotter that evening, hadn't you?'

'No comment.'

'Don't deceive me. You met up with him, didn't you?'

Martin shrugged, but remained tight-lipped.

'Now here's my problem,' said Holt, shaking his head. 'We know you messaged Joseph Trotter at precisely three-twenty-two. What you don't know, or perhaps you do and are not letting on, is that Joseph Trotter is an undercover police officer.'

Martin's face dropped. 'It was just a bit of fun.'

'Fun, Mr Martin? This isn't some sort of chat show, and I'm not a TV host sitting here. That's how you always meet up with your men, isn't it? You message them on Internet chatroom sites and build up a friendly rapport.' Holt held eye contact. 'I'd say you were grooming them... isn't that how you win over your victims?'

'I enjoy chatting to people. There's nothing wrong with that.'

'No, I suppose not,' Holt agreed, 'but what worries me is what goes on behind closed doors after you've taken them home with you.'

'What are you inferring?'

'Well,' Mason began. 'What did you intend to do with Joseph Trotter after you'd met with him that night?'

'He was an interesting guy.'

'I bet he was. Just like the other young men you

chatted up.'

Martin sneered back at them. 'No comment.'

Holt raised an eyebrow as he stared hard at him. 'The night Thomas Wilkinson was murdered, you were the last person seen with him. We're not stupid, Mr Martin. After you'd teamed up with him outside the Globe bar in Railway Street, you'd met up with him later that evening.'

'You're making this up. It's utter bollocks,' Martin said, turning to his solicitor.

'But is it?'

'You know it is.'

'You took advantage of him, didn't you?'

Martin's solicitor leaned forward. 'Those were your words, Sergeant, and not my client's.'

Mason stared at Martin for signs of weakness, then slid another vital piece of evidence towards the suspect. 'For the tape, I'm showing Mr Martin exhibit AD69. It's a still image taken outside Islam Khan's corner store in Dean Street, Byker.' Mason glared across at Martin and tapped the image with his pen. 'That's you in the picture, is it not?'

Martin said nothing.

'The night you met Thomas Wilkinson, you wore a black hoodie, jogging bottoms, and white Nike trainers.' Savage paused for effect. 'And do you know what? This person is wearing the same clothes that you wore that night.'

'It's not me.'

'How can you possibly say that? I haven't provided you with any information about the time this picture was taken or any other details about it. You're lying, Mr

Martin, and you're making this really difficult for yourself.'

'Perhaps we should take a break, gentlemen,' Martin's solicitor announced. 'I need to talk to my client.'

Holt leaned over and switched off the tape.

'Of course,' Mason replied irritably. 'Take your time. Your client will soon have plenty of that on his hands.'

'Let's not get facetious, Chief Inspector. My client is completely innocent, and you people know it.'

Mason's grin broadened. 'Surely that's up to a jury to decide, not me?'

'True,' Martin's solicitor acknowledged, 'but before you consider going down that avenue, perhaps you should ask my client where he was on the night Colin Henderson was murdered. Had you done so, then you may have approached this interview differently.'

Mason glared across at Martin's solicitor, realising he must have reasonable grounds to prove his client's whereabouts.

Bugger! he groaned. Surely not.

CHAPTER FORTY-TWO

Wasp braked hard the moment he spotted the marked patrol car – *just in case.* He needn't have bothered. The officer inside looked docile, but you could never be too careful with these idiots. Much to his relief, except for a few security lights guarding the back of the hospital grounds, this part of the complex was in darkness. No cameras to worry about – they were all at the front of the building. There was always the Fat Controller's room, but he'd deal with that later.

The moment he slid into the designated parking lot, there was an air of orderly calm. His first task was to secure the escape route; without which he was toast. Working at speed, he dragged the folding ROAD CLOSED sign from the back of the vehicle and erected it close to the approach road. Next, he slid the ramp into position and rolled out the wheelchair. One last check. Perfect. He was ready to rock and roll.

Deep into the night, he heard sirens wailing. This place never slept. There was always plenty to keep the hospital staff occupied, no matter what time of day it was. Breathing heavily, he trundled the empty wheelchair towards the rear of the staff accommodation wing, double-checking the curtains and smiling. All that remained now was to prise open the fire door – the one he'd wedged earlier. Once inside, it would all run like clockwork. Nothing to worry about, he laughed. Everyone was asleep.

Wearing a clean white shirt, navy slacks, and a comfortable pair of black shoes, Wasp felt a million dollars in his new porter's uniform. His wig was a tad uncomfortable, and a little too tight. If anything, he was more than pleased with the Swiss medical watch he'd nicked from the local charity shop. God, it was awesome.

Gripped by uncertainty, Wasp hung back in the shadows. Nerves jangling on edge, he swore he heard a high-pitched beeping sound the moment he entered the building. Physically shaken, he stood for a moment and listened. They had to keep security tight, so almost every door in the building was alarmed. Slowly at first, he lifted the wheelchair brakes with a resounding click, and listened. Everything worked flawlessly, just as he'd planned.

The route he took was less than two-hundred metres away from his intended target. Crammed full of cameras, this was dangerous ground to cover. Deep in the shadows, he could see the operating theatre, and chilled. Some people were circulating a myth that it was possible to reattach limbs to another person's body up to four days after amputation. Why bother going to medical school when you naturally possess surgical skills like his? Hand-eye coordination and manual dexterity came naturally to him. After all, he was well-practised in the art of cutting up bodies.

He'd read somewhere that a physician had transplanted a healthy hand from a dead patient to a living one, which he thought was awesome. How it would work with fingertip recognition he had yet to decide, but he was willing to give it a go. Being a surgeon meant you could perform amazing procedures, but it wasn't much help if you were dead.

He was about to move when two men came scurrying along the corridor, their footsteps echoing their arrival. One was carrying a human organ box, the other was wearing green scrubs. Given their status and fame, he was hoping they'd notice a fellow genius. They didn't, of course, leaving him absolutely gutted.

Annoyed, he wiped his face to remove the wetness and stood for a moment. It was then he noticed the neurological ward. Directly in front of him, slightly to his left, how things looked different in broad daylight. Night-time was full of surprises. Nasty places where strangers shouldn't go.

He tried the door. It was locked.

Nerves on edge, Wasp peered in through one of the glass panels just as a middle-aged woman joined him. Wearing blue scrubs, she looked at him oddly. Had she rumbled his disguise? If she had, it would be a first.

Hold your nerve!

Then, much to Wasp's relief, she punched a series of numbers into the push button keypad, and he made a mental note of the code. As the door swished shut, she turned to face him.

'How can I help?' she asked.

'I'm here to pick up a patient.'

'Which one?'

'She's due at the Imaging Department in twenty minutes.'

Building in confidence, he patted the empty wheelchair with assurance.

'Do you have a name?' she asked.

'Umm—'

'A bed number, perhaps?'

She looked him up and down, causing him to drop the clipboard he was carrying. He recovered it and pointed up at the list of names that were present on the patient board.

'It's the foreign lady I always have difficulty in pronouncing.'

'Ah, you mean Angelica Glebova?'

'Yes. That's the one.'

She glanced down at the computer screen. Something was wrong, and whatever it was, she was making him nervous. Wasp drew himself into the scene and tried not to think negative thoughts. He'd covered a lot of ground and wasn't giving in that easily. Even though he couldn't see his little sweetie, he still sensed her presence. Her cute little face. Her sweet, girlie voice. Excitement gripped him, and he was holding back the tears.

Then, glancing up, he spotted the armed police officer. Meek looking, and dressed in a familiar black combat uniform, he was standing in the doorway.

'Who sent you?' the duty staff nurse asked in a sombre voice.

'Why, is there a problem?'

'There seems to be some sort of mix-up. Ms Glebova has had another subdural haematoma and is back in intensive care.'

'Intensive care...' whispered Wasp.

'Yes. The doctors are in with her now.'

'Dearie, dearie me. I hope she's not in a lot of trouble.'

Niceties dispensed with, the duty staff nurse looked directly at him. 'I can check with the Imaging Department if you want,' she said, her hand hovering over the telephone receiver. 'It's always best to err on the safe side.'

Wasp forced a smile as he turned to leave.

'Best not waste any more of your precious time,' he said, using a well-rehearsed, sympathetic voice. 'I know you are extremely busy.'

'We are,' the duty staff nurse smiled.

Concealing his anger, Wasp punched the red door release button and watched as the doors swung open. Having remembered the security code, he knew he'd be back later.

'Best to err on the safe side,' he mused.

He rather liked that. It had a nice ring to it.

CHAPTER FORTY-THREE

Dragged out of bed at an unearthly hour, Jack Mason wasn't in the best of moods. Someone had breached hospital security, and the chief inspector was livid. Not only did someone attempt to snatch Angelica from her sickbed, but the entire area was now in a state of heightened alert. Worse still, he wasn't in radio contact. It was 06:00 and a shift change was imminent.

'Where the hell is the Controller?' Mason screamed.

Blue spinner lights flashing, his phone buzzing in his pocket, sergeant Holt stood before him, dripping with sweat. 'We've covered every inch of the ground, boss. Except for the staff car park, there isn't a lot more we can do until the dog teams arrive.'

'What about the rest of the buildings? How do we know he isn't posing as a patient?'

'We don't,' Holt shrugged.

'Who's in charge of checking them?'

'That's down to each individual ward.'

Mason peered at his phone for messages, then stood for a moment. 'Did no one think it conceivable that he would try such a daring mission? The woman was a major risk Goddammit – the killer's accomplice.'

The arrival of Stan Johnson had brought a calming effect. If there were flaws in their plans, the SOC manager would fix them. Stan was dependable and never missed a trick when it came to managing a crime scene.

Johnson stood for a moment, pondering.

'If the suspect wasn't a genuine hospital porter, how come he knew the security code to the neurological ward?'

The scene of the crime officer had asked a question that no one else had that morning, and it had taken them by surprise. It was Holt who was the first to react.

'The duty staff nurse should know the answer to that, boss.'

'If he's not a member of staff, he'll not hang around longer than necessary.'

Johnson shot Mason a glance. 'If it was the Estonian woman he was after, what did he intend to do with her?'

'God knows. She's in no fit state to move, let alone someone push her around in a bloody wheelchair.'

'Not now. She's back in intensive care,' added Holt.

Mason sucked in the air. 'There are far too many unknowns for my liking, Stan.'

'Whoever's in charge of security is facing an internal enquiry. That much is certain. If safety measures have been breached, then we must ensure the public's safety.'

'You're right, Stan,' Mason replied, grateful for some sound advice.

'What does your gut reaction tell you?'

'It's time we threw a security cordon around the entire complex.'

'I'd go for it, Jack. If he's posing as a hospital porter, and not a member of staff, it shouldn't be too difficult a problem to fix.'

There followed an awkward exchange of glances between them.

'Surely it's down to these people to vet their own staff?'

Johnson looked at him guardedly. 'I would have thought so.'

Mercifully, the incident did not cause any injuries to anyone. They'd been lucky. Had someone seriously challenged the killer, then God knows what would have transpired.

Johnson stared into the distance, thinking. 'Whoever he is, he's obviously familiar with the security layout.'

'That had crossed my mind.' Mason nodded.

By nine o'clock, the sun appeared, and it promised to be another beautiful day. In what had been a damp and dismal June, the warm weather had come suddenly. It was Race Week, and Mason was looking forward to some quality time off. Just when he thought he'd got to grips with the case, everything had turned on its head. Even Tom Hedley's team had thrown up very little in the way of fresh leads. These crimes took time. He realised that. Nothing was straightforward anymore. Loath to admit, it was time to get the profiler involved and bring some lateral thinking to the team.

He reached into his pocket and pulled out his phone.

'Ah, if it isn't Inspector Jack Mason,' a familiar voice called out.

The moment he clocked Christopher Sykes, Mason's stomach lurched. Never on speaking terms, where Sykes got his information from beggared belief. The trouble was, newspaper reporters had a way of finding things out.

He took a deep breath. 'What can I do for you?'

Pen poised at the ready, Sykes habitually brushed the flecks of dandruff from his jacket and said, 'Excuse the pun, Inspector, but there seems to be a rather large gathering of police officers around the complex. Would it have something to do with this Suitcase Man?'

'What suitcase man might that be, Mr Sykes?'

'Mind telling me what's going on?'

He pretended to act dumb. The last time he'd spoken with Sykes, he'd ended up complaining to the independent press standards about running an inaccurate story about a major crime case he was working on. He'd got nowhere.

'Why don't you check with hospital security?'

'I already have. I just thought I'd run it past you, that's all.'

Mason refused to be drawn in. Sykes was weird, and not to be trusted. Rumour had it he had been caught messing around with teenage girls in one of the local park toilets. Nobody could prove it, and that was the problem. The most likely scenario, as far as Mason could determine, was that people were trying to get their own back for salacious reporting.

'What do we know about this intruder?' the journalist asked.

'Not a lot. Why?'

'That's odd. I'd heard he'd tried to snatch the patient from their sick bed. Came through a rear fire door, apparently.'

'What else have you heard?' Mason sneered.

'Some say it was this Estonian woman he was after.' Sykes dribbled. 'Could be mistaken, but you know me. I always try to keep my readers informed.'

Like hell, Mason thought. Sykes' only interest lay in selling headline stories, no matter how many people he upset. It's what sold newspapers, what made scumbags like Sykes such an enemy of the police. It was time to put the record straight.

'Okay,' Mason began, 'don't quote me on this, but a few of my trusted lieutenants are currently out searching for him.'

'Anywhere in particular?'

Mason lowered the tone of his voice and pretended to check over his shoulder. 'We've received reports he's heading for the Quayside.'

Sykes stared at him and laughed. 'Why is it I don't believe you, Inspector?'

'It's Detective Chief Inspector, actually.'

'Yeah, well. The trouble is, if my readers get wind, there's a lunatic running amok on the streets of Newcastle, they'll demand answers.'

Mason glared at him, annoyed. 'No doubt you'll think of something to say.'

Sykes' bottom lip quivered. 'Don't tempt me, Jack.'

'You asked, and I delivered,' Mason groaned.

'Like you, I'm only doing my job.' Sykes swivelled on his heels. 'Which reminds me. Andrew Martin, the latest suspect you brought in for questioning...'

'What about him?'

'A reliable source informs me they have dropped the charges against him. Mind, his solicitors aren't happy. I'm told they've written to the Independent Police Complaints Commission about their client's abusive treatment. Having spent two nights locked up in a Gateshead police cell, you'll be hearing from them, no doubt.'

'You should have been a detective,' Mason groaned.

'No thanks. I'll stick to what I do best.'

'And what's that, Christopher?'

The moment DC Manley joined them carrying a large plastic forensic bag in his hand, Sykes made a note of it. 'One last question. Is anywhere off limits?'

'If you're looking for a kidney transplant,' Manley scoffed, 'the surgical suite's still open.'

The reporter's face darkened.

'Don't push me, Constable. I'm in no mood for cheap talk.'

Mason burst out laughing. 'You've done it again.'

'Done what?' Manley frowned.

'We're having steak and kidney pie for dinner.'

Sykes didn't see the funny side and stormed off towards the hospital admissions building. What tomorrow's headline story would bring, Mason dreaded to think. One thing was for sure, Manley's quip had certainly brought a smile to his face.

CHAPTER FORTY-FOUR

Tommy Nolan was a slightly built man, mid-forties, with a high forehead and a long, hooked nose. Dressed in a blue open-necked shirt, grey suit, and black brogue shoes, he certainly looked the part. Mason had a notion about slick car sales agents, believing they could sell snow to the Inuits. It was this aspect, among other things, which had brought him here today. Close to the A1, and two miles north of Newcastle city centre, the car dealership showroom reminded him of an oversized greenhouse. It had a fine range of high-end luxury cars on display, and there were plenty to choose from. Mason sat quietly for a moment, weighing up the prices. There was none to suit his wallet, though he did fancy a test drive in an Audi R8 coupe he'd spotted.

'Okay,' the chief inspector began, as he sat back in a plush leather upholstered seat that stank of saddle polish and squeaked when he moved around in it. 'After Auto Parts Distribution went into liquidation, you tried your hand as a supermarket manager. When that didn't work out, you ended up here.'

'That's correct, Inspector.'

Nolan was irritatingly chatty and didn't know when to keep his mouth shut. The advantage from Mason's perspective was there wasn't a thing Nolan didn't know about the distribution business. The man was a mine of information, and having read about them in Companies House, he was trying to catch Nolan off guard. If an ex-employee was the serial killer, he was determined to weed him out.

The chief inspector peered lovingly at the exquisite Audi R8 coupe again. It had beautiful contour lines, a luxurious interior, and a full range of fancy gadgets. As he let his mind drift, Mason could fancy himself parading up and down the High Street, watching people drool.

'How long did you say you worked for auto parts?'

'Three years.'

'And how many people did the company employ?'

'There were fourteen of us in total. It was a mixed bag. Sales mainly, and a smattering of backroom staff.'

'And you worked in the warehouse, you say?'

'That's correct. Me and a bloke called Bob Stanton. He came from Liverpool as I remember. Married with kids. Nice guy, not the sort to cause trouble.'

Mason cocked his head to one side. 'Friendly atmosphere, would you say?'

'Yeah, you could say that.'

'What about staff turnover?'

'We only had one, as I recall, and that was because of ill health.'

Mason sat quietly for a moment. 'Apart from the owner's wife, I take it the rest of the staff were mostly male?'

'They were.' The senior sales manager looked at him quizzically. 'Mind telling me what this is about, Inspector?'

Pleased in the knowledge he was finally getting somewhere, he hoped it would continue. Mason wasn't usually sentimental about the victims, but the image of Kevin Price's dismembered body had indelibly etched itself on his mind. It could have been his daughter lying in the freezer, or any of his friend's kids. The attempt to erase the memory wasn't working, and Mason was determined to put a stop to this monster's killings.

'Sounds like it was an excellent company to work for. Were you in it from the start?'

'I was. I joined as the distribution manager. Well, that's how they initially described the job in their advert.' Nolan's eyes dropped. 'It was a strange affair.'

'In what way?'

'The owners were setting up a distribution hub in Yorkshire and looking for a new manager to run it. It never materialised, unfortunately.'

'No doubt you complained to the owners?'

'Yes, bitterly. And on more than one occasion, might I add?'

'And how did they react?'

'They were extremely apologetic.'

'Any reason they never went ahead with setting up this distribution hub?'

'It's a cut-throat business, Inspector. Besides, the company had cash flow problems, as I recall. It had something to do with ninety-day payments.'

Mason nodded, already knowing the answer to that. 'And that would be an accounts problem, I presume. Nothing to do with the rest of the staff.'

'Yes, it was,' Nolan acknowledged.

'I see. And what exactly did your job entail?'

'We spent most days making up shipment orders for the distribution drivers. Apart from re-ordering and replenishing stock, the job was warehouse-based.'

'Tell me,' Mason said, thoughtfully. 'Apart from you, what did the other members of staff get up to? What were their roles?'

Nolan went to great lengths to explain the company's set-up. Its customer base, turnover, distribution, sales, everything about it. By the time he'd finished, Mason was more than happy with the way things were going.

'These distribution outlets?' the chief inspector quizzed. 'where were they located?'

'All over the North East and as far south as Sheffield. At one point, there was talk of expanding into Nottingham.'

Mason's ears pricked up. 'What about Leeds?'

'Yes, we had an excellent customer base there,' Nolan confirmed.

'Were all of your delivery drivers involved with the Leeds distributions?'

'No, only three of them were.'

Mason made a note of it and turned to face him.

'Did anything out of the ordinary occur in Leeds?'

'Like what?'

'You know what I mean. Men always like to brag about their conquests after a few drinks.'

'No. There were none of those shenanigans going on, to my knowledge.'

Mason took a sip of coffee and gathered his thoughts. A family man, Nolan didn't have a bad word to say about anyone – let alone kill someone. This was far more complex than he first thought, and a lot had happened since the company had gone into liquidation. If the killer was an ex-employee, it certainly wasn't clear from what Nolan was telling him.

Then Mason remembered. 'Tell me,' he said, pen poised. 'Did auto distribution ever deal in heavy duty duct tape?'

'It was one of our most popular brands.' Nolan shuffled awkwardly, as if a memory had resurfaced. 'It's funny that you mention Leeds, as that's where we sold the majority.'

'To whom exactly?'

'A spray paint company in Seacroft.'

Alarm bells ringing, Mason jotted down some notes.

'These Leeds delivery drivers you talked about. Did you ever stay connected with any of them?'

'Yes, I occasionally meet up with one of them. Why do you ask?'

'Married, I presume?'

'Yes. He is.'

Mason remembered what Carlisle had told him about the killer sticking rigidly to set routines. He knew it was a longshot, but still went ahead all the same.

'After the company went into liquidation, did any of the employees ever go back into the distribution business?'

'A few did as I remember, and—'

'Would you know who, exactly?'

Nolan reeled off a couple of names, but Mason was reluctant to divulge why he required such information.

If the press ever got hold of it, they would blow his investigation out of the water. He glanced lovingly at the blue Audi R8 coupe again.

'Nice car,' he said, pointing to it. 'What would something like that set me back?'

'Interested in buying one, Inspector?'

Nolan had automatically switched into sales mode, and Mason had picked up on it.

'No, just curious, that's all.'

'Around one-hundred and twenty-grand, but they're a beautiful car. Three hundred and ninety-seven horsepower, nought to sixty-two in three point two seconds, and a lot of extras thrown in. It certainly looks your type of motor. Like to test drive one?'

Mason gave him a look that said, *you must be joking, bonny lad.*

'Just for the record,' Mason said, standing to leave. 'Did anyone at auto spares ever team up with an Estonian woman?'

Nolan repeated the question and stared at him, bemused. 'Not that I'm aware of. Why do you ask?'

'Internet chatrooms, that sort of thing?'

'Hell no. Besides, it's not what somebody at work would discuss.'

'No, I suppose not,' Mason grinned, 'but it's what someone would brag about.'

Nolan shook his head, as if puzzled by it all.

'Can't say as they ever did, Inspector.'

Mason extended a hand. 'Thanks for your time. You've been most helpful.'

He left the showroom, casting one last lingering gaze

at the stunning blue Audi R8 coupe. *One-hundred and twenty thousand pounds,* he groaned. He would need to reach chief of police to own that sort of vehicle, and there was little chance of that happening. Not with his track record, there wasn't.

CHAPTER FORTY-FIVE

It had rained briefly that morning, and damp puddles still clung to the pavement. The estate had changed little over the years. Not exactly the Ritz, it still carried an element of hopelessness, as though stuck in a time warp. From what Mason could gather, there was quite a mix of houses in the street, and those unoccupied had overgrown gardens full of junk. Across the street, he spotted a rusty Ford Escort jacked up on bricks. Its wheels were missing, and the exhaust pipe had fallen to the ground like a jouster's broken lance in battle. The people who lived here didn't give a damn about the material things in life, only drugs.

From the outside, the house looked deserted. All the upstairs curtains were drawn, and junk mail was sticking out of the letterbox. Peering in through the broken window blinds, Mason's attention focused on the unkempt clutter. The place was a tip. There were no other words to describe it.

He checked his phone for messages. There were none. Strangely enough, Mason was having a quiet day. All his clear thinking had paid dividends. He'd made a few calls, eliminated several people from their enquiries, and made his presence felt. Approaching thirty-six, Patrick Stanley was the last of the three distribution drivers on his list to be interviewed. And that, he told himself, was the purpose of his visit here today.

'No one's answering,' Carlisle announced, appearing from the side of the building.

'He's probably in bed and smacked out of his mind.'

'It's not the nicest area, Jack.'

'No. I can agree with that.'

The chief inspector stepped forward and banged on the door. He'd been over this ground many times. People with secrets to hide always refused to answer. Curious, he peered in through the frosted window, but could see nothing.

'Who are you guys looking for?' an unfriendly voice called out from a neighbouring fence.

'Police,' Mason replied. 'And you are?'

'I live here. What do you people want?'

Mason gave him a withering look. To call him stout would have been ungenerous. His centre of gravity was located around his mid-riff like an overgrown Teletubby. Then, out of the corner of his eye, he caught movement. It wasn't much, but enough to draw his attention towards the dishevelled dog. Hostile looking, it was baring its teeth at them. If he wasn't mistaken, it looked like a pit bull terrier, and one of the four breeds banned from the UK.

Mason flashed his warrant card under the man's nose and watched the frown lines ripple.

'Does Patrick Stanley live here?'

'He's out. Why do you ask?'

'Out where?'

'How the hell would I know?'

Mason checked the door. It wasn't locked.

'If Stanley returns,' said Mason, stepping into the building. 'Tell him he's got visitors.'

They entered a long, narrow passage, their shoes squelching on wet carpets. Flicking on the hall lights, he slipped into detective mode. Whilst Carlisle checked the downstairs rooms, the chief inspector dashed up a short flight of stairs to gain the element of surprise. On reaching the landing, something stopped him in his tracks.

'God!' he gasped.

'You okay?'

Stood frozen, fear engulfed him. 'Touch nothing,' the chief inspector shouted. 'This is a murder scene.'

Eyes clouded over, Carlisle stared up at him from the bottom of the stairs.

'What have you found, Jack?'

'Best look for yourself.'

Mason took another deep breath and steadied himself against the banister rail. The bathroom door was ajar, but what lay beyond sickened him to the pit of his stomach. Slowly at first, he pushed the door open with the toe of his shoe. It was then the smell hit him.

'It's a slaughterhouse up here,' he said, swallowing hard. 'There's blood everywhere, and what appear to be chunks of human flesh lying in the bath.'

'Any footprints?'

'There's plenty of those.'

'Blimey!' the profiler gasped as he joined him.

Mason gestured towards the hallway. 'Let's suit up and secure the building before the rest of the cavalry arrives.'

***

Twenty minutes later, the estate resembled an impregnable fortress. Mason's instincts as a working detective told him they were closing in on their killer. Wherever he was, he had few options left open to him. There were hundreds of officers out searching, and more on their way. Mentally shaken, the chief inspector watched as a team of forensic officers methodically crawled over the suspect's rear garden. Amongst other things, they were looking for body parts or buried clothing from previous victims. These operations took time, but time was a luxury they could ill afford. They had jobs to do, fresh plans to be set in motion, and new lines of enquiries to explore. Once they'd conducted a thorough examination of the property, it was a simple matter of legwork.

'I never expected this.'

Mason spun to face the profiler. 'Me neither. It takes some believing.'

'I had a hunch we were close. But not this close.'

'If I didn't know you better, I would have thought someone had tipped you off.'

'It's not over yet, Jack. The killings may have stopped, but he'll be difficult to pin down.'

Mason blew out his cheeks, his eyes fixed firmly ahead. 'No doubt the Acting Superintendent will want to go public on this one.'

'Let's hope not, as it could spark all kinds of problems inside his head.'

'I know,' Mason sighed, 'but I doubt she'll listen. Sutherland's more concerned about what Mad Frankie Wiseman will do once he finds out who killed his ex-wife. The man's unpredictable, and there's no way of knowing how he'll react.'

The profiler stared at him, perplexed. 'You're right. I'd almost forgotten about Wiseman.'

'I wish it was that easy.'

'Nothing is ever straightforward. You, of all people, should know that.'

'More importantly,' Mason said, the concern showing in his voice, 'Where the hell is he?'

'Stanley can't be too far away. I'm positive of that.'

'We need to get to him first... before the criminal fraternity does. Once word gets out that the police are knocking at his door, he'll go into hiding.'

The pair fell silent.

Deep in thought, Mason put a pen against his lips as he racked his brain for answers. Stanley was bound to make life difficult for them. He had no other option. Not with Frank Wiseman breathing down his neck.

'You're right.' The chief inspector said stoically. 'Do you think he'll head for Leeds?'

'Who knows? He has contacts there, so he might.'

'He'll get far less hassle in Yorkshire than he will here. Perhaps that's what lies behind Sutherland's thinking.'

'Could be.'

'Bugger,' Mason groaned. 'I was hoping for a quiet life, but this is far from peaceful.'

'Serial killers are always one step ahead of us, Jack. Just when you think you have them in the palm of your hand, they slip through your fingers.'

He gave a little shake of the head. 'No doubt the Chief Constable will want to get involved, which leaves little room for manoeuvre.'

'Our biggest threat is the media. Once those maggots get hold of the story, we'll be catapulted into the stratosphere.'

'Spare a thought.'

'How to put a stop to it,' the profiler said, staring into the distance. 'Stanley's becoming a celebrity monster. His total disregard for life is feeding the public's insatiable fascination for the macabre.'

'You don't pull any punches, my friend.'

'Like it or not, it's a fact.'

Mason shuffled awkwardly. 'I'm more interested in what forensic throws up.'

'I doubt they'll uncover anything we don't already know.'

'No. You're probably right.'

There was nothing either of them could do, not until the crime scene manager had given them clearance. Entering the hall, the serious expression on Tom Hedley's face immediately caught their attention. Carrying a large brown paper bag in his hand, Mason sensed trouble.

'What's up, Tom?' he asked nervously.

'You two should look at this,' Hedley insisted.

They both stared at one another.

'Don't tell me you've found more body parts. I can't handle much more of this bastard's handy work,' Mason groaned.

'True, but what's hidden beneath the floorboards

would surprise you.'

'Really?'

Hedley opened the brown paper bag, and Carlisle stuck his head inside.

'Well, I'll be dammed.'

'What the hell is it?' Mason insisted.

'It's a surgical saw.'

'Bloody hell!'

'Exactly.'

'What else have you found, Tom?' asked Mason.

'Not a lot, but we're working on it.'

The chief inspector shrugged as he turned to face them. 'Why leave a crime scene without trying to get rid of the evidence? It makes little sense.'

Carlisle wrinkled his nose. 'Isn't that why you employ a profiler, Jack?'

CHAPTER FORTY-SIX

The damp getting to his bones, DS Savage shuddered inwardly. He'd encountered Tony Fox's nefarious organisation on more than one occasion these past few months and could think of far better places to meet on a windswept night. The dimly lit back streets of Low Fell weren't exactly the safest place to hang around in. Not at any time. The problem was, if ever they were going to make inroads into catching the man responsible for such heinous crimes, they would need to take risks. DCI Mason's meeting with Tony Fox had initially set the wheels in motion, but Fox had gained the upper hand and was giving the police a run for their money. With claims that Patrick Stanley had once worked as a barman at Fat Sam's nightclub, could the gangster be bluffing?

Fists clenched, legs slightly apart and ready to spring into action, the detective sergeant stood perfectly still for a moment. He'd been in this situation many times and knew not to lower his guard. Deep down there was a much darker side to this, and one involving a serial killer. His boss was right, he should have agreed to back up instead of going it alone. He hadn't, and now he faced an even bigger challenge.

Then, just when he was about to make his move, a figure emerged. A man in his late forties wearing a baseball cap pulled low over his face was moving towards him.

'I assume you're Mason's man?'

'And you are?'

'That's none of your concern.'

The stranger glowered at him. Dark alleys had a ghastly habit of throwing up all kinds of nasty problems. Regardless, his priority was to establish a serial killer's whereabouts. Do that, and the team might put a stop to a spate of vicious killings.

'You came alone?'

'Just as arranged,' the detective replied.

'I'll be brief.'

Savage was under no illusions where this was heading. There was hostility in the stranger's voice, enough to throw him off balance. Over the years, the sergeant had been involved in many secret meetings. It was never easy, and the rules of engagement were complex. No weapons, no concealed recording devises, and no hidden agendas. Fail to conform and the consequences could be catastrophic.

'How do I know we can trust you?'

'You don't,' the stranger replied. There followed an awkward impasse between them, a coming together of minds. 'I'm reliably informed that you people are seeking Patrick Stanley's whereabouts?'

'We are.'

Another uncomfortable silence befell them.

'What assurances do we have?'

'Fat Sam's stays open.'

The stranger gave a nervous flick of the tongue,

wetting his lips. 'He's here in the city.'

'Where exactly?'

'Not so fast. There are a couple of things that we need to talk about first.'

'At least tell me which part of the city he's in.'

'Not until you agree to our terms.'

'Terms! What terms are these?'

The moment the stranger reached into his pocket, the detective's heart sank. Everything was happening quickly, and he had to react swiftly.

'What are you after?' asked Savage.

'Written assurances,' the stranger replied.

'Regarding what?'

The man moved into the light and handed him a crumpled envelope. 'If you wish to know Stanley's whereabouts, you're to sign this.'

'Why haven't you people gone to Jack Mason direct?'

'It's not my call.'

'Whose call is it, then?'

'Like you, I'm just the messenger.'

Still curious who was pulling the strings, the officer wracked his brains. Besides Tony Fox, the nightclub gangster, who else knew where Stanley was? There were the Eastern Europeans, of course, but that was highly unlikely.

'So, what's the deal?' Savage insisted.

The stranger pointed to the envelope and dropped into the shadows. 'If you agree to our terms, you're to call that number.'

'And what if we don't?'

'What do you mean, don't?'

'Like you, I'm merely the messenger. I can't answer for Mason.'

'Let's just say he'd be unwise to refuse.'

There was a menacing urgency in the stranger's voice. Plea bargaining with gangsters always carried an element of risk. An awful lot was at stake here, and failure wasn't an option. Get it wrong, and the outcome could be catastrophic.

'When are your people expecting an answer?' the sergeant asked, playing on his words.

'Within the next ten hours. No more.'

'That's cutting it short!'

'There are no guarantees. The whole damn city is looking for this serial killer.'

'I take it he no longer works at Fat Sam's?'

The stranger's eyes were the giveaway. Patrick Stanley, alias Wasp, was no longer employed by Tony Fox. That much was obvious. Besides, Fat Sam's was now under twenty-four-hour surveillance and no longer a haven for miscreants to congregate.

With the narrative coming together, Savage tucked the envelope into a back pocket and tried not to dwell on it. After seventeen years in the force, his instinct was to believe nothing. His boss was right: too many people were searching for the killer, and all for different reasons. Time was of the essence, and ten hours wasn't a long time.

No sooner had the stranger melted into the night, then Savage pressed the call button.

'Jack Mason?'

'It's me, boss. DS Savage.'

The connection went silent for a few seconds.

'How did your meeting go?'

The sergeant sucked the air in anticipation. 'You'll not believe this...'

CHAPTER FORTY-SEVEN

Wasp lit up another cigarette, took a deep drag, then blew out a long smoke trail. He'd packed up smoking years ago, but after losing his partner, the urge had finally got the better of him. Sleep did not come easy. After another restless night cooped up in the old bottling plant, he was suffering from claustrophobia. Not that he was complaining any; he wasn't. Hell, he'd not felt this safe in a long time. Besides, it didn't take a rocket scientist to figure out the police were out looking for him. The entire area was crawling with armed officers. What would they do all day if they didn't have people like him to chase? Maybe the system would collapse. Maybe it wouldn't; who gave a toss anyway?

The room was small and stifling. Despite the open windows, the stale air hung heavy and unchanged. Bats in the loft, mice everywhere, and a million dust mites to contend with. Strange, he should call this place home. When he was a youngster, he came here after school. His foster mother worked at the plant, lifting heavy bottle crates and stacking them onto long wooden pallets. Nan was a happy-go-lucky woman with a wonderful sense of humour. The men were friendly, too. Kind souls, every single one of them. Such fond memories. What he wouldn't give to have them back again.

As another long smoke trail drifted aimlessly towards the ceiling, he eased back in his seat. Wasp wondered if they had transferred Angelica to another hospital. One he'd not visited yet. He would need to act swiftly. Whisk her out of there and back to Estonia, where she had contacts and friends. That thought excited him, and he was gaining in confidence with each passing day.

What to do with the bodies was the conundrum. Some without arms and legs, others he'd forgotten about. Damn cockroaches, every one of them. People like Thomas Wilkinson, who'd preyed on vulnerable young women as if they were pieces of human meat. How many more innocent lives would they destroy to fulfil their sexual fantasies? The police couldn't handle it, and it was down to him to take care of the problem.

Annoyed, Wasp crushed the cigarette butt in a saucer and sat back. There was nothing of value here. Only security. He had a makeshift bed and could boil a pan of water on an old camping stove if needs be. For what more could he wish? Sometimes he questioned why people complained. If you'd never had a television, you were none the wiser of what was going on in the world. He still missed the hourly bulletins, though. Listening to the anchor man talking about his exploits and how good he was at killing his victims.

God, he was brilliant. A crazy killing machine.

Transfixed, Wasp stared at the jar of human fingers. Each carried a ring, each a proud moment in another person's life. A shiver ran down his spine as his skin crawled. He'd loved slaughtering these people, although it wasn't always that way. Some were his chums, friends who had crossed a red line. He'd intended to keep them alive, punish them to within an inch of their lives. That was before he met Angelica. She was such a calming influence in his life and had taught him so many things about the human anatomy. Not just collecting fingers in a jar, this was far more complex.

Somewhere in the distance, he heard a helicopter. It was out searching for someone. Those scumbags never gave up. Sometimes he wondered why they even bothered. They would never catch up with him. Not in a zillion years.

As he stood in front of the mirror, a fresh surge of urgency washed over him. Using a cotton pad soaked in an alcohol solution, he carefully wiped away the oils from his forehead, leaving his skin feeling refreshed. Then, holding the back of the wig with both hands, he slid it over his head in a front-to-back motion. Finally, he aligned the ear tabs to ensure the front hairline was in place.

God, he looked amazing.

Wasp lit another cigarette and took a deep drag. Money talked, it got you into places where other people couldn't go. That was incredibly important to him. Once he'd cleared the backlog here, they would catch the overnight ferry together to Amsterdam. First-class, executive suite, the best that money could buy. It wasn't a brilliant plan, but he knew it would work. And, if he wasn't mistaken, once they'd crossed the English Channel, Angelica's friends would take over from him.

His companion had never gone back on a promise. That's why he had to snatch her out of there.

To keep his promise to her.

He thumped the table with the flat of his hand and stared at himself in the mirror.

Don't give up on me now, my little sweetie.

CHAPTER FORTY-EIGHT

The focus of attention that morning was damage limitation. As usual, the moment the lead detective read out his summary to the assembled team, you could have heard a pin drop. The story had made all the headlines, prompting dozens of people to come forward. So far, the police had arrested ten individuals, released three, and two of those released were now out on bail. Acting on a tip-off, the team had conducted dozens of raids on properties in Newcastle and Gateshead, having seized numerous items of interest. All that remained now was to sift through the detail, including a large quantity of data found on the killer's computer.

It was a mixed bag of officers who had gathered in Meeting Room One that morning, but Carlisle knew most of them. There was almost an air of expectation, as if something big was about to happen. Now that Carrington had returned after a short firearms training course, the profiler was looking forward to working alongside her again. Despite all the negativity, there was at least one silver lining in his favour.

To everyone's surprise, Tony Fox had completely disregarded Mason's arrangements and was refusing to cooperate. Everything that could go wrong had gone wrong. They'd been conned, big style, and the chief inspector had been left with little option other than to continue harassing the gangster.

'Okay,' Mason announced. 'Everything's in place for tonight's raid on Fat Sam's, and we now have search warrants to that effect. If Fox hasn't kept to his bargain about Stanley's whereabouts, we'll revoke his nightclub licence at midnight.'

A loud cheer broke out.

As Mason sped through the summaries, Carlisle pondered over the last message found on the killer's computer. If someone were harbouring Stanley, it would be highly relevant for profiling purposes. Upon further reflection, had their suspect found another unsuspecting victim to target? Anything was possible.

'What if the killer has fled to Leeds?' suggested Manley, his plastic coffee cup poised close to his lips. 'We know he has contacts there.'

Stoney-faced, Mason's voice deepened. 'It's highly unlikely. Stanley's major interests lie in Newcastle.'

'Well, that's what I'd be doing if I were in his shoes.'

Mason considered this.

'What are your views, David?'

Carlisle looked up at the large street map now covered in post-its. There were thousands of places to hide. Too many for his like. The game plan had changed, and everyone was feeling the strain.

'He'll not leave the city, not whilst Angelica remains here. Besides his deep resentment towards young men, Stanley's territorial and will stick to his comfort zones.'

'Will he attempt to snatch her from the hospital?'

'Looking at past killer partnerships, the Moors Murders are a classic example of how this type of crime unfolds,' the profiler replied. 'Serial killers have a real affinity with power, even when caught, and they know the game is up. Stanley is a possessive narcissist who likes to exert his control over people. In his mind, he probably sees Angelica as the real mastermind in all of this. Even to the point of blaming her for his own sadistic wrongdoings.'

'Sounds like the gang of flying monkeys,' Manley chuckled.

Mason glowered. 'What the hell are you on about?'

'It's a scene from the Wizard of Oz, boss. When the Wicked Witch of the West sent her flying monkeys to do all her dirty work for her, she couldn't stop laughing about it.'

Mason shook his head. 'Sometimes you frighten the life out of me, Harry.'

Rob Savage suddenly chirped up. 'What about our undercover team at the hospital? Have we had anymore feedback?'

'Nothing much in the way of information,' Mason acknowledged. 'Angelica's lawyers are presenting an opposing viewpoint and arguing that she is not mentally fit to be interviewed.'

'Compos mentis, and all that,' Hedley remarked.

'Bollocks more like,' Manley chuckled.

'What about Stanley's neighbours?' asked Holt.

'If they know anything, they're not letting on.'

Savage cleared his throat. 'It's about time we applied some serious pressure, boss.'

'And how do you propose we do that?'

Seize the day, thought Carlisle. *Carpe diem.* It was the

first time in a while that Savage had stirred up their imagination and he was eager to share his thoughts. 'What if we informed Sykes we're about to make an arrest? The press are as much in the dark as we are as to the killer's whereabouts, so he's bound to make a headline splash.'

'That's not a bad idea,' Mason agreed, pointing a finger at the evidence board. 'It may force Stanley out into the open.'

Hedley leaned forward, his brow furrowed in deep concentration. 'But will Sykes swallow it?'

There was a knock on the door – soft knuckles by the sound. Seconds later, Sutherland emerged from the doorway, her uniform adding an air of authority.

'When you have a spare minute, Chief Inspector. The Area Commander wishes to speak to the two of us about tonight's raid.'

'We're almost done here, ma'am,' Mason replied.

'Good,' she smiled, reflecting her approval. 'I'll be up in my office.'

As the meeting ended, no one was any the wiser as to the killer's whereabouts. It was a roller-coaster ride, and Stanley was proving an elusive figure to track down. But that was the nature of the beast, and it was causing havoc amongst senior backroom staff.

***

Stepping from the shadows, twenty officers drawn from the police's special tactical unit stormed through the nightclub front entrance. Still early hours of the morning, the ground underfoot felt damp. Dressed in their familiar black armoured vests and wearing black balaclavas, ten officers from the police's special tactical unit secured the building within minutes. The speed and execution of the operation was breath-taking, surprise took even Jack Mason.

Under the codename "Operation Peppercorn," officers had been stealthily collecting information about Fat Sam's for weeks. With its growing reputation, the nightclub had become a mecca for celebrities and those yearning for a taste of the glamorous lifestyle. Not all patrons were here for the music, of course. That much was obvious.

Scurrying across the dance floor, Mason bumped into one of the nightclub bouncers. A muscular man, with a mouth full of gold teeth and a face like a Pitbull terrier. He was standing next to the DJ's booth with a cheesy grin on his face. The music full volume, the lead detective swore he could feel the floor vibrating under his feet. Undeterred, he pushed through the steel security door leading to the basement and ran down a steep flight of stairs.

'If you're looking for the gaffer, he's not here,' Rolex Roy announced.

'Where is he?' Mason demanded.

'What is it with you people?'

Amidst the confusion, Mason felt his ears were about to pop. Even in the fortified confines of Fox's basement sanctuary, the noise levels were unbearable.

'Do yourself a favour, Roy. Tell your friends upstairs

to turn the fucking music down. It's doing my head in.'

The doorman glared at him as if about to throw a punch. Then, unexpectedly, the door to Fox's office flew open. Naked apart from a pair of boxer shorts and black socks with garters, the Newcastle gangster gave a look of surprise.

'What's all the noise about?' demanded Fox. 'What's going on?'

'We have visitors,' said Roy.

'Like whom?'

'It's the filth.'

Fox looked at the doorman, then across at Mason, before glancing back into his office. 'Get dressed, Polly. Try to look respectable... there's a good girl.'

Mason grinned but said nothing. He'd seen enough for one night.

CHAPTER FORTY-NINE

'I hear last night's raid was a complete success,' the acting superintendent began in a low, subdued voice. 'Has Tony Fox said anything to you about Stanley's whereabouts?'

'Not to me, he hasn't,' Mason replied.

'What about the others who we questioned?'

'We've made ten arrests for possession of class A drugs, but nobody has seen hide nor hair of Stanley.'

'I thought he worked at Fat Sam's?'

'He did. He worked as a barman there but quit shortly before the killings began.'

'Someone must know of his whereabouts, surely?'

'Apparently not, ma'am. Despite having dozens of eyewitness accounts confirming Angelica's visits to the nightclub, there is a notable lack of specific detail.'

'Have we checked camera footage?'

'We have, ma'am.'

'What about Fox? What does he have to say?'

'His lawyers are a right pain in the arse. Unless we drop charges against their client, they are refusing to cooperate.'

Sutherland ran a finger over the charge sheet and then remarked. 'His solicitors are looking for a way out, it seems. In which case, perhaps we should contact the prison governor at Durham jail and find out what Mr Wiseman is up to. No doubt the bush telegraph will be red hot after last night's raid.'

'I agree, ma'am. That could be beneficial.'

Sutherland sat back, as though puzzled. 'Even if we close the nightclub down, we're still a million miles from uncovering Stanley's whereabouts. Do we have any thoughts?'

'Carlisle believes he's still in the area.'

'What about Leeds?'

Mason was quick to react. 'No, ma'am. The profiler's convinced he's hiding in Newcastle, and I agree with him on that. Just on the off chance he does travel south, I've contacted the West Yorkshire Police to keep an eye out on all artery roads.'

'The sooner Stanley's brought to justice, the better for all concerned.'

'I wish it were that simple, ma'am. The killer is elusive and is proving difficult to pin down.'

'He's out there somewhere.' Sutherland rested her hand on the edge of the desk as she stood. 'What are your thoughts about getting the media involved?'

'We've already started the ball rolling. We've met with a group of resident journalists to drum up local support.'

'This wouldn't involve Christopher Sykes?'

'Yes, ma'am. Do you have a problem with that?'

'No, but after your last run in with the Independent Press Standards, I would have thought you'd have learnt your lesson. Besides, I was thinking more on a national scale.'

'I don't think that would be a wise move at this stage, ma'am.'

'Oh, and why not?'

'The last thing we need is to spook Stanley into going into hiding.'

Sutherland checked her notes. 'Speaking of local interests, this council property that Stanley was renting in Gateshead. Have forensics found anything that might uncover his whereabouts?'

'Not yet, they haven't.'

'I would have thought there would be plenty of hard evidence available?'

'There is.'

Silence filled the room. The only sound was the gentle flapping of the window blinds.

'What about this message found on his computer?'

'Meet ya soon!'

She nodded, as if to confirm his response. 'Do we have any idea who the intended recipient was?'

'No, unfortunately.' Mason blew through his teeth. 'It's a strange one, as we have found no links to Stanley's close associates either.'

'What about this alias he goes under – Wasp?'

'Nothing of interest has shown up on social media. As far as I know, the tech boys are dealing with taking down Stanley's Facebook wall.'

'Pity, I was hoping there might be a connection here.' Sutherland shook her head dismissively. 'We're missing a trick here, Chief Inspector. Perhaps now's the time to tighten up our investigatory procedures.'

The tension was building, and Mason was feeling the pressure. Okay, he wouldn't tolerate incompetence, not at any level. If mistakes were made, he would admit to them. They hadn't, and this type of comment was totally unwarranted. Besides, he disliked the sudden change in Sutherland's tone. She was desperate for answers, and no one had any to give. Pity, he thought. Just when they were building up a favourable rapport, this had to turn up. Could one of the senior backroom staff be pulling her strings?

'It's a bit of a minefield, if I'm honest.'

She silenced him by raising her hand. 'It's time we stopped pussyfooting around.'

'Ma'am?'

'Fox knows more than he's letting on. That much is obvious.'

Mason smiled wryly and raised an eyebrow as if in agreement. 'I know it's not much, but the profiler believes Stanley is using some of his old thespian skills to slip in and out of society. If he's using disguise as a weapon, he'll be difficult to pin down.'

There was a loud, forceful knock on the door, and Savage confidently breezed into the room.

'Yes, Sergeant?'

'She's gone.'

'Who's gone?' Sutherland demanded.

'Angelica Glebova, ma'am.'

The acting superintendent stared at Mason, and then back at the sergeant.

'Gone where exactly?'

'God knows, but she's disappeared from the hospital.'

'People don't just disappear, Sergeant. She must be there somewhere.'

'With all due respect,' Mason interrupted, 'we can't predict the future.'

'This won't do,' Sutherland said, slapping her palm on a pile of case files. 'Both suspects are missing, and neither of you has the faintest idea where they are.'

'That's down to hospitals security, ma'am. Surely?'

'But is it?'

'There's obviously a weakness in their system.'

'What do you mean, *weakness?* I thought you had everything covered.'

'We do, but hospital security chiefs keep hitting us with the Human Rights Act.'

'I thought we had round-the-clock security in place to protect the public, especially after Stanley's previous unsuccessful attempt to abduct her.'

'We have,' the sergeant insisted.

'It's all very well saying she's gone missing, but it's me who's answerable to the Chief Constable.'

Get a grip, Mason cursed. If this bastard were to kill again, she'd assign him to a desk job for the rest of his days. The only person most likely to know the answer to Stanley's whereabouts was the profiler. He stared at his phone screen and thought about making the connection, but it was Savage who interrupted his thoughts.

'According to the security manager, Angelica was on her way for a CT scan when she went missing.'

Mason stared at his watch. 'What time was this?'

'Barely fifteen minutes ago, boss.'

'And what have we done in the meantime?'

'A team is on their way over.'

'And uniforms?'

'They're out covering the hospital grounds,' the sergeant replied.

Mason had to think quickly, but he excelled at doing so in these situations.

'What about Road Traffic?' he asked.

'The last I heard, they were setting up road checks on all access roads to the hospital.'

Mason recalled the last time Stanley had tried to snatch Angelica out of the neurology ward, and fifteen minutes didn't seem a long time. Sutherland was right. Maybe the pair were lying low inside the hospital grounds somewhere.

His mind running amok, he leaned in closer. 'Let's get hospital security involved – close all exit points in and out of the complex.'

'Sounds like a plan,' Sutherland acknowledged. 'Do we know what sort of physical shape Angelica is in?'

'Not a good one, I'd wager.'

Sutherland drummed her long fingernails on the desk as she spoke. 'Who's behind it, Jack?'

'Patrick Stanley no doubt.'

'I agree. There's no way she could walk out of there on her own accord.'

'Which raises the question, what is he intending to do with her?'

'Looking at the case files, Stanley didn't have a very good upbringing, and that could be part of his problem. His father's frequent incarcerations, which had made him well known to us, ultimately led to Social Services stepping in after his death. The sad thing is, they brought up young Stanley in foster care on a rough council estate in Byker, so he knows the area well.'

'A loner with an attitude problem doesn't bode well, ma'am.'

'What did he do after leaving school?' she asked.

'He failed miserably at every job he did until working for Auto Parts Distribution.'

'There has to be a connection in there somewhere.'

'The profiler believes there is.'

'You're right. The pair of them are in this together.'

Mason leaned closer to express his frustration. 'Apart from Mad Frank Wiseman and a couple of Fox's cronies, I can't think of anyone else who fits the frame.'

'Which brings us nicely onto Fox.'

'In what way, ma'am?'

Sutherland glanced at her case files. 'If Fox is giving Wiseman the run around in connection with this takeover bid, could he be using Angelica as a screen?'

'What, trying to smuggle her out of the hospital?'

'And why not?'

'I wouldn't go as far as that, but the longer this goes on, the less chance we have of catching her,' Mason said, staring at his watch.

'What about his mental state? What are Carlisle's views?'

'The profiler believes Stanley has a split personality and is living out a double life.'

'And what are your thoughts?'

'I must admit, Carlisle has an incredible knack of getting inside other people's minds and has been right on more than one occasion in the past.'

'That is interesting. We could be up against a Jekyll and Hyde's personality here.'

'We are. Having failed miserably at drama school, Stanley is trying to prove a point. Hence his use of disguise, it's all down to this thespian malarkey.'

'It's time to give Mr Carlisle a wider role... a free hand in trying to track Stanley down.'

'We already have, to some extent, ma'am.'

'Where's Carlisle now?'

Mason stared at her, then across at Savage. 'He's with Carrington. They're currently looking into old case files. Stanley's predictable, and the profiler believes he may return to his old hunting grounds.'

'In which case, we'd best leave well alone.'

Mason stood to leave. 'No disrespect, but there's plenty to be getting on with.'

'Yes, of course.'

The lead detective picked up his case files and smiled cheerily. 'In the meantime, I'll reach out to the West Yorkshire Police and explore what technical help they can provide.'

With hesitation, Sutherland nodded reluctantly and said. 'In which case, I'll inform HQ what's going on at the hospital.'

Mason gave her a look that said it all.

CHAPTER FIFTY

Tucked away in one of the many backrooms in Gateshead's Metrocentre was the Retail Crime Unit. An inconspicuous building, its small team of plain-clothes security officers covered every inch of the mall. One of the largest shopping centres in Europe, with over three-hundred and forty stores, this was a shoplifter's paradise. Not today. Security was tight, and nothing could get under their radar.

Now taking centre stage, the man's image that exploded across a dozen monitor screens seemed to cut a familiar figure with David Carlisle. Dressed in a pair of black tracksuit bottoms, hoodie, and sporting dark Ray-Ban Aviator sunglasses, the suspect was heading towards the Red (shoppers') multi-storey car park as though he owned the building.

'How long have you people been monitoring him?' the profiler asked.

'Ever since we first contacted you?'

'That's almost thirty minutes ago,' said Carrington.

The controller proffered a smile. 'Twenty nine.'

'What drew your attention towards this man?'

'Central Control asked us to look for any males fitting this man's description.' The controller tapped an image pinned to his screen. 'We believe he's wanted in connection with a series of murders in the city.'

'He is,' Carlisle confirmed.

'Is it him?'

'I'm not sure. What do you think, Sue?'

'It certainly looks like him. Same age, same height, and identical clothes. Can we put a marker on him?' Detective Carrington asked anxiously.

The moment the suspect entered Level Three car park, he glanced over his shoulder. There was purpose in his stride, as if in a hurry. Trying to predict his intentions was impossible, but the profiler believed he was heading for a black Peugeot 308.

Seconds later, he was inside it and heading down a steep spiral exit ramp.

'He's descending into Level Two,' the controller announced.

'Is there no way of stopping him?'

'We've circulated the car's registration number, make and model to your people. The best we can hope for is that he's held up at the next set of traffic lights.'

Carrington smiled faintly, as she relayed her findings back to roads policing. Still no signs of the Peugeot showing. The tension was building.

'It's Road Traffic,' she whispered, turning to face Carlisle. 'The vehicle was stolen from Byker yesterday morning.'

The profiler felt his stomach tighten.

'It has to be him.'

'They've already put a marker on it and are setting up road checks.'

'If he heads towards the Angel of the North, there's fixed camera units all the way.'

'Fingers crossed,' she smiled.

Then, from beneath the ground floor of the multi-story carpark, a black Peugeot emerged. Slowly at first, it inched its way forward towards the mainstream traffic before pulling to a halt at the lights.

'What other cameras do you have covering the Red Zone?' asked Carrington, turning to face the controller.

'Just what you see,' he replied. 'Once he joins the circular, he'll be out of camera range.'

His mind running amok, Carlisle tried to piece together the possibilities. Using geographical profiling could be highly valuable, especially in predicting the whereabouts of a serial killer. Knowing the suspect as he did, Byker immediately sprang to mind. That's where Stanley grew up in foster care, and he knew the area well. The pieces were coming together, but this man was unpredictable.

'The Red Zone is now closed to all traffic,' the controller announced.

Carrington pointed to the central bank of monitor screens. 'What about the other zones?'

'Your people are dealing with it.'

'It's down to us then,' she smiled.

Everything was a blur as events unfolded rapidly, making it challenging to stay on top.

'There,' the controller said aloud, 'he's moving again.'

'Jesus! He's heading in the opposite direction.'

Within seconds, the Peugeot disappeared from view, leaving behind a lingering cloud of exhaust fumes.

***

The profiler sat thinking as DC Carrington pulled up outside his house in Whitburn. It was seven o'clock, and he was utterly exhausted. Having spent the best part of the afternoon looking for a stolen black Peugeot 308, the search had finally been called off. So much for his theory of the killer returning to Byker – Stanley was nowhere to be seen.

Carrington turned to face him. 'Aren't you going to invite me in?'

'Sorry?'

'I thought you might at least introduce me to this new partner of yours.'

Not believing his ears, Carlisle tendered a smile. 'You mean Benjamin?'

'Why, is there someone else in your life?'

'No. Why do you ask?'

'I'm dying to see him,' she said.

The moment Carlisle stepped into the kitchen, the young kitten ran towards him. It had been a long day, and Benjamin seemed more than pleased to see him back at the house. Acting on instinct, he grabbed a bottle of Chardonnay from the fridge and two glasses from the kitchen cabinet.

'Wine?' he asked, 'or would you prefer coffee?'

'Wine's fine,' she smiled.

Surprised at Carrington's forthright approach, he moved into the living room and made himself comfortable. As the conversation inevitably turned to

Patrick Stanley and his partner, Carrington eagerly joined in.

'Make yourself at home, that's if Benjamin approves.'

'He's fine,' she replied. 'It seems I've made a new friend.'

'He can be a demanding little bugger.'

'Cats don't normally take to me like this,' she admitted. 'They're usually very choosy who they make friends with.'

'Benjamin's not normal, I can assure you of that. I'm positive he thinks he's a dog.'

'Really?'

'Try throwing something for him to fetch, and he'll bring it back to you.'

'That's hilarious,' she giggled.

Moving towards the sound system, Carlisle felt a fleeting moment of calm as he put on one of his favourite tracks from JJ Cale's *"Really"* album. 'I'm trying to wrap my head around Stanley's sudden disappearance.'

Carrington sighed and gave him a withering look. 'Does that brain of yours ever shut down, or is that a profiler thing?'

'Sometimes, but rarely,' Carlisle had to admit. 'It's fascinating how the mind works. Most people assume our memories are accurate records of what has happened to us. The trouble is our brains tweak and alter our memories all the time. We recreate partial recollections, imagine different outcomes, and change an existing memory until it's quite different to what actually took place.'

'Try giving it a rest,' Carrington groaned. 'We've done enough running around for one day, and *my* brain is in bits.'

Carlisle walked over to the window, and Benjamin followed. 'Can I ask you a personal question?'

'You may, but whether I answer is another matter.'

'Do you like Indian food?'

'Of course. Why wouldn't I?'

'Good, would you mind if I order us a take-away?'

An hour later, their food arrived. Delivered by a middle-aged Asian woman who arrived on a red scooter carrying a large white box strapped on the back of it. Neither of them had eaten since breakfast, and apart from grabbing a quick coffee between enquiries, they were famished.

Sitting with a tray resting on her lap, Carrington tucked into her starters. The food was not only delicious but incredibly filling. By the time they finished the main course, he felt as though his stomach could burst.

Carrington reminded him of his late wife. Her easy going nature and outgoing personality made her instantly likable. As they finished their second bottle of wine, her words flowed more freely, and he could see the excitement in her gestures. They talked about many things that evening, and he pleasantly discovered their shared interests. Below the angelic charm, there was a definite mean streak — an obvious choice for close protection selection.

Deep down, Carlisle felt relaxed in her company. Not pushy like some, she was intelligent, incredibly quick witted, not to mention a slightly wry sense of humour. Not that it ever showed in her work, but her parents were well-to-do people, which may have accounted for her confident outlook on life.

She stood suddenly, gazing at her mobile. 'Blimey! It's almost eleven-thirty and I'm well over the legal limit. I'd better phone a taxi and pick up the pool car tomorrow morning.'

There was panic in her voice.

Carlisle thought about it, but not for long. 'There's a spare bed in the boxroom. It's not exactly the Ritz, but you're more than welcome to stop the night.'

'The perfect host,' she replied coyly.

'I wouldn't say that,' he confessed. 'But you may have company during the night.'

She looked at him warily. 'What do you mean... company?'

'Your new-found friend.' Carlisle smiled, pointing to Benjamin, who was now comfortably curled up on her lap.

She flashed her big brown eyes at him. 'Let's drink to that.'

CHAPTER FIFTY-ONE

Mary Leech lived in a terraced house just off Shields Road in Byker, and within easy walking distance of the local Metro station. Her presence reminded Carlisle of his late mother, emanating a sense of pure innocence and kindness. Such a sweet old lady, with her dyed auburn hair and deep blue eyes, she had captivated him with her remarkably retentive mind. For the past twenty years, Mary had been a foster parent to no less than seventeen children, all of them through Social Services. No stranger to problematic teenagers, Mary had a knack of rebuilding young people's lives. With a heart overflowing with kindness, she showered every foster child with the love and affection they so desperately craved, treating them as if they were her own. Not so in Patrick Stanley's case. As her story veered into a dark and disturbing place, a chilling silence filled the room.

Emotionally detached and unable to connect with others, young Stanley had shown little or no empathy towards other people's suffering. Aged ten, he'd set fire to the neighbour's garden shed, having slaughtered all of their pet rabbits. His evil knew no end, and after he stole the poor box from the local parish church, he spent all the money on cigarettes.

Carlisle remained silent as Mary's incredible story unravelled. A troublesome child, Patrick Stanley had always unnerved others by his abnormal, remorseless behaviour. Unquestionably violent, he didn't care how many lives he destroyed – just that he got his own way.

'Excuse me for asking,' asked Carrington softly, 'when you first took charge of Patrick from Social Services, how would you best describe him?'

The old lady looked a little nervous, as well as she might be.

'When he first arrived in my care, he displayed impeccable manners. He was such a pleasant child, it was as if someone had raised him in a palace.'

'Was he a lovable child?'

'At first he was, but that all quickly changed.'

Carlisle couldn't help but think about the recent crimes Stanley had committed and the person he had become. 'When did you first sense that something was amiss?' he asked.

Mary leaned back and regarded him quizzically through narrowed eyes. Despite being in her mid-seventies, she lacked confidence and displayed a self-conscious shyness. Her foster children described her as strict but fair, and many of them stayed in touch with her over the years. Not so in Stanley's case. On the day he left home, he had turned his back on all the acts of kindness she had given him, erasing her from his memory.

'Patrick was an extremely challenging boy, and difficult to keep in check. None of his school teachers possessed the expertise to manage his wild behaviour, intensifying the issue.'

'In what way?'

'Whenever you tried to bring him into line, Patrick would throw a tantrum, stomping his feet and unleashing piercing screams. The negative impact on the other children in his class was not surprising. Schools can be peculiar establishments, with peculiar rules enforced by intellectuals who have little patience.' Her eyes dropped as if living a dark moment. 'If something happens out of the ordinary, they have weird ways of dealing with it.'

Carlisle could not resist feeling sorry for the old woman. There were so many factors to consider, and every one of them was complex. Having told them so much about Stanley's troublesome past, it had undoubtedly taken its toll.

'I take it he had serious anger issues?'

'Yes, he did. Unlike the other children we took into care, you could never reach out to Patrick. Nobody could. Not even Social Services.'

'Did he ever threaten you at all?'

'He frightened me, especially when he couldn't get his own way.'

Carrington checked her notes. 'And what did Social Services say about that?'

'Not a lot. They referred him to a specialist doctor.' Mary gave them a long-suffering look. 'For anxiety management, of all things.'

Having spent the previous evening going back over old case files, Carlisle was more than familiar with the details. Stanley had shown little or no emotional attachment towards his foster parents, having isolated himself from them. The child's fear of embarrassment made it impossible for him to handle any kind of criticism, even if it was helpful. And if anyone dared to challenge him, he didn't have the social skills to cope. Perhaps that's why he reacted as he did. It was his way of dealing with it. Thinking about this, all the little idiosyncrasies were there. Interpersonal dominance, aggression, excessive self-esteem – it took little.

He tried to think rationally. Some experts believed anxieties could manifest themselves in a variety of ways, which were based on a psychological response to a threat in the environment. It was this response that maximised the body's ability to either face danger or elude it. People had misread Stanley's reactive behaviour to an uncomfortable situation as anger or opposition. However, no one had picked up on the problem in his adult life and no one had addressed the uncontrollable anxiety attacks. He'd obviously gone into meltdown, a ticking time bomb that had laid dormant till someone pressed the trigger.

Grave mistake!

'How did Patrick respond to his treatment?' asked Carlisle. 'Did his disruptive behavioural patterns finally come to a halt?'

'At first they did, but they quickly returned.'

'It sounds to me as though you dealt with the problem on your own.'

Mary stared back at them. 'Sometimes I felt totally incapable of handling the situation. At first I thought it was me. It wasn't, of course. Whatever I did, the tantrums and unacceptable behaviour seemed to get worse. It was as if Patrick enjoyed embarrassing me.'

'The only real failure is failing to try, Mrs Leech.'

Carlisle shook his head sympathetically. 'You did your best, and under very difficult circumstances, you coped admirably well.'

She blushed. 'Yes, I tried my best.'

Carrington remained silent. Whether she understood the underlying warning signs, he could not tell. His primary aim was to establish Stanley's childhood comfort zones, and which environments he felt most safe in. When confronted by authority, most serial killers would retreat into themselves. It was their way of dealing with it. If Stanley had gone into hiding, he may have returned to his childhood roots. He realised the risks, but anything was worth trying at this late stage.

'What about Patrick's friends?' asked Carlisle. 'What can you tell me about them?'

'He had no friends,' Mary replied unreservedly. 'Patrick never mixed with other people; he isolated himself from them. If he couldn't get his own way, he became aggressive.' She stared pitifully across at them. 'The other children called him Wasp. It was a name that stuck with him throughout his teenage life. Who would want to mix with someone like that?'

The early signs of power and control were all there. Stanley had obviously developed into what he now was – a narcissistic freak who was prone to violate the rules of society.

'Tell me, what did Patrick do with himself apart from school? Did he hang around in his bedroom all day?'

'He spent most of his spare time down at the bottling plant.'

Carlisle's ears pricked up. 'Bottling plant?'

'Yes, I worked there for several years. Patrick used to hang around there.'

'Excuse me for asking, but I thought you said he had no friends.'

'Not at school, he didn't. He got on with some people at the plant and used to run errands for them.' The old woman shuffled awkwardly. 'At a price, of course. They gave him their loose change and unwanted sandwiches they couldn't eat.'

'That explains everything,' Carlisle smiled. 'I presume the bottling plant is down by the River Tyne?'

'Yes, but it closed many years ago.' Mary thought for a moment. 'To tell you the truth, I'm not sure if it's still there.'

'I'm forgetting,' said Carlisle, shaking his head and smiling, 'this all happened fifteen years ago.'

'Time waits for no one, Mr Carlisle.'

He sat quietly for a moment, thinking. 'When did you last see Patrick?'

'Not since he left my care.'

'And neither of you have met or spoken since?'

'No, we haven't.'

Mary told them more, then flopped back in her chair as though utterly exhausted. There was nothing more to be gained here, and the old woman had told them everything they'd wanted to know. After all, this wasn't a police interview, more a fact-finding mission.

'If Patrick ever contacts you,' said Carrington, handing her a business card, 'you're to ring this number.'

The old woman's face darkened. 'Is Patrick in some sort of trouble?'

Carlisle smiled thinly as he stood to leave. 'We don't wish to cause you alarm, Ms Leech. But if you have any concerns, please contact that number.'

'Yes, I will.'

They left the estate with mixed feelings, hoping she would never need to contact them again.

Somehow, he doubted it.

CHAPTER FIFTY-TWO

As DC Carrington drove north along the Western Bypass, bright sunshine bathed the city. Newcastle Quayside flourished as the rejuvenation programmes breathed fresh energy into the area. Spending long weekend breaks in the North East seemed to be effortless for the middle class in England. As the affluent south poured into the metropolis nightlife, Geordie hospitality was alive and kicking. But there was a darker side, a side where tourists never ventured.

Ten minutes later, Carlisle's instincts told him they should turn left at the next junction, but they had to make a brief detour first. After descending a steep bank, they journeyed past a row of dilapidated buildings before finally arriving at their destination. There were no gates at the front of the old bottling plant, just a narrow back lane leading to another part of the complex. Most of the surrounding units had been demolished, but a few terraced houses still stood.

Pulling up behind a mud-spattered dumper truck, Carrington switched off the undercover car's engine. Not twenty metres away, two men dressed in Hi-Vis jackets were digging a hole in the middle of the road. One guy was short and lean, the other was stocky, with a weather-beaten face. Neither paid much attention to them.

'Are you sure this is the right place?' asked Carrington, sliding out from the driver's seat.

Carlisle frowned. 'According to the satnav, it is.'

She stared at him quizzically. 'I think we should get uniforms involved.'

He knew what Carrington was thinking, but ignored her.

No sign of life came from within the old bottling plant, and there were no vehicles parked outside. If Stanley was here, he was obviously covering his tracks. That much was clear. As they moved down a cobbled lane together, Carlisle stopped at the first door he came to. Boarded up and covered in graffiti, he swore quietly to himself. Upon closer inspection, someone had sealed all the ground floor windows with bricks. The vandals had been there recently, as evidence of their mischief was everywhere.

'What's up now?' Carrington shrugged.

'I'm not sure.'

'Why don't we try the rear of the building?'

All kinds of emotions tugged him, and none of them curiosity. Then, close to an old boiler house, they found a door. Carlisle placed the flat of his hand on one of the central door panels and gave it a gentle push. It wasn't bolted, and a single mounted lock held it in place. Taking a step back, he employed a forceful, well-placed kick to the side panel and watched as the door crashed inwards.

Within seconds, they were inside and staring into a vast, open abyss.

'This must be it,' said Carlisle, gazing up at the skylights. 'There's a small courtyard at the rear of the complex, and several buildings beyond that.'

'We'd better check them out.'

The upper floor, which was built on two levels, was set back from the rest. Considering the building had lain empty for more than a decade, the structure was in remarkable condition. Some of the old factory units had been demolished, while black boarding covered the ones that still stood, concealing any internal openings. Moving through what appeared to be an old office block, someone had decked out the floors with cheap black-and-white tiles. He tried the lights. None of them worked. It was then Carrington spotted a large brown suitcase propped up against one of the office doors. She pointed her torch beam towards it and stepped back a pace.

'What the hell is that doing here?' she asked.

As his grip on the handle tightened, he felt his pulse race.

Oh shit! Please don't let there be a body inside.

That wasn't all. It was something in Carrington's voice that sent shockwaves down his spine. From the darkness within, she pointed to the office walls. Someone had daubed a big red smiley face on all of them, but none of them were in blood. Crude as it was, alarm bells were ringing inside the profiler's head. Everything was surreal, as if living out a nightmare.

His entire world spiralling out of control, Carlisle prepared for the inevitable. This was a crazy idea. Carrington was right; they should never have entered the building without backup, as there was no way back from here. If Stanley was lying low, they would need to confront him.

The detective stood perfectly still as her eyes toured the interior.

'We should check the upper floor level,' she said a little nervously.

Daylight pouring through the skylights, together they moved up a narrow flight of stairs. Treads creaking underfoot, all that remained was to hope the killer wasn't lying in wait.

'There,' Carlisle whispered.

To their left was a small annex, beyond that a sliding door. Nerves jangling, Carrington pointed her taser gun towards the opening.

'There's someone inside,' she nervously whispered.

The profiler took another deep breath and tried to steady himself. Looking for Stanley was like searching for the Holy Grail. The man was an elusive predator who wouldn't think twice about killing them.

They inched their way closer.

After he slid back the partition door, the profiler immediately noticed a powerful, pungent odour permeating the air. It wasn't a spacious room. It had two narrow slit windows and a bank of office cabinets running the entire length of one wall.

He stood for a moment, transfixed.

'Over there,' Carrington insisted, pointing her torch beam at the corner of the room.

Carlisle had difficulty in focusing, and the shapes were nebulous, the features hazy. Then he heard a whimpering noise. Pitiful, like the cry of some wounded animal. The next thing he noticed, after he stooped to inspect, was the terrified look on the young woman's face.

As fear ripped through him, he stepped back.

From what he could make out, her wrists had been bound to the wheelchair rests with heavy duty duct tape and her ankles strapped to the side frames with rope. Still conscious, she was breathing shallowly, and her pulse was weak. It was then he noticed the IV bag hanging over the wheelchair backrest. It was empty. Whatever lifesaving fluids had been flowing into her veins were no longer keeping her alive.

'Angelica,' he whispered.

Her lips moved to speak, but her words were inaudible.

'Where's Patrick Stanley?'

She craned her neck, as a look of fear swept over her ghost like features.

'It's okay. Help's on its way.'

Drifting in and out of consciousness, her arms were so badly swollen that Carlisle could barely look at them, let alone touch them.

Carrington reached for her phone and frantically pressed the call button.

'I want full forensic deployment, and the entire area sealed off.'

As the profiler checked out the rest of the rooms, he heard sirens wailing. Faint at first, but rapidly growing louder. Then he heard another, pursued by a third. Moving towards the sliding door, a splinter of blue light flashed past his eyeline. Suddenly, the whole courtyard was bristling with police vehicles.

***

First, the ambulance arrived, closely followed by a Mercedes Sprinter full of police officers. Kitted out in full body armour, a stern-faced sergeant slid from the passenger seat and ran towards the front of the building.

'I want every inch of the ground covered,' the officer shouted.

Minutes later, Jack Mason appeared in the doorway, and it was Carrington who spoke first. 'This woman is badly in need of medical help.'

The chief inspector took a step forward and stared into the suspect's face. Then, just when he was about to apply his handcuffs, he thought better of it.

'Her circulation's restricted,' Mason said, matter of fact.

'Shall I cut her free, boss?'

'No, Sue. Leave that to the medical experts.' Mason peered into the gloom. 'Has anyone searched the rest of the building?'

'Only this complex, boss.'

'Any sign of Stanley?'

'No. Nothing.'

'How long have you two been here?'

'Not thirty minutes. I called base the moment we found her.'

Mason caught the detective's eye. 'Well done. You did the right thing.'

The air was heavy with the smell of machine oil and dust. Then, out of nowhere, a man's voice cut through the atmosphere. It was coming from the lower level of the building.

'Are you there, Jack?'

'I'm up here,' Mason shouted back.

Seconds later, a small group of officers ascended the stairs. Six in total. Each of them wore a white, sterile paper suit, their equipment slung over their shoulders. The senior officer nodded, his eyes darting between his colleagues as they exchanged crucial information.

'We've cleared the upper level but have found nothing,' Mason reported.

'What about Stanley? Do you think he'll return?'

'I doubt he's left her to rot here.'

'No, I wouldn't have thought so,' the senior officer replied.

'What are we doing about search teams?' asked Mason.

'They are on their way. Try not to touch or disturb anything. We'll be back in a jiffy.'

Carlisle said nothing; Mason's expression said it all. Over the years, he'd grown accustomed to this kind of rhetoric, which usually meant the suspect was long gone. The trouble was, the chief inspector lacked patience and was straining at the bit to take charge of proceedings. Not so in this case. Not until the crime scene manager had given them clearance.

As he let his mind drift, Carlisle detected an evil sensation in the pit of his stomach. They were close, and Stanley would only have one thing on his mind – to liberate the woman now fighting for her life.

As he drifted towards the open doorway, the profiler closed his eyes to concentrate on positive thoughts.

'Where are you, Patrick?' he murmured.

CHAPTER FIFTY-THREE

Wasp looked on in confusion. His world turned upside down, it wasn't looking good suddenly. Blue spinner lights everywhere, marked patrol cars on every street corner, and a shitload of armed police officers to contend with – what was he to do?

Abandoning the stolen Peugeot, he made his way towards the old bottling plant. The master of disguise, Wasp, knew his waterboard outfit would keep him out of trouble, at least for now. Even he was amazed at some of the incredible disguises he had recently come up with. He should have been a make-up artist, as that's where his future lay. It was good to dress up, and he had a favourite costume, like the black hoodie he always wore on night manoeuvres. Everyone's favourite, he mused. Now a national treasure – the Suitcase Man had finally reached celebrity status.

He smiled inwardly. *'Whoever had dreamt that up was pure genius.'*

The road ahead was long and exposed, with only a handful of red-brick buildings offering protection. There wasn't much he didn't know about the local community. This was his territory, his domain, a place to call home. On reaching the blue and white police cordon tape, Wasp suddenly felt vulnerable. No stranger to police officers, this was where the bad guys spent time together.

He loved this part of the city. It was incredible. The shipyards had long gone, but it was a past he knew very little about.

It was the gravelly voice that shattered Wasp's concentration. A stout man, with bushy sideburns, and inquisitive brown piercing eyes that cut through him like laser beams. Next to him, and dressed in a grey pinstripe suit, stood an alert man who he took to be a senior detective. This was a large gathering, which made him feel important.

As excitement gripped the air, Wasp could barely breathe, let alone contain his emotions. God, this was awesome. No matter where he looked, network satellite vans were tipping the skyline. Not all had gone to plan, of course, but nothing was ever straightforward where the police were concerned. He checked his pocket, pulled out his phone and switched it to the camera. Lifting his arm high above the crowd, he fired off a couple of shots. He liked to keep a record of everything, just for posterity. Not that he was narcissistic – he wasn't. His plans falling into place, the recognition he so desperately craved was finally coming to fruition.

Then he spotted the ambulance. Stationary, its back doors flung open, the driver was nowhere to be seen. He knew from experience that this was a serious response call. As the minutes ticked by, a stocky, fit-looking man in his late forties entered the scene. He carried a large black bag in his hand and was barking out instructions to nearby police officers.

Then two paramedics appeared. Dressed in their familiar green uniforms, they were pushing an EMS stretcher towards the back of the stationary ambulance. He knew she was alive and could see the fresh IV drip line they'd attached to her arm. He would follow them, find out which hospital they were taking her to. Newcastle General seemed the most logical choice, but there was always the Freeman, a hospital he knew inside out.

Wasp glanced at his watch.

'Time to be off, my little sweetie!'

CHAPTER FIFTY-FOUR

DCI Mason had just finished his meeting call with the acting superintendent when there was a sharp rap on the door and DS Savage entered.

'What can I do for you, Rob?' asked Mason.

'We may be onto something here,' the sergeant said, casting a beady eye around the room. 'We're getting reports of a stolen white Transit van travelling on Dutch number plates.'

'Where is it now?'

'It's about to board the DFDS ferry *Ijmuiden* for Amsterdam.'

'If you haven't already done so, you'd better inform the port authorities. No doubt they will aspire to be involved.'

'There's something else you should know,' said Savage excitedly.

'What is that?'

'The van driver is wearing the uniform of the Royal Dutch Touring Club ANWB. It's the equivalent of the UK's Automobile Association.'

'What is this, a bloody fashion show?'

'No, but one of the security officers at the ferry terminal reckons the guy's an imposter.'

Mason put his pen down. His interest levels heightened. 'Where's the driver now?'

'The last we heard, he'd boarded the overnight ferry.'

Mason moved from behind his desk and picked up his jacket. Until now, they'd heard very little from the port authorities, but all that was about to change.

'Grab half a dozen men and meet me down in the car park in five minutes.'

The sergeant's grin broadened. 'Do you suspect it's Stanley?'

'Chance would be a fine thing.'

Within minutes, two unmarked police cars were speeding east towards the Royal Quays ferry terminal in North Shields. His foot hard to the floor, the needle on the wrong side of one hundred, Savage seemed determined to show off his driving skills.

Big mistake!

'Easy on the cornering,' Mason demanded. 'We need to get there in one piece.'

'I'm only doing a hundred and ten,' the sergeant chuckled.

'Seems more like five hundred and ten from where I'm fucking sitting.'

When Mason caught sight of the ship's DFDS funnel markings, a wave of relief washed over him. Thirty minutes from now, and they'd be staring at an empty quayside. Still loading, the undercover car inched forward in a long queue of waiting lorries before being redirected to a holding bay.

'Morning,' a ship's officer announced, as he moved from behind the check-in desk. 'I'm Lars Anson, the ferry's Chief Engineer. How can we help you, Detective Chief Inspector?'

Pleasantries exchanged, Mason handed Anson a

photograph of Patrick Stanley. 'We believe this man may have boarded your ferry. He's travelling on stolen number plates and wearing the uniform of the Royal Dutch Touring Club ANWB.'

'That's a new one,' Anson grinned. 'Smugglers prefer to dress up in crew uniforms these days.'

Mason gathered his wits. 'Stanley's no drugs runner. He's wanted in question about several brutal murders he's committed.'

'And you believe he's boarded our ferry?'

'According to the port authorities, he has.'

'In which case, he shouldn't be too difficult to track down,' the ship's officer confirmed. 'May I suggest we continue with our loading, then go into ship's lock-down?'

'Sounds good to me,' Mason shrugged, none the wiser.

'I'll get one of the staff officers to check the van's whereabouts, and we'll take it from there.'

'One other thing,' Mason said, trying to curtail his excitement. 'Stanley's a desperate man and may carry a bladed weapon. If he is, he won't be frightened to use it.'

'Thank you, inspector. I'll warn the rest of the crew members.'

Anson radioed the ship's bridge and spoke directly with the captain. It was a tense moment, and Mason was keen to get going. There were things to be done, plans to set in motion, and a lot of maritime protocols to adhere to.

'Here's the plan,' said Anson, with an air of authority. 'The captain advises that once he's ready to set sail, he'll conduct the mandatory lifeboat drill. Whilst the crew clears the car decks, your men can check on the assembled passengers.'

'Thank you. I'll inform my team of your plans.'

'First, we must secure all escape routes,' Anson confirmed.

'Yes, of course.'

They moved onto the vehicle loading deck and split into two groups.

'How many men do you have with you, Inspector?'

'There is six in total.'

'That's perfect.'

Twenty minutes later, plans in place, the ship made ready to slip from her moorings. Seven short blasts of the ship's horn pierced the air, replaced by the heavy clanks of the ferry doors closing. As passengers assembled at their muster stations, two teams of officers moved into position.

Anson raised a cautionary hand and turned to face them. 'Let's work in tandem,' he instructed. 'Team One will search the forward part of the vessel. Team Two the aft. Once we've cleared the bottom two decks, we'll close the watertight doors, and only then do we move up to the next level.'

'There's only one way he can go,' Mason said, pointing up to the heavens.

'Yes. It's like squeezing a tube of toothpaste.'

Well, that was the theory.

Within minutes of securing the two lower decks, the crew had traced the stolen white van. Whoever had driven it on board was the person they were now looking for.

'Time to move up a deck,' Anson said, closing the last

of the watertight doors.

Keeping in close contact with the rest of his team, and wearing a bright orange lifejacket, DCI Mason climbed the ladders to the next level. Split into smaller groups, the teams worked their way through the accommodation decks. It was painstakingly slow work, as every cabin on the ferry had to be checked for signs of life.

Anson swung to address Mason. 'Before the ship's captain gives his all clear on the lifeboat drill, you and I must clear the Columbus Deck.'

Mason nodded. 'Anything you say, Lars.'

'I doubt your man will be there, but let's not underestimate his cunning.'

'There can't be many more decks left,' Mason insisted.

'No, but there are plenty of places to stow away.'

The moment they reached the Columbus Deck, Mason instinctively poked his head around the double glass doors. Much larger than expected, the lounge had an enormous dance floor, central stage, and what looked to be a well-stocked bar. Now void of passengers, the place reminded him of the Marie Celeste.

Then, out of the corner of his eye, Mason caught movement. It wasn't much, but enough to draw his attention towards it. Handset switched to silent, Mason pushed it to the back of his mind as they crept towards the lounge bar. Struggling to breathe, he thought he heard a scraping noise coming from behind the bar.

Anson, stocky in stature with broad, rounded shoulders, had heard it too. Tiptoeing across the dance floor together, the ship's engineer signalled his intentions before peeling off in the opposite direction. Then a figure emerged – screaming at them like a madman possessed.

Mason spotted the knife.

Fists clenched, feet spread slightly apart, Mason instinctively shifted his weight to the balls of his feet. Quick as a flash, he lunged out and grabbed a tight hold of Stanley's knife arm. Realising his terrible mistake, the lead detective lashed out at him with both feet. When that didn't work, he twisted his body sideways to throw his assailant off balance. It was a tense encounter and each time he tried; the killer continued to resist. Wedged between drinks cabinet and bar, they were now locked in mortal combat.

Hemmed in on all sides, the chief inspector faced a maniac whose eyes glinted with a twisted determination to cause him a terrible harm. As he desperately clung onto Stanley's knife arm, he head-butted his assailant. Nothing had prepared him for this, and as he lashed out with both feet, he tried to bring him to ground. Then, just when he thought he had the upper hand, the killer caught him a lucky blow to the right cheek. Dazed, Mason staggered to his feet and caught the knife blade flashing towards him. Seconds later, he let out a terrifying scream.

'You bastard!' he yelped.

Staring into his assailant's crazed eyes, Mason felt the steady trickle of warm blood running down his sleeve. Pinned down and unable to move, his whole body was on fire. If only he'd carried a gun, he would have blown the bastard's brains out without the slightest hesitation. He hadn't, and now he was staring certain death in the face.

Exhausted, and desperately fighting for his life, he tried to break free from the killer's firm grip. Stanley was having none of it. Swinging him around by the ankles, Mason felt the rush of blood to the head. He was toying with him as a cat plays with a mouse before it moves in for the kill. Then, to his left, he saw the knife arm retract again.

Oh shit. Oh no.

Lars Anson wasn't a tall man, but he was nifty on his feet. Picking up the nearest bar stool, he smashed it over Stanley's head. As the killer's feet buckled from under him, he dropped to the deck like a stone. Blood spurting from a huge gash in the top of his head, he thought the ship's officer had slain him.

'You okay?' Anson called out.

'The bastard's stabbed me, Lars.'

The ship's chief engineer bent down to inspect and immediately radioed for help. It was another tense moment of madness, and with his head spinning three hundred sixty degrees, Mason felt physically sick. Then, just when they thought it was over, Stanley rose to his feet. Pure hatred filled his eyes, their intensity betraying a mind consumed by chaotic thoughts.

Terrified, the ship's engineer ducked sideways as he desperately tried to defend himself against a crazed killer. As the knife blade disappeared deep into the officer's chest, he let out a gut-wrenching shriek. The sight of blood spurting out in torrents left Mason feeling helpless, knowing there was nothing he could do.

Enraged and frothing at the mouth, the killer's knife arm rose once again.

Seconds passed, and suddenly the doorway was swarming with crew members, their presence filling the air with a sense of urgency. They were yelling abuse at their attacker, goading him, and trying to drag the ship's officer to safety. Outnumbered and hemmed in on all sides, Stanley was far from finished yet. Eyes still burning with hatred, head gushing with blood, he continued to lunge out at them with the knife.

Determined to inflict the maximum harm to those closest to him, panic spread like wildfire. Nobody had predicted this, and as the ship's crew scattered in all directions, a massive gap opened up.

One hand gripping the handrail, the other wielding the knife, Stanley flung himself headlong over the side of the ferry. He was gone, but the gut-wrenching scream he let out as he plunged headlong toward certain death resonated throughout the ship. Seconds later, as his head struck the lifeboat winching crane, it catapulted his whole body sideways.

First the splash.

Then silence.

***

Within minutes of the ship's lifeboat being launched, the river police arrived. Two launches, each desperately searching the waterline for signs of life. Shouting broke out, but still no signs of Stanley surfacing.

Confused, Mason gripped the handrail for all he was worth. Unsteady on his feet, he scanned the river for signs of movement. Nothing. Only the black murky depths of emptiness remained visible.

Above, a helicopter clattered, its thermal imaging camera pointing down at the water's edge. Then, one hundred feet below, a ghostlike figure emerged. It was staring up at them like the stone face of a child on a cathedral tomb. At first, he thought he was imagining things, but others had witnessed it too.

Water lapped and bubbled as the river's notorious undercurrents took charge. Slowly at first, Stanley slipped silently from view and into the shadowy depths below. It was over, and the Suitcase Man's terrifying reign of terror had finally ended. All that remained now was to recover the body and the pieces would fall into place.

'You okay, boss?' a familiar voice called out.

The moment he saw Rob Savage sprinting towards him, Mason knew then he was in serious trouble. He tried to stand, but the pain in his side was unbearable. He tried lifting his head, but his muscle controls continued to shut down. Drifting in and out of consciousness, he felt a whirlwind of strange and surreal sensations. He imagined he was floating on a silver cloud and peering in on himself as if from another dimension.

The next thing he saw, after opening his eyes, was a team of masked surgeons peering down at him. Confused at first, he desperately tried to make the connection. Something was very wrong, and as he reached out towards the outstretched hand that was drawing him ever closer towards a bright silver light, he slipped into the dream again. It was surreal, unimaginably beautiful, and yet more powerful than anything he'd ever witnessed.

As his life flashed before him, he felt his eyelids becoming heavy, as if someone had attached lead weights to them. He wanted to say something, anything, but could not form the words. Then he heard his father's voice telling him there was nothing left to fix here anymore. He was free, and it was time to let go.

Then Mason's world sank into inky blackness.

CHAPTER FIFTY-FIVE

Two months later.

Having found a parking space on Benton Front Street, David Carlisle walked the short distance back to the Ship Inn. A man's pub, the profiler had always felt at home here. Eight long weeks had passed since his involvement in Operation Walrus had come to a close. Not surprisingly, he missed the workplace banter, the camaraderie, and the feeling of togetherness. Being a private investigator had its advantages, but his involvement in the operation ended once they had apprehended a dangerous psychopath. Not all was despair, though. He now had a much needed pay cheque tucked in his back pocket, and enough money to pay off his creditors.

Despite a huge search operation, which had lasted several weeks, Patrick Stanley's body had never resurfaced. Missing and presumed drowned wasn't the result that Jack Mason had been hoping for, as it always left an element of doubt. The River Tyne was notorious for its strong tidal undercurrents, particularly around the ferry terminal. There were differing opinions about Stanley's fate: some thought the sea had swept away his body, while others believed it lay trapped underwater, decomposing.

'Took your time,' Mason said, checking his watch.

'I got held up in heavy traffic, but I could sorely murder a pint.'

His colleague conveyed his agreement with a brief nod. 'Talking of homicide, we've formally charged Glebova on two counts of murder.'

'Two counts?'

'Yes, and I'll be making a statement to that effect at tomorrow's press briefing.' Mason did his usual funny little jig like dance. 'Her solicitors' are claiming she's suffering from retrograde amnesia and can't remember a damn thing. It's utter bollocks, of course. Glebova's a devious bastard, and it wouldn't surprise me if she pleads not guilty before the trial.'

'She's obviously playing the system.'

Mason laughed, confident that she would make no progress. 'Not according to the CPS. She won't.'

Against all advice, and barely eight weeks after nearly losing his life, Jack Mason was back at his desk. He'd had a remarkable escape and had it not been for the type of life jacket he was wearing, he could easily have ended up as Stanley's last victim. Mason was old school, a no-nonsense copper determined to fight his corner. As for Lars Anson, the ferry's chief engineer, he was back sailing again.

The drinks arrived, along with a bag of crisps.

'Stanley had charisma,' Mason chuckled, his laughter filling the room. 'His next-door neighbour reckoned he could charm a vulture off a carcass.'

'That's how most serial killers operate. They know who to make friends with.'

'Let's hope the crabs strip his body clean and the bastard rots in hell.'

'Well, at least the killings have stopped.'

'Thank God,' Mason muttered.

Carlisle gave him a serious look. 'Recovering the murder weapon is one thing, but it's a pity you never found his body.'

'He's dead, all right. I saw the bastard go under, along with hundreds of other people.' The chief inspector took another swig of his beer. 'Once they list the trial date, the press will have a field day. Those cockroaches never fail.'

Carlisle shook his head slowly. 'What really puzzles me about Stanley's last movements is why he left Angelica behind as he did?'

'It's a strange one. Mind, if he wanted her dead, he would have done it long ago.'

'There's no doubting that.'

'Theirs was a strange partnership which had all the ingredients of a Greek tragedy.'

The profiler nodded in agreement. 'Having experienced the childhoods from hell, it's little wonder they teamed up as they did. They were definitely an odd couple.'

Mason raised his glass to his lips and paused for a moment. 'She's bound to talk at some point; most usually do. I can think of a dozen cases where that has happened in the past. Once they realise they're banged up in prison for the long haul, they look for a way out.'

'You surprise me, Jack.'

'Nah. Even the Moor's murderer, Myra Hindley, severed all contact with Ian Brady. Throughout her life, she relentlessly proclaimed her innocence, fighting tirelessly to regain her freedom.'

'That's not a bad analogy, actually,' admitted Carlisle. 'At least it answers a few questions.'

The chief inspector looked jaded, heavy around the eyes. Having almost lost his life in a vicious knife attack, his return to work seemed foolhardy. But Mason was tenacious, and the day he retired would be the day they broke the mould on old-school detectives.

'There's something you should know,' his colleague said, his voice barely above a whisper. 'Hedley insists that someone dismembered Lawrence and Price in Stanley's bathroom. He also believes that Angelica was the driving force in the partnership and now has the evidence to prove it.'

'What about Stanley?'

Mason cradled his glass in thought. 'There's plenty of trace evidence and footprints, according to the latest forensic report. The thing is, we know Stanley always wore rubber gloves.'

'And Hedley is adamant Angelica had a major role in all of this?'

'He is.'

'What about dismembering Price's body?'

'Not all is as it appears,' Mason shrugged. 'We know she was the last person to touch Lawrence's body, as her DNA and fingerprints were all over the suitcase we found on open waste ground.'

'Why hasn't any of this information come out in the open before now?'

Mason shrugged. 'I suspect the CPS are building a case against her and keeping it back for the trial.'

Carlisle nodded. 'It makes sense.'

'The coroner's report suggests they were both murdered over the same weekend. What is of major significance is that DNA tests carried out on the surgical saw show a ninety-nine percent probability match to Angelica Glebova.'

'God! I would never have expected to hear that. Is that why you're charging her with two counts of murder?'

'Some people never cease to amaze. I don't subscribe to the evil in the world, but I worry about sending my daughter out into it.' His colleague's shoulders slumped. 'It's their victims I feel sorry for, as none of them saw it coming. Once Angelica hooked up with them on the Internet chatrooms, they thought they were onto a good thing.'

The profiler cocked his head to one side in thought. 'There's obviously a lot more to come out of this case by the sounds.'

'Absolutely. If nothing else, it proves they were both in this together.'

'Who would have thought that six months ago?'

Mason proffered a smile. 'That's why I'm the copper and you're a profiler, my friend.'

'Let's not forget that Stanley was the dominant partner in all of this, and it was he who had overall control over everything. The problem with Stanley was, a knife entering a human body sexually aroused him. The appalling nature of his crimes, and the twisted way in which his warped mind worked, was plain for all to see.' Carlisle paused in reflection as he put his glass down. 'That's how Stanley fulfilled his fantasies...

dismembering his victims' bodies.'

Mason took another sip of his beer, as if pondering his statement. 'Perhaps we'll never know what really went on behind closed doors.'

'Probably not, but it certainly changes my thoughts as to the killer's motives.'

'Stanley was always an enigma,' Mason frowned. 'Let's leave it at that.'

Outside, the streets were bustling with people. Clear blue skies, a smattering of cotton wool clouds, and pleasant sunshine. Mason was right, serial killers were control freaks and perhaps that's why he left Angelica to die as he did. Daft, as it seemed, he probably didn't have the heart to kill her himself.

'What's the latest crack on Mad Frankie Wiseman?' Carlisle asked casually.

'In what respect?'

'The last I heard, he was seeking revenge.'

'Nah. Now he knows her killer is dead, he will quieten down a tad.' Mason's stare hardened. 'How he'll react once he finds out this Estonian woman was involved is a different matter, of course.'

'Yes, but Angelica didn't kill Jennifer Oakwell.'

'True, but Tony Fox has more than an interest in the case, and we all know what that bastard can get up to.'

Mason filled him in on the latest developments, and Wiseman's reactions towards Fox's takeover bid. Fox was a cunning sod and knew how to play the system to his advantage, but Mason still had an ace up his sleeve. CCTV footage recovered from Fat Sam's nightclub proved beyond all reasonable doubt that Patrick Stanley had once worked there. Not only that, two of his victims had regularly frequented the nightclub having hooked up with Angelica. It wasn't over yet, not by a long chalk, even though Fox denied all knowledge of it.

'What are the Area Commander's views?'

'Sutherland is loath to get involved with the CPS at this stage. The problem is, Fox has influence in high places. Given the opportunity, he'll no doubt make another huge donation to a well-known local charity and that will be the end of the matter.'

'Pity,' Carlisle said, wrinkling his nose. 'Putting Fox behind bars would have been the icing on the cake.'

They chatted a while, about everything and nothing.

Mason glanced at his watch.

'Now that you've received your payment, what will you do with yourself?'

'It's back to the grindstone, I'm afraid.'

'Each to his own.' Mason clanked his empty glass on the bar to attract the barman's attention. 'How's your old man keeping, by the way?'

'He's doing fine, thanks.'

'Do you still go fishing together?'

'We do, and I'm taking him out on a sea fishing trip this weekend.'

'Sounds like fun.'

'As long as the North Sea doesn't finish him.'

Mason chuckled. 'Does that involve hiring a boat and a skipper for the day?'

'Fortunately, an old family friend owns a sixty-foot converted motor launch and has promised to take us out in it.'

'That makes life a lot easier.'

'The odd thing is, he keeps it moored up in St. Peter's Wharf.'

Mason's jaw dropped. 'Shit! That's Wharf Butcher country.'

'I know, and barely a stone's throw from the North Shields ferry terminal.'

Mason raised his glass and smiled. 'Here's to your weekend sea fishing adventures. If you bump into Patrick Stanley on your trip, you're to give him my regards.'

They both fell about laughing.

CHAPTER FIFTY-SIX

One month later

The Café Frontline in Amsterdam sat on the edge of the notorious red-light district. Like most bars housed in the area, it had a lively atmosphere and played excellent music. Unfortunately, it wasn't one of his favourite bars. Working his way through a crowd, the stranger ordered a bottle of Amstel beer, sipped, and watched the world go by. It was seven o'clock, and the place was unusually busy. The streets outside were lively too, and a few hours from now, Café Frontline would be rocking. It was that kind of district, dynamic, and always had a friendly atmosphere.

'*Hoe kan ik helpen*?' the pale-faced barman asked, in a gruff Hollander voice.

'I'm looking for a man called Jack Mason. Do you speak English?'

'A little,' the barman replied. 'What do you want?'

'I have some valuable information I'd like to share with him.'

'And you are?' the barman asked.

'I'm an old schoolfriend of Jack's.'

The tall man standing next to him sucked in the air as he turned to confront the stranger. 'If it's Jack Mason you're looking for, I may help.'

The stranger's eyes widened a fraction. 'Do you know

his whereabouts?'

'I do. What is it you wish to speak to him about?'

'It's personal...'

'I see. And your name is?'

'I'd rather not say,' the stranger smiled, 'but I'm told Jack has been looking for me.'

'Without a name, how do you expect me to help you?'

Annoyed with himself for having been discourteous, the stranger swore under his breath. He should have known better, done things differently. These things took time. He realised that now. He stood for a moment and tried to gather his wits. Some things were best left unsaid, and the least people who knew of his presence here the better. Moreover, he had an important commitment later that evening and was in a hurry to leave.

'The name's Doctor Ballantine,' the stranger said, trying to recover the situation. He held out a welcoming hand. 'Jack and I go back a long way.'

'Well, Mr Ballantine. I'm sorry to inform you that Jack Mason isn't in town at the moment. He's a very busy man.'

'I'm sure he is.' The stranger stared at him, the disappointment showing. 'When was he here last?'

'A few days ago. He was visiting a friend?'

'Police business?'

'I've no idea. Besides, it's none of my concern.'

The stranger stood for a moment, thinking. 'A few days ago, you say?'

'Yes, he was here for the Rolling Stones' Two concert.'

'The Rolling Stones Two?'

The man standing next to him furrowed his brow, giving him a quizzical look. 'It's a local tribute band. No doubt you'll have heard of them.'

'Sounds fun.'

'It is,' the barman smiled, his eyes twinkling with mistrust as he continued about his business.

The stranger, visibly irritated, turned towards the man standing next to him and shoved a crumpled envelope into his hand. 'When you catch up with Jack Mason again, tell him to ring that number.'

'I will—'

Happy in the knowledge he'd finally set the wheels in motion, the stranger slid an empty beer bottle across the bar and walked off into the night.

You've turned the last page, but it doesn't have to end there ...

If you are looking for more action-packed reading in the Jack Mason crime thriller series, there's a whole new series in store.

'Once again, the author has delivered another gripping tale of murders that leaves the reader wanting more. Very believable, gruesome, well-written and engaging to the end.' ***Dan Brown.***

Acknowledgements

All my DCI Mason and David Carlisle novels are works of fiction based in the Northeast of England. There are so many people without whose help and support it would have been difficult, if not impossible, to write with any sense of authenticity. Having dyslexia as I do, my grateful thanks go out to the late Rita Day and my dear late wife Pauline, whose belief and inspiration never waned.

I am indebted to Detective Constable Maurice Waugh, a former member of the Yorkshire Ripper Squad, and Ken Stewart, a former member of South Shields CID. Their technical help of how the police tackle serious crime has allowed me a better understanding of what takes place. Their efforts have helped me enormously.

To single out a few other names who helped make the difference to this book, I would like to thank Paul Foster and Lynn Oakes for their encouragement and unqualified support in developing the initial cover graphics. Finally, I would express my heartfelt appreciation to the Beta reader team: Jan Duffy, Dan Line, Mark Duffy, Daniel Inman, and Brenda Forster, without whose help this book would never have made the bookshelf.

Michael K Foster
www.michaelkfoster.com

MICHAEL K FOSTER

Printed in Great Britain
by Amazon

eac56e37-60c1-4df8-8175-0deecacfcebeR01